Spring Rain

SPRING RAIN

a novel

BET OLIVER

HORSDAL & SCHUBART

Horsdal & Schubart Publishers Ltd.
Victoria, B.C., Canada

This is a work of fiction. All the characters are creations of the author's imagination, and any resemblance to persons living or dead is purely coincidental.

The cover is a painting by Josephine Crease, courtesy of the British Columbia Archives and Records Service (catalogue number 3372), Victoria, B.C.

The chapter-head line drawings are by Suzanne Prendergast, Ganges, B.C.

Horsdal & Schubart Publishers Ltd. thank The Canada Council for giving financial support to our publishing program.

This book is set in American Garamond.

Printed and bound in Canada by Printcrafters Inc., Winnipeg, Manitoba

Canadian Cataloguing in Publication Data

Oliver, Bet, 1953-
Spring rain

ISBN 0-920663-49-4

I. Title.
PS8579.L56S67 1996   C813'.54   C96-910436-7
PR9199.3.O395S67 1996

CONTENTS

MARIANNE: February, 1990

S HE IS SITTING beneath a narrow, rain-streaked window, the only light in the room. Tony has dropped me off to meet her, his Grandma Em. She's good at finding the answers to things, Tony says. Her house is at the far end of the Reserve. I would not have felt comfortable walking through on my own.

Her fingers fold strips of cedar bark in her lap. Coloured grass lies in strands on the table, between remnants of tobacco and tea. Tony says she has been making baskets all her life. It looks as if she has been sitting here forever, beneath the window, in the gloom. She raises her smoky old eyes. "Tell me a story," she says.

A story!

For a long time I watch her, listening to the bark in her hands. It is she who must have the stories; as for me, all I have are dreams, fragments of dreams without meaning, shadows in a dark wind.

But she waits. Somehow, I begin.

The captain's letter is in the pocket of my jacket. The letter was what brought me out to the coast, and the dreams started on the very first night I spent here, in the cottage beside the Reserve.

1

I had gone to bed early, trying to get used to the sound of the sea lions yelping and braying offshore. Every so often a bull would bellow horrendously, and I was picturing him, king of the reefs, with an enormous gut and a cigar. It had just started to rain.

My voice grows stronger as Grandma Em's head dips approvingly; she knows the sea lions, and she knows the rain.

I explain how I had written ahead from Vancouver, asking the Chamber of Commerce for help finding a place. Rentals were scarce, and I hadn't expected to end up beside the Reserve. The cottage is on a slight ridge, next to a giant cedar tree, and Jimmy Joe, the care-taker, lives next door. I'm not used to having a man so close. Jimmy Joe has eyes like a chicken, no teeth, and he's been around for as long as the cottage, I guess. The cottage overlooks the river where it widens into the salt water, lap-lapping all that night as I lay in bed, thinking: if it rained, I would surely sleep.

I could have been in Portugal that night, or on a cruise, those places women go to, in the sun. Instead, I was at that point on the map where provincial pink meets Pacific blue, right down along the gravel beach out front. Except for the shelter of the spit, I could have been hearing breakers along the shore.

When they learned where I was going, the other nurses and the orderlies on the ward, everyone laughed just at the name of the place: Squally Bay. They thought I'd picked a hideaway to recuperate and I didn't correct them, not even Barbara, whom I'd worked with for twelve years. I had been asked to take a medical leave.

Angrily, I agreed to three weeks. Mrs. Vincennes had caught me full on the mouth with the meal tray. Timid and pleasant for decades, she had plunged into dementia with a wild, nasty strength; the force of that tray loosened my front teeth. In the commotion, she received a small injury to her chin. Of all the stupid scenes: me down on the blood-speckled linoleum and Mrs. Vincennes in her wheelchair, blub-bering through cream of celery soup.

The very next day, she died of a stroke. Barbara, head nurse, arranged my leave.

I endured the three weeks, the bad jokes, and a thousand dollars of dental repair. Then suddenly my mother passed away, and I felt ridiculous with loss and rage. Mrs. Vincennes had gone out with a bang, my mother with less than a whimper. For years my mother had hardly spoken, crippled with disappointments, and a wasting muscular disease. I had looked after her, bent my will to hers, day after silent day in the house we shared.

A child is born deserving a history or at least some larger memories, I tell Grandma Em. To my embarrassment, my voice is a little shrill. Grandma Em doesn't seem to notice, preoccupied with her work.

I sold the house, got rid of all the stuff in it and, to Barbara's astonishment, for I had one of the best employment records in the hospital, I went back and arranged more leave.

Everything in that house was junk; I couldn't get rid of it fast enough. On my last trip through the attic, with the vacuum cleaner, I came across a wooden box. It was shoved in the corner and was so cracked and dirty, I had just never paid attention to it before. But the wood had once been finely finished, evoking the era of distinction my mother had clung to in her frugal decline. The initials E. H. on the clasp belonged to my mother's grandfather, Edwin Hume. He was one of Vancouver's early physicians; his name is engraved on a plaque at the hospital where I trained. His only son, my mother's father, did poorly in stocks and died around 1930 when she was very young. I assumed that this was why we had nothing to do with the original family residence, a severe-looking stone mansion off Granville Street which is now a soup kitchen and a depot for recycling restaurant food.

Inside the wooden box was a tunic of navy blue wool. The tunic was crumbling, but there was a man's faint odour and creases beneath the arms, as if it had been worn only a short time ago. I ran my fingers over the braided trim and the dull metal buttons; then I saw an envelope, tucked underneath. I turned off the vacuum cleaner and carried the box over to the light.

The envelope was addressed to Edwin Hume. It was fastened with twine and crammed with the thin, brittle pages of a letter which I spread out and read on the attic floor. The letter had been sent to Edwin in Boston, in 1876. It was from his grandfather, inviting Edwin to join him aboard his schooner on the northwest coast.

I reach for my jacket, pulling out the letter to show Grandma Em. She squints across the table, shaking her head at the antiquated script. I'm not going to read her the entire letter, though by now I could recite parts from memory. Far more than an invitation, it was the summing up of the old captain's life.

Except for a few returns to his wife and family in Boston, Captain Hume had spent his life roaming at sea. His apology for his long absences was lost in his eloquence; page after page described the grandeur, the hospitality, and the freedom awaiting young Edwin, should he take a break from his medical studies and become his grandfather's mate. Captain Hume's first commission to the coast was on a fur-trading ship in the summer of 1816. He crossed the Pacific in many different ships, and by 1853 had saved enough funds to have the sixty-foot, black-hulled *Coast Princess* built in San Francisco. Shallow drafted, with a large freight hold, she had put in over twenty years of service along the northwest coast and Captain Hume was very proud of her.

He proposed that Edwin should join him in the lovely, sheltered anchorage where the *Coast Princess* was accustomed to spending the winters. He promised a small but civilized settlement, with plenty of game and fish. In the tiniest print in the atlas I had located the place he was writing from: Squally Bay.

His letter was what led me here, to Grandma Em.

She sighs, setting the basket down. I have been watching her fingers as I speak. Her stained fingers, her blackened eyes, my voice raw in the gloom ... I hardly know where I am, why I have come. What did I expect ... the hulk of the *Coast Princess?* There wasn't a single Hume to be found in the phone book, and Grandma Em's face has been blank each time I mention the name. She nods, making a sympathetic noise in her throat, and I think back to the cottage, to the early morning rain.

I had been lying there, stunned with exhaustion, unfamiliarity, the heaviness of the air. The mattress was damp and the room was saturated with the scent of cedar. Drips ran down the silvery shakes, along the gutter and into the rusting barrel tended by Jimmy Joe, who would take care of me. The rain would take care of me. I would be cared for, and I would sleep. It felt like a night I had been waiting for, for thirty-seven years.

Grandma Em nods, smoothing paper for a cigarette. I twitch with hope: she is listening, she understands. Tony's truck is out on the road. I can hardly continue, so huge is the urge to hide my head and weep.

Grandma Em strikes a match, puffing clouds of smoke. Tony's door slams; he is on his way up the path. Quickly, I must finish.

It was almost morning and the rain had freshened. Out in the darkness I sensed something, I heard something, close to me, then distant, beyond the rustling shore. Closer it came, and I fell back on the pillow, my heart flapping against my ribs.

4

An owl trilling softly, sadly, in the rain.

When at last I slept, the little owl came inside and entered my dream.

I dreamed that ghostly, painted faces bobbed all around me, fading and reappearing through the fog. Children screamed with terror and Jimmy Joe rose up, grinning, then dropped soundlessly away. I lurched awake, not recognizing where I lay, and the owl trilled again.

Since then I have dreamed a thousand deaths — on the spit, out in the water, beneath the trees. Every night I wait for the little owl. The worst of it is, I have come to believe that the owl was waiting for me.

Across the table, Grandma Em sits very still. Her head slowly lifts, and by the look in her eyes I see that this is a story she already knows.

~~~:~~~

KAHAMMIS: 1815 - 1816

INTO THE HEART of the ancient cedar crept Kahammis, as the rain began. Biting her fingers, she snarled at the moans rising from Sa-sat-kis below. Old fool! She could not think amidst the fumes of his fear. With a downward hiss, she parted the boughs and peered out over the bay.

It was almost time. Beyond the delta to the east of the village, grey mounds of hills emerged in the faint, first light; beyond the spit, along the reefs, the fat sea lions barked and brayed. Kahammis rubbed her arms and legs, dropping to the base of the tree. She kicked Sa-sat-kis upright, whispering her plan. When Sa-sat-kis crumpled forward, she grabbed him by the hair, as her father would have done, yanking him close, close enough to feel, despite the murk and the rain, the fire in her eyes.

Then she was gone, and Sa-sat-kis knew by the stirring of spirits where; he clung to the trunk of the mighty cedar with the plea that he at last be set free. Immediately Kahammis was back with two war clubs, shoving one into his hands. Her eyes glinted as he fingered the shaft and found his bony, balanced grip, and then they both stiffened, a soft trill floating down from the canopy above.

The owl was returning to roost; it was time.

As the hills arranged themselves around the bay, two heads appeared over the ridge behind the village: the chief's daughter, and the chief's oldest slave. Among the coast dwellers only the most vigilant — the preening mink, the tiny screech owl — followed those two heads as they separated, encircling the bay like a net, tightening not on a salmon but on the victorious war party sleeping along the spit.

Sa-sat-kis caught his breath in a thicket of alder at the swampy corner of the bay where the spit began. On the sheltered side of the spit, above the tideline of seaweed, a cluster of canoes took shape in the early morning mist. The few remaining teeth in his mouth started clacking as Sa-sat-kis heard, over the surge, a hooting trill.

Kahammis had landed, calling like the screech owl to Sa-sat-kis. She had slipped around the bay through the trees and the salal, until she was abreast of the spit. She had thrown off her cape and knotted the war club around her neck, sliding into the water silent as a harbour seal. Not for nothing had she challenged her brothers across this swirling channel, until her shoulders were almost as broad, her hips as narrow, as theirs. She scrambled up the end of the spit and flung back her hair, touching the copper rings in her ears and nose.

Then she signalled Sa-sat-kis.

Rain rippled the bay.

Time for Sa-sat-kis to choose: stay, or flee.

Kahammis could feel the indentation of the Thunderbird on the handle of her father's whalebone club, solid and heavy as a winter wave. She had taken the club from its sacred place in the lodge, and now, clutching fiercely, she addressed the Thunderbird in the name of her massacred family. Crawling through the grass, waiting for Sa-sat-kis, she sniffed out her first pair of warriors, snoring on their backs. All through the night the warriors had plundered the food boxes; then they retreated to the spit, gorged into a stupor of triumph. A keg lay tipped over nearby; beyond the keg protruded another pair of feet. The warrior nearest her mumbled in his sleep, rolling away from the rain.

From her tree, she had counted sixteen. One had been stabbed by her mother, and four lay speared on the beach. She had been in her tree at dusk when the canoes burst into the bay. Barbaric chants froze the villagers, who were banking their fires and settling their children for the evening. Faster than a careening kingfisher did those hulls hit the beach below the lodges, out leapt the warriors with their red and black faces and terrible howls. Despite the dances that had enthralled Kahammis during the feasts, despite the imagining and pretending with her brothers, nothing had prepared her for the violence of that landing. Only Sa-sat-kis escaped; he had been sent up to the ridge by her mother moments before, to bring Kahammis down.

Her mother had died huddled with her two youngest daughters in the farthest corner of the lodge. From high in her cedar tree Kahammis listened to their screams, screams which had not stopped echoing, back and forth, between her ears.

Now she stiffened as over the rain and the surf came the owl's mournful reply: Sa-sat-kis! She sprang forward: smash, smash! Turn and smash! She was onto the main camp, five bodies sprawled around a smouldering firepit. The grass parted, revealing Sa-sat-kis. Groaning with relief, she brought down her father's club as if she were splitting a kelp ball. Death alerted its neighbour, a head craning in alarm. She swung the club with a sickening whack, while Sa-sat-kis worked his way around the pit, swift with terror.

Kahammis gestured to Sa-sat-kis: how many left? Sa-sat-kis shuddered and shook, and a gull squawked as a dazed warrior lurched through the rain-beaded grass. They knocked him to the ground, but before they could recover their balance, three more appeared. Sa-sat-kis felled the first, while Kahammis threw herself with such force onto the second that she bounced into the third. He blundered over his dying companion to seize her by the throat. Fighting to lift her club, she locked eyes with a boy no older than her brothers, his breath rank and his brows plucked, his cheeks smeared with ochre and charcoal. Just as her lungs were about to burst, his hold slackened: Sa-sat-kis, beloved Sa-sat-kis, had shattered his spine with a single blow.

Suddenly a rock skimmed past, then another, exploding against her ear. Rasping and reeling, she watched Sa-sat-kis crumple without a sound. The whalebone club flew out of her hand, into the shadow over Sa-sat-kis. The gulls shrieked and the ground slammed up to meet her, and daylight spilled feebly over the eastern hills.

When she awoke, to a raucous chorus from the crows and gulls, it was past noon. She was facing a cedar box, stained with roe, her family's crest of the Whale and Thunderbird painted on the side. In bewilderment she studied the box. The tide had receded, and the sky was dense with rain. A raven sat clucking in the lone pine tree at the end of the spit. Close by her nestled Sa-sat-kis, as if caught in a nap.

Through the roar in her ear, she heard the raven announcing around the bay that she was alive. Away whirled the afternoon as she lay gazing at the milky sky, the only safe place to look. A young gull hopped closer, emboldened by her glassy stare. She staggered upright, and the raven clucked sympathetically.

The birds assembled over the village cocked their heads, watching her and listening to the raven cluck. The screams between her ears had been replaced by a dull, aching emptiness, and she wondered if, during the early morning carnage, the owl had flown off with her soul.

~~~:~~~

A generation ago, the raven had paid a visit to her mother's village, half a day's paddle north. The village was called Klinniklinnikaht, built around a lagoon at the back of a channel full of islands and bends. At that time, the Klinniklinnikaht people claimed a great stretch of coast, almost as far south as Nootseetaht, where Kahammis lived. Not only did they claim the coast, they also claimed its abundance: the clam beds, salmon runs, otter colonies, rivers, and vast forests that had sustained them for thousands of years.

The raven flew up to Klinniklinnikaht during a war which had shaken the people of Nootseetaht for an entire cycle of seasons, with no winners, yet. Like a dreaded storm from across the southern straits had come the Wewksah, to avenge the expulsion of their ancestors from this rich coast, and to establish rights lost in battle, in particular the rights to Nootseetaht, renowned for its shelter and its salmon.

The fortunes of the coast people shifted like the sand beneath the tides. As Kalowish, Nootseetaht's chief, lay dying, the raven flew north to consult with Paquacheenish of Klinniklinnikaht. The raven reminded Paquacheenish that the Wewksah would make terrible neighbours, far worse than Kalowish. Paquacheenish agreed, and departed at once with a flotilla of warriors and supplies. When the sentry's cry sounded, and the majestic Klinniklinnikaht prows rounded the spit, the villagers sagged in fear of further attack. Then they roused themselves, for instead of murderous chanting, there was respectful silence from the Klinniklinnikaht warriors, who were wearing ceremonial cloaks of pale gold bark, their heads sprinkled with eagle down, a tribute to the dignity of Kalowish as Paquacheenish awaited the welcome of the dying chief. Kalowish

9

recovered long enough to see his hereditary lands come under the protection of Paquacheenish, with his eldest son established as the new chief. When the mourning was over, this son also became known as Kalowish.

Since Nootseetaht had been ravaged by war, the naming ceremony took place at Klinniklinnikaht, during the winter feast. Here the young Kalowish fell in love with the daughter of Paquacheenish, who was leading the women's welcome dance for the first time. She undulated and sang and Kalowish crouched, transfixed, in the position of honour in his family's section of the lodge. As children, they had been promised to other partners through a lengthy process of diplomacy and gifts. With no one of sufficient rank to intervene on his behalf, Kalowish moped hopelessly until the winter of the following year, when Paquacheenish gave in to pressure from all sides and paid out the previous agreements. The marriage quickly took place, further strengthening ties between Klinniklinnikaht and Nootseetaht, and Kahammis, the cherished first daughter, grew up secure in the knowledge of the powerful ally just half a day's paddle north.

For Kahammis and her brothers and sisters, the sun shone and the seasons turned like a benevolent wheel across a universe defined by sea and sky, food and play. Until the Wewksah came back, to finish what they had begun.

~~~:~~~

The day before the massacre, Kalowish had been hunting otters off the spit when he caught a glimpse of white sails. No ship had yet attempted the treacherous entrance into Nootseetaht, tucking instead amongst Klinniklinnikaht's sheltered twists. The coast people thrived on trade, and Paquacheenish provided fresh water, fish, and female slaves. The vessels returned to him every summer, bolstering his reputation and wealth.

Kalowish had scanned the dappled ocean, thinking that the good weather would soon be ending, along with the opportunities for trade. Paquacheenish had confided that the ships were visiting less in recent years, and that they were all the same: the Boston men, in a hurry, with little formality and many kegs.

Not only were the ships visiting less often, but it was getting harder and harder to find the otters. If there were no otter pelts, the ships might not come at all. Kalowish had sighed as he reached for his arrow and bow, steadying his canoe. The coast used to be lined with otter colonies, especially around Quatlukaht, north of Klinniklinnikaht. The kelp beds off Quatlukaht were nearly empty, now. Chief Quassoon of Quatlukaht had permitted his hunters to lure the female otters with the cries of their dying babies, a ruse that Kalowish would never have allowed.

His gaze had gone back to the sails: yes, the ship was aiming straight for Klinniklinnikaht. His own village had pelts, meticulously dried and stretched under the supervision of his wife, and stored in the bentwood boxes against the walls of his lodge. In the nineteen years since the Wewksah siege, his people had slowly healed. Once again the Nootseetaht beaches resounded with children's laughter and the crunch of loaded canoes. For this, he was indebted to Paquacheenish, who had loaned them the strength to survive. He decided to go north immediately; he would show those Boston men that they did not visit in vain.

Back at the village, Kalowish organized his best paddlers into three canoes. Aneetsick, his eldest son, took charge of one; Hasallum, master carver and brother of his wife, took charge of another. His younger son he kept with him. His wife, brilliant at bartering, handed aboard baskets of food and called out with advice until the men began to make faces and snicker, relieved she was staying behind.

From her cedar tree, Kahammis had watched them leave. Her brothers sat proudly, especially Aneetsick, tall and composed like Kalowish. He could bring her a looking glass. If he brought coloured beads she would hurl them into the sand.

She had seen a ship once, in the channel at Klinniklinnikaht. She was now the same age her mother had been when the ships first appeared, and still her mother chortled to recall the outrageousness of the white skins, the strange smells. What Kahammis would have given to join the journey at her father's side! Only when the three canoes were specks in the distance did she sullenly climb down from her tree.

The women were working in the lodges, preparing for the move upriver to the winter camp, away from the storms and the wind. Kahammis helped, sweat trickling between her breasts down to her loose, swinging skirt of shredded cedar bark. The surface of the water glowed like a scallop shell when she went outside to swim. Charging to the spit and back, she floated, spent, beneath the woodsmoke and wafts of the clam broth bubbling away for the evening meal.

It was not until the next afternoon that Kahammis had suddenly felt worried, out on the delta with Sa-sat-kis. The river was low and Sa-sat-kis busied himself picking up twigs while she dawdled along the banks, gathering grasses for the weaving that would occupy the months ahead. Sa-sat-kis was careful to keep her in sight; the virtue and safety of the girls was his responsibility, and not even the witless toddlers tested his patience as did Kahammis. She was betrothed to the grandson of Patlowah, the most trusted adviser at Klinniklinnikaht, and Sa-sat-kis was counting the days until her marriage, in the coming spring when she turned sixteen.

Wisps of cloud trailed over the hills, but down on the delta, amidst the cheeping sandpipers, the air was unnaturally still. As Kahammis was following the riverside dance of a dragonfly, her knees had begun to shake. It was a shaking that seemed to originate from within the earth, just a quivering, then the birds had fallen silent. Everything continued as before — the dragonfly's hum, the hustle and bustle around the lodges, the snuffling of Sa-sat-kis — except for the sandpipers shooting like smoke into the sky.

All at once, to the astonishment of Sa-sat-kis, Kahammis had dropped to the ground. She jumped up, slinging back her hair, then again she fell. Sa-sat-kis fumbled with his bundle of twigs, confused. "Can't you hear?" she hissed, pushing his head into the wet mud. Sa-sat-kis looked around, ready for one of her tricks. But she had pointed north, wild-eyed with fear.

She ran straight for her cedar tree, and there she would remain, Sa-sat-kis balefully reported, until her father came home. Her mother had nodded and smiled, bringing out delicacies to celebrate the return of the trading expedition: boxes of sun-dried berry cakes, baskets of nuts, and camas bulbs from farther south, carefully hoarded for such an event.

Then, gliding low behind the spit, the Wewksah warriors had burst into the bay. Kahammis had known they were Wewksah, from the legendary markings on their faces and their prows, markings which had haunted the memories of her people since the siege. And she had known instantly: the Wewksah would not have dared come if her father were alive.

What had happened to Kalowish?

~~~:~~~

12

Kahammis was in her canoe, heading north. The canoe was a gift from her uncle, Hasallum; together they had scorched, oiled, and rubbed the hull with dogfish skin until the outside shone glossy black, the inside ochre red. With eyes narrowed to contain their pride, she had watched his chisel mark out not only the family crest but a shower of dancing lines which made the canoe hers, and hers alone: Kahammis, of the spring rain.

At her knees in the canoe lay the whalebone club, retrieved from the grass beside Sa-sat-kis, crusted with Wewksah blood. She had gathered strings of dried clams from plundered food baskets, her head averted, sick with despair at her inability to provide the burial her people deserved. Though she could not have remained at Nootseetaht another night, she had barely been able to attend to the details of her departure: fishing line, fur-trimmed cape, a blank study of sea and sky. Beyond the spit, the paddling song came unbidden to her lips, a broken wail in the breeze.

As darkness fell, the swell increased. No longer could she ignore the lowering sky, the splattering rain, and the wind that came out of the southeast, a wind they called with contempt "the belch of the Wewksah." She glanced around fearfully, altering course to avoid being driven onto the rocks during the night. Except for a few straggling cormorants, she was alone with the dip of the blade and the unceasing rhythm of the waves. It was as alone as she had ever been.

The hours passed and the final band of light disappeared below the horizon, and the rain continued, slantwise and steady. With each stroke, drips slid down the insides of her arms to the warmth beneath her cape. The wind began to roar and the rain slashed her cheeks; she thrust out her paddle, tipping and toppling over the crests, into the troughs, up and down, until it seemed that each wave would be her last, and she would enter the abyss, her fingers welded to the paddle as if also carved out of Hasallum's yew. Unable to defend herself, she cowered in the bottom of her canoe. She would surrender to the hideous two-headed serpent that lived beneath the sea. She would join her slaughtered family, as had been intended all along. Sheltered from the wind and the needle-sharp spray, she waited for the serpent to rise.

She woke to a world of absolute calm.

She could hear voices, which came as no surprise; the sea monster's victims were numerous along the coast. The sky was pure blue, the sun a caress on her skin. She jerked upright, jostling the canoe. She was drifting into a wide bay, where smoke was curling above houses on a beach shaped like a crescent moon.

The voices came from a crowd of excited villagers climbing into canoes. She fell back, horrified, realizing that she had been swept past Klinniklinnikaht. Within moments the villagers were upon her, brown faces peering alongside, strong hands seizing the bow. All too well did she understand their chatter, and when she heard to whom they were delivering her, this treasure from the sea, her heart turned over in her chest.

Quassoon of Quatlukaht: she would have preferred the serpent's embrace.

~~~:~~~

From the far edge of the platform bed, under the luxurious reach of the otter-skin robe, Kahammis followed the sound of Quassoon's wife, Yatintala, muttering along the central passage of the lodge. Every second counted, her ears shutting out the racket of the birds, her bones absorbing the blissful heat of bodies and fur, trying to store enough warmth to get through another day. Quassoon stirred, and she caught her breath; his leg kicked out and she tumbled off the sleeping platform with a stifled gasp. Yatintala snorted over the hearth, where shreds of dry cedar snapped alight. Amidst the groans and distractions from neighbouring firepits, Kahammis pulled on her cape and her burden basket, and scuttled like a hermit crab out the door.

Grey wavelets lapped at the cold, grey sand. A glance up the inky slopes was all she needed to confirm another day without sun, or hope. She ran along a bramble-lined path into the forest, emerging moments later with a load of branches. She returned to the lodge and dropped the bundle beside Yatintala, darting out for more.

This was the winter camp of Yuhktu. With the passing of the first storm of the season, the southeaster that had swept Kahammis to Quatlukaht, the lodges along the crescent beach had been dismantled from their supporting frames and packed into canoes. All the boards and belongings of the village had been ferried north, to an inlet at the head of an island-filled sound. On a flat strip of land beneath the mountains, the lodges were reconstructed around the sun-bleached beams and posts waiting from previous years.

How Quassoon gloated over his prize! Hooting over her account of the massacre at Nootseetaht, verified by spies sent down the coast, screeching over her revenge on the war party, and worst of all, fondling the sacred crest on the handle of her father's whalebone club, Quassoon had found his winter sport. When he was bored, he tapped Kahammis with his lance until she recited her bloodline so far back that even Yatintala was impressed. Already he was plotting how to show her off at the feasts.

Yatintala had expressed little interest in Quassoon's dallying with female slaves, until Kahammis arrived. When she resisted Quassoon, in the beginning, everyone in the village had been greatly entertained, but now, Quassoon swam nightly into this frigid fish and behaved during the day as if caught on one of his own barbed hooks. Yatintala was disgusted, and determined: Quassoon would have only one wife.

Kahammis knew there was no chance of escape or rescue in this desolate place. And who was left of her family, to care? Quassoon had also been at Klinniklinnikaht, that fateful day her father had seen the white sails and gone up to trade. She cursed herself for the way she had fallen onto Quassoon, when the villagers dragged her in from the bay. She had sobbed for news of her father, and the roar had gone up around the village: Chief Kalowish is dead! The key to Nootseetaht lay begging at Quassoon's feet! But what of her brothers, her uncle, she had cried? Quassoon had laughed and laughed. "Boom, boom!" the children had shouted, hopping around Kahammis, kicking their legs with glee.

Then she remembered the quivering on the delta, and the rumours of weapons on the ships, worse than thunder and fire. Quassoon had picked her up and thrown her over his shoulder; neither ally nor enemy of Paquacheenish and Kalowish, he could not resist claiming such a delicious little asset of the mighty clan.

For more than a month now, she had been trapped at Yuhktu. Returning to the lodge with her second load of branches, she shrank from the eyes that watched her: vengeful eyes, greedy for the sight of the granddaughter of Paquacheenish running errands. Her forehead was creased from the tumpline on the burden basket, and her yellow cedar cape had become grimy and frayed. Yellow cedar was the mark of nobility; she could not bear to think of when her cape fell to pieces, when she would wear the red cedar bark of commoners and slaves. Soon there would be nothing left but memories, when she crouched in the shadows at night, until Quassoon's enormous hand sought out her bowed head, stroking her neck, yanking her up to the sleeping platform.

Yatintala observed her silently from the hearth. Yatintala was a tiny woman with hair that stuck out in tufts and a ferocious stare which she used to control her section of the lodge. Her fingers slid across a frame, weaving mats. Kahammis had woven mats since she was a child, and as she built up the fire with branches, her thawing fingers yearned to feel the coarse bark strands. She was, however, being punished, blamed for the loss of Yatintala's favourite loom. During the move from Quatlukaht, the canoe in which she had been travelling had been thrashed by a tide rip in the sound, and the loom had slipped over the side. Squashed amongst boxes, baskets, and nets, Kahammis had been closest; lives had been sacrificed for less. When they disembarked at Yuhktu, Yatintala had consulted with the Shaman, whose assessment of Kahammis's unworthiness was absolute, further binding her to the burden basket and the lowliest chores.

Since her capture, the Shaman had been much in demand. To Kahammis he seemed to be everywhere, peering through the mats and stacks of boxes that divided the lodge, ranting and rattling and sending chills from her neck to her knees as he reached into the lurking, murky underworld just beyond mortal touch. It was a world that had closed in on Kahammis since the massacre, a world of unresolved spirits hovering above her head like a cloud of bees. She hid her face at the smoking hearth, until Yatintala's sharp cough reminded her to widen the gap between the roof planks with the pole.

All day she had roamed with her basket, bringing back wood. The women called out to their families as they prepared the evening meal, and children appeared in hungry clusters, although there were no children at Quassoon's hearth, only slaves. Tonight Quassoon was also hosting a crowd of commoners, a small feast in anticipation of the large feast, the dramatic, week-long winter ceremonies. The essence of celebration was abundance, and Yatintala brought out salalberry cakes which had been soaking in oil since dawn. By nature acquisitive, Yatintala struggled in her role as the chief's wife, for Quassoon was expected to be good to his people, his generosity a reflection of their worth. Quassoon was a strong chief, descended from warriors and whalers of renown. In the fifteen years since his father's death by drowning, he had not gained in stature, but neither had he lost. With each passing year Yatintala's forehead had become more furrowed with the strain of squinting into the future, while her husband indulged his chiefly whims.

Quassoon reclined against a pile of boxes and mats at the hearth, facing the entrance, the premium location in the lodge. This was his favourite time of the day and the season, surrounded by supporters, recounting successes, awaiting supper, planning the winter feast. Because of his size and strength, both physical and inherited, he was at forty an utterly confident man. Yatintala bustled around him, setting out wooden bowls of eulachon grease, but he ignored her, smacking his leg and whooping at a riddle a cousin had just composed. His bare chest gleamed, and his hair swept back thickly over his shoulders, from a crown elongated at birth. The shaping of heads by cradlepads was the distinguishing feature of the coast aristocracy, to which Kahammis also belonged.

Kahammis attended to the mussels brought by fishermen from the mouth of the sound. Using wooden tongs, she lifted red-hot stones from the fire and dropped them into a cedar cooking box. When the water in the cooking box boiled, she submerged the basket of mussels, covering the box with a mat. She shut out distractions and concentrated on her work; overcooked, rubbery mussels would be another excuse for Yatintala's wrath. Although Yatintala owned several iron pots, traded from the ships, she did not trust them and instead used the stones and the bentwood boxes which had served her people from the beginning of time. Since the pots went directly into the fire, eliminating the fuss of stones, Kahammis thought these old ways were ridiculous and longed for the day she would have pots of her own.

She heaped the mussels onto trays, passing them through the noisy crowd. Soon an argument began, between Yatintala and Quassoon. A slave belonging to one of Quassoon's cousins had fallen ill and died, and his body, flung out the door, was attracting huge flocks of gulls and crows. Yatintala warned that the ruckus would wake the bears hibernating in the mountains behind Yuhktu. Quassoon, who owned the bear crest, countered Yatintala's complaints with increasingly lewd jokes. The real issue was Yatintala's resentment of all the cousins living with Quassoon; although they were older and more experienced, not one of them had brought in a whale for an entire handful of years. Cleverly they manipulated the conversation, their laughter thinning, heads bending close. Kahammis heard the murmurs: raiders, from the north. Nothing united the villagers more effectively than a grudge outstanding, an insult perceived. Last spring, an expedition from Yuhktu had been ambushed by northerners while checking the herring run in the sound. Five slave paddlers had been abducted, and two fishermen had been killed. The farther north, the fiercer the weather and the warriors; life in the south was easier, and so was the prey.

Kahammis edged away from the hearth, wondering if she would ever feel safe again; her only security was her status beneath Quassoon. With a pang, she thought of old Sa-sat-kis, snatched from his home village as a child. At death, commoners and slaves descended to a place where the wind always blew and the ship-traded blankets were full of holes. Because Sa-sat-kis had fallen defending her, might he not go to the peaceful resting place in the sky? Now that she shared the nothingness of Sa-sat-kis, this question had begun to plague her, along with memories of the years of teasing he had endured. She swallowed the berry cakes doled out by Yatintala, and her face twisted with the sorrow of nevermore, on winter nights like these, hearing his beloved voice.

Around the great room, the air had grown thick with yelling and fumes. Laughter went up nearby: Tatoosch, Quassoon's only son, was picking lice out of his hair and popping them into his mouth. Smacking his lips gustily, he fingered the nape of his neck, his ear ornaments jingling and jangling in the firelight.

Nineteen or twenty years of age, Tatoosch was hulking and hirsute like his father, although he lacked the canniness that quickened Quassoon's face. His eyebrows were heavy and wide, darkened with paint, his nose a flat triangle above protruding lips. He had recently been married, but his wife had returned to her village in the sound, and her father, the chief, had sent a message saying that she would not be back. It was whispered that Tatoosch had mistreated his young bride. Yatintala, who had looked forward to reigning over a daughter-in-law, and who even in her worst moments would have welcomed children around the hearth, berated Tatoosch constantly for this disgrace. Tatoosch wandered the beaches or occupied himself with painting complicated patterns of charcoal and ochre on his face, and Kahammis avoided him with extreme care.

When the eating was over, Yatintala passed around soft, shredded cedar bark to wipe away the grease. Out came the rattles and the hollowed planks, which the men hammered on with hard, polished sticks. A song began, melancholy and sweet, then louder and faster, rising up the lonely slopes to the snow-covered peaks. On went the

18

singing, the consulting, and the scheming, into the night. Head against her knees, Kahammis heard mention of Paquacheenish, invitations, grand plans. Finally Quassoon beckoned her to bed where, to her relief, he immediately fell asleep. She lay with her ear to the wallboards, listening as a breeze lifted the fir boughs, the waves slapping at the sand in reply. Towards morning a shower went over, and she dreamed that she was curled beside Sa-sat-kis, under the rain on their Nootseetaht roof. She woke to the racket of the birds, and Quassoon's hands encircling her waist.

~~~:~~~

It was the day before the winter ceremonies were to begin. The weather, blustery during the weeks of preparation, cleared just in time for the visitors, and the sun appeared above the inlet like a brilliant, fleeting flame. Kahammis crunched along the frosty paths with her burden basket, scattering the woodland birds. While she gathered sticks, she examined the shoreline for a bloated corpse that might have washed up in the night; the dead slave had been dragged down to the beach during the storm. Yatintala had swept through the lodge like a storm herself, ordering Kahammis to haul out mats laden with fishbones, ashes, and empty shells. The mood was anxious; Quassoon and the cousins had disappeared up the stony creekbed with their deerskin pouches of amulets and potions, to cleanse themselves and pray. The women assembled boxes and dishes, and baskets of shredded bark, shaking out their jewellery, oiling and plaiting their hair.

Stacked beside the lodges were supplies of firewood, and fragrant evergreens for sleeping on, and rolls of mats which would unwind from the entrance of Quassoon's lodge down to the visiting canoes. Above the beach, a row of carved welcome figures extended their arms in a stiff but universal gesture of goodwill. Yes, the village was ready, and the villagers felt worthy of the honours about to come their way.

Kahammis emptied her basket by the hearth, taking the water containers Yatintala gave her to fill at Quassoon's private pond. The fresh air drew her onwards, along a deer trail which wound past the marsh where the geese overwintered, past Quassoon's pond, until she ended up, unexpectedly, in a grove of conifers far behind Yuhktu. Massive, mossy columns surrounded her, beneath a canopy of green and gold. Here and there, shafts of sunlight slanted to the forest floor, a cushion of needles that had sifted down over the centuries and absorbed all sound. With her brothers, Kahammis had ransacked the forest around Nootseetaht, always one step ahead of the imaginary imps and monsters, and with her mother she had travelled the bark-gathering paths, but it had not been like this, silent and seemingly empty, yet serene. She sank against the trunk of a giant cedar, a distant relative of the tree on the ridge above Nootseetaht. A chirruping squirrel broke the spell, and she got slowly to her feet.

She pushed her way back towards Quassoon's pond, through salal which grew to the height of the tallest man and was impenetrable except along the animal trails. As she knelt beside the pond, reaching out with the dipping box, a glint on the surface of the water caught her eye. Puzzled, she looked up. Tatoosch was perched in the fork of a fir snag across the pond, extracting hairs from his chin with a pair of mussel shells and a little mirror. When he grinned lazily, she was too surprised to move. Now was the time for purification; the success of the winter ceremonies depended on the sincerity of the hosts, who bathed, abstained, and understood that the outcome of events could be altered by the smallest improper act. Not only was Tatoosch preening at his father's private pond, he should have been up in the mountains, praying with the men. Was he here because he knew that she came each morning with water containers to fill?

So ingrained were the purity taboos that she could not comprehend what he was doing when he unwound himself from the snag and dropped to the ground, flipping aside his cape, his pink-tipped penis throbbing in his fist. Letting go of the dipper, she sprang to her feet. Tatoosch hurtled after her, crashing through the underbrush. She looked over her shoulder, terrified by his nakedness and by the penalty to her, accomplice to his wrongs. Within minutes she had outdistanced him; though well-developed in his upper body from paddling, Tatoosch was not a runner, wheezing and dragging behind.

For the rest of the afternoon she stayed close to the village, searching for sticks with trembling hands. Her only wish was that she could let go, and float through the opening on top of her head, where souls escaped, to join her family. Cosseted daughter of a chief, she had been groomed for a lifetime of duty and reward with Patlowah's grandson at Klinniklinnikaht. Children of the chiefs were expected to be humble and kind, mediators, an example to their peers. Above all, girls were expected to be chaste, with the onset of puberty the central event in their lives. Her own puberty had been marked by symbolic dances; purifying water had been poured at her feet, and she had spent days fasting in seclusion behind a screen at the rear of the lodge. At the final feast she had given up her childhood name to become Kahammis, of the spring rain. After puberty, sanctions and supervision were very strict, a drain on Sa-sat-kis, who had wondered if he or Kahammis would last until her marriage. Then, with less than a year to go, the massacre had changed the course for them all.

Sanctions and sacrifices, for the benefit of Quassoon? How victoriously he had held forth to his people that first night at Quatlukaht, with Kahammis attached by a leather thong to a housepost, lest she repeat her crazed outburst upon hearing of her father's death. Finally it was bedtime, under a quarter moon glimpsed as she was led to the urinal box kept by the entrance to scare away evil spirits during the night. The entire village had held its breath when Quassoon shoved Kahammis onto his sleeping platform, Yatintala a motionless lump in the shadows nearby.

Kahammis had felt a rush of heat beneath the magnificent robe. Groping and grunting, Quassoon shredded off her skirt and fell on top of her, suffocating her with his weight. He split her thighs so forcefully that she screamed, clawing at his face. Suddenly he collapsed, with a tremulous squeak. Gasping for breath, she had been certain that she would be killed, in penance for killing the chief. But within minutes he revived, rolling onto his back, and she had become conscious of the stinging trickle between her legs. Everyone in the lodge exhaled, settling in to sleep. Silent tears had soaked her hair. An hour later, adrift in a terrifying dream, she awoke to Quassoon slurping at her breasts. Since then his need for her had been insatiable; the nights he spent away with his men were her only reprieve.

At noon the next day, the first guests arrived.

The men had emerged early in the morning, scoured and subdued. The women, up before dawn, flitted from hearth to hearth with baskets and boxes, glancing out at the inlet, praising the clear skies which held, and pinching the cheeks of the children, who were tripping over each other in anticipation of the festivities.

A cry signalled specks in the distance, dark specks that took on the shape of canoes under the scrutiny of the villagers gathered outside the lodges, their hands shading their eyes. Quassoon assumed a regal pose, his robe of the finest yellow cedar bark wrapped under his left arm and fastened over his right shoulder. His hair was oiled and pulled into a topknot, stuck with a hemlock sprig. All of the men of high status had sprinkled their heads with eagle down, including Tatoosch, at his father's side. Copper pendants swung from his ears and nose, and there was a smirk on his freshly decorated face as he succeeded, with much effort, in catching the attention of Kahammis. She withdrew on the pretext of helping Yatintala, who, not a big woman to begin with, was so laden with strings of cylindrical, ivory-coloured shells that she could barely stand upright.

The shells Yatintala staggered beneath were dentalia, obtained offshore where nature and hereditary right permitted their harvest. Weighted poles, tipped with twigs, were lowered from canoes into the muddy ocean bottom, snagging the dentalia which were then cleaned and sorted into the standard lengths for trade. Yatintala's necklace was a confirmation of her wealth and position, and Quassoon glanced at his scrawny wife with pride.

A murmur went up: Mannakaht! Now it was Tatoosch who tried to withdraw, shuffling from foot to foot until stilled by his father's scowl. Chief T'isharth, in the lead, was the father of Tatatoe, Tatoosch's reluctant bride. T'isharth represented three small villages on the islands clustered at the mouth of the sound. Less privileged and more exposed, these villages had experienced many setbacks, and T'isharth's struggle to balance foresight with hindsight had given him a faceful of nervous tics, ridiculed by Quassoon. Although Quassoon could not ignore his neighbour, he made sure that T'isharth knew his place. Yet, T'isharth had bravely come to the aid of the herring fishermen hijacked last spring, and he had supported his daughter's rejection of Tatoosch, despite the cancelled gifts, so that the loss of honour ended up in the house of Quassoon.

The Mannakaht visitors drew nearer and the villagers could hear them singing, striking the sides of their canoes with the butt ends of their paddles while the gulls wheeled noisily along the banks of the inlet. The song sank, trailing into silence as the high, carved prows slid up the beach and T'isharth stepped ashore. With his topknot and fur-trimmed robe he was as stylish as Quassoon, who came forward to guide him to the lodge on clean, new mats. The Mannakaht guests followed the two chiefs inside, where ushers hovered, ready to carry out the much-discussed seating plan.

Drummers took their positions beside a line of young women at the far end of the lodge, on a stage defined by mats suspended from the beams. When the drums boomed, the women began to sing and dance with gentle, lyrical movements of their arms, their palms upturned in welcome. The song closed to a crescendo of drumming, voices straining through the smokeholes into the sky, then the performers bowed their heads while the visitors took their places. No sooner were they seated than from the beach sounded another cry, and the villagers excitedly reassembled, Quassoon in his pose.

This time it was Ewona, chief of the Sheshalam, from the north arm of the inlet, with a summer village on the outer coast. Like Quassoon, Ewona had become rich trading ôtter skins and was renowned as a hunter of whales. He was, therefore, Quassoon's equal, though not in physique, for he was squat and swarthy with legs even more bowed than usual amongst the males of the coast. He sped shoreward with a tremendously loud rendition of the paddle song, in an entourage of black canoes. He brought his wife and eldest son, setting Yatintala ajiggle beneath her shining shells.

Kahammis watched from behind a corner of the lodge, gnawing at her fingers, searching for a familiar face among the arrivals. When Ewona was settled, with a repeat of the welcome song, Yatintala shouted for her slaves. In late fall, she had supervised the digging of fern rhizomes which had been dried and were now steaming in a large pit. While it was still dark, Kahammis had built a fire in the stone-lined pit. She and Yatintala had dumped in baskets of wet seaweed, then rhizomes, then more seaweed and rhizomes, until the pit was filled. Served with salmon roe and berry cakes, the starchy underground stems rounded out a plain but plentiful meal.

The three chiefs were cleaning their hands when they heard an urgent call from the beach: Wikkosum was coming, in command of the Wasquimaht, making fast time despite his long journey. Wikkosum was Quassoon's most northerly ally, fierce and possibly treacherous, for if he joined up with the raiders or divulged tactical information about Quatlukaht or Yuhktu, Quassoon would be doomed and this they all knew.

As the Wasquimaht canoes approached, a hush fell over the crowd. Wikkosum had brought his wife, sons, and daughters. Yatintala almost swooned, and Quassoon was swollen with importance, his broad nose pointing into the breeze. Wikkosum's portly wife wore an even heftier mantle of dentalia, and the faces of the Wasquimaht men bore elaborate red and black designs, applied several miles back, where they had stopped to regroup and prepare.

The third welcome song nearly raised the roof beams, and the ushers dashed between the hearths to properly arrange the newcomers. From where she tended the cooking pits, Kahammis watched the inlet. The sun had crossed over, and shadows were sliding down the slopes when a distant speck on the water broke in half, then half again, and a cheer went up for the final guests, travelling against the tide and the fair-weather wind yet still capable of a rousing song. Not until the canoes reached the beach was Kahammis reassured that they were from Klinniklinnikaht, with ravens and whales entwined along the high prows. She counted a dozen men, accompanied by their short-haired slaves. Could that gaunt, solemn leader be Patlowah, grandfather of her betrothed? She crept closer, reckless with certainty, until tinkling shells warned her of Yatintala's approach. Yatintala snapped at her, ordering her back to the pits.

So the assembly was complete: not the biggest feast Quassoon had ever hosted, nor the smallest, three years in the planning, accumulating, and inviting. While his lodge would be used for the performances, visitors were billeted according to rank and family connections. Warriors from each visiting party were delegated to sleep in the canoes as guardians of the gifts, lest some careless impulse mar the happy mood.

For Yatintala, the stockpiling and serving of food was an overwhelming challenge, but one that must be met for the week to be a success. She thrummed like a hummingbird in a gale and without her hard-working slaves she would have spun into orbit, while the wives of the cousins nattered amongst themselves about who should do what next.

The breeze died away as evening fell, and the inlet glimmered beneath the amber sky. Smoke spiralled over the rooftops and hung in soft grey layers, undisturbed except by tardy flocks of ducks beating their way home to the marshes for the night. Such a spectacular beginning could only mean that the supreme powers were pleased, that sufficient respect had been paid to the laws of the natural world.

Out by the cooking pits, Kahammis overheard the cousins' wives speculating on the absence of Paquacheenish, convinced that his health had failed. She turned her back on their gossip and edged closer to the lodge, listening through the cracks in the wallboards to the Song of Gladness; at Nootseetaht, she would have been leading that swaying line.

The huge crowd was excited and impatient, soothed by the deep voice of Quassoon's Speaker as he greeted each guest with a speech on the honour brought to the hosts. When it was time for the main evening meal, Yatintala kept Kahammis busy outside, heaping more steamed roots into tubs which required two men to lift. Baskets of clams, stored in salt water, were brought inside to roast. Bowls were piled with sweet, chewy strips of dried salmon, and Yatintala filled ornate dishes with oil for the chiefs. Slaves ran back and forth, bearing water and shredded bark. The guests ate without hurry, for there was so much food that each family would carry out leftovers at the evening's end.

Beneath the starry sky, beside the open door, Kahammis nibbled at strips of fish she had hidden in the folds of her cape. The mat dividers were down and she had a clear view into the lodge. Patlowah and his delegation had been positioned directly across from Quassoon, in deference to the greatness of Paquacheenish. The families of Wikkosum and Ewona lined the central aisle, and T'isharth had been put closest to the door. Wikkosum's wife was a popular woman, her jokes about her appetite sending ripples of laughter through the crowd. Wikkosum, also a hearty eater, crammed his hands into the overflowing trays, grease dripping down his chin. Across from the Wasquimaht, Ewona chewed methodically while his wife assessed each detail of Yatintala's domestic wealth. Tatoosch belched and spat, sizing up the other young men. The Mannakaht sat quietly, and although T'isharth covered his twitching jaw with his hand, his charcoaled eyebrows shot upwards at random, giving a comical twist to his otherwise thoughtful face.

As Patlowah ate, he also searched the crowd. Kahammis noticed his casual but thorough examination of the commoners and slaves bunched around the food trays against the walls. Her capture at Quatlukaht would have been relayed to Klinniklinnikaht by the trading parties which travelled the coast year-round. With Kalowish dead, what losses and gains to rival chiefs would decide her worth? Patlowah's presence at the feast was significant, for it was his grandson's bride who had been snatched away.

She inched forward from the doorway, willing Patlowah's eyes to keep going, to meet hers, and they did, in a split-second of recognition. Then he bowed to a query from Quassoon and she sank back, hugging herself. Watching Quassoon entertain his guests, she was not fooled: his grins and guffaws belied his iron grip. She was out in the cold for good reason, lest Patlowah or anyone else get too close.

Yatintala rose to divide up the leftovers, flushed with benevolence and the blaze. Her slaves took away the empty dishes, and the singing resumed, reaching Kahammis at the edge of the inlet, where she knelt rinsing dishes.

Songs were the personal property of individuals and families, presented with immense ceremony and meaning, reaching far back in time and ritualized year after year, empowering their owners with their understanding of who they were, and what they had become. Some of the songs were in the ancient language, and some were in dialect; some rang with victory, and some were resonant with grief. Kahammis listened and wept, her lonely heart washed with tears.

All through the night, the plank drums pounded and the birdbone whistles shrilled. Hoops strung with shells and deer hooves rattled and clacked, and the slaves stoked the fires. Sparks shot through the roof-boards to the stars, an infinite amphitheatre beneath which Kahammis slept, curled on a mat over a cooking pit, warmed by the underground coals.

Isolated by hard labour in the days to come, she lived on tidbits grabbed from the tubs, enduring taunts and snickers, and sleeping with the other slaves. She made many detours to avoid Tatoosch, who wrestled in the sand with the visiting young nobles, their laughter punctuated by roars of triumph and defeat. When they were not testing each other's strength, the young men gambled with sets of black and white bones concealed in their hands, and again Tatoosch flaunted his winnings. At night, Kahammis watched between the wall-boards as masked dancers writhed through the coast mythology: Eagle and Whale, Thunderbird and Wolf, Raven and Frog, and more. Baffled by the riddles of the jesters, she concentrated instead on the faces: Patlowah grave, Quassoon aglow. Then, when it seemed that the cere-monies had been going on forever, it was the evening of the last day.

The chiefs donned their carved head-dresses, the muscles in their oiled shoulders gleaming in the flames. Tatoosch had sprinkled powdered mica onto his grease-layered cheeks, his ego running rampant after a week of success at the bone games. The wives were queenly, this being Yatintala's crowning meal.

Fishermen had been sent out to the deep waters of the sound, trolling for spring salmon which had been boiled in the cooking boxes until reduced to a thick broth. Bundles of bitter cinquefoil roots dug from the tidal flats were steamed for hours and served with eulachon oil. Small fish greasy enough to ignite, the eulachon were harvested in spring by the northern villages and profitably traded south. After the roots came succulent mussels, then camas bulbs, sweet and mealy and expensive, stored since summer and steamed overnight. Wikkosum's wife beamed with satisfaction, and Yatintala beamed with relief.

Now Quassoon's grandest hour began, the distribution of his wealth. To give was to receive, perhaps many times over in future ceremonies, but most importantly in the esteem of his people and his guests. The Speaker discoursed once again on the glory brought by all assembled, then, at prearranged drum signals, the gifts were carried forth. Patlowah was first, nodding sombrely at the stacks of new blankets from the ships. Inlaid boxes contained smaller boxes of buttons and beads, and, incongruously, a seaman's cap. There were baskets of dried food, each basket a work of art in itself. And there were muskets, though inferior to the bow and unreliable, known to misfire. Wikkosum counted up his muskets with a relish not lost on Quassoon. When it was Ewona's turn, his wife held up each piece of copper, each coloured bead. Bolts of ship's cotton were laid at the feet of the women, and sheaves of bear grass, for their best weaving.

T'isharth accepted his share with an uncertain face; there had been no mention of his daughter's marital difficulties. The blankets he received would be divided amongst the Mannakaht villages, much needed as capes and covers now that the otters were harder to find. It would take several lifetimes to match Quassoon's largesse, but did this compensate for the behaviour of Tatoosch?

The gifts continued in diminishing value even to the commoners, followed by the responses of appreciation. Restless from sitting, the audience was waiting eagerly for the music when Patlowah raised his hand. He had gifts of his own, he said. He summoned his assistants, who held up twenty perfect lengths of dentalia shells. His heart was like that of a little bird, said Patlowah, in the face of Quassoon's majesty. Quassoon leaned forward as Patlowah lowered his voice. Therefore, murmured Patlowah, a giant of a man like Quassoon would think nothing of freeing a slave.

A hush flattened the fidgeting crowd. Outside, Kahammis sensed this sudden shift: Patlowah was calm, and Quassoon was a study of innocence, but Yatintala's eyes slid revealingly to the door. It was the will of Paquacheenish, continued Patlowah, that Kahammis be returned. One by one, twenty more ivory lengths were laid before Quassoon, who shook his head. Kahammis watched, giddy with hope, and Patlowah beckoned to his assistants, who held up otter pelts, the crowd gasping as the pile grew. Quassoon's crafty eyes thinned and again, imperceptibly, he shook his head. Patlowah seemed mystified; Yatintala's gaze was riveted on her husband's face. A lone figure bobbed in the shadows: the Shaman. Kahammis stared into the lodge, clutching the doorpost for support.

Quassoon jumped to his feet and shoved the pelts and the dentalia back to Patlowah, barking for his warriors. He whispered instructions, and his men ran down the central aisle, past Kahammis quivering in the dark. His guests looked anxiously at each other, and at their chiefs, swivelling again to a commotion at the door. Six warriors on each side carried Quassoon's most prized possession, his whaling canoe. When she saw the canoe, Yatintala nearly fainted into the fire. Reverently, the warriors set their load between Patlowah and Quassoon, dismissing themselves.

Quassoon stretched his arms, surveying the packed lodge. Then, with powerful swings from prow to stern, he demolished the exquisite canoe. Patlowah's face was closed; Kahammis slipped down the post to the ground. For once and for all, Quassoon was demonstrating the force of his refusal, and his disdain for material wealth. He had taken the great risk, however, of angering the Thunderbird and the Whale. His tool of destruction was none other than the war club which had belonged to Kalowish.

Fog rolled up the inlet through the night. The next morning, along the dank shoreline, the canoes sat heavily with their bounty as the Mannakaht, the Wasquimaht, the Sheshalam and the Klinniklinnikaht visitors prepared to leave. Kahammis crept off with the water containers, to the sounds of the Song of Farewell, repeated as each convoy swung away from the beach and was swallowed up. A pall settled over the village, more penetrating than the weather, mixed with awe and the tension that presages change.

Yatintala spent the day on the sleeping platform, the Shaman at her side. Kahammis gathered wood until dusk, and when she came in with her burden basket she heard the Shaman chanting through her own fog, the fog of despair. She had been certain that when Patlowah left, she would be aboard his canoe.

Supper at Quassoon's hearth was spartan, with Yatintala refusing to get up to cook, and all the leftovers given away. Kahammis's last hopes were extinguished when Quassoon ordered her to eat from his dish. Tatoosch sniggered at this gesture of intimacy, while the cousins and their wives choked over their dried fish. Remnants of the whaling canoe still littered the central aisle. Evenings following feasts were usually an opportunity for the participants to recount their successes, but tonight Quassoon impatiently tapped his fists, tugging at the pendants around his neck. He thanked his people for their loyalty and told them that they must be very tired after all their work. With a yawn, he rose for bed.

Ahead of him, he pushed Kahammis. The mat dividers were back in place again, and in the privacy of his corner, he commanded her to undress. She had just bared herself when he leapt off the platform in a rage. She cringed, but he lunged past her, through the mats. There was a yelp of pain and surprise as he landed on Tatoosch, who limped away from his observation hole, groaning and holding his head.

Many nights had gone by since Quassoon and Kahammis had shared the otter-skin robe. He fell onto her, thrashing like a wounded bear, finished almost before he began. But he was too aroused to sleep, caressing her silky hair, her breasts and thighs, as if discovering her for the first time. Then he was onto her again, his clumsy attempts at tenderness most revolting to her of all.

Southeast winds brought back the grey — skies, water, trees, and sand. Yatintala and Quassoon reached some sort of agreement: Kahammis slaved for one during the day, for the other at night. Repeatedly at dawn she dreamed that she heard the screech owl, coming to claim what might be left of her soul. Her thoughts became unclear and her cape was in tatters; her canoe lay exposed to the rain. She had begun to wander far from the village; having lost her fear of the forest, she had more range than the other slaves, who were suspicious and scornful but left her alone. Several times she found herself in the grove behind Quassoon's pond, not remembering how she got there, drooping with helplessness and fatigue.

Then it snowed heavily through one night. The villagers were confined to their lodges except for the children, who burst outside,

29

chasing snowflakes with their hands and tongues, sniffling and rosy-cheeked when their mothers called them back. On the second day, the slaves were sent out for fuel. The landscape had been transformed by the whiteness and the weight of the snow, branches rebounding with plumes of spray as they released their load. Red berries stood out on the frozen bushes, the undropped leaves furled against the cold. But for Kahammis red meant violence: blood on her baby sisters, blood on her fingers, blood on the spit at Nootseetaht. Shivering, she turned away.

She had reached the grove and was dozing against a big cedar when a slight sound caused her to glance up. A young woman stood close to the tree, watching her, incredulous. She was wearing a cape unlike any Kahammis had seen, made of soft, pale wool, fastened in the front with a carved piece of antler. Her hair was braided with wool and her legs and feet were wrapped with deerskin.

She pointed to herself, smiling. "Sheebo," she said.

Kahammis could not speak, overcome by shock, and then shame at her own torn cape, her tangled hair. When a woodpecker drummed insistently, not far off, the young woman turned and ran through the trees. Kahammis stared after her, crouching over her footprints in the snow. She pulled on her burden basket in a daze, and returned to Yuhktu.

All through the next day she waited in the grove, half-believing that she had imagined those smiling eyes, dragging herself away at dusk. Yatintala kept her in the lodge the following morning, and by the time she reached the grove, it was too late. At the base of the cedar tree she found the antler tine which had fastened Sheebo's cape. It was carved into the shape of a loon, decorated with pearly chips of shell. Weeping inconsolably, she tucked it into her fur collar.

She visited the grove every day, in the hope that Sheebo would appear again. At night she listened to the storytelling around the hearth; some of the elders spoke of hapless villagers lured by spirits into caves up the slopes; some spoke of strange tribes compelled to wander through the inner forest, in penance for an offence. Furtively she touched her collar, reassuring herself that the little loon was real.

Winter passed in a flurry of wind-driven rain, fog, and more wind. Then, on a sunny afternoon, the herring fishermen departed for the islands in the sound, where they would camp, waiting for the clouds of gulls which signalled the spawning runs. Now the villagers had something to anticipate, the feast honouring the herring, setting off a cycle of harvest which would last until late fall, when the storage boxes would once again be full.

Sixteen years earlier, Kahammis had been born on such an afternoon. She knew this because her mother had sung to her, commemorating her arrival into the world. Now, pausing to watch the fishermen, she suddenly noticed the light sparkling on the waves; tight buds had emerged on the boughs arching overhead. Like the stripped branches, she had bent but endured; one day, her hands would again feel the loom and she would weave herself the finest cape on the coast. She was designing the cape's border when a squabble broke out nearby: two crested jays and a nest-building crow, in competition for a twig. The crow was so indignant, and the jays so cocky and mischievous, that Kahammis chortled aloud. The birds abandoned their dispute and hopped closer to this enchanting new sound, and her laughter spun out over the inlet, a salute to the hope that comes with spring.

~~~:~~~

Kahammis was miles from Quatlukaht, running along the sand until she was far enough away to feel free. She ran just out of reach of the surf, racing the lines of swell which drew nearer and nearer, turning from ripples into mounds and then into thundering walls, dispersing to nothing along the shoaling shore.

Although the weather had improved and Quassoon had moved his people to the outer coast, Kahammis had given up her fantasies of rescue, telling herself repeatedly to accept her fate. With each passing month this became even more difficult as Quassoon's obsession with her worsened; he had begun to walk with a strut when she was present, not unlike his son Tatoosch. And how he loved to preen with mirrors, winking at her as she tugged a wooden comb through his mane of hair.

It was the whaling season, and she was grateful for the rites of purification which forbade a whaler from taunting the spirits with his sperm. Only when Quassoon was out hunting did she feel anxious: would Yatintala have the nerve to sell her north? The other slaves had been titillating themselves with the possibilities; apparently both Ewona and Wikkosum had taken a fancy to her at the winter feast.

31

The villagers would support Yatintala, for despite the prestige associated with capturing the granddaughter of Paquacheenish, they were afraid of her, and afraid even more of the effect she had on their chief.

Yatintala's strategy was simple: exhaustion. Since the day in the spring when the fishermen had reported the first herring, Yatintala had been caught up in a frenzy of work. With Kahammis replacing her under the robe, Yatintala's value was defined by the accumulation of food, all the more necessary since the excesses of the ceremonies.

Not even Tatoosch brought pleasure to his mother; after weeks of absence he appeared in the bay, his canoe low on the waterline.

"What are those?" asked Yatintala, inspecting the trinkets and muskets he carried up to the lodge.

"Trade," he evasively replied.

"Bone games!" she muttered to herself.

She had begun to rely on the Shaman, and his beady eyes glistened with importance. He was an enormous worry to Kahammis. The only magic-maker she had known had been the impartial old crone at Nootseetaht, who healed sick babies and could throw her voice, and imitate the call of any bird Kahammis and her brothers could name.

Thinking of her brothers reopened the wounds of loneliness for Kahammis, and she slowed to a walk, gazing pensively across the waves. Fog was forming along the horizon, as it often did during the summer months. Somewhere out there was Quassoon, on his third expedition for whales. The task of assisting him had drained Yatintala; for many days, she prayed with him to the ocean, to the four winds, to the moon. Wearing a headband woven and painted by his wife, Quassoon had fasted and scrubbed himself to get rid of distasteful human smells. The whale must want to die, to be admired and appreciated; through songs, the whale must be subdued so that none of the whalers would be killed. The progress of the hunt depended on the chief, who was judged by the higher powers as to the purity of his goals.

Yatintala had collapsed onto her sleeping platform, attended by her slaves. If she ate or drank, the whale would not be pleased. If she had a pain, perhaps the whale had been hit, or if she could not breathe, the whale might be diving deeply into the sea. She lay rigidly, for this was Quassoon's third attempt. Until he brought in a whale, no other hunters could lift their harpoons, and Quatlukaht did without the most important harvest of all.

The herring rakes and the salmon nets had come up full, and the hemlock-branch fences set under water had been retrieved loaded with spawn; they had feasted well, and dried what they could not eat. Then had come the shift to Quatlukaht, and the search for the otters. Pelts were thickest in the spring, and the people were looking forward to the taste of otter oil. The men had gone out in small canoes at dawn, skirting the kelp beds over the reefs, while back at the lodges, the women readied the scrapers and the stretching frames.

"Your bow is twisted?" Yatintala had asked sarcastically, when the hunters returned the first day. At the end of a week they had cleaned less than a dozen skins. Quassoon had shrugged, but his back and shoulders were bloody from purifying, and his face was haggard in the noon glare. Without otters, there would be no blankets or muskets or eulachon oil to make up for what they had given away. Week after week the men went out, but the otters had disappeared.

"To where?" asked Yatintala, a question which echoed across the hearths.

One of the cousins wondered aloud, "What if Paquacheenish sneaked up to our reefs before we came around from Yuhktu?"

"Shut your mouth!" growled Quassoon, and Kahammis had winced at the hostile stares.

But the halibut eagerly sought the longlines baited with octopus, followed by the salmon — chinook, sockeye, coho — wave after wave of fish, and a rhythm of cleaning, cutting, and drying that would culminate with the dog salmon run in the fall. While the men were out on the water, the women were busy gathering bulbs and berries and roots, making use of every minute of the lengthening days. Kahammis's ankles were crisscrossed with scratches from snagging vines, and her fingers were stained purple from the berries. Her neck was wrenched from keeping watch over her shoulder in the meadows behind the village, for the dark rump of a bear, or worse, for Tatoosch.

As she scanned the fogbank offshore, questions tossed around in her mind like chunks of driftwood in the swell. During the hunt, Quassoon did not sleep in the lodge; he went to his sacred pool along with his crew. The previous night, before he left, she overheard him conferring with Yatintala at the other end of the sleeping platform.

"Make her stay on the mat with you," he whispered.

There was a scuffling as Yatintala pulled herself upright. "Absolutely not! Do you want to confuse him even more?" She was referring to the whale, Kahammis understood. "You've insulted him with your second-best canoe," hissed Yatintala, and Quassoon had stormed out, Kahammis quaking beneath the robe. Was she going to be blamed for this, too?

Quassoon was only a few miles from shore, at the edge of the fog which advanced and retreated, swirled and descended over the four ghostly, whaling canoes. Each vessel was forty feet long, rendered with maul, chisel, and adze by the finest craftsmen from a single cedar log. Quassoon crouched in the bow with his hand resting on the shaft of his harpoon. He was sweating beneath his bearskin robe and his bulb-tipped, conical hat. He sucked morosely at the water box, disoriented from lack of food and sleep, from the rise and fall of the swell.

Never in his life had he felt so conflicted: burdened with his heritage, maddened by lust for Kahammis, frustrated with Yatintala, the otters, the whale. He must prove himself as a chief and a man, to quiet Yatintala and win Kahammis the proper way. Lately, he had been tormented by a longing to make Kahammis his wife. Married, her usefulness to him increased a thousand times: an alliance with Paquacheenish, access to her vast wealth, and the sons he deserved, to perpetuate his name. The issue of sons grieved him constantly, for he could understand neither the flaws of Tatoosch nor the failure of Yatintala to bear more heirs. With Kahammis at his side, he could rule the coast. Kalowish was dead and Paquacheenish was ailing, and already Kahammis had achieved legendary status with her beauty, her bloodline, and her revenge on the Wewksah, a revenge which thrilled him all the more as he mounted her during the night. Somehow, though, every turn seemed to bring obstacles and doubts. He tightened his hold on his harpoon, mouthing a prayer. His crewmen were getting worn down; it was a miracle he needed now.

He was ready to give up when he heard a cry: Kwatyet, from the bow of the farthest canoe, shrouded in fog. Pausing with suspense, then chilled with wonder, the hunters inhaled the whale's ripe, whooshing breath. Suddenly the whale was upon them, an enormous, barnacle-backed grey which rolled over and surveyed the black canoes with a knowing eye.

Quassoon cut through the waves, bracing himself as he approached from the side and behind, at the mercy of his steersman, his heart nearly leaping out of his mouth along with words of entreaty and hope. Tensing the muscles in his right shoulder and arm, he aimed, hesitated, the steersman swerved, then almost too late he thrust, the barbed point of the harpoon driving deeply into the flesh behind the left flipper. With a grunt of elation he fell back, his paddlers instantly reversing as the injured whale rolled, and rolled again.

Lunging for the line, Quassoon guided out the oiled, knotted lengths of bull kelp while the steersman avoided the flailing tail. Quassoon's father had been knocked overboard by a mighty fluke, the worst disaster that had ever befallen the family: the chief was dead, and no humpback or grey had been taken for six subsequent years. The water foamed crimson with every thrash, then the whale stilled, gathering strength to sound as the paddlers scrambled to pay out the line to which the sealskin floats were attached.

As the whale dove, Quassoon screamed himself hoarse with prayer, his men poised with floats and harpoons. After what seemed an impossible wait, the whale surfaced, rolling and blowing in a maelstrom of blood. Quassoon closed in with another harpoon thrust, the canoe almost swamping while the paddlers frantically paid out the second line. The whale veered offshore, pulling strongly despite its injuries and its load, a triumphant Quassoon beneath the bearskin leading the chants of comfort and glory to their dying friend.

Kahammis glanced at the afternoon sun, realizing that she had been away for too long. Sprinting back across the sand, she tried to prepare herself for Yatintala's fury if the hunt failed. Quassoon would clench his fists, and his people would be even more glum and watchful. She pushed through a shortcut in the salal, emerging on the village beach. Then she saw visiting canoes pulled up below the lodges. Quickly, she shrank out of sight.

But wait! These were Mannakaht canoes, and she recognized T'isharth from the winter celebrations at Yuhktu. His canoes were loaded; since this was the trading season, he must be on his way home from the ships at Klinniklinnikaht. Had T'isharth found the otters, then?

The Mannakaht men lounged in the sunshine, resting on their journey and exchanging news with the villagers. Kahammis circled behind the lodges, afraid to show herself, lest Yatintala get the idea of swapping her first to the Mannakaht and from there north to Wikkosum. She was forced back into the trees by the sound of approaching footsteps. A man stopped close to her and urinated into the salal. She bit her fingers when she saw who it was: T'isharth!

"Chief T'isharth, of the great Mannakaht," she whispered.

Startled, T'isharth reached for the club at his waist.

"I am Kahammis, daughter of Kalowish." She stepped out, not looking up until he relaxed his hand. Her composure disintegrated at the sight of his face. "What has happened to my father?" she cried.

T'isharth cleared his throat, glancing around. He moved closer, and she knew that she could trust him; his first loyalty would be to Paquacheenish, who controlled the coast trade.

"I have spoken with Hasallum," murmured T'isharth.

Hasallum! Her uncle who had gone north with Kalowish on that fateful journey, to intercept the ship. Hasallum was alive? Kahammis could hardly breathe.

"There was a fight in the channel," continued T'isharth, referring to the anchorage in front of Klinniklinnikaht. "The Wewksah were there. Three times, the Wewksah have burned the ships visiting their own shores. Now they must cross the straits to Klinniklinnikaht, for no ship will come to them. The furs they brought were not as good as your father's; he made excellent trade. The Wewksah became resentful and demanded kegs. When the ship was ready to leave, they were already drinking from the kegs. But," gulped T'isharth, holding his jaw, "the drink was not strong enough for those angry Wewksah."

Recalling discussions around the hearth, Kahammis guessed that the Wewksah might have tried to pass off the inferior pelts of the river otters, a ruse common at dusk or when business was done in a rush. The men on the ships would have retaliated by watering the liquor in the kegs.

"The Wewksah attacked the ship!" T'isharth shook his head, as if in disbelief. "The ship aimed guns into the channel." With his hands he described the cannons mounted on the ship's stern. "The guns fired," sighed T'isharth, "and the Nootseetaht canoes were in the way."

Kahammis struggled to remain standing, to hear what T'isharth had to say.

"The ship left quickly. Your brother Aneetsick was not hurt. He tried to go after the Wewksah, but since he was so outnumbered, the Klinniklinnikaht men held him back. The Wewksah slipped out of the channel and headed south."

"They stopped at Nootseetaht," sobbed Kahammis, "to finish what they had begun!"

"A village is only as strong as its chief," nodded T'isharth. "Kalowish was dead." His face twitching sorrowfully, he returned to the beach.

Kahammis lay for a long time beneath the sun-dappled leaves. When her tears were exhausted, she remembered Aneetsick setting off so proudly from Nootseetaht, in his own canoe. Could she and Aneetsick rebuild Nootseetaht, as their father had done? She must get back, but how? How much longer must she remain with Quassoon? He had known all along that her father had been an innocent casualty, and that her brother survived as the rightful heir. Yet he had humiliated her from the moment she had been dragged ashore and thrown at his feet. A true chief would have been chivalrous, his eye on future gain.

She lurched up, slapping mosquitoes, straightening her skirt. "He's nothing more than a brute," she whispered, seething. "And I am Kahammis, not his slave!"

Quassoon and his whalers were on their way home. The sun, behind them, was a vivid orange ball. The breeze had paused briefly between the cool water and the warm land, and the sea was calm except for the swell. Beneath the bearskin in the bow, Quassoon reflected on the kill he had just made, a kill which would become magnificent in the retelling, a kill by which to measure a chief.

The whale's mouth had been sewn shut, the carcass kept afloat with inflated sealskins, and the paddlers were perspiring heavily as they pulled. The whale had led them in a valiant chase and was now at rest, awaiting the celebrations which would fill the coming days, honouring the passage of life into death.

But as they drew shoreward, Quassoon's agitation grew. "Just let Yatintala try and stop me," he growled, interrupting his towing chant. Guiltily, he thought of Yatintala's sojourn on the mat, praying for his success. The whaler's hat she had woven for him bore on its rim the best depiction of the hunt which anyone had ever seen. Still, lesser men than he took additional wives, sisters usually, to minimize the rivalry around the hearth. In a burst of optimism, he decided that Yatintala and Kahammis could learn to like each other; he would enlist the Shaman's help.

Furthermore, he reasoned, squirming beneath the bearskin, marrying Kahammis would make things right with Paquacheenish. He had felt a few twinges of conscience following his flamboyant exhibition at the winter feast. He had sent spies south to check out Patlowah's grandson, who had apparently been intended as a husband for Kahammis. This was a relationship he had known nothing about, until Yatintala coldly informed him of it, the morning after the feast. Surely a marriage proposal from the great Quassoon would persuade Paquacheenish to overlook the way Kahammis had been treated during the past year. What more fitting resolution to the strange but fortuitous events that had delivered her into the bay he now approached with his men, paddles smacking the sides of the canoes.

The cry went up and the people danced with joy at the spectacle of the whalers framed against the setting sun. T'isharth and his men had left with the tide, sorry to have missed Quassoon but eager to reach their village before dark. Children climbed to the roof ridges, beating the boards with sticks, and Yatintala flew down to greet Quassoon.

As the whale was drawn ashore, the villagers outdid themselves praising its bulk and its length. Teams of cutters set to work separating the blubber from the meat, cheering and then cursing as knives slipped. Precise rules governed the distribution of the carcass, with Quassoon taking the first piece, a wide saddle around the dorsal fin. His own paddlers accepted their rations, and the families from the three accompanying canoes lined up for their turn. There was enough for everyone, with plenty to spare.

Butchering continued through the night and into the following day, while the women prepared the blubber for a feast. Quassoon and his crew prayed to the spirit of the slain whale, and he found time also to provoke the Shaman; Kahammis heard them quarrelling, then saw the Shaman stomping into the trees. Since her chance encounter with T'isharth, her heart had burned like a cooking stone. Quassoon had not come near her, though she felt his eyes on her constantly, hotter even than her simmering heart.

On the evening of the feast, she rested against a log on the beach, listening to Kwatyet's fourth or fifth account of the hunt. The weather had been unusually fine, heightening the jubilant mood of the villagers, and the sand glittered beneath the stars.

Quassoon came around to where she sat. Without warning he yanked her up, dragging her to the far end of the beach, where they dropped behind a bank of salal. Although Kwatyet resumed his story, he had lost the concentration of his audience: the blatancy of

Quassoon's need, set aside during the forced abstinence of the hunt, turned corners in their minds. Yatintala locked eyes first with Tatoosch and then with the Shaman, a venomous triangle. Quassoon suddenly bellowed, a shocking sound. Everyone drew closer to the crackling fire, Kwatyet's voice wavering as he continued his account.

Quassoon bellowed when he was kicked by Kahammis. He clouted her across the face, and her head snapped back; for a terrible moment he was sure he had broken her neck. But she twisted away, and he ripped off her cape, exposing her skin to the starlight, pawing at her breasts, her sloping belly, the soft mound at the join of her thighs. As he drove into her, she was stiff, unyielding, spitting blood. He was a hero, conqueror of the coast: how dare she not treat him so? He rolled off, spent, staring into the night.

Beside him lay Kahammis, cold and clammy as a clubbed seal.

~~~:~~~

Quassoon ordered the canoes loaded. Kahammis heard him through the early morning mist, stooped over her burden basket, flinching at his shouts. On the night of the blubber feast, she had slept, finally, where he left her in the sand. The following night, on the sleeping platform, he had punched her unconscious; since then she had not been able to pull back her shoulders, wheezing painfully with every breath.

When she was worn out from hating, her mind raced with plans. She had polished her canoe, moved with the others between Yuhktu and Quatlukaht, with handfuls of horsetail, sheltering it with a mat from the sun. If ever she could catch the wind and tide and elude the prying eyes, she would flee. But her dreams were always cut short by a vision of Quassoon in his bearskin, looming behind.

She picked up a few more branches, skirting the commotion on the beach. The men were sorting trade goods: bladders of oil, baskets of food, and a single box of otter pelts that went straight into Quassoon's bow.

Quassoon lumbered out of the mist, knocking the firewood from her arms. "Get in!" he barked, gesturing at his canoe.

She edged towards the lodge, thinking of her cape which she had left on the sleeping platform. Quassoon caught hold of her, seating her between two of his paddlers. The steersman began to chant, and the paddlers pushed off through the surf. The mist thickened into fog, and then Kahammis gasped in surprise: the bows were swinging south!

Down the twisted coast they flew, her excitement rising with every surge, falling with every slide into the troughs of the swell. Nothing exhilarated her more than such a ride; as a child, she had hugged the gunwale in her father's lee, delighted by the startled plunges of the sea ducks. The trees along the shore were stunted and sheared by the wind, and by the surf smashing at their roots in the fissured rock. Great had been the rewards to young eyes that sighted a lone wolf, or a family of bears rummaging amongst the debris thrown up by the tide. Now she looked around worriedly as Quassoon's canoe veered close to the reefs, the steersman checking his bearings in the fog. What if Quassoon intended to cross the straits and sell her to the enemy Wewksah?

But they sped steadily southward, past the white-streaked cliffs where the cormorants roosted, past the kelp beds which the men scrutinized for otters. The fog gave way to sunshine, and the paddlers continued without a break, mile after mile, until they reached Klinniklinnikaht. Masts protruded above the trees beyond a bend in the channel; the presence of the ship explained the pelts and food Quassoon had brought to trade.

As they turned into the channel, Kahammis became aware that Quassoon was watching her, with an odd look on his face. She turned away, gazing disdainfully out to sea. Quassoon snorted, leaning over to confer with his steersman.

They wound through the channel towards the familiar spread of lodges and, as always, countless canoes were pulled up around the lagoon. Just as Kahammis was bracing for their landing, they swerved towards the anchored ship. She glanced entreatingly at the crowd gathering on the mudflats, about to raise her hand and call out when Quassoon yelled loudly, alerting the ship's crew.

Quassoon and several of his men swarmed up the side of the ship while the rest remained below, passing up boxes and baskets. Only because of the excellent reputation of Paquacheenish were any of the coast people permitted on board, carefully supervised by pale men in outlandish costumes. Kahammis cringed from the whiskery faces peering down at her, spouting gibberish, but she was astonished to understand a few local words as they greeted Quassoon.

Her father Kalowish had approached trading with caution and rituals. Here, Kahammis heard no songs of welcome and saw no ceremony between chiefs. Quassoon was already in an argument with a tall man wearing the most dazzling outfit on the ship. To her embarrassment, this man leaned over and examined her. More debate ensued, while she cowered self-consciously and wondered what was to come. She remembered her father telling of an incident when a ship had exchanged dentalia for pelts, but the shells turned out to be made of a strange, unnatural substance, provoking chaos amongst the warriors in the canoes.

Quassoon threw a prickly rope over the side of the ship. Urged by the paddlers, Kahammis took hold of the rope and swayed above the water until Quassoon hauled her up. She had been wedged in the canoe for so long that her legs were numb, and she collapsed onto the deck to roars from the crew.

The tall man bent down and lifted her gently, leading her through a dark tunnel; no one spoke as they went. Kahammis put one foot in front of the other in the certainty that she was going to be taken away and dropped off the side of the world, out of reach of her spirit family, who would never know where she had gone. She was guided into an enclosure lit by a round, blurred hole, then a door swung shut with a creak that raised the hair on the back of her neck. She sat where she was directed, covering her face with her hands.

When the man knelt close to her, she parted her fingers, peering at him in the diffused light. Never had she seen such eyes: they were like fragments of the delicate, dawn sky. He touched her bark skirt, making an exclamation. Though his manner with Quassoon had suggested authority, he seemed to have become as timid as a boy. She could hear the Quatlukaht traders outside; they had not left yet.

When the man stood up and took off his hat, she dropped her hands in amazement at his hair, which was the colour of boiled crab. He unfastened the shiny buttons on his chest, and her jaw dropped at his nakedness; he was as slim and white as a freshly peeled alder pole. He took her by the shoulders and laid her against a ship's blanket, smoothing her hair, tracing the bruises on her cheeks.

She shivered at his touch, propelled along part of life's journey that not even her most frantic dreams could have foretold. Having been brought so close to salvation, on the threshold of Klinniklinnikaht, then snatched away, she could only withdraw to that place inside of her without wish or fear. She gave herself up, as she had done in her storm-battered canoe.

41

Even so, she was aware that the man pressing against her was utterly different from Quassoon. Though he wanted the same thing, he pushed between her legs with restraint, all the while studying her, eye to eye. She felt him shudder and prepared for a bellowing crush, but he held himself lightly, and she exhaled with relief. He lay for a few minutes then quickly straightened her skirt.

As he fumbled with his clothes, a button fell off and tinkled onto the ship's plank floor. Kahammis grabbed the button, holding it up. He shook his head, flustered, when she tried to give it back, and she tucked it into the waistband of her skirt with a shy laugh.

Quassoon was waiting for her, scowling impatiently. He lowered her into the canoe. Slumped between kegs and boxes of muskets, she could not bear to lift her head as they sped off, with shouts and clattering paddles, Quatlukaht style. But when she felt the bow meeting the swell in the channel, she turned for a last, anguished look.

A canoe emerged from the shadow of an island, running parallel with them across the channel. Heads pivoted, and for a second the Quatlukaht paddlers lost their beat. Despite the distance and the glare, Kahammis recognized the distinctive Nootseetaht prow: it was Aneetsick!

"Forward!" screamed Quassoon.

They surged out into the open ocean, and Kahammis fell back, expressionless. She would die before she would let Quassoon know what it cost her to be heading north again.

~~~:~~~

Quassoon laughed all the way home.

He laughed to save face with his men. No, he laughed at the memory of the face on Kahammis, disappearing inside the ship. No, he laughed at himself: Quassoon the buffoon, who had set off to better Patlowah's deal with a deal of his own, a deal Paquacheenish could not have refused, but had ended up selling Kahammis to the ship's captain, instead. He had been driven to it — by her indifference, by Yatintala's nagging, by the Shaman's disapproval, so close on the heels of his victory with the whale. Prostituting Kahammis showed his strength, thwarting her pride, and Yatintala's jealousy, and the Shaman's almightiness. Though he knew there would be a price for his actions, he felt confident of his standing with the supreme powers; after all, he was the chief.

Initially the ship's captain had not wanted Kahammis, but Quassoon had very much wanted the captain's hat, particularly after giving his favourite seaman's cap to Patlowah, during the winter ceremonies. The captain was young and inexperienced, which was good for trade, but he was wary of the diseases which he told Quassoon lived under the skirts of the women Paquacheenish sent out to the ships. Although the captain did not believe that Kahammis was the daughter of a chief, or untouched, he did agree that she was not local, and Quassoon knew that he had won the hat after a single look.

As for Paquacheenish, he was not going to be around for many more years. Kahammis was worth more than pelts or dentalia; her true value was yet to be defined. She was going to bear Quassoon's children, ensuring his dynasty.

~~~:~~~

The days grew shorter and the nights cooler, the people making haste with their harvest as nature's provisions came ripe. The leafy trees behind Quatlukaht blazed with colour, and the village was cluttered with racks of drying fish, and berry cakes. The cakes were made of layers of berries and roasted clams, compressed by a plank on which the stoutest women in the village were invited, with much hilarity, to sit. They were using the last of the thimbleberries, seedy but sweet, picked from thickets along the creekbeds.

The dog salmon run was the best he could remember, declared Quassoon. Speared, or guided through weirs into baskets made from cedar slats, the salmon were easy prey as they returned to the rivers and streams of their birth to spawn. Quassoon and his cousins owned the rights to the rivers between Quatlukaht and Yuhktu. The men came back singing at dusk, paying homage to the Great Salmon, whose people had died so that they could live. The women also sang as they emptied the canoes, wiping the fish clean with handfuls of moss, slashing off the heads and tails and splitting the flesh, scooping out the spawn. The dog salmon dried the most rapidly as it contained the least oil, while the spawn was dumped into boxes to ferment, a tasty treat.

Tatoosch appeared one evening; he had left when the hard work of the harvest began. He was empty-handed but indolent as always, with only two of the three slaves who manned his canoe. Yatintala fussed happily, but within days Tatoosch and his father were bickering;

43

Quassoon wanted to know the whereabouts of the missing slave. Tatoosch had been making free with the kegs acquired from the ship at Klinniklinnikaht, which up until his return had been hidden away. The villagers would have avoided the kegs anyhow, so dramatic was their effect on Tatoosch: he lurched through the lodges, spewing like a deranged beast. After a week, he took his remaining paddlers and left again. He also took a box of muskets and several full kegs, infuriating Quassoon. The missing slave was supposedly staying with Wasquimaht relatives; Quassoon suspected that he had been bartered off during a losing streak at the bone games.

Despite his bravado, Quassoon was feeling a vague, creeping unease. He decided to restore his relationship with the Shaman by asking for advice. The Shaman, however, was on a vigil in the forest, nowhere to be found, so Quassoon brought out the last keg and drained it with the cousins in one night. Later, under the robe, he hurled himself at Kahammis for what seemed like hours; she dozed fitfully while Yatintala nearly bounced off the other end of the sleeping platform.

Since the trip to Klinniklinnikaht, an enormous lassitude had taken hold of Kahammis. When she failed to find firewood, Yatintala would comment scathingly, but what did it matter if the burden basket was empty or full? She would be fed, or not fed, craving not food but endless sleep. Now and then she would notice the early morning sky, recalling the captain's eyes, mulling over some detail of her intimacy with him on the ship. She had fastened the metal button inside her cape, close to the carved loon. There were times when she wondered if she would have been safer with the captain than with Quassoon.

Fall swept forward, the leaves stripped off by the wind. Then, the Shaman returned from the forest. He commanded Yatintala to prepare a feast, and she rushed to do his bidding, for a Shaman's feast was a rare event. Towering fires were built in the hearths, and the villagers anxiously took their places, Kahammis dozing against the wall. The Shaman spun bare-chested along the central aisle, trilling on his whistles, grey tassels of hair whirling over his head, strings of elk hooves clattering around his waist. As his audience reeled with the effort of following him, he jerked to a stop.

"Daughter of Kalowish!"

Quassoon, Yatintala, and the cousins craned their necks, afraid to breathe. Kahammis suddenly awoke, blinking in confusion.

Again the Shaman spun, and the people clutched each other. All at once he launched himself upwards with an eerie screech: "Kahammis carries the seed!"

Nothing could have stunned the people more. Quassoon leapt ecstatically, and now the feasting began: bubbling tubs of spawn, whole sides of salmon, berries, roots, and bulbs. Propped between Yatintala and Quassoon, Kahammis refused to eat; her throat was filled with bile.

Shortly afterwards, Quassoon announced that it was time to relocate to Yuhktu. The canoes departed in convoys between squalls, with Quassoon's lodge the last to leave. On the morning of the move, Kahammis woke before dawn as she often did, listening for the little owl. She was certain that her prayers would be answered: one day the owl would reunite her soul with the souls of her family. But now, hearing nothing, she slid from beneath the otter-skin robe, tiptoeing outside. She had not adjusted to her most recent status: Yatintala solicitous instead of scathing, Quassoon his magnanimous, old self. Everyone seemed satisfied, Yatintala most of all. Unknown to Kahammis, Quassoon had promised Yatintala the ownership of this first child.

Kahammis drifted along the shoreline, pulling at her cape, shivering in the autumn chill. Yatintala was weaving her a new cape, for which she had no desire, but she was forbidden to weave herself lest a tangle foretell a knotted umbilical cord.

Along the sandbars the gulls cried hauntingly, speeding night on its way. Kahammis turned back to the village, struggling to gather her thoughts, to gather strength for the coming move. The moon lay above the dark ridge of trees behind the lodges, a slender, golden crescent, with a single star close by. Bright star and moon, perfectly balanced in the pale sky. Gazing in wonder, she asked herself: what could it mean, such a beacon of beauty shining over her despair?

She was not ready for the little owl, not yet.

~~~:~~~

45

MARIANNE: June, 1990

LIGHT FROM THE June afternoon filters through window glass coated with cobwebs and dust. Grandma Em pokes at a jumble of buttons in a frayed, woven tray on the table between us. She is attaching the buttons along the edge of a scarlet blanket draped over her lap. The room is thick with the smells of drying grass and smoke.

"Who is it for?" I ask.

"Elsa."

Her youngest granddaughter, Tony's sister. Elsa doesn't live at Squally Bay. I met her one night at the pub up from the main wharf, in the basement of the hotel. She has the same cheekbones as Tony, high and flaring beneath hard, black eyes.

"She dances on the weekend," says Grandma Em. "In town. People from the whole northwest."

She is referring to celebrations for the Bicentennial. Two hundred years ago, a Spaniard, Manuel Quimper, was the first white man recorded to have set foot on this part of the coast. He explored the shoreline from Squally Bay south to what is now the town of Port

46

Albert, fifty miles away, connected to Squally Bay by a winding road famous for frightening tourists, myself included, the day I arrived.

"I was invited, too," chuckles Grandma Em. "Elsa can go."

Rummaging through the tray, I arrange buttons in rows. Some of the buttons are shaped from bone, and some are from what looks like abalone shell. Grandma Em spreads out the blanket, kneeling on her mat; today she is as straight and sturdy as a first-growth fir.

I think about the Bicentennial and calculate in my mind: two hundred years. Who would have been here as a witness: Grandma Em's great ... great ... great-grandmother?

Grandma Em bites off a piece of thread. Tony says that she used to sing. He says she went on and on for hours; he and his sister never understood a word. I wonder if she ever sings anymore.

It is a miracle she welcomed me back, after that first visit. She asked me for a story and I told her about the owl, and then I just ... fell apart. When I got hold of myself, I was in a quilt by the wood-stove, with her watching me and Tony making tea. My mother's death, selling the house, all those years on the ward ending with that stupid, nasty scene ... I had been trying to explain to Grandma Em that I had come out to Squally Bay to make a new start.

"You found it!" cackles Grandma Em. She takes the button I have picked up and places it on her palm. Much less interesting than the others, this button is made of metal, tarnished and grimy from the bottom of the tray.

Suddenly I remember the buttons on the tunic in the wooden case. "Can I have another look?" I rub the metal against my sleeve; the insignia is the same. Handing her the button, I ask, weakly, "Where did you get this?"

Grandma Em shrugs over her work. She has a quiet, inner place she goes to, when she doesn't want to speak. She hesitates for a long moment, then sets the button on the blanket, reaching for her needle. A single tear slides down her wizened cheek and splashes on the metal, which shines, ever so fleetingly, in the gloom.

~~~:~~~

The tide has receded enough for me to take a shortcut to the cottage, along the beach that fronts the Reserve. My head is booming with questions: did the button belong to Captain Hume?

Why was it in Grandma Em's basket? Would she tell me, and does she even know?

Tony's truck is in the yard by the cottage, and Tony is up on the porch, talking with Jimmy Joe. Jimmy Joe lives in what looks like little more than a poultry coop, just inside the border of the Reserve. As well as keeping track of me, he does chores for the elderly woman who owns the cottage and lives in the big farmhouse farther back up the hill.

Beyond the spit, the sun spills over the water at the close of a glorious day, all the more glorious following months of rain. It has been raining, in sheets or varying mists, since last November when I arrived in Squally Bay. Tony, a salmon fisherman, speaks of systems and fronts; this clear weather is apparently the result of high pressure building in from the northwest. True enough, after lying low all winter, Squally Bay has turned euphoric in the sun. Children play around the pilings beneath the wharves, hacking off worms for bait, while in the distance I can hear cars racing back and forth between the bridge and the dairy farm where the paved road ends. On the weekends, these rusting, cavernous cars veer through a bright parade of jeeps and station wagons, families from Port Albert, out for a drive. Groups of girls have gathered, giggling and demure, in the parking lot that services the grocery store, the bowling alley, and the Community Hall. Farther along, a couple of Mounties catch a quick supper at the cafe. Tony says that the fields behind the village were once all covered with forest, which is hard to believe.

I met Tony at the main wharf where the trollers and seiners tie up. Not for weeks after my arrival had I ventured out, except for food and mail. The terrible dream — filled with death and confusion and a crying owl — had been more oppressive than the weather, trapping me in the cottage and causing me to question why I had come at all.

On the day that I met Tony, a gale was blowing across the spit. The wharf timbers groaned against the pilings, rigging clanged, and tire bumpers creaked between the white-hulled fishing boats which shifted restlessly like the rumps of workhorses in stable stalls. I lurched from float to float with the gulls shrieking overhead, stationary in the wind. My scarf ripped away and I looked up into a creased, smiling face. It was a smile so unexpected that I stepped back, nearly falling off the dock.

I'll never know why he invited me aboard, me whose pleasures in life are so few. I collapsed without grace onto a bunk next to a rusting stove. In different circumstances, I would soon have been asleep, so cloistering was the contrast between the troller's cabin and the gale outside. Since then I have learned that the interiors of fishing boats on the coast all smell the same, and like no other place in the world: diesel fuel, wet wool, grease and coffee grounds, with the undertones of the fish carcasses in the hold.

Thus I met Tony, at the Government Wharf in Squally Bay. He is waiting for me now with his canoe on top of his truck. Barbara has written from the hospital, wondering when I will be back. How can I tell her: Barbara, I am compelled to stay by the shades of grey cedar in the fog, and the soothing patter of rain?

"Been to Grandma Em's?" asks Tony. Jimmy Joe scuttles off, and I wish he was a little less nosy. Wisely, Tony ignores what he does not understand. "I've brought sandwiches," he says. "Let's go!"

Of course I have never been in a canoe. We launch upriver and drift down towards the bay. Tony's canoe is made of green fibreglass, with moulded wooden seats. Closing my eyes, I visualize the two of us in the carved dugout at the museum in Port Albert; I am a pioneer, and Tony is my guide.

Before Squally Bay, the closest I had come to a coast native was during my training at the hospital, in the dimly lit hall next to the emergency ward. Leo, no more than twenty but a regular on the ward, had picked me up by my starched bib and pinned me against the wall, his puffy face inches away, red-eyed and spitting with rage. For a long moment, the tips of my carefully polished, sensible shoes grazed the floor. When finally he dropped me, I staggered into the supply room and locked the door. My specialty has been geriatrics, and I have never met the likes of Leo again.

Tony points with his paddle. "Fishing long-legs." We laugh as the heron flaps squawking through the shallows, and then I catch sight of three ungainly brown creatures tumbling along a shady bank. "River otters," says Tony. He explains that sea otters are different and have been hunted out; there are only a few left, in colonies re-introduced along the coast. We are silent; I know so little, and most of what Tony knows, he keeps to himself. We pass beneath the metal arches of the bridge, sweeping along the silted delta, swinging with the current against the Reserve. Sound travels so clearly that we can hear the squeal of jacked-up tires beyond the village, and someone working late with a power saw. We circle the bay and reach the end of the spit, marked by a beacon and a single, wind-sheared pine. The current is very strong and suddenly we are surrounded by swirling eddies, whipped-over waves.

A breeze hits us broadside, and I ask, "Is this how Squally Bay got its name?"

Tony chuckles reassuringly. "Grandma Em says there is a different name, but it's been Squally Bay for as long as I've been around." He nods at the ship silhouetted against the fluorescent orange and pink horizon. "Freighter, bound for Japan."

We hurtle past the spit, into the ocean swell. The canoe seems very insubstantial and I am mentally measuring the distance I used to be able to swim. Tony aims for a shell beach behind kelp-streamed reefs where cormorants dry their wings. The bow crunches onto shore and I leap out, my relief tempered by the reminder that we must return the way we came.

We eat the sandwiches and sit back on the blanket and I feel indebted to Tony, for landing us in the canoe, for teaching me the differences between the gulls, for taking me to Grandma Em. I wouldn't mind a glass of wine, but Tony does not drink. He, too, has other chapters in his life; his son Andrew attends high school in Port Albert, and I try not to make assumptions about his ex-wife.

The symmetry of his face is offset by a scar which slices through both of his lips. Watching the scar in the cabin of his troller, the *Paquacheenish Point*, the morning we first met, I knew for certain that here was a man I could never kiss. Later, I recalled the mess of my own jaw before it was repaired. Now, as the sun slips away and Tony's mouth touches mine, nothing seems certain, anymore.

~~~:~~~

The clear skies continue, and one morning I am sweeping the porch when I see that the lichen-covered railing is entwined with rosebuds. A rose bush as big as a tree is laden with partly opened buds the colour and shape of apricots. I set aside the broom and sit on an upturned barrel, astonished that the cottage could offer such charm. Out of the corner of my eye, I notice Jimmy Joe limping across the yard. Tony says that Jimmy Joe was injured at the sawmill, the same mill that closed down not long after Tony quit school to work on the greenchain, along with most of his friends. That was when an hourly wage was more important than an education, and everyone thought those jobs would last at least another century.

Sniffing the rosebuds, I feel that I should come up with a plan. The hospital would like to know the date of my return, and although my savings hold steady, seven months is a long time to read and roam and stare at the sea. Today I am going to hike upriver to a midden just below the falls, described by Tony and vaguely confirmed by Grandma Em. I have been exploring the countryside and making trips to the Squally Bay library. Soon I will be decorating driftwood with feathers and rocks; already strings of shells hang above the porch, clacking in the wind.

Once or twice a week, I find myself on the potholed road to the Reserve. I had brought the wooden case with me from Vancouver, and yes, the buttons on the tunic matched the one in Grandma Em's basket. But I don't know how to ask her about it; I'm afraid she will withdraw from me again.

On her good days, she tells me where the best grass grows, how the strips of cedar are harvested from the mother tree. And she weaves me into her legends, no less skillfully than she weaves her strips of bark and grass. According to Grandma Em, there is a presence watching over Squally Bay, a mythical, heroic female who has been around here for many years. She speaks for justice, and justice twists a powerful thread along this coast; people often hear her out on the water, by the spit. She leads Grandma Em's list of protectors; how I wish that I had been born with a few, something to throw in the teeth of the dreams. I am thankful that months have passed since I last heard the owl's cry; perhaps it was only in my imagination, after all.

After breakfast I set off on the trail which begins on the other side of the bridge, near the dilapidated farmhouse where the owner of the cottage lives. Jimmy Joe gives her my rent money; we have not yet met. The house is on a knoll surrounded by orchards and fields, and black and white cows watch me cross the dew-wet grass. The wide verandah is covered with a mass of apricot roses, the same as on the railing of my own porch. I am drawn closer to this profusion of fragrance, about to sneak away again when the door to the verandah flies open and a face appears, and I freeze as if caught with a candy-bar at the local store. An elderly woman sticks her head through the roses; she is wearing an old-fashioned print dress, and her hair is a pure white halo around a perfect widow's peak.

"Hallo!" she cries. "Just in the nick of time!"

I glance behind me but there is no one else in the yard.

She waves impatiently. "I'm not waiting forever! Through here."

I squeeze between the thorn-studded stems. "I was just admiring the roses," I explain lamely. "What are they called?"

She gives me a blank look. "Oh those," she says, sticking her head back outside. "Those are Evangeline's."

I follow her along a hall into a darkly panelled room where tea is laid on a table covered with an oiled cloth. Beside the china pot is a fan of heavy spoons and a cluster of dripping bottles: mustard, vinegar, and sauce. She offers a chair, and tilts the pot, but the tea is cold. With the gay abandon of the hostess, she gives me biscuits from a tin. As I nibble self-consciously, she pounces on a pile of newspapers by the stove.

She presents me with a clipping. "Father said I was the most reliable person in Squally Bay!"

A striking young woman is standing on what appears to be the verandah I have just crawled through. She is posing proudly with a vintage telephone. Above the door is a sign: Squally Bay Post Office. She has the same fluff of hair and could be wearing the same dress, although the collar is slightly different. She is Miss Agnes McPhee, descended from the first family to settle Squally Bay. The yellowing print notes that the McPhee sawmill supplied the poles for both the telegraph and telephone lines linking Squally Bay to the rest of the world.

I gaze at the clipping, thinking back to Captain Hume, who must have known those first McPhees. Could he have left anything else besides the button, any connection to me?

Thoughts have been creeping forward lately, into the spaces vacated when my mother passed away. For years I carried her truisms: never complain, there is always someone, somewhere, whose sufferings outnumber yours; in any case, life is meant to be a struggle. My father drank himself to death when I was small, leaving her with a mortgaged bungalow in one of the suburbs that emerged like mushrooms in the fertile fields around Vancouver, after the war. Back she went to her bookkeeper's job at the trucking company, where she and my father had met. By the time I completed nursing school, she had progressed with unspoken grievances from walker to wheelchair to bed, while I worked out the truisms, at the hospital and at home. This was not a past to dwell upon. Yet the past has a peculiar buoyancy, and ever since I found the button I have been hounded by a sense of almost tripping over something, something not quite there, but so close.

Agnes snatches the clipping. "Where are you going?" she asks.

"Upriver." I cough nervously. "To the falls."

She mutters, shaking her white halo dismissively. Now that our tea is finished, she can't get rid of me fast enough, and I step onto the overgrown verandah just ahead of the slamming door. My desire to explore has been extinguished, replaced by a loneliness, a rootlessness which hits me like the storm waves against the spit. It is a condition that must be foreign to Agnes, who knows exactly where she belongs.

When I was looking after my mother, I once or twice asked her what I had been like as a child, hungry for some anecdote, some lost image of brighter, happier days.

"You were a good girl," was all she would sigh.

And what of my father? He would vanish for weeks, months, then tap at the door, sickly and trembling with excuses and gifts. During one of his absences, a neighbour woman drove my mother and me in her ponderous sedan, across bridges and through streets lined with cloudy pink trees. We circled slowly while my mother went into a building which took up most of a city block. I pressed my nose to the car window as she came back down the stone steps in her grey coat and dressy white sandals with the thick soles. When she got in, the two women exchanged guarded glances. The following spring, bravely asking if my father would be home for my birthday, I learned that he had died.

Not until I came across the wooden box in the attic did I even wish for more. By then it was too late; all I had was the long-forgotten letter of an old sailor, and now Agnes McPhee, reminding me of people like Mrs. Vincennes, from whom I have run.

I find myself turning into the Reserve, past the unpainted houses, through the gate, up the oyster-shell path which leads me to Grandma Em. Elsa has danced in the button blanket, and Grandma Em is back to her weaving again. She looks frail in the light through the open door, and I am ashamed to be bothering her. But when I sink beside her onto the mat, she smiles as if she has been waiting for me. In her palm is a miniature basket with a domed lid. "For you," she says.

A chill washes over me. The months slip away and I am back at the house in Vancouver; my mother has just died. I see myself standing at the fireplace, holding a plastic garbage bag. With my arm I sweep through the dusty relics along the mantel, and a tiny basket tumbles downwards; as it disappears, an even tinier moon and star revolve around the lid.

Now my fingers trace the moon and star Grandma Em has woven, but I cannot speak. Grandma Em nods, pleased with herself, reaching for my hand. I feel as if I am falling, floating into the space between the two baskets, and all that keeps me in the room is her ancient, bony grip.

~~~:~~~

KAHAMMIS: 1816 - 1843

ONE MORNING IN the darkest heart of winter, a morning indistinguishable from all the other mornings, like the grey trees fused in the fog, Kahammis knelt at the pond, watching the dipping box sink as it filled. Although her hair had been oiled and plaited by Yatintala, her eyes were dull, her complexion sallow. She poked at the dipping box, leaning out with melancholy absorption; a little farther, and she would fall in.

Wings swooped across the water, then Kahammis heard an owl's whistling trill. Barely did she stir to the sound, sickened not only by her pregnancy but by the events unfolding back at the village: manic plans for her marriage, the prelude to a lifetime of mothering for Quassoon. How would Paquacheenish extricate her from those bonds? With a groan she let go of the dipping box and followed the owl's call. Either way, she was about to lose her soul.

She stumbled through the salal, pursuing the owl until she reached the grove of trees on the mountain slope. There she waited, and waited, almost weeping when at last she felt the soft brush of wings. Lifting her head, she saw not the owl but Sheebo. She put out her hand, certain that she was in the presence of an apparition. When she touched Sheebo's warm skin, her vision blurred and she thudded to the ground.

She recovered to find herself on a rough path in the crusted snow, winding upwards through the mist. She was supported between Sheebo and an older man who stopped frequently, glancing back and rubbing the marks left by her dragging heels. Waking to the possibility that her spirit journey had begun, she suddenly understood that she was in the care of people as real and vulnerable as herself. She shook free, determined to walk on her own. Finally they crossed the summit, and she hobbled with the desperation of the refugee, for whom whatever lies ahead must be better than that which looms behind. Down the far slope they went, through fog-shrouded trees which seemed to repeat themselves like a supernatural trick, and she shivered at her temerity in thinking she could escape Quassoon, or the Shaman.

Daylight was fading when they stopped at a clearing beside a small lake. Her fingers searched for the carved loon in her collar; she knew that the birds came to lakes such as this one, to mate in the spring. She unfastened the little loon and showed it to Sheebo, who responded by flinging her arms around her with a joyful shout. Faces appeared at the doorways of lodges flimsier than the temporary shacks put up for berry-picking expeditions on the coast. An elderly woman stepped close, murmuring in admiration as she ran her hands over Kahammis's yellow cedar cape and up to her regally shaped head.

Sheebo helped her into one of the shacks, where a hearth beckoned with its common language of comfort and warmth. Children wiggled through openings in the walls, Sheebo good-naturedly swatting them away. She offered a bowl of broth, which Kahammis sipped tentatively, hardly daring to believe that she was safe. Who were these people? What crimes had they committed to consign them to such a remote, closed-in space?

Despite her fears, she slept soundly and discovered the following morning that she had been wrapped in Sheebo's cape. She sniffed the smoky wool, hearing voices in the clearing outside. The older man, whom she assumed was Sheebo's father, was describing once again how she had been found. Although puzzled by certain phrases of his dialect, she recognized many words. Sheebo lay nearby, watching her closely. She buried her face in the cape, for to be looked at with such gentleness was more than she could bear.

Within days, though, her time with Quassoon had taken on the quality of a distant, despicable dream. She lounged by the hearth, refusing to think beyond the next meal, listening to Sheebo's chatter as if it was all that mattered in the world.

"We live here in winter," explained Sheebo. "We travel when the weather dries." She opened a cedar box, setting out chunks of black rock, and a mottled green stone which reminded Kahammis of the tree frogs she and her brothers used to trap. "This is what we trade, for food and things." Sheebo pointed to the elk stomachs, plump with oil, secured to the rafters overhead. "First we go north, then south, then back here again." She sighed wistfully. "South is best. We have so much fun there."

"Tell me more," urged Kahammis, remembering the stories of Hasallum, her uncle, master carver at Nootseetaht. Hasallum delivered canoes to prominent southern families, returning with descriptions of meadows bluer than the summer sky with camas flowers, where the rain clouds vanished from moon to moon.

Sheebo twisted the black rock in her hands. "My mother came from the south. Her parents let her marry for the price of many valuable stones. I would stay there," she shrugged, "but you can see how my father needs me here. In any case, my head was not flattened with cradleboards, and I would not fit in with everyone else." Her fingers squeezed the rock. "We got caught by a blizzard on a pass. My mother fell over the side. Her feet never became used to the snow, my father said."

Kahammis nodded, aching for Sheebo's losses, and for her own. In a burst of flame from the embers, she glimpsed the eyes of the owl that had led her away from Quassoon's pond, to Sheebo. How, she wondered, could she repay such a gift?

The only connection to her previous life, and a worrisome one, was the infant growing in her womb. When Sheebo pointed out that soon they would be travelling the trade routes, and Kahammis would need a cradle basket, she reluctantly agreed. Even looking at her body reminded her too much of Quassoon — his hands, his crushing weight, his jeering laughter on the ship. Her few moments with the young captain would have seemed unreal if it were not for the button, which she still carried in the collar of her cape.

Sheebo sorted through her supplies, unwinding a honey-coloured ball. "I was searching for these roots last winter," she told Kahammis,

57

"when I saw you in the grove. I was picking out the best cedars to harvest in the spring."

Her voice dropped to a whisper. "Father was very angry. He let me join a hunting party, warning me to stay away from the inlet. But when I was coming down the mountain, I just had to go into that grove." Her laughter filled the shack. "I told my father I would return, the next year. I wanted to get my loon back. It has special powers, you know." She patted Kahammis on the hand. "You keep it, of course!"

They laid out the frame of the cradle, and Kahammis watched, entranced, as Sheebo designed the cover, using bear grass to outline a loon. They stuffed the cradle with rocks and tested it on Kahammis's back, and the children were greatly entertained by Sheebo's imitations of an infant's disgruntled shrieks.

Preoccupied with the weaving she had so missed, Kahammis failed to notice that the weeks were slipping away, like the fog which ebbed and flowed from valley to coast. She was jolted awake one morning by a melodious announcement: the sparrows and wrens were commencing construction on their nests. Sheebo's father returned from a hunting expedition with a sprig of red-flowering currant tucked into his belt, and on the following day, they dismantled the camp. Each house was taken apart mat by mat, pole by pole. The hearths were raked and bundles of belongings were hidden in caves at the other side of the lake.

They packed the carrying baskets and laid out the tumplines, and the children tangled excitedly as they spread their sleeping mats on the ground for the last night. A journey's beginning was celebrated with singing to the muted beat of the deerskin drums, soothing anxious travellers of all ages beneath a bright, round moon. Sheebo sat through the night with her father, praying to the many spirits which must be appeased on the hazardous route to the north.

"First we go north," Sheebo had said. Kahammis imagined herself, waddling and enormous, every step taking her farther from Nootseetaht. What if they encountered the raiders, or Wikkosum, or Tatoosch? She fell asleep only to wake moments later, dreaming that she had plunged over a cliff.

In the morning, shivering and sighing, she searched for her cape. The children waited, bursting with suspense, as Sheebo pulled a bundle from under a mat and gave it to Kahammis. It was a cape like the one Sheebo wore, fringed with rare mountain-goat wool and trimmed around the neck with otter fur. Kahammis touched her cheek to the creamy wool.

"For the daughter of a chief," Sheebo said softly. "I switched collars during the night." Kahammis swung the cape over her shoulders, fastening it in the front with the carved loon. A cheer went up, and the woodland birds fell silent, rebounding moments later with even lustier tunes.

They assembled to take on their baskets, Sheebo's father in the lead. Kahammis carried the cradle, into which she had lovingly folded her worn, bark cape. She also carried a pannier of household goods, the tumpline settling into its familiar crease around her forehead. They left the lake and ascended steeply, not stopping until they reached a mossy ridge. Kahammis climbed slowly with the unaccustomed load. She eased off the tumpline, welcoming the breeze that lifted her braids. The ground was spongy with melting frost, and the sun was directly overhead.

Her gaze turned southward, across the hazy, undulating slopes to a narrow finger of fog. "Yuhktu?" she asked Sheebo, pointing nervously.

Sheebo nodded. "Come with me." She took Kahammis to a granite outcropping where her father had knelt, praying, when they had reached the ridge. Chiselled into the granite was a series of weathered, concentric circles, joined by short rays.

"Mountain spirits," murmured Sheebo, glancing around. "Father knows the way," she added. "It isn't nearly as bad as it looks from here."

They turned their backs on the snowy peaks and reclined on the moss, chewing strips of venison from the baskets. The haze below them extended all the way to the ocean, to the sound where the Mannakaht lived, on islands floating like green ships in the fog. Again and again, Kahammis's gaze slid from these far islands to the milky finger which terminated at Yuhktu.

Sheebo's father sat separately, staring out over the sound. Soon he was urging his people up, and the children tugged at Kahammis, exclaiming playfully at her weight.

She reached for her tumpline. When she hesitated, Sheebo was instantly at her side. "Let me help."

Kahammis shook her head, clutching the cradle. She could not meet Sheebo's eyes.

"What's wrong?" Sheebo's voice rose. "Is it the baby?"

"I'm going home," blurted Kahammis.

"No!" Sheebo gasped, the colour draining out of her face. "Are you mad? If you go back, you'll be a slave for the rest of your life!"

"If you make it back at all." Sheebo's father spoke grimly. "The path is steep and there are many obstacles. And the mountain cat never sleeps."

"I'm not going back to Quassoon." Kahammis straightened her shoulders. "I'm going home to Nootseetaht." She turned to Sheebo's father. "My canoe is waiting for me at Yuhktu. I'll sneak through the village at night, they'll never know." She held up her hand as Sheebo protested. "I'll go to the Mannakaht, at the mouth of the sound. Chief T'isharth is a friend to my family."

"Chief T'isharth, of the Mannakaht," Sheebo's father said, with a tremor in his voice, and again he stared over the fog-blanketed sound.

Sheebo clung to Kahammis, crying and pleading with her father. "You can't let her go!"

He led Kahammis to the circles chiselled in the granite, explaining the landmarks she would pass. "At the second set of circles, turn to the ocean, and you will go down to Yuhktu." He glanced at the clouds behind the peaks, and Kahammis jumped as he clapped his hands together. "The weather can change like that! You must run, to reach Yuhktu by night."

He made sure that her cradle was packed with berry cakes and venison, and added a container of water at the top. Then he helped fit the cradle to her back.

Sheebo still held Kahammis. "I'll never see you again," she wailed.

"You will." Kahammis put her cheek against Sheebo's stricken face, unable to say more. With a swish of wool, she was gone.

But as she went, Sheebo's father muttered to himself, "Run, and find her way? I should not have let her go."

Sheebo sobbed, trying to catch a last glimpse of Kahammis, and the children blubbered against her knees. Slowly they gathered up their baskets, leaving faint imprints in the moss where they had lain. Turning north, they began their long summer's trek.

Her ears ringing with warnings, Kahammis sprinted through the scrub pines, over rocky outcroppings which frequently gave way to banks of shale. Although she had crossed this same trail with Sheebo and her father, it seemed even more steep and slippery now that she was alone. She reached the first set of circles and paused to rest, when she noticed clouds surging up over the closest peaks. She set off at once, her chest aching in places she had not felt since her escape from Quassoon. Faster she ran, tripping and skidding, and the clouds also advanced, masses of purple and grey, lit from below. Branches creaked and her cape flapped in the wind, and soon the sky was solid with cloud, except for a rim of violet light along the horizon. Her strength had almost given out when the trail ended at the base of a rock cliff. She forced herself up, crevice by crevice, and came upon the second set of circles, barely discernible in the dwindling light.

Yuhktu was directly below. Down she raced, into the grove of conifers. She collapsed against a familiar trunk, slinging off the cradle, feeling the baby inside her, heels drumming on her ribs. Finally the baby quietened enough for her to sleep.

The moon flashed through the forest canopy, waking her abruptly. The clouds were rolling out to sea, and she must follow, while the people of Yuhktu were snug on their sleeping platforms. She set off towards the pond, smacking into a tree which for a terrifying instant seemed to be none other than Quassoon. The impact knocked her backwards, and as she lay recovering, a riffle of wind on her face felt like the breath of a forest prowler: the Shaman! No, even worse ... the mountain cat! She cowered in dread, but when she raised her head, a shaft of moonlight revealed that she was alone.

She pushed through the salal to the pond, and memories of Quassoon flooded back as she hurried past, half-expecting the dipping box to bob up from where it had been dropped. Her heart almost stopped at the sight of Quassoon standing naked, his arms lifted, but it was only the snag where Tatoosch had perched with his mirrors.

The air was clearing behind the storm as she cautiously approached Yuhktu. Then she stared, in disbelief. The village had been abandoned and all that remained were its bleached, moonlit bones. The people had left for Quatlukaht, out on the coast. The lodges had been dismantled, exposing the posts and beams. Raccoons foraged through the piles of garbage, watching her with shiny, resentful eyes. The herring must have shoaled early, and Quassoon's people would have been eager to move, to leave the site of her disappearance three months before. She sagged against a doorpost, knowing only that she must get to T'isharth.

The raccoons woke her, scurrying amongst the mounds of shells. Streaks of light were spreading down the slopes, and short, fast waves snapped along the inlet in the wake of the storm. She searched the empty ramps where the canoes were kept, fighting off panic. At last she picked out a shape in the bushes beyond the ramps, an old mat which had been tossed away. She yanked the mat aside and there, buried in the salal, was her canoe.

~~~:~~~

On the day that Kahammis vanished, no one even noticed her absence until the evening meal, when Quassoon and Yatintala eyed each other accusingly. Then Quassoon charged outside, straight for the canoe ramp. He found the little canoe that belonged to Kahammis and hurled it into the salal, tearing back to the lodge. Yatintala met him with the news that Kahammis had last been seen on her way to the pond. Guided by torches spitting with pitch, Quassoon and the cousins set off, bellowing her name.

Clusters of villagers emerged from the lodges, running helter-skelter, no one certain what had gone wrong. Yatintala's screeching eventually broke through the confusion; she assembled the crowd, who filed sheepishly back inside, except for Quassoon's warriors, who were fanning out with their clubs along the shore. They understood that the disappearance of Kahammis might indeed signal danger to themselves and to their chief, for her revenge on the Wewksah had grown more fantastic every time the story was told. Scowling down the dark inlet, they braced for attack.

Yatintala cornered the Shaman with a torrent of bribes and threats; if he knew about Kahammis's pregnancy, surely he knew how to find the lost heir. The Shaman retreated into one of his trances beside the hearth, where he could sit for hours cross-legged, not moving so much as an eyelash, staring into the flames.

Dashing between the hearth and the door, Yatintala awaited Quassoon's return. But his bellows continued all through the night while his warriors kept their vigil on the beach. In the damp, grey morning, the people dragged themselves around the lodges with murmurs of folly and greed, while Quassoon stalked the sand, berserk with frustration, his warriors giving him a wide berth.

Mid-morning, a scream pierced the gloom. Jaws dropped and the warriors tightened their grips, and the children whimpered against their parents. The Shaman had come out of his trance! Yatintala flew to his side.

"Stolen!" he spluttered, swaying and barely coherent.

Yatintala screeched for Quassoon.

"Stolen?" repeated Quassoon, aghast.

The Shaman vibrated with effort, amulets dancing on his wrinkled chest.

Yatintala and Quassoon gave each other a look of furious blame. "How can we get her back?" they pleaded, but the Shaman was silent, and they crept away from his amulets, his acrid smell, his fire-glazed eyes.

Just then, a warning sounded outside. Quassoon bolted through the lodge, brandishing the whalebone club, rallying his men with unearthly cries. A canoe appeared out of the fog: Tatoosch, neither seen nor heard of since his drunken departure from Quatlukaht.

"It's me!" squeaked Tatoosch, crouched between his bewildered paddlers.

Quassoon stared, slack-jawed. Yatintala rushed down to welcome her son, who still gaped at the warriors positioned along the beach. Quassoon turned away, in disgust. For a moment, it seemed as if he did not know what to do, then he staggered off in the direction of the pond.

The next day, he announced that the winter festivities would be cancelled, to the disappointment of many, including Tatoosch, who thought he had timed his return well. Yatintala continued to hound the Shaman, who had nothing further to say. The cousins' wives gossiped incessantly, predicting that someone important would be killed. When a person of high rank died, a slave could be sacrificed, to appease the higher powers and compensate for the loss. So which had Kahammis been, royalty or slave? Had she died, or had she been transformed by terrible forest spirits, and would she come back to haunt her tormenters? For days these questions consumed Quassoon's people, while he seemed eaten alive by questions of his own. Bored and confined by the weather, Tatoosch occupied himself teaching the young boys to gamble, and regaling them with tales of his exploits. Meanwhile, Yatintala brooded over how to inform Paquacheenish that his granddaughter had slipped out of their grasp.

One morning, between squalls, Quassoon drifted towards the pond, repelled by companionship and indifferent to the cold. Endlessly he searched for answers as to why Kahammis, delivered to him at his prime, had been snatched away. He had honoured his people and all the neighbouring people, and they had honoured him. The finest whale in the ocean had swum to his harpoon. What had gone awry?

Reaching the pond, he brusquely wiped his hand across his eyes. To his astonishment, he was not alone. A surly-faced Tatoosch stood at the edge of the water, poking deeply with a long stick.

"What are you doing?" Quassoon roared. Then he understood: Tatoosch was probing for the drowned body of Kahammis.

Seizing the stick, he whacked it across his son's back, and Tatoosch crawled off. Quassoon stared into the pond, overcome, but all he was able to see was his own reflection, wavering and grotesque.

~~~:~~~

Twice Kahammis set out in her canoe, and twice she was pinned against Yuhktu by the churning waves and the rising tide. Futile though it was to fight with the ocean, she fumed along the beach all morning until the tide slackened at noon.

Her shoulders loosened when she began to paddle, and she chanted with pure joy, her voice echoing between the inlet's conifer walls. Nothing restored her sense of self more profoundly than the dip and hiss of the blade, pulling her home. Flocks of wintering mallards rose up quacking, and rafts of pintails and buffleheads parted in consternation as she glided through their midst.

When the sun fell to the level of the trees, she steered towards a strip of shell-speckled mud. She would have gone ashore, but the surrounding forest smelled of bear, and she returned to the security of her canoe. She found a cedar tree which angled out over the water, and wedged her stern amongst the lowest branches, anchoring herself against the current.

The descending sun illuminated the inlet with a rosy glow. She was close to where the inlet widened, and soon she would be amongst the Mannakaht, who occupied their islands year-round. The worst of her journey was behind her; she had navigated the narrows safely, through whirlpools where vessels bigger and braver than hers had been swallowed without a trace. She leaned back, relaxing, watching a family of eagles nearby. The eagles were fishing the tide rip, and the gawky, mottled yearling cheeped impatiently beneath the soaring wings of the adult birds, their tails flashing pink in the last of the light.

When a woodpecker rattled against a rotting stump, she sat up, startled; the drumming woodpecker had been the signal between Sheebo and her father, behind Yuhktu. Where were Sheebo and her father now? How easily they could slip off the side of a mountain, or more likely, fall into the path of marauders. They had rescued her, but who would be there for them?

The night settled heavily over her, seeping with fears: the bear, the Shaman, Quassoon. Even her own brothers used to jump out at her, with whoops and child-sized spears. She lay alert to every sound, until fatigue pulled her into sleep.

Two Mannakaht fishermen spied her at dawn. She woke to the clink of their paddles, and immediately demanded that they take her to T'isharth. They complied, hardly taking their eyes off her as they escorted her to their chief. She set the pace and refused a tow line, determined to avoid a repeat of her capture at Quatlukaht.

T'isharth's village was a spread of low houses along a small bay. A group of carvers stood with their mouths hanging open as Kahammis stroked towards them, then she raised her head, laying her paddle across her knees. The two fishermen leapt ashore, running to the chief's house.

T'isharth recognized Kahammis, his face contorting with the tics that had plagued his tenure as chief, poised as he was between the whims of Quassoon, Wikkosum of the Wasquimaht, and Ewona of the Sheshalam. He shuffled down the path to the beach in a paroxysm of doubt: to whom should he be loyal, now?

His people had already heard the story of Kahammis's disappearance, told by Quassoon when he had stopped overnight during the move to Quatlukaht. Quassoon had poured out his sufferings at T'isharth's hearth, Yatintala at his side, more pinched and shrunken than ever. Conspicuous by his absence was Tatoosch, who had been gone since the altercation by the pond. Every village along the coast was in an uproar, for when Paquacheenish learned of his grand-daughter's disappearance, he sent deputies to interrogate not only Quassoon but T'isharth, Ewona, Wikkosum, and all the other minor chiefs, his rage more than equal to Quassoon's grief. Then, on a peaceful spring morning, who should land on T'isharth's beach but Kahammis, the very source of the rumours, the mystery, the blame.

Regally she waited, in her canoe.

T'isharth took a look at her and scurried off, without a word, to his thinking stream. Foremost in the minds of his people, as they watched, was the certainty that anyone who could take revenge upon the Wewksah, survive a southeaster at sea, bewitch Quassoon, then simply ... vanish, could also turn their already insecure lives upside-down. Fortunately, Chief T'isharth's daughter, Tatatoe, possessed great common sense. She had stood up to Tatoosch during their brief marriage, and she had no reason to fear this young woman in the canoe. She invited Kahammis ashore, frowning at the villagers until they resumed their activities, muttering and shaking their heads.

Kahammis was led into a lodge similar to those at Quatlukaht and Yuhktu, matted against drafts, cluttered with baskets and tools. She sat at the main hearth, smoothing her cape self-consciously over her bulging middle. Tatatoe settled close by, curious about the cedar-root cradle and hardly able to keep her hands off the fringe on the cape. Neither spoke, and each was wondering: what had it been like with the brutal father, the brutal son? T'isharth had taken his daughter back even though it meant breaking a marriage pledge made when Tatatoe was a child. Surely, Kahammis told herself, T'isharth was a compassionate man.

She glanced around the lodge. The poles holding up the roof beams had been elaborately carved, and she was taken aback to see that T'isharth's crest was dominated by the Raven, claimed also by Paquacheenish, whose bond with the bird was legendary along the coast.

"What is this?" she asked, tracing the long tail weaving through the raven's wings.

"Mountain cat." Tatatoe pointed to the bottom of the crest, brightening. "And here is our herring. We Mannakaht are gatekeepers to the best runs on the coast."

Gatekeepers for Ewona, Wikkosum, and Quassoon, Kahammis mused to herself.

Tatatoe's expression changed, as if she knew what was in Kahammis's mind. "At one time, we also owned Yuhktu."

Kahammis lowered her eyes to hide her amazement. She studied T'isharth's crest, struck by a thought: had Tatatoe's marriage pledge been made to re-establish her family's rights?

A pair of T'isharth's advisers came into the lodge, and Kahammis threw back her shoulders, lifting her chin as they sidled past; not for a minute was she going to behave like a slave. It was this gesture, so evocative of her grandfather, that the advisers hurried out to report to

T'isharth at his thinking stream. T'isharth forced himself to move beyond his local allegiances and consider Paquacheenish, who had lost his daughter, son-in-law, and grandchildren to the Wewksah, and then lost Kahammis to Quassoon. Coast justice was simple, and severe: violence begets violence, spinning down through the generations as each chief sought his own version of revenge.

So it had been in T'isharth's own life, when the Mannakaht had relinquished their rights to Yuhktu. Forty years before, T'isharth's father and Quassoon's father had been allies, both of them strong and ambitious chiefs. They had instigated a retaliatory raid on the northern thieves, a raid which was tragically bungled, with T'isharth's father and many of his warriors killed. Since T'isharth and his older brother were at that time merely children, the Mannakaht people fell under the guardianship of Quassoon's father. Quassoon's family gradually shifted from their own winter camp, a dismal site at the rear of the sound, to the camp of the Mannakaht people, which was Yuhktu. Crowded out and made to feel unwelcome, the Mannakaht were forced to occupy their summer villages year-round. To this broken group, T'isharth eventually became chief. It was a responsibility he bore alone, for his older brother, a proud and sensitive youth, had been so humiliated by Quassoon's family that he had departed long ago, with a handful of close friends and slaves. Then, T'isharth's young wife had died while giving birth to Tatatoe. For many years, his losses seemed immense, his gains few. Tatatoe's failed marriage had been a terrible blow, eliminating his only hope of reclaiming Yuhktu.

Now, here was Kahammis.

Here was the opportunity T'isharth had been waiting for, to make a deal with Quassoon. He must be dreaming! A deal with Quassoon would unleash the wrath of the mighty Paquacheenish! He clutched his jaw, and his advisers hovered in the bushes nearby.

Kahammis and Tatatoe strolled through the village, their heads bent together as they discussed the construction of the cradle and the cape. Tatatoe did not share her father's dilemma; a few moments alone with Kahammis were all she needed to align herself with the beautiful and, to her mind, heroic escapee. It was only her good manners which kept her from asking: where on earth had Kahammis been? That was the question for her father to ask, when he was ready.

T'isharth tossed pebbles into the ferny stream, grateful to be away from the distraction of his people's never-ending needs. He lost himself in the spreading ripples, alone with the clicks and clucks of his friend the raven, who always seemed to know when T'isharth was troubled.

Around and around rippled the thoughts in T'isharth's head.

"Make a deal," whispered the ghost of his slain father, yet to be avenged.

"Careful!" His advisers twittered through the trees. "She acts as if her nose is connected to the sky!"

"Believe in yourself, T'isharth, believe in yourself." These were the last words of his brother, as he left.

T'isharth gulped and stood up, shouting out loud so that he could not change his mind: tomorrow he would take Kahammis to Klinniklinnikaht!

But tonight, a feast!

Kahammis sat in the position of honour at the hearth, outwardly demure, inwardly dazed with relief. Beside her, Tatatoe peeled cowparsnip stems with a mussel-shell knife. She handed Kahammis a sweet, stubby stem, beaming as she shook the green skins out of her lap. Nothing pleased a coast woman more than the preparations for a feast: the ritual unpacking of the boxes and baskets which contained the ceremonial dishes and spoons, and the bounty of the land and sea. Children and slaves ran for water and fuel; red-hot stones fell sizzling into the cooking boxes, along with the day's harvest of chitons pried off the rocks and crabs speared at low tide, filling the lodge with succulent steam.

T'isharth had moved beyond doubt to the calm centre of his destiny, a place he had never before achieved. When he finished eating, he wiped his mouth with shredded bark and lifted his head, gesturing to Kahammis. A hearty meal was in progress, but the chewing stopped at once and not a sound was to be heard. This was the moment everyone had been waiting for: Kahammis must speak.

Kahammis gnawed her fingers, studying the silent crowd. How could she appease the Mannakaht without risk to her rescuers behind Yuhktu? The crowd was equally apprehensive, despite their full stomachs and their devotion to their chief. What mischief would Kahammis now reveal?

Their eyes narrowed suspiciously as she fumbled at the collar of her cape. "I have been with the forest people," she whispered. She pulled out the little loon, thrusting it at T'isharth.

T'isharth's reaction galvanized the crowd. "This belongs to me!" He jumped up, holding the loon to the light of the flames. "I gave it to my brother when he left!" He turned to Kahammis, his face twitching wildly. "My brother! You have seen him!"

Kahammis looked at T'isharth, dumbfounded. Suddenly she understood, remembering how Sheebo's father had gazed over the sound, his voice breaking when he spoke of the Mannakaht. Now she knew why she had been able to go with him across the mountains, into the unknown. She had trusted him, just as she had trusted T'isharth.

T'isharth listened to the story of her rescue, sighing and turning the little loon over and over in his hands. Then he placed it on her lap. "For luck," he said, and her heart was wrenched by his goodness, and his pain.

They departed at dawn, Kahammis in the chief's canoe, her own vessel towed astern. She had been awake all night with long-suppressed emotions and sat numbly, the water and the sky around her shimmering with the colours of the early morning, ephemeral colours which haunted her, taking her back to the ship, to the captain's eyes.

Klinniklinnikaht was as far south of Quatlukaht as Quatlukaht was south of the sound, a journey that would test the stamina of the Mannakaht paddlers, born as they were to the wind and the wave. On other voyages they would have stopped at Quatlukaht; now, T'isharth directed them well offshore. They passed the crescent bay, and even as far out as they were, they could smell the woodsmoke, the drying fish, the warm land. T'isharth basked in the sunshine, enjoying the thought that he would never again have to grovel to Quassoon. Of course Quassoon would be angry, but Paquacheenish would be pleased, and Paquacheenish was far more important to T'isharth. He was about to direct the paddlers back towards the coast when a whoosh from behind took them all by surprise. A family of killer whales, dorsal fins rising in unison, crossed their wake. Kahammis spun around, and her laughter rang out over the water; these were the whales of the Kalowish crest, severing her northern servitude as surely as the cut of a knife.

She sang with Tatatoe through the long afternoon, and T'isharth jested with the seabirds and shouted down to the two-headed monster with such irreverence that his men forgot their fatigue. The sun had just touched the horizon, with a flash of ruby light, when they reached the channel at Klinniklinnikaht. The eagles and the ravens were on their roosts and the breeze was stilled, the ocean and the earth converging harmoniously in the dusk.

Kahammis braced herself for the sound of the sentries, commencing their howling from point to point, and the paddlers grinned, for the Klinniklinnikaht warriors were very sharp, instantly identifying their northern neighbours despite the glare of the setting sun. They sped up the channel, and Kahammis gripped Tatatoe's hands. Across the lagoon they flew, to the beach below the chief's lodge. Summoned by the sentries, Paquacheenish emerged, ever the accommodating host.

He walked slowly to the beach, so slowly that for a moment Kahammis thought he would collapse.

"Kahammis?" he asked, as if mistrusting his old eyes.

A young warrior pushed through the crowd. Kahammis recognized Aneetsick, who so resembled their dead father that she felt faint with shock.

"Kahammis?" called Paquacheenish, stretching out his arms.

Behind her, the paddlers rested with whistling breaths. T'isharth endeavoured to compose himself, and Tatatoe blushed as she helped Kahammis disembark.

Kahammis felt her bare toes sinking into the mud. She could not take another step, but it no longer mattered, for she was in her grandfather's arms.

~~~:~~~

Kahammis sat beneath the spreading shade of her cedar tree, sorting strands of bear grass. Taking form in her mind was a basket, small and round with a curving lid; on the lid would be a waning moon, tipped backwards towards a single star. What freedom it was for her to weave, to dream, to inhale each moment without fear.

Just in time, she turned to catch a brown body hurtling beneath the branches. Her son squealed in her arms, narrowly escaping Aneetsick, who growled behind him on hands and knees. Kahammis hugged him, laughing as she pushed Aneetsick away.

She had agreed to stay at Klinniklinnikaht until her son was born. He was unusually long and thin for a coast baby, and bald, but his eyes were very black like his mother's, and she had named him Hoptooyak. She was amazed at how rapidly he grew, except for his

70

hair, a coppery fuzz which delighted the village elders, particularly Paquacheenish. The matrons watched Hoptooyak closely and commented amongst themselves, with satisfaction, that they could find no similarities to Quassoon. Everyone knew that Kahammis had been put with the young captain on the ship; this, however, like her relationship with Quassoon, was not discussed. Nor was it mentioned that the captain had returned several times with his ship to Klinniklinnikaht, looking out for the Quatlukaht canoes.

Paquacheenish delayed the resettlement of Nootseetaht through the fall and winter; better to start strong, he said, in the spring. The truth was, neither he nor his doting wife could bear to lose Kahammis again so soon. For Kahammis the wait had seemed endless, yet now on this bright, summer afternoon, she felt as if she had never left.

She set aside the bear grass, tracking Hoptooyak's unsteady progress down the ridge towards his uncle, who had gone back to repairing one of his canoes. The tiny basket with its moon and star was already finished in her mind, and she was eager to begin weaving, even though she had been on watch all night, and berry-picking at dawn.

"Go to sleep!" Aneetsick called teasingly from the beach. "Don't worry, I will protect the Warrior Prince!"

Kahammis waved and lay back. Beside her was a bouquet of fireweed she had collected from the burned-off slopes behind the village, where the best blackberries grew. She studied the blooming spires, vibrant purples and pinks, wondering how to reproduce such colours with dye, something livelier than the traditional hues. Though her eyes drooped tiredly, she could not shut out the hopes and ideas crowding her mind.

When Quassoon learned that a baby boy had been born, his rightful heir, he swore eternal revenge upon T'isharth, Paquacheenish, and Kahammis, who had slipped away like smoke yet still consumed his imagination, and the imagination of his people. His rumblings reached Paquacheenish, who issued a warning, delivered by a hundred painted warriors lest the meaning be misunderstood: stay away from Kahammis or you will never trade again. Quassoon's massive shoulders twisted with impotence; the otters were gone and what was left to sell, raccoons? If Paquacheenish kept him from the ships, and kept the ships from him, he was ruined, for the economy of the coast had become dependent on the stacks of blankets, the guns and the kegs.

As for the defence of Nootseetaht, Aneetsick had begun his own collection of muskets, organizing a strategy of retreat to the caves upriver. When he and Kahammis moved home they were joined by Hasallum, their uncle, who had taken on the role of chief until Aneetsick came of age. They were joined also by many young families who were glad to leave the congestion at Klinniklinnikaht and make a fresh start. The men kept watches, concealed across from the spit, a duty which Kahammis insisted on sharing. She sat through the darkness, and when the owl trilled, or the woodpecker rattled against a tree, she thought of Sheebo trekking the mountains far away.

Honorary chief and master carver, Hasallum had brought a steadiness and strength to the rebuilding of Nootseetaht. It was Hasallum who, three years before, had supervised the removal of the bodies after the massacre, burning the bones of the Wewksah on the spit. Also removed, to Klinniklinnikaht for safe-keeping, were the boxes, baskets, planks and tools, until the day they were needed again. So when Kahammis did return, there were no more bloodstains on the sleeping platforms and the paths, and no more angry, buzzing clouds.

Now, resting beneath the cedar tree, she was remembering how preoccupied Hasallum had been several days earlier, as he was preparing for a trip north. She hoped he would be back soon, with news of her grandparents; Paquacheenish had limped down to the lagoon to see them all off in the spring, and her grandmother had been sniffling as she handed over Hoptooyak.

Kahammis rubbed her eyes, sitting up. Aneetsick had grabbed Hoptooyak and was running around the bay, towards a cluster of boys who were pointing and shouting on the spit. Climbing the lower branches of the tree, Kahammis saw a large grey lump floating beyond the outer shore. Aneetsick waded into the waves, and by the time Kahammis arrived, the carcass was already wedged on the beach, a mature humpback, freshly dead. She and Aneetsick inspected the ridged throat and along the flippers to the white underside of the tail, but they could find no wound marking the carcass as the property of a neighbouring chief. The whale was theirs to keep! Such providence was almost unheard of, all the more miraculous coming at a time when they lacked the resources to mount a hunt of their own.

"An omen!" cried Kahammis, and Hoptooyak crowed, waving his little fist.

"He'll be our best harpooner yet," grinned Aneetsick.

Kahammis turned away, blinking happy tears.

~~~:~~~

Nine years later, Hoptooyak hurried deep into the forest behind Nootseetaht, until his great-uncle Hasallum restrained him with a smile. Hoptooyak was searching for the cedar tree which would become his first real canoe. Hasallum steered him towards the river, towards a specimen he had selected months before.

"We'll sail your tree downstream," he told Hoptooyak, adding with a wink, "you can be the captain."

Hoptooyak's face lit up. Every summer when he saw the ships, his mother promised that one day he would be allowed aboard. He strode ahead on his long, spindly legs, and behind him trotted Kleeshin, three years younger, Hasallum's son. The two boys held their spears at the ready, lest they encounter anything bigger and fiercer than themselves.

The mystery of Hasallum's preoccupation, years earlier, had been solved when he announced his marriage to Tatatoe; he had been north visiting the Mannakaht, presenting his suit. On the evening when T'isharth had delivered Kahammis to Klinniklinnikaht, Hasallum had been working over a canoe behind his father's lodge. His adze dropped from his hands as he caught sight, not of Kahammis, but of her blushing companion. His former bride had died from an infected tooth, and he had been uninterested in substitutes, until Tatatoe appeared. The marriage was an excellent alliance for the Mannakaht, causing T'isharth to further reflect on the peculiar luck brought to him by Kahammis's escape from Quassoon.

T'isharth often turned his thoughts, as did Kahammis, to Quassoon. The thwarted chief was only biding his time and sooner or later, he would strike.

Kahammis smiled as she followed the two boys into the forest, so endearing did they look in the conical hats, several sizes too big, which they had begged from Aneetsick, hoping to borrow some of his idolized status. She wished that Aneetsick would also take a wife, if only to give him something to think about apart from the muskets accumulating in the boxes stashed upriver. Aneetsick had been promised to a girl who had been killed in the massacre, and Kahammis feared that he would let no one take her place.

73

Kahammis was annoyed with Aneetsick because of the Wolf Mask he had sold in the fall to a ship. "See what they paid," he told her, stacking guns in flannel sheaths, handing her a bolt of cloth decorated like a spring meadow. The mask had belonged to their father and she knew it had been wrong to let it go, just as it had been wrong to sell her baskets to the same bossy captain; he had snatched them away while she was still sorting the salmon they had contained.

Hoptooyak was dashing impatiently from trunk to trunk, his rain hat shaking as he and Kleeshin noticed some imperfection that would mar his canoe. "Uncle! Uncle!" he cried suddenly, galloping back along the path. "We've found the one!"

Hasallum looked around, feigning skepticism as the boys guided him to the tree they had chosen, its trunk tapering smoothly to a high, branched crown. Now was the time for cutting, before the sap ran. Hasallum was so confident of this tree that he would not bore a test hole for rot, and when he smiled his approval, the boys cheered.

"You and I will return at dusk," he informed Hoptooyak. "We will pray that we are worthy of our task."

Hoptooyak agreed with such enthusiasm that the brim of his hat slipped over his nose, and his mother turned away, trying not to laugh. The boys raced homeward, and she and Hasallum followed more sedately, along the trail beside the river. They skirted the abandoned winter camp, where houseposts leaned, unsupported, and the hearths were already overgrown with salal. They no longer moved upriver in the fall, so that they could defend Nootseetaht year-round.

A family of mink rose up on hind legs, whiskers twitching as Kahammis and Hasallum went past. Kahammis thought back to old Sa-sat-kis, whose stories of the mink had enchanted the winter nights of her childhood. She turned to Hasallum, her voice quavering, "Where is Sa-sat-kis?" It was the first time in years that she had spoken his name aloud. "Is he warm and safe?"

"Of course," Hasallum replied gruffly. His pace quickened as they neared the delta, where the river, swift and muddy from the rain, widened and flattened into a rich feeding ground for the wintering birds. They saw Tatatoe waiting outside the lodge with her new baby, Neetsa, and the two excited boys.

Kahammis settled at the hearth. She was unravelling pieces of the cape Sheebo had made, working the scraps of wool into a new cape of golden bark. She often dreamed of Sheebo, remembering the hours they had spent together by the lake. Paquacheenish had known of Sheebo's father, as he knew of everyone, and he warned Kahammis that these were people who existed from season to season, no more. She had hardly been able to listen, covering her ears like a child.

The loon pin was kept on a bed of eagle down, inside the tiny basket with the moon and star on the lid. Weaving had come to consume Kahammis; she craved the feel of the bark and the grass and her thoughts raced constantly to the next design. Already she had pushed far beyond local styles, not without offending some of the elders with her experimental dyes. Paquacheenish, however, purchased everything that she did not keep and proudly gave her work away as gifts.

Hasallum and Hoptooyak spent the afternoon readying their tools. Hasallum tested his iron chisels, acquired from the ships, superior to the stone and antler chisels which he seldom now used. Kahammis could recall her father tossing out iron chisels in disgust, because they shattered in the cold, but Hasallum's chisels were strong, lashed to hardwood handles with cedar withes.

At dusk Hasallum took Hoptooyak into the forest, and Kahammis paddled across the bay to keep watch. She sat quietly in the thickening darkness, in the hope of hearing the otters amongst the reefs. Sometimes she went out in her canoe just to see the otters groom and play, pleading with Aneetsick to spare the last, small colony that survived. Prices had risen so dramatically that Aneetsick thought her mad, but he was not chief yet.

Only a few ships traded now at Klinniklinnikaht, for pelts of river otter, mink, marten, and the occasional fur seals hunted offshore. Kahammis passed close to the ships when she visited her grandparents; she caught a glimpse, once, of a man tall and slim like the young captain, talking with Paquacheenish on deck. She turned away instantly, for with the memory of the captain came the cruel, jeering memory of Quassoon. There were times, though, when she glanced into Hoptooyak's face and caught a certain angle of bone and skin which left her breathless and vanished even as she looked, like the sky at dawn. The round metal button had fallen off her cape and disappeared when Hoptooyak was a toddler, and then, amazingly, she found it a year or two later when she was raking the hearth.

As the ships decreased, so did the risk from the cannons and the volatile cargo of kegs. There had been terrible incidents to the north and south, ships and villages attacked, but for Paquacheenish's people it seemed that their worst misgivings about the white strangers had come to naught. Since it was the otters that had lured the ships out of nowhere, with fabulous rewards, the people trusted that when the ships were all gone, the otters would return.

Kahammis never ran out of thoughts to keep her awake, wrapped in her cape and shifting constantly to lessen the chill. She enjoyed her independence, and chuckled at Tatatoe's hints about possible husbands; Tatatoe was no doubt encouraged by Hasallum, Aneetsick, and Paquacheenish, who were all hopeful that Kahammis would become someone's wife. Patlowah's grandson now had two pretty daughters; she had seen them cavorting in the lagoon. She was pleased for him, and was just as pleased with her own life.

When Hasallum and Hoptooyak came back from the forest in the morning, they recruited volunteers to help bring down the tree. Although cedars were often felled by a controlled burning, this time Hasallum and his helpers built a cutting platform above the wide base of the trunk. The splitting out of the pungent wood continued through the afternoon, and the women came to watch, singing respectfully, appreciatively, to the cutters and the tree. Standing behind her son, Kahammis could see the effort he was making to keep up with the older men. The felled tree would be stripped of branches, bark, and sapwood, and floated downriver, shaped into a rough hull, and left to mature until late spring. Hasallum looked forward to teaching Hoptooyak how to adze in rhythm with his heartbeat; they would work side by side until the final polish, as he had worked with Kahammis so many years before.

They proceeded homeward through the twilight, Hoptooyak flagging, Hasallum deep in contemplation of the moods of the forest, variables that despite decades of study he did not fully understand. The moment of the fall was always the longest in his life: a creaking shudder as the tree gathered momentum from the severed trunk to the wavering crown, ripping through the adjacent trees, then a thunderous crash, bark and branches exploding on impact. He and his men would stand back silently in the settling debris, stunned with relief and awe.

For days a curtain of mist had hovered over the coast, and now, as the women and the tree-cutters emerged onto the delta, the clouds far across the ocean lifted to reveal the sun's dazzling light. The curtain again descended, and the gilded horizon was erased from sight.

Hoptooyak took his mother's hand, exclaiming at the unexpected show. But Kahammis stiffened, hearing the sentry's call as a trio of canoes careened around the spit.

This was not the season for casual journeys, and only those with local knowledge would arrive late, against the tide. Her fears were confirmed as the visitors streaked towards the village: huge and dishevelled, smeared with grease and paint, Tatoosch leered out of the lead canoe. With him were his blank-faced slaves and gambling companions, among them a young man from a high-ranking family at Klinniklinnikaht. The young man had stayed briefly at Nootseetaht during the rebuilding of the houses; it was he, no doubt, who had prompted Tatoosch.

The villagers flocked outside to the sounds of the sentry and the striking paddles. Hasallum strode forward from the delta; tradition required that travellers receive food and shelter at rest stops along the coast. Aneetsick remained at the entrance to his lodge, a wary expression on his lean face.

Tatoosch bounded out of his canoe, losing his balance and splashing into the water, and the villagers watched from the grassy slope, bemused. Hoptooyak still held his mother's hand, and he was surprised by her reaction: she hung back, as if she wanted to hide. She looked around in a panic for Tatatoe, who had stayed out of sight.

Two years earlier, Tatoosch had found a wife he could keep. There had been a tournament of the bone games at Klinniklinnikaht which had almost culminated in a riot, with Tatoosch banned from the village, but not before he had won fourteen-year-old Oweena, daughter of a drunken opponent. Home to Yatintala he took his bewildered bride, and now he was father to a newborn son.

"Have you heard the news?" slurred Tatoosch, swaying and peering around the slope. His companions backpaddled in the shallows, waiting for the invitation to come ashore.

"The Wewksah are destroyed!" Tatoosch hooted, throwing up his hands. "Destroyed by the spots!"

Kahammis stepped out from behind Hoptooyak. The Wewksah of their nightmares, destroyed by ... the spots?

Hasallum folded his arms across his chest, noticing the keg tipped over in the canoe. "What is spots?" he asked.

Tatoosch belched, and one of his companions spoke caustically from the bay. "Burning spots which burst out all over the Wewksah, even the babies! Two or three days, then they collapse, dead."

A shiver spread over the slope, mothers clutching their children, creeping closer to hear more. Hasallum's questions were interrupted by Tatoosch's hiccups, and his companions were still awaiting permission to disembark.

Tatoosch's hiccups ceased abruptly. Kahammis ducked behind Hoptooyak, but it was too late, Tatoosch was charging up the slope. "Whore!" he screamed. "I knew you were around here somewhere! I knew I would catch up to you one day!"

Aneetsick stepped forward. "Go!" he commanded Tatoosch.

"Who is the brat?" sneered Tatoosch, poking at Hoptooyak, who stood, face drawn, in front of his mother.

"Go now!" Aneetsick's hand was on his club.

"My men need rest," whined Tatoosch.

Aneetsick raised his club. Tatoosch stormed down to the beach, his slaves readying their paddles, impassive in the gloom.

"What kind of village is this?" shouted Tatoosch as he went by Hasallum. "A village of sandfleas?" He sprawled into his canoe. "I'll come back. I'll crush you, sandfleas!"

The three canoes spun away, picking up speed. "You too, Kahammis," roared Tatoosch, with an obscene wave. "You too!"

Long after he left, the villagers stayed slumped along the slope, torn between the offense of their inhospitality and the offensiveness of Tatoosch. Kahammis stood with the cold rain splattering her neck, holding tightly to her son's hand. She was listening to the echo and hearing not Tatoosch, but Quassoon.

~~~:~~~

A slender, white moon lit the waters of the bay as Hoptooyak loaded boxes into his canoe. Hoptooyak had now attained his full height, at sixteen years of age, and his canoe fit him perfectly, to the amazement of all but Hasallum, who had been alone in his prediction of just how tall Hoptooyak would grow. The canoe's flaring bow had been decorated with the crest Hoptooyak would inherit when he became a man and assumed the name of his grandfather, Kalowish. This decision, made by Paquacheenish and Aneetsick, filled Kahammis with pride in her lanky son, who no longer allowed her to brush the flyaway, coppery hair out of his eyes, and whose artistry with wood had come to match her own with the bark and the grass.

78

Hoptooyak was helped with the boxes by Kleeshin, with long-suffering sighs. Kleeshin's day had begun when his younger sister Neetsa emptied a water container onto his sleeping face. Now she and her friends hurtled over the frosty slope, taunting the boys on the beach.

Aneetsick, Nootseetaht's chief, inspected the contents of each vessel, ensuring that nothing was left behind on this momentous occasion: the celebration of his marriage to Chee-uxqua, of a genteel family at Klinniklinnikaht. He urged everyone to paddle strongly as they filed past the spit; the breeze, barely ruffling the bay at dawn, would by noon blast their faces and raise the westerly chop. Hoptooyak and Kleeshin skimmed ahead, eager to lead. Six-year-old Neetsa shouted farewell to the remaining villagers, so reckless in her enthusiasm that Tatatoe feared she would fall overboard.

Kahammis travelled on her own; she still kept her watches across from the spit, and Tatatoe had given up trying to turn her into a bride. In the bow of her canoe was the box of treasures she took everywhere: combs that had belonged to her mother, rare shells and feathers, the metal button, and the little basket with the loon pin. She sat erect, paddling briskly, measuring the current by watching the cormorants poised on a distant, floating branch. Except for the fine lines around her eyes, she could have been the girl setting out from Nootseetaht half a lifetime ago.

Tatoosch had spoken the truth: the Wewksah had been eliminated. The southern nations insisted that the sickness had been brought by a ship, a concept so deadly as to spread terror through every village along the coast. Not long after delivering his news, Tatoosch had taken his wife and child south to a gathering place of many ships. Tatoosch drank from the kegs and caroused as always, and on the return trip, Oweena erupted with ugly sores, the same sores that had plagued the women Paquacheenish used to send out to the trading crews. When they saw her, Yatintala and the Shaman refused to allow her ashore. They kept the baby Moochinnick and sent Oweena back in disgrace to Klinniklinnikaht. To everyone's relief, the sores ended with Oweena's death, and the fears of disease gradually decreased as even fewer ships ventured north.

When the westerly wind was just curling the wavetops, Hoptooyak steered his canoe into the channel at Klinniklinnikaht. Chee-uxqua and her family waited nervously; Hasallum had overcome his natural reticence to approach them on Aneetsick's behalf, offering gifts and reiterating the rights that the bride and groom would share. The women at Nootseetaht had been weaving mats and filling boxes with berry cakes, roots, and fish. Hoptooyak had carved bowls and spoons, and Aneetsick had exchanged a superb pelt for the dentalia that settled his suit. He and his hunters had rounded up the last colony of otters, the pelts too valuable to pass off as a sentimental sight.

Paquacheenish stood in welcome at the head of the lagoon. He addressed Aneetsick in his throaty growl, leading him to the place of honour at the hearth. Aneetsick glanced around despairingly: the lagoon was a hubbub of laughter and greetings, considerably less dignified than he had wished. He looked fiercely handsome in his golden bark cape, his eyebrows blackened and his hair tied up with spruce, copper pendants in his ears and nose. He had inherited the cheekbones of Paquacheenish who, bešidè him, seemed to have shrunk.

Kahammis and her grandmother watched them go. "All yesterday, he sat in the hotsprings," murmured the old matriarch, smiling as Paquacheenish nimbly ushered guests into the lodge. "Just to be able to walk like that! He sleeps on a bed of blankets," she added, sighing, "when he sleeps at all. The ravens are back."

Kahammis glanced up into the trees lining the lagoon, where the ravens roosted on their coastal flights. The ravens had been speaking to Paquacheenish for sixty years; what were they telling him now?

"He has forbidden the kegs, you know. Oh yes!" Her grandmother nodded at Kahammis's surprise. "In the cutting season." She was referring to the fall run of the dog salmon. "A ship came, from the far islands." She gestured offshore, where she had been told that the ships spent their winters, on islands surrounded by days of ocean in every direction. "They wanted fresh water and fish, and we had plenty." She chortled indulgently. "You know how Paquacheenish loves to visit with the captains."

Paquacheenish owned three fancy garments covered with buttons and trim, which he wore, layered over each other, when a ship was in.

His wife's voice grew shrill. "Well, you know how the buying goes better with kegs. The captain's best musket went missing and where was it found? In one of our canoes! Certainly things go missing now and again, but this time, the captain ordered Paquacheenish off the ship!" Her wrinkled cheeks were pink as she finished her story. "Never have we been so insulted! I'll be happy if we never see a ship again!"

Kahammis could not help thinking that if Paquacheenish had banned the kegs long ago, her father would still be alive. However, as her grandmother had pointed out, whisky smoothed the trade, and trade had made them rich.

The westerlies blew for the next three days, and the eagles soared, and the crows clung tousled and protesting in the trees below. For three days Paquacheenish surpassed even his own standards of generosity and abundance, ensuring that all up and down the coast his reputation would remain intact, despite his brittle joints, despite the moments of chagrin when the names of his dearest friends would not come to his tongue. Never had the blankets been heaped so high, and never had the pots, muskets, and bolts of cloth been strewn around his lodge with such abandon. How the guests cheered at each shake of the rattle, delivering some new privilege, trinket, or steaming tub of food.

When Chee-uxqua danced before her husband, only the rigid line of his jaw betrayed the importance of this milestone in Aneetsick's life. The burden of his choices weighed heavily on him now that he was responsible for Nootseetaht. Would he listen to those around him, wondered Kahammis? She knew that at times she seemed more like a conscience to him than a sister, and she met his eyes reassuringly across the enraptured crowd.

When he stood to reply to his bride, even the crows ceased their protests, and the eagles spiralled on their wingtips as the hereditary wedding song rose through the roofboards and was carried away on the westerly gusts. Lest the mood become too serious, Paquacheenish summoned the village jesters who had been rehearsing all year. Neetsa giggled wildly, nestled on her grandfather T'isharth's lap. She was sucking a hollow kelp stem filled with treacle, and Kahammis could recall her own first taste of the sticky brown syrup, when she had been no older than Neetsa and just as greedy. She had drained the entire kelp ball and fallen to the ground, tingling from her fingers to her toes.

At the close of the third extravagant day of feasting, a wolf yipped behind the village. Everyone fell silent, and soon the surrounding forest resonated with eerie howls: the Wolf Ceremony was about to begin. Hoptooyak turned to his mother with an ashen face.

"Howeee!" Closer came the wolves, yip-yipping in the darkness, and Hoptooyak resisted with all his youthful courage the urge to dive behind his mother, while beside him, Kleeshin crumpled at the mercy of his fear. The crowd flattened against the walls as six creatures sprang

81

through the entrance, wolfskins dangling over their blackened limbs, carved snouts searching out their victims: six bug-eyed boys, including Hoptooyak and Kleeshin, who were dragged off into the night.

When they were gone, to a frenzied battering of the drums, Kahammis reached for Tatatoe's hand. The lodge vibrated with the roars of the crowd, calling the boys back. The drummers held their sticks in suspense as from the forest came the answering howl: the boys now belonged to the wolves! Then the speeches began, berating Kahammis, Tatatoe, and the other mothers for their carelessness in allowing their sons to be stolen. Kahammis hung her head, aching with the knowledge that she had indeed lost Hoptooyak; he was her child no more. Yet still she could feel, as if it were yesterday, the curve of his baby cheek imprinted against her breast. Why had no one warned her how fleeting that embrace would be?

For three more nights the masks rattled and the drums rolled, and the villagers beseeched the wolves to give back the boys. The boys had been taken to a remote lodge, where they were learning the sacred songs, the duties, and the rights they would inherit. At night so realistic were the sounds of the wolves gnashing their teeth outside that each boy, in his heart, felt convinced of their presence a mere wallboard away.

On the evening of the fourth day, shouts of alarm shattered the calm lagoon. The boys had been sighted by sentries, adrift in strange canoes. A daring rescue was staged, and although the wolves fought terribly, the boys were saved. They were paraded through Paquacheenish's lodge, their faces stained red and black, their bodies entwined with hemlock sprigs. A hushed, grateful crowd accepted their songs and dances, and marvelled at the rights of ownership: the clam beds, the halibut banks and whaling grounds which established them as men. Most important was the presentation of family crests, and Hoptooyak received his adult name: Kalowish.

"You mustn't call me Hoptooyak anymore," he admonished Kahammis, when the ceremonies were over. Tossing his hair, he eyed her severely. "Did you know? Well, I suppose you wouldn't have told me, even if you did!" He leaned closer, confiding. "Actually, I was very brave. Everyone else was scared out of their wits!"

Kahammis choked back a laugh, but she touched the smear of paint he left on her chin, and her laugh turned to a sob. "Kalowish," she whispered as he rushed off to join his friends. Hasallum had promised an expedition to hunt ducks; now he must prepare his bow, as a warrior, not a boy.

During the festivities the wind had shifted, sweeping down the mountains to the whipped-up sea. By the morning of the hunt the lagoon was glazed with ice, and the children broke the surface with rocks, admiring each other through crystalline panes.

A dozen youths gathered around the canoes, where Aneetsick was distributing a case of shiny new muskets. Kahammis watched her son reach out eagerly, cradling the gun in his arms, his yew bow falling to the mud. For the previous year Hasallum had been helping the boys refine their archery skills; his own son Kleeshin could already pull back on the braided whale sinew and release the feathered arrows with the precision of the expert marksman. Kleeshin had become Kleeshinnin during the naming ceremony, after an ancestor famed for his accuracy with the harpoon.

The hunters crackled through the ice, heading up the channel to the marshes. Kahammis went inside to sit with Paquacheenish, who had been seeing off guests since daybreak. He nodded wearily to Kahammis, patting the mound of blankets where he reclined. His stick-like legs were covered with a mat; a slave had packed seaweed compresses against his knees.

Neetsa was busy with a half-frozen mouse she had cornered, intent on taking it back to Nootseetaht. Tatatoe sat quietly on the sleeping platform; she had just said goodbye to her father T'isharth, who was hurrying home to his people in the sound.

T'isharth, too, had been bothered by the ravens. Far into the last night of the ceremonies, Kahammis listened while the two old chiefs ruminated on what they heard. T'isharth had clicked and clucked like the bird on his crest; Paquacheenish's deep baritone, raw from all the speeches, grated like gravel in the tide.

Kahammis inhaled the smell of the hot seaweed, shifting closer to the hearth; even the fire could not hold back the north wind's chill. The crack-crack of shooting bounced along the channel, and she wished that she, too, was on her way home.

"So the kegs are gone," she murmured to her grandfather. "The ships are almost gone, as well, and I'm glad."

"The ships are not gone," rasped Paquacheenish. "They're down south. Ships full of white men who go ashore and put up houses and plan to stay."

"What does it mean?" asked Kahammis, astounded.

"They eat enormous quantities of fish, to begin with, which we supply," shrugged Paquacheenish. "Even without the otters, there will be trade."

Kahammis could feel her thoughts swimming like the salmon, struggling upstream through the weirs to spawn. "What if they learn to fish for themselves?"

Paquacheenish snorted, then he noticed her dismay. "Kahammis," he said reprovingly. "Remember that we are strong, and only through strength are we treated as equals! Aneetsick is right, you know. We need muskets, just as we need trade."

Kahammis lowered her head.

"We are strong!" Paquacheenish thumped the blankets emphatically, finding the voice that for generations had gripped the will of his people.

"This is for strength," exclaimed his wife, passing out bowls of broth, which Kahammis accepted, thankful for the distraction. But the broth was bitter on her tongue, tainted by her doubts.

Neetsa squeezed closer to the hearth, grinning impishly, her little hands wrapped around her new friend. "Get him away from my soup!" cried Kahammis.

"Not even one teensy sip?" Neetsa kissed the grey nose peeking between her thumbs.

Paquacheenish tilted his head to the sound of a commotion outside. The lodge quietened, everyone realizing that the racket of the muskets had ceased.

Kahammis jumped up, rushing outside with Tatatoe. Kalowish had pulled his canoe to the edge of the lagoon, and Hasallum and Aneetsick were helping lift Kleeshinnin from the bow. They carried him inside, lowering him onto a mat by the hearth. A sigh fell over the lodge as Tatatoe drew back his bloodied cape, revealing the bones and tendons of his forearm through scorched skin.

Tatatoe opened her medicine basket with shaking hands. She folded the remnants of skin over the wound, making a dressing out of pale green sphagnum moss which the slaves had brought in from the forest. Then she bound the dressing with strips of fabric from a bolt given to her at the feast. No one spoke, and Kleeshinnin seemed asleep. Tatatoe covered him with a fur robe and lay down with her mouth to his ear.

Paquacheenish led the men away. "What happened?" he asked Kalowish.

"We were just the two of us, in my canoe," mumbled Kalowish. "We'd never seen so many birds, we didn't know where to shoot. Kleeshinnin saw one of the swans way back in the marsh. I steered, Kleeshinnin took aim." Kalowish moaned. "The gun went off like a blast of fire. Kleeshinnin fell backwards. Pieces of the gun sank away."

"If anyone is to blame, it is I!" Aneetsick slammed his fist into his hand. "Is this the price of putting our faith in the white man's guns?"

Kahammis left the lodge, walking aimlessly, ending up on the windward beach. The clear skies of morning had been replaced by cloud, and the beach was as bleak as her thoughts. Had the boys paused, even briefly, to address the spirit of the hunt? Or had they been too smitten with their new weapons, their new status, forgetting their place amongst all creatures of the earth? With the bows, the rituals were ingrained. She could imagine the cool metal against Kleeshinnin's cheek, a cheek hot with the anticipation of feathers exploding over the marsh. She heard a noise of distress, turning around to see Neetsa weeping amongst the rocks. She took the child into her arms, wiping tears with the fringe of her cape.

"Will he die?" gasped Neetsa. "I never meant to tease him so much, truly I didn"t!"

Kahammis held her, comforting her, until Neetsa jumped to her feet. "I'm starving!" Hand in hand, they made their way back to the lodge.

The clouds brought snow, enclosing the village in a soft, white cocoon. Kleeshinnin battled with fever and pain while his family fought their own battle, to move beyond recrimination. Tatatoe nursed him, and Paquacheenish spent most of his time meditating alone. Then, the clouds shredded to nothing out over the ocean, and Kleeshinnin's smile returned, and once again life became rich with possibilities. Aneetsick and Kahammis prepared to leave for Nootseetaht; Hasallum and Tatatoe were staying until their son was fully healed.

On the morning of departure, Aneetsick's bride Chee-uxqua tried out her new role, supervising the loading of the many gifts. Chee-uxqua was stout and placid, with a thick braid of hair that swung over her bottom as she worked. Kahammis lingered beside Tatatoe, who looked drawn and fragile in the bright light; all her energy was directed towards the recovery of her son.

85

Chee-uxqua bashfully took her place in the chief's canoe. Led by
Aneetsick, they set off to the songs of farewell: songs of tribute to
Chee-uxqua's family, to the boys who had survived the wolves, and to
Paquacheenish, their magnificent host. Kahammis reached out vigor-
ously with her paddle, each stroke pulling her home.

Late in the afternoon, as they could see the blue hills behind
Nootseetaht, Aneetsick noticed a canoe ahead. The canoe rapidly
drew nearer, and larger, and he shouted in warning. Almost at once
they were abreast of a huge vessel carrying at least twenty people and
cargo: these were the northerners, navigating the coast in any
weather, at any time of the year. Keeping her distance from the forked
prow, Kahammis tried to hear the conversation between Aneetsick
and the big man standing in the stern, unfazed by the rolling swell.

Kahammis had been close to northerners once before, at
Klinniklinnikaht, where Paquacheenish welcomed everyone to his
lagoon. Now she watched in amazement as the big man resumed his
seat, ordering his paddlers to follow Aneetsick. He must have requested
to break his journey, a request which Aneetsick could not refuse without
damaging his reputation, for Tatoosch had complained loudly and
bitterly about being sent away from Nootseetaht without even a meal.

One by one the canoes rounded the spit, but the joy of arrival was
dampened for Kahammis by the size and boldness of the northerners
as they stretched and gazed around. Except for the coincidental
meeting, they would have passed by Nootseetaht. Kahammis recalled
stories of the raiders, stories she had grown up on, and she reassured
herself that by morning they would be gone.

Sparks from dry branches shot through the smokeholes as the
women hustled to prepare food. Aneetsick settled at his hearth with
the northern leader, Gitti-kang, a good-looking man with slanted eyes
and the light, smooth skin characteristic of the northern race. As the
evening progressed, it became clear that he was also a fine guest,
familiar enough with the local dialect to converse expressively. The
women served a meal of bulbs and berries, and the meat of the most
tender salmon, the silver-sided spring. When he had eaten, Gitti-kang
wiped his face and hands with bark, to the approval of the crowd.
Then he reached beneath his cape, withdrawing an elaborate carving
which he held up to the firelight.

"A pipe," he explained, pointing out the drilled stem and the
hollowed bowl. But a pipe unlike any other, of lustrous black stone

with mythical creatures entwined along the stem. The pipe was passed around to exclamations of awe, and he brought out another piece of stone, similar to the pipe but with a flat, engraved surface.

He chuckled at the expression on Aneetsick's face. "Fort," he said, tracing his finger along the rows of sticks and houses with oddly pointed shapes. The food in her stomach tumbled as Kahammis wondered: were these the houses of which Paquacheenish had spoken?

She slipped outside, gazing around the starlit bay, but all she could see were the sticks in Gitti-kang's engraving, marching through the village in sharp, forbidding rows. She shook her head, appalled, and then remembered her box of treasures, still in her canoe. Her bare feet found the path down to the beach.

As she was bending over the storage compartment in the bow, she heard a cough. She scanned the slope and the bay and saw nothing amiss. Again she heard a cough, which seemed to originate from Gitti-kang's canoe. She retrieved her box and approached hesitantly; a head popped up, and in the silvery light from the stars she could make out a boy's face.

She backed away and hungry eyes pursued her, out of a face which could have belonged to her own son. He must be a slave, she thought. Slaves were the property of their owners, to do with as they pleased. The look on the boy's face reminded her of what it had been like to live without rights: her ribs and her thighs had been forever seared by Quassoon. From the lodge the plank drums boomed, voices picking up the beat as the evening's entertainment began.

"Wait!" she whispered. She rushed up the slope, returning with chunks of salmon which she thrust at the boy.

Coughs bubbled up from beneath a heap of mats in the canoe. Torn between pity and revulsion, she asked, "Who is that?"

"My mother." The boy's mouth was crammed with fish.

His chewing stopped as Kahammis leaned over and pulled back a foul scrap of blanket. A woman coughed violently, struggling to lift her head.

"She's blind." The boy swallowed, tearing off more fish. "We belong to Gitti-kang," he said matter-of-factly. "They didn't want us at the fort."

The lyrical strains of Aneetsick's wedding song floated down the grassy slope. Kahammis stared into the canoe, feeling as if she were trapped in a nightmare carved out of Gitti-kang's stone. "What is her name?" she whispered.

"Sheebo," said the boy.

At the sound of her name the woman once more tried to rise, while Kahammis sagged against the side of the canoe. The boy stiffened, glancing up the slope.

Gitti-kang had come out during a break in the singing. "What are you doing?" he yelled to the boy, who dropped out of sight.

He strode down to the beach. Kahammis pointed at the heap of mats. "I want to buy her," she said, in a strangled voice.

Gitti-kang whooped derisively. Before he could speak, Kahammis tore open her box of treasures and shoved the tiny basket into his hands. He lifted off the domed lid, poking his finger into the eagle down. He held the carved loon to the starlight and laughed, satisfied. "She's yours!"

He threw Sheebo over his shoulder as though she were weightless, and Kahammis led him to her sleeping platform, everyone pausing, disconcerted, as they passed.

No matter how many blankets Kahammis added during the night, Sheebo's hands and feet remained as cold as shards of ice. She prepared teas and tonics but Sheebo was beyond thirst, the potions spilling over her cracked lips. Her hair hung in sweat-matted ribbons, and her skin was chalky. In the morning, through her panic, Kahammis heard the northerners getting ready to leave. Suddenly, she remembered the boy.

She ran down to the beach, where Aneetsick stood with Gitti-kang. "You must buy him!" she cried, grabbing the boy, who cowered in the canoe.

Aneetsick frowned. "Is he for sale?"

"Anything is for sale," laughed Gitti-kang, not about to reveal that he had obtained the boy for the price of removing the sick woman from the fort.

Kahammis raced back to Sheebo. Aneetsick came into the lodge shortly afterwards, scowling and dragging the boy, who gaped at his mother on the sleeping platform.

Kahammis summoned Kalowish. "Now he belongs to you," she said, indicating the boy. Deliberately she met Aneetsick's eyes. "He will be called Sa-sat-kis."

Sheebo's coughing worsened throughout the day. Towards evening she began to wheeze and flail, fighting with the blankets. Repeatedly she reached for Kahammis, murmuring her name. The pulse in her neck thrummed faintly, and more faintly; her soul was straining to move on. Kahammis held her as she died.

The next morning, Kalowish prepared a burial box. Sheebo's body was wrapped in clean mats and folded into the box. Her head was positioned towards the corner with the joint, so that her soul could escape and return to the sanctuary of the forest.

Kahammis asked Sa-sat-kis where his people lived. He shuffled and edged closer to Kalowish; during the burial preparations, he had not strayed from Kalowish's side.

"Your mother's people?" repeated Kahammis.

Sa-sat-kis shook his head, perplexed. "This is the farthest north we've ever been. Sometimes we stayed on the ships," he added, grinning at Kalowish, who nodded with envy. "Biscuits and treacle!" His grin revealed the gaps of his missing teeth.

Rain was falling at dusk when Kahammis directed the two boys to load the burial box into her canoe. The clouds had not yet obscured the horizon, and the sun laid its last rays over the sea. Kahammis steered past the spit, past the sentry's knoll, to a shell beach behind the reefs. She rode through the shorebreak and Kalowish followed with Sa-sat-kis, in his own canoe.

The boys lugged the box across the beach to a natural cavern between jutting ridges of rock. Accessible only at the lowest tide, this was the cavern where Hasallum had buried the victims of the Wewksah massacre. The boys crawled far back with the box, and when they came out, wan and shaken, the sun had disappeared.

For days, Kahammis kept to herself. She sheared off her hair and blackened her face with ash. Hasallum and Tatatoe came home with Kleeshinnin, and Chee-uxqua stopped missing her family, and it seemed that Sa-sat-kis had been with them always. Early one morning, as she lay on her sleeping platform, the screech owl called from her cedar tree.

She listened, and knew that Sheebo was safe.

~~~:~~~

The forest behind Nootseetaht was interlaced with soft, rust-coloured paths, paths which had been formed by millions of conifer needles and trodden by centuries of passing feet. It was on one of these paths that Kahammis strolled soundlessly, roaming with her memories.

89

Although six years had gone by since Sheebo's death, she still felt her presence, partly consoling, and partly a confirmation of grief.

A hummingbird darted over her shoulder, straight into a salmonberry bush, gathering nectar from the blooming pink tufts which enticed the tiny birds to the coast each spring. Kahammis had also come into the forest on a seasonal task, to pull cedar bark, keeping to the section of trees allocated to her family by hereditary right. The mild winter had set the sap running early, so that the bark lifted away easily from the wood underneath, and for this she was thankful; she was finding the work more strenuous every year.

She chose her final tree, an immature yellow cedar, its pale branches drooping in the diffused light. She marked the trunk at the height of her waist, chipping into the bark with her iron-bladed adze. Taking hold of the loosened edge, she slowly backed away, twisting as she pulled, watching the bark rip higher and higher, narrowing, splitting off and cascading down into the underbrush. She pulled two more strips, exposing a swath of dripping sapwood which would harden to a permanent scar. With a prayer of gratitude, she left the tree to grow in peace.

She found a patch of sunlight and squatted with her antler knife, separating the inner and outer layers of each bark strip. Her fingers were sticky with sap as she folded the precious inner bark into her burden basket. Though few women bothered, she also bundled up the coarse outer bark, for the hearth. Never had she forgotten the drudgery of collecting fuel, and never did she fail to pick up a dry stick. When her basket was full, she heaved it onto her back and headed home.

Neetsa would help spread the inner bark to dry, and helping Neetsa would be Paonea, the chubby young daughter of Aneetsick and Chee-uxqua, huffing and puffing in her efforts to keep up. Neetsa had almost reached puberty and was trying hard to prepare for the coming rituals; she reminded Kahammis of herself at the same age, climbing trees and canoeing fearlessly along the floodwaters, defying the older boys.

After a week of drying, the bark would be soaked in tide pools around the delta, weighted with stones, for two more weeks. Then Kahammis would take the whalebone beater Kalowish had made for her, and pull the wet strips over a flat rock, smashing the bark into layers. She would oil her hands and twist the layers into silky strands, setting them aside to cure.

The finest strands would be woven into a cape for Kalowish. On the inside of the cape would be his crest, as befitted his status now that he was a married man. His bride was the graceful Hiyuyah, great-grand-daughter of Patlowah, the elderly adviser at Klinniklinnikaht. If Kahammis found irony in this match, no one knew. She would have been part of Patlowah's family herself, had it not been for the Wewksah and Quassoon.

Next on her list of projects was a whaling hat for Aneetsick, who brought humpbacks into the bay every summer without fail. Though Chee-uxqua laboured over her hats, the bulb tips invariably ended up skewed, unsuitable for a chief. Next she would make a pouch for Hasallum's rattles, and a holder for Kleeshinnin's fishing hooks. Kleeshinnin had matured into a robust young man despite his withered arm, and he was famed for his success with his dipnets and lines.

The women always needed more baskets, and Sa-sat-kis needed a tool carrier. Sa-sat-kis had transcended his humble beginnings through his apprenticeship to Kalowish. Every mask they carved was valued for trade, and used in ceremonies all along the coast. Kalowish had never learned to treat Sa-sat-kis as a slave; like Kleeshinnin, he was a cherished friend.

Trudging back to the village with her bark, Kahammis thought sadly of Paquacheenish, for whom she would weave no more. She heard a muffled wail and noticed Tatatoe sitting on the riverbank, her basket by her side and her face in her hands. Within days Tatatoe, Hasallum, and Neetsa would be leaving Nootseetaht, so that Hasallum could assume the position vacated by Paquacheenish. Although this was a position too big for Hasallum, too big, indeed, for anyone, the vacuum left by the death of Paquacheenish would fill with chaos if his only son did not return.

Tatatoe sniffled as Kahammis came down the bank, then her wails began anew. She was broken-hearted at moving and also at losing her father, who was with Paquacheenish, in that exalted place in the sky. The Mannakaht had once more been caught in the coastal crossfire, and T'isharth's luck had come to an end.

Quassoon had struck, after simmering for two decades.

The trouble had begun innocently enough the previous winter, when Moochinnick, son of Tatoosch and Oweena, had been invited to Klinniklinnikaht by the family of his deceased mother. He stayed all winter, and winter had turned into spring, and he ignored the messages from Quassoon, ordering him home. It had not taken him long to notice how much more fun life was at Klinniklinnikaht than at home where his grandfather ranted like an enraged grizzly, where Yatintala shrivelled like an unwanted salalberry, and where no feast had been held in many years. Spring became summer, endless days of adventure for a young boy. For Quassoon, however, this prolonged absence was a crushing humiliation, and he declared that Moochinnick had been kidnapped: once again, the heir had slipped away.

Quassoon called upon his old allies: Ewona of the Sheshalam, and Wikkosum of the Wasquimaht. Concealed by the summer fog, the three chiefs assembled with their warriors at the rear of the sound. They daubed themselves with paint and bolstered themselves with remembering all the insults to their power and prestige. Highest on Quassoon's list was T'isharth, for rescuing Kahammis. He led the charge through T'isharth's village late one night, killing everyone but the chief, for whom they hunted high and low. T'isharth had been saved by the raven; that very night, the black-winged trickster had beckoned his venerable old friend to the thinking stream. T'isharth woke, beneath the ferns, to the howls of doom. He crawled through the woods to the far side of the island and escaped in a fisherman's canoe, paddling south as fast as his arms would go. He intercepted a pair of seal hunters off Klinniklinnikaht and told them his story, laying down his paddle, too weary for another stroke. The hunters took him under tow, but T'isharth was dead by the time they reached the lagoon.

Paquacheenish then sent his swiftest messenger to Aneetsick, who mobilized his men and reached Klinniklinnikaht shortly after dark. No one actually believed that Quassoon would attack. Even so, the mere thought of him on the rampage with the stolen war club was more than Paquacheenish could tolerate, and he ordered every warrior into the channel, where they waited through the night.

Fog filled the channel, drifting out to sea, then in again, distorting sounds and shapes. A cough, the inadvertent clink of a paddle, sent terror surging through Kalowish, Kleeshinnin, and Sa-sat-kis, sheltered behind a bend with Aneetsick's fleet.

Just before dawn, in that hour of utmost vulnerability, Quassoon managed to goad Ewona, the vain, swarthy chief of the Sheshalam, into leading the attack. Ewona came through the channel like a rogue wave, catching the defenders dozing, lulled by skepticism and the swell. Ewona was finally halted on the threshold of the lagoon. Losses on both sides were calamitous, warriors drowned or speared as they clung to their shattered canoes. Aneetsick held his men back despite the closeness of the battle; Kalowish and his companions listened to the screaming and discovered that their fantasies of valiant combat had been eliminated, never to return.

After Ewona retreated, an awful hush settled over the channel, shifting with the fog. Before the defenders could properly regroup, Wikkosum was upon them in a frenzy of musket fire. For a few long moments it seemed that Paquacheenish had underestimated his enemies, a tactical error that would cost him his career. Then, out burst the Nootseetaht warriors, hurtling across the channel like a pod of voracious whales. They had been drilled relentlessly by Aneetsick, and Kalowish made his second discovery: beyond terror lies absolute calm. He shot with the precision required by the most intricate detailing on one of his masks, and Kleeshinnin and Sa-sat-kis took courage, and shot with similar care. Wikkosum's bluster collapsed, and he swerved out to sea with fewer than half of his men.

So Kalowish waited and waited, startled by the quack of a duck, the splash of waves along the shore. Ewona and Wikkosum had been held off, and they waited now for Quassoon. The wind picked up and the fog dissipated; all at once, the sun appeared directly overhead.

The ocean was empty; Quassoon was gone.

Moochinnick never went home. Aneetsick was vindicated, after all those years of stockpiling muskets and ammunition. He made sure that Kahammis understood her son's bravery, as if, she reflected, bravery would make the battle more noble in her eyes. For she was sickened by the losses and by their cause; better than anyone, she knew Quassoon. His fury had not abated; she could feel it in the rustling trees at dusk, in the bite of the wind. Paquacheenish summed up the battle by surmising that Quassoon had at least been taught a lesson, and the people speculated as to what Ewona and Wikkosum had learned.

For days, canoes, weapons, and bodies washed up around Klinniklinnikaht. Paquacheenish ordered the enemy heads retrieved and mounted on poles in the mud around the lagoon, where they rotted in the heat and were picked apart by the birds.

It was the death of T'isharth that Paquacheenish minded the most. Shortly before his own death, a few months later, he made Hasallum promise to carry on the fight. Hasallum wrestled with this promise every night before he slept; neither warrior nor diplomat, he wanted only to build canoes.

Tatatoe wanted only to remain at Nootseetaht, but watching the river and weeping with Kahammis would not pack the moving boxes, and the two women slowly rose, slinging on their baskets. They crossed the delta, where the men were working over a cedar log. Kalowish's wife, Hiyuyah, was collecting leaves of seaweed exposed by the falling tide. Hiyuyah seemed even more frail than usual, though she smiled and waved at Kahammis and Tatatoe. She is pregnant, realized Kahammis, unprepared for the way her heart fluttered at the thought.

Just then, Kleeshinnin shouted from the ridge, "Quick! The Smoking Tree!"

The villagers dropped what they were doing and raced around the bay to the spit, converging from all directions, pointing to the ship offshore. The ship was rumbling south, trailing clouds of white smoke from a black column on the deck. A month ago they had watched, slack-jawed with curiosity, as this same ship passed heading north.

"Going back to the fort," commented Aneetsick, and the men around him nodded gravely. From their conversation Kahammis learned that the ship had set into Klinniklinnikaht, where the captain had asked for wood, huge quantities of wood, to feed the fire beneath that smoking tree.

Kahammis saw her son standing with Sa-sat-kis and Kleeshinnin, the three of them utterly focused on the streaming white flag which grew smaller and smaller as the ship churned out of sight. Reluctantly, the villagers returned to work, except for Kahammis, still gazing across the water.

A pair of black oystercatchers ran back and forth along the spit, peep-peeping in distress. Year after year the oystercatchers formed their nest, no more than a shallow depression, somewhere amongst the stones on the shore. Year after year they defended their speckled eggs against high tides and rapacious intruders with what to Kahammis seemed a hopeless dedication, running side by side, back and forth, with their red beaks outstretched.

Every year it was the same.

But was it?

The oystercatchers shared the earth with the ship that had just passed by. Perhaps they ran so agitatedly because they sensed the ship's tremor beneath their feet, no less ominous than what Kahammis had once sensed, out on the delta with her old slave.

~~~:~~~

A late summer sun slanted across the ridge, warming Kahammis as she shaped bark strips over a wooden frame. Her hair was streaked with white, and she wore a cape she had woven recently, decorated with bits and treasures of capes past. She was surrounded by smouldering alder fires and racks of drying salalberries, which she had been up early to pick. They would eat well tonight, pulling clusters of the grainy, blue-black berries with their teeth, chins dripping oil.

Nootseetaht was flourishing, and Aneetsick had proved to be a capable chief. Though his skin was leathery and his hair glinted like metal, his body was still lean and virile, with the tension of a man who always holds part of himself in reserve. His ten-year-old daughter Paonea had become so like her mother, stout and loyal, that she was referred to as "Little Chief's Wife." Lacking younger siblings, she challenged her maternal instincts with Callicum and Sea-ossum, the twins born to Hiyuyah five years before. Invariably someone would remark on how peaceful the village used to be, and eyes would slide to these two copper-haired boys. Their parents were frequently confronted by an outraged fisherman holding up his tangled gear, or by an indignant cook, opening a box to find nothing but juice-stained fingerprints. The twins would blink at these charges, and Kahammis guessed that they did indeed see themselves as blameless, at the mercy of their appetite for life.

Kahammis shared her oasis on the ridge with Hiyuyah, who was again pregnant, due any day to give birth. Hiyuyah was keeping a lookout for Kalowish. He had gone south with Aneetsick and Sa-sat-kis, visiting a place they called Port Albert; the name in their mouths was as unfamiliar as the idea that such a place could exist, put up in one short summer, on camas grounds beside a village belonging to a great southern clan. Paquacheenish had been right: the people on the ships were coming ashore and staying. Kahammis was grateful for the long day's paddle separating Port Albert from Nootseetaht; she had already seen the lines of pointed sticks on Gitti-kang's stone. However, the construction of the fort pleased the coast chiefs; trade was at its slowest in generations, and Aneetsick was determined that Nootseetaht would not be left out.

Hiyuyah shifted restlessly beneath the shade of the cedar tree. "Nothing feels right," she sighed.

"Go down to the lodge, where it is cool," suggested Kahammis, helping her up. "And stop worrying. The men will be home this evening, for sure."

Kahammis hummed to herself, threading grass. During the rainy season, her hands were too clumsy except for the coarsest mats, but now, with the combined heat of the fires and the sun, her fingers flew over the wooden frame. She glanced upwards as a pebble smacked into her lap, bouncing off onto the grass. A raven was clucking at the top of the tree, and she wondered: was this a message from Paquacheenish? Sadly, his wife had also died, outliving him by less than a year. Suddenly another pebble landed, accompanied by loud cackling, this time on Kahammis's head. She yelped and looked up, catching sight of her grandsons clinging to the crown.

It was all she could do to keep a stern face, so infectious was their pleasure in their trick. They clambered down, running to the beach. Kleeshinnin was coming through the gap in his canoe; he was easy to identify by the way he paddled, compensating for his arm. He had moved to Klinniklinnikaht to help his father, though he returned frequently to visit with Kalowish and Sa-sat-kis. He greeted the twins and presented them each with a bone fish hook. Immediately they launched their boat, a sodden log they had hacked into shape with chisels. They were stalking an elusive codfish which lurked in the shadows of the bay.

Kleeshinnin climbed up to the ridge. Kahammis set aside her weaving, delighted to have company, then she noticed the look on his face. "What is it?" she asked anxiously. "Is it Hasallum? Is it Tatatoe?"

Kleeshinnin's expression was the strangest she had ever seen. He shook his head. "No," he said. "It's Quassoon."

~~~:~~~

Quassoon had been out whaling the previous week, in a dark, condensing fog off Quatlukaht. He had smelled his prey's krill breath, homing in with a ferocious thrust, his paddlers gasping with fear and excitement as they paid out the line.

He groped for the war club knotted around his waist. The club was his luck, his last link with Kahammis, whom he would pursue to the ends of the earth. For he was a hunter and a hero; this season alone, four docile greys had delivered themselves to his harpoon. Now he had just skewered his fifth whale, a majestic humpback, and he welcomed a battle worthy of a chief, a chief in turn worthy of the adulation, the feasts.

A scream from his steersman jolted him out of his reverie. Too many seconds had passed, the coiled line still slack in his hands. A mammoth, knobby head surged through the waves, aiming directly for the canoe. Too late, the steersman swerved; the whale rammed the bow. Quassoon thudded backwards in the splintering crash. The whale slid over the canoe and dove, and the tangled line tightened around Quassoon's thigh. Down, down, plunged the whale, and down spun Quassoon, into the clutches of the two-headed sea monster, mistress of the murky underworld.

~~~:~~~

"Dead?" asked Kahammis, dry-mouthed and barely trusting the word.

Kleeshinnin nodded. "The paddlers survived. They have been killed in penance, of course. The question is, who will replace Quassoon? One of his lazy cousins? Or worse, Tatoosch." Kleeshinnin's lip curled. Tatoosch was despised along the coast for his gambling, and for abandoning his dying wife. "He stopped by Klinniklinnikaht last summer, did you know? He picked up Moochinnick, who's been hiding out with us for years now. Quassoon sent messages, but Moochinnick had caused so much trouble for his grandfather, he was afraid to go home. I don't blame him," snorted Kleeshinnin. "Anyhow, he went south with Tatoosch and we haven't seen either of them since."

Kahammis was scarcely listening. Would she nevermore wake before dawn, wondering: was this the day Quassoon would come? Kleeshinnin began to fidget, sighing loudly, and then she remembered his family's latest predicament. "Neetsa?" she asked. Rumours had been circulating ever since Neetsa's refusal of the marriage her parents had arranged. Kahammis had never married, stated Neetsa, and nor would she. Hasallum and Tatatoe were too kind to force her, and only once had they become angry, when Neetsa had begged to join a whale

97

hunt. Tatatoe prayed that Neetsa would learn restraint before she jeopardized her father's reputation, or even his life.

"I worry about her," admitted Kleeshinnin, "but right now I'm more worried about the three visitors we had yesterday at Klinniklinnikaht. Did they come here?"

Kahammis shook her head.

"They are seeking a special kind of rock, which burns. They say that this rock even burns in the Smoking Tree."

Kahammis almost laughed, imagining the prospect of setting fire to stone.

"They've put up a camp at Hoxem." Hoxem was a stream-fed cove midway between Klinniklinnikaht and Nootseetaht. Kahammis had played there as a child, while her father dove for abalone nearby.

"They're white, but with a different way of speaking." Like many of the younger men, Kleeshinnin was fluent in the language of the traders. "At least they know how to handle a canoe. They were wearing bright stretches of cloth around their waists. And their manner was different. Not like this," Kleeshinnin screwed up his face, mimicking the suspicions of the traders, "but proud, all the same." He got to his feet. "I'd better rescue those boys."

Callicum and Sea-ossum had drifted across the bay and now gazed longingly at the village, wondering why their bellies felt so empty, and the air felt so much colder on the far shore. Kleeshinnin lifted them off their log, and into his canoe. He opened his baitbox and helped them pierce wriggling minnows with their new hooks. The leaders on their kelp lines were made of nettle fibres, dyed brown for camouflage. Just as they were about to fling their lines over, Kleeshinnin removed a small pouch from his belt, rubbing it against the new hooks. "For the spirits," he told them. Gingerly they lowered their lines, and he reclined, with a contented yawn. "Now we wait."

Kahammis collected her weaving supplies and went down to the lodge. Hiyuyah lay on her sleeping platform; her pains had begun, and Chee-uxqua hovered close by. They could hear shouts across the water; sure enough, the boys had landed a gigantic, gratifyingly ugly ling cod. When the men returned from Port Albert, in time for the evening meal, they were triumphantly presented with the ragged fillets.

With them the men brought Moochinnick, whom Kahammis had not seen before. He was big and hirsute and bore more than traces of his paternity, with a look of experience beyond his eighteen years. He was billeted in a distant lodge with relatives of his mother, one of the families that had helped resettle Nootseetaht.

After the meal, Kleeshinnin revealed the story of Quassoon and the whale. Kahammis avoided looking at Aneetsick; she knew that he had never gotten over the shame of her relationship with Quassoon.

What the men wanted to talk about most was their trip to Port Albert. Aneetsick described the extraordinary commotion they had encountered upon arrival: northerners, southerners, foreigners, all trading in the excitement of the new place. As he spoke, Kahammis heard the struggle in his voice; he was torn between condescension and respect, searching for meaning in all that he had seen. The fort, he explained, was ruled by a hierarchy of chiefs who even in their absence exerted total control. He drew walls with his hands, outlining the cedar pickets surrounding the fort. The local villagers had provided the pickets, in exchange for blankets. Where the rows of pickets met, small houses had been constructed to hold the same cannons which toured the coast on the decks of the ships.

Kalowish was impressed by the tools. "Everything is done in a hurry. A tree falls in hours, not days." The forest was being peeled back, he said, with great, horned animals pulling out the trees and dragging sharp pieces of metal through the soil. The green fields were forbidden to the local people, who faced muskets if they ventured too close.

"How hard the white men work," murmured Sa-sat-kis. "Harder than slaves." The fort was more civilized than he had anticipated; in his vague, early memories, he and his mother always seemed to be on the fringe of hunger, rejection, and cold.

The Nootseetaht men had camped on the outskirts of the village, near the picket wall. Visitors swarmed everywhere, staying in hastily erected lodges or canvas shelters held up with poles and ropes. It had not taken long to hear all the opinions and speculations on the inner workings of the fort. Sightings of the animals, housed in their own building, had been the source of much amusement; no one, however, even breathed as two white women appeared, gliding like busy clouds. A man followed them, carrying a pail of white liquid which was, amazingly, coveted as much as the contents of the kegs.

Conversation ceased at the mention of kegs, and Kahammis heard a moan from the birthing hut, in the woods behind the lodge. Though she knew that she should be with Hiyuyah, she could not miss the men's talk.

Through the sale of masks and canoes, the Nootseetaht men were friends with the village chief. He told them his fears for the flimsy encampment, for the warriors who fought with their own brothers, for the whisky in the kegs that flowed endlessly and fueled the trade, the excitement, the fights. He was an old man, he told them, squinting worriedly into their faces as if they might know what the future held.

Clearing his throat, Aneetsick resumed his tale.

On the second morning, skirting the encampment, the Nootseetaht men had gone to check their canoe. The fort was beside a harbour deep enough for anchored ships, and wide enough for the hundreds of canoes which Kalowish scanned with a trained eye. Though he felt ready to go home, Aneetsick wanted to spend another day studying the fort. They picked their way through the dust and the garbage, amongst the gulls and the crows squabbling over fish carcasses ripening in the late summer heat. Bad-tempered dogs snapped at their heels; the southerners bred the dogs for wool, the same creamy wool Sheebo had used for Kahammis's cape.

They came to a man and a woman sprawled in the entrance of a crude shack, and Kalowish nudged Aneetsick. The woman snored on her back, her bark skirt twisted to expose her thighs. The Nootseetaht men hurried by, turning their heads aside.

Kalowish had noticed a rough-looking youth near the shack. He caught up with Aneetsick, who strode on ahead.

"Wasn't that Moochinnick?" asked Kalowish. He remembered seeing the youth at Klinniklinnikaht.

Aneetsick spun around angrily.

"Moochinnick!" Kalowish pointed to where the youth had stood.

A glint came into Aneetsick's eye, and he retraced his steps to the drunken couple. Beneath the grease and the filth and the vomit, he recognized Moochinnick's father, Tatoosch.

"Get up!" snarled Aneetsick, giving Tatoosch a kick.

Tatoosch made no effort to rouse himself, mumbling belligerently and snuggling against his companion. Kalowish urged Aneetsick away.

Early the next morning, Kalowish sniffed the ocean, eager to be heading home. They had a final word with the chief, who seemed willing to consult with anyone. "What should I do?" he asked Aneetsick querulously.

"Move!" Heads bobbed around the shadowy lodge, the audience recoiling from the harshness of Aneetsick's reply. Move? Move to where?

Leaving the old chief, the Nootseetaht men crossed through the crowded encampment. Tatoosch still lay in the entrance to the shack; the woman was gone. They were readying the canoe when Kalowish turned at the sound of footsteps on the beach. Moochinnick stood behind them, sullen but clearly in distress. He gestured for them to follow; grumbling, Aneetsick went with Kalowish and Sa-sat-kis. He led them to the shack.

Tatoosch was dead. Flies crawled over his face, around his nostrils and into his mouth. A rumpled, fair head appeared through the blanket draped over the entrance of the shack. The Nootseetaht men stared in surprise: it was the worker from the fort who had been carrying the pail.

"Get rid of him," growled the man.

They stood dumbly, then Sa-sat-kis knelt, grappling with Tatoosch's shoulders. Kalowish tried to keep the revulsion out of his face as Moochinnick seized his father's bare legs. They carried him to the canoe, cramming him into the bow. Ships moved at anchor in the harbour, masts protruding through the mist. "You might as well come with us," Aneetsick said to Moochinnick. "This is no place for you."

They dumped Tatoosch into the first swells beyond the mouth of the harbour, just as the sun rose over the distant hills.

Kahammis gazed into the flames. Tatoosch and Quassoon had died within days or even hours of each other; in her mind she saw them together, plunging down into the underworld.

The night passed quickly for the Nootseetaht people, troubled as they were by Hiyuyah's moans and by so much news. Kalowish fretted over his tools at dawn, accosting Kahammis when she came out of the birthing hut.

"Why so long?" he asked miserably. "Even the twins were nothing like this. It's not fair."

"There's nothing fair about birth." Kahammis recalled her own labour, when she had pleaded with her grandmother to rip open her womb and let her die in peace. "Soon," she promised.

At noon, a daughter was born. Chee-uxqua pronounced her perfect, and Hiyuyah smiled dreamily. Kahammis swaddled the infant with shredded bark, settling her in the cradle with pads to shape her forehead, as befitted her aristocratic birth. Already she showed her mother's dark, delicate beauty, her little mouth puckered like a flower bud in spring.

Hiyuyah was very weak. She dozed fitfully throughout the after-noon and the night, and the women encouraged her to take some broth. Paonea had been allowed into the birthing hut; she touched the baby's curled fist with a reverent sigh. The following morning, Chee-uxqua grew concerned, examining Hiyuyah. She called Kalowish to the wall of the hut, and he begged Hiyuyah to wake up, to drink the broth.

After a long wait, Hiyuyah stirred. "I have been thinking," she whispered suddenly. "We will name her Pali, my mother's name when she was a girl." Obediently, she took a sip of broth.

Later in the day, the strangers from Hoxem came into the bay, riding easily through the gap. They were met on the beach by Kleeshinnin, who had extended his visit on account of the birth. Aneetsick waited to be introduced, in the guarded pose Kahammis recalled from when their father was chief. Two of the men were older and grizzled, but the third was about the age of Kleeshinnin, with whom he stood companionably. He was massively built, with a chin even more bushy than the faces Kahammis remembered from the ship. Circling his waist was the brightly coloured sash which Kleeshinnin had described. He and the other two men stared around the village, speaking in a blend of languages, asking about rocks, game, and fish. Aneetsick, however, did not invite them to stay. They departed in good humour, and as their canoe rounded the spit, Kahammis realized that they had not asked permission to camp at Hoxem. Although it was a formality, and of course Aneetsick would have agreed, not one of them had thought to ask.

She went back to the birthing hut. Hiyuyah's face was waxen, and Chee-uxqua wept quietly. Kahammis had known that Hiyuyah would be leaving them; even so, she sat for a long while, mustering the strength to tell her son.

Sadly, through that final summer night, their voices floated across the water. The men chanted, beating on the plank drums, and the women poured out their mournful harmonies, not just for Hiyuyah but for the universal losses of motherhood that defined their lives. Chee-uxqua and Paonea had taken over the care of baby Pali, assisted by a nursing mother from a neighbouring lodge. As Kahammis sang, her eyes sought the sleeping platform where Hiyuyah had lain. Callicum and Sea-ossum peered out from the darkness; they had gone to bed but no one had thought to clean their faces, tracked with dust and tears for their mother. They stared out at the singing crowd, so woebegone that Kahammis gathered them into her arms, and within minutes they were asleep.

In the grey light of morning, the bentwood burial box was carried down to the canoes. Clouds of sandpipers rose up over the delta as the convoy crossed the bay. Kahammis navigated through the reefs, waiting offshore while the men landed on the shell beach and ducked into the cave.

Kahammis waited, with weary eyes. Here was where life's journey ended, amongst the boxes and the bones, the wash of the tides. The men came out of the cave and they returned to Nootseetaht on a rippled, leaden sea.

~~~:~~~

MARIANNE: May, 1991

GRANDMA EM HANDS me a plate of stubby green stems, arranged like celery around a sugar bowl. She nods as I savour the taste. "Elsa picked them. Cow parsnip, from the bush past the river."

She glances beyond the open door to the first promising day after months of ceaseless damp. A bee flies in, bumbling and torpid, drawn to the basket in Grandma Em's lap. The basket is overlaid with vibrant patterns of crimson and aquamarine. "No more dyes from the forests and the fields," says Grandma Em. "Now they come in packets from Cam and Max's hardware store." The hardware store was bought out by a chain a few years ago but is still referred to by the names of the original owners, Cam and Max McPhee.

This is one of Grandma Em's good days, fingers flying, black eyes frisky as she tucks bark. I think back to Mrs. Vincennes, fuming in her wheelchair. Such is the serendipity of life: without that hurled meal tray, would I have come to Squally Bay?

"Who taught you to weave?" I ask.

"Could've been my mother, though she died pretty young."

104

"How did she die?"

"Worn out!" exclaims Grandma Em. "Twelve babies."

"What was she like?" I speak carefully; it doesn't take much for Grandma Em to close down, intent on her work.

"Small and gentle. She grew beautiful flowers. And she loved to sing. Oh yes, did she love to sing! Her songs were her stories, about when she was young, her parents, the old times."

"Stories!" I sigh. "How fortunate you are."

Grandma Em frowns over her work.

"Was this their house?" With renewed interest I gaze around at the rough cedar walls, cobwebs strung from the corners to the beams.

"This is my house. I married a man upcoast, and we moved back to Squally Bay when we had our children." Grandma Em's voice is rich with remembering as the years roll away. "My mother, Evangeline, her family didn't live on the Reserve. They lived up the river. Her father was a Frenchman, you see."

"A Frenchman," I repeat, astonished. "Out here?"

Grandma Em chuckles. "Came across the country, in canoes."

My mind expands from west to east and back again as Grandma Em goes on talking, holding the basket to the light coming through the door, snipping stray tufts of grass. Her work sells at an exclusive waterfront shop in Port Albert, where the cruise ships unload. Tony took me there, and we stood watching as tourists swarmed the glass cases with rapturous cries.

"Tell me about Tony," I ask, "when he was a boy."

Tony has been preparing for the fishing season, a brief, intense battle for the salmon which grow scarcer every year. This past week his boat has been up on the ways. I hadn't realized that a boat is like an iceberg, so much underneath.

"Tony." Grandma Em speaks his name with satisfaction, smoothing the basket with her hands. There is nothing she is prouder of than her grandchildren.

Tony was raised on the Reserve. His father Earl is Grandma Em's eldest son. Sometimes Earl goes out trolling with Tony, though he is retired and no longer keeps his own boat. Tony's mother, Winnie, came from Port Albert. Her face is flatter and rounder than the faces of her children. She works at the beauty salon in Squally Bay, and has the most unaffected laugh I have ever heard.

Tony's family has been taken aback by his interest in the woman who rents the cottage from Agnes. I realize that to them I must seem insipid; my pale blue eyes and my ignorance of the coast make me an outsider in every way.

My standing improved slightly when Dr. Conaliki offered me a job. Dr. Conaliki has recently replaced Dr. Doyle, who passed away after practising medicine in Squally Bay since before Tony's birth. Dr. Conaliki and I have spent hours sorting and deciphering Dr. Doyle's charts, in which he recorded not only his patients' pain but also a poetic commentary on their lives. I have severed ties with the hospital; no longer is it possible for me to imagine going back.

Grandma Em pokes around the clutter on the table, for her papers and tobacco.

"That Tony, he built models. Ships, planes, anything he could put together. Cam at the store brought out whatever was the latest from Port Albert, for Tony and his friends." Thoughtfully, she tips the tobacco pouch. "Tony had his heart set on a particular model. I don't remember what, except that it was the biggest and fanciest on the shelf behind the cash register, where Max always stood." Grandma Em squints at me through puffs of smoke. "You never met them McPhee brothers. I put a snake down Max's shirt once, when we were kids. Crabby old Max." She laughs gustily, rocking on the mat.

"For months, Tony saved up his money. He was a serious child. He worked at the wharves, cleaning boats." Grandma Em puffs. "It was a Saturday morning. Earl was out fishing, Winnie must have been at the beauty shop. I noticed Tony sitting over there, on the porch." She points through the doorway to Earl and Winnie's house across the road. "Earlier, I'd seen him heading off. He didn't look so good. I called, finally he came over. He'd gone for the model, was ten cents short. Added up wrong, I guess." Grandma Em thumps the basket. "He'd die before asking a McPhee."

Quietly she adds, "He never built another model."

In my mind I see Tony's face, unforgiving of himself or Max. I see him walking the long mile home to the Reserve, and I feel so tired, I wish the day would end.

All winter I have slept and slept. Grandma Em has been encouraging me not to be so afraid of the dreams. "Those dreams you had when you first came, they connect you," she told me. "There were some terrible things happened here, a long time ago. We know from the songs. In dreams, the spirits speak."

Upon waking, I am filled with misery, more misery than I ever had during those years of looking after my mother and nursing on the ward.

Such pain, for what and for whom? For the spirits in the dreams?

~~~:~~~

We are in the pub, in the basement of the McPhee Hotel.

Tony was waiting when I returned from Grandma Em's. We had supper together, as we often do, although Tony has his own house on the Reserve.

This is a Saturday night, a working man's pub, thick with noise and smoke and camaraderie. Tony greets acquaintances while I scan the cavernous room; I am not too tired to know how grim it must look in the morning light.

Tony orders coffee, indifferent to the booze hurtling past him on dripping cork trays. His acquaintances have accepted that we are a couple. We sit at a small, round table covered with red terrycloth, spotted with stains and burns. Tony leans back in his chair, his right leg resting across his left knee. Studying this classic male pose, I think how lovely some men are in the angles of their bodies, the echo of their forearms to their thighs.

Not a conversationalist, Tony is one of those enviable people who mean what they say and never say what they do not mean. For me it will be a long night, better only than the solitude of the cottage. I see Elsa bending over the pool table, dangling silver jewellery; she works in Port Albert and spends weekends with her family on the Reserve. It is she who markets Grandma Em's baskets, along with carvings and masks made by cousins, equally in demand. Elsa is polite but aloof, and her hair has an unusual copper sheen, which I thought at first was artificial. Tony explained that Grandma Em's mother also had copper hair, even brighter.

Spring has officially arrived, Squally Bay being this week's destination of a busload of visitors, the season's inaugural mystery tour. We passed a large, sleek coach in the parking lot outside the hotel. Most of the tour passengers are elderly and female, enjoying dinner in the dining room upstairs, which has a panoramic view over the bay and the spit. A few have ventured downstairs, bunched around the tables with courageous expressions, dwarfed by their glasses of beer.

Midway through the evening, Tony begins to talk, provoked by an argument between two of his friends who are sitting with us, one a logger and the other a fisherman. Sections of the argument repeat themselves over months of Saturday nights.

The fisherman is defending his stance against the opening of the watershed to logging, which would create jobs for the coming years. This is a part of the country where making a living off the land has been a birthright for generations, and Tony tells me that the logger, descended of pioneers, lost a brother to the woods. The fisherman is Dr. Doyle's son. Both men attended school in the village, where their own children now play.

Annoyance flickers across Tony's face. Much of his free time is spent far up the inlets, removing debris from the spawning streams. Logging has left many of these streams muddy and inhospitable to the salmon seeking the clean, gravel beds of their birth.

Tony swivels back to his coffee, leg crossed over his knee, and I continue my study of the crowd. The mystery tour ladies have retreated upstairs, except for a final pair at a table nearby. Somehow they have ended up sharing their table with a young man who hangs around the Reserve; the locals call him "Turkey," and I do not know his real name. The first time I saw him, the double doors of the pub crashed open and there he stood, grinning hugely, his pants at his knees. He comes and goes between Port Albert, Vancouver, and Squally Bay. I pass him on the wharves, big-boned but sly and wasted, tossing back his long, greasy mane of hair. But at night, in the half-light, his face becomes lean and alive beneath the embroidered headband, and I fear that he evokes something out of a legend to the ladies on the mystery tour.

It is springtime and one of the ladies is wearing, incongruously, a turquoise beach hat. Thrilled and bewildered, she has found herself at the heart of the Squally Bay nightlife. Her companion, an overpermed matron in golfing casuals, nods into her beer as if she is still feeling the effects of the winding bus ride.

Turkey shifts closer to the turquoise hat. The air is gritty and the ashtrays are overflowing; the noise level has swollen to a roar punctuated by the shouts and clinking glasses that define Saturday night. Every so often the pub doors fly open, jolting the crowd with blasts of fresh air.

From where I am sitting, I see Turkey's fingers ascending and descending along the spine of his new friend. Though she squirms nervously, a girlish blush spreads from her powdered cheeks to her straw brim. Turkey's fingers slide around to her breast, and he smirks, leaning back in his chair.

I look across at Tony, who broods over his coffee.

Soon Turkey is on the move again, exploring the edge of a gabardine skirt. After a few moments of squirming and whispering, Turkey persuades his friend to leave the table, making for the dimly lit stairwell which leads up to the lobby of the hotel. Their companion, realizing that she is being abandoned, lurches to her feet, knocking over her chair. The roar is briefly suspended as everyone swings around, in case they are missing a fight.

Turkey stands at the entrance to the stairwell, gesturing gallantly for the women to proceed. Then he waves to the crowd with a grin so cunning that I choke over my drink, and Tony glances blankly between me and the empty stairs.

Later, Tony comes up the steps of the cottage, his hand against the small of my back. I remember Turkey's grin, and the foolish smile beneath the beach hat, a smile yearning for something real, something to take home from the mystery tour. I can feel Tony's tiredness and his tension, and I know the pleasure of a body next to mine. But I pull away, and stand alone on the porch, watching his headlights turn into the Reserve.

I, too, yearn for something real, the scrape of a dark cheek against my skin. Backwards and forwards I have been pulled by this yearning, a pitiless pull, towards the possibility, only the possibility, of being loved. Perhaps it was the father's touch that deserted me before I was ready, before I had the mechanisms for survival in place.

For I cannot remember so much as a hug or a book in a lap, not even the comfort of mending hands after a fall. My mother was consumed by her own losses; she had squandered a lifetime on that mostly absent touch. So I learned to do the giving, at home and at the hospital, and for almost a decade I was mistress to a married man, a surgeon, driven and remote like myself.

I sit on the porch amongst the apricot buds until I am half-frozen, and sleep not with Tony but with wretched, labyrinthine dreams.

~~~:~~~

Tony is out trolling with the fleet when Agnes appears at Dr. Conaliki's clinic, one day in June. Occasionally I have come across her walking beyond the village; she carries a mesh bag and peers over fences, and the black and white cows regard her placidly but the children give her a wide berth.

Dr. Conaliki emerges from his office with Agnes, looking even more flustered than usual. He has emigrated from a tropical island which shares the same ocean as his patients, and little else. Agnes is wearing one of her print dresses and her hair is a stiff halo despite a plastic kerchief wet with rain. "Why haven't you come for tea?" she asks sharply, confronting me behind the counter.

I don't know what to say.

"I'll see you at three!" She adjusts her kerchief and marches out, leaving the waiting room empty. Squally Bay is storing its troubles, slowly gathering confidence in Dr. Doyle's replacement.

"You know her?" asks Dr. Conaliki.

I nod, and shudder, recalling the time she caught me admiring the roses on her verandah. The visit had ended abruptly, and I had gone straight to Grandma Em. She had woven me a little basket with a moon and a star on the lid. No sooner did she give me the basket than the room swayed, as if the floor was dropping, and later I wondered if Agnes had put something in the tea. Whatever it was, I felt shaken for a week. Grandma Em didn't seem surprised when I told her that a similar basket had sat on my mantel; she had sold hundreds of them over the years. She showed me the original basket, where she had got the idea for the design. It was so fragile that I hardly dared lift off the lid. Inside was a piece of antler, amber with age, carved into the shape of a bird. A loon, Grandma Em said. She said that the basket and the loon had brought luck into her life.

At three o'clock I am waiting outside the farmhouse when Agnes comes swishing through the orchard with a stick.

"For the nettles," she says firmly, as I step back. "We're going upriver. Never mind those clouds!" She brandishes her stick at the sky.

Agnes is wearing rubber boots; my jeans are quickly soaked by the unmown grass. A narrow rut leads through fields and stiles, following the river. Agnes seizes a branch of ocean spray, and we thrust our noses into the cascading, creamy blossoms. The fields become forest, where lichen hangs in beards from branches above the old, mossy path. The rains this past spring seemed endless, and in places along the riverbank the lush growth reaches our waists. Agnes fells stinging nettles with ruthless swipes. She slows as we enter a natural glade, and waves her stick, scowling. "Father says this belonged to the Indians."

In fact, it is part of the Squally Bay Reserve, marked on the map on the wall in the municipal office, which I noticed while the clerk was renewing my driver's licence.

Agnes speeds up, beating through the salal. We follow the river, coming upon a cabin which at first glance seems part of the bush, constructed of slabs of logs still ragged with bark. Moss carpets the shakes on the roof, and saplings jut through the porch. Shutters over the windows have been ripped off, and beer cans glint where the steps have fallen away. Crowning all this decay is a tree of apricot roses, climbing over the acid-green moss to the sun. We stand in the outer circle of their scent, inhaling deeply, sweating and prickling in the sudden heat.

After a few minutes, Agnes sighs. Her cheeks cave in and her eyelids droop, like a child who has eaten too many sweets. We are standing in what was once the garden, overlooking the river. I hear Grandma Em's voice describing this cabin, where her mother Evangeline was born, nurtured by vegetables and roses, by venison and grouse caught by a Frenchman who had crossed the country in his canoe.

Agnes straightens, thrashing through the ferns and the salal. A fallen post crumbles beneath her stick. "Fence," she mutters, "six foot high, for the deer." I suspect she is regretting my company, all this explaining when she so clearly prefers to be on her own.

"People say she talks to plants, and that I should do something," Dr. Doyle had written, in his mellow script. "The plants are her only companions; she has alienated herself from the village with her stick. Perhaps we need a Miss Agnes amongst us, no less worthy and no more tamed than the hedges along the roadside in June."

She stomps through the glade, stuffing slain nettles into her mesh bag. The nettles are delicious when they are steamed, unrelated to store-bought greenery wilting in cellophane.

"Agnes," I call out. "Thank you for bringing me here, for showing me all of this."

"Don't you get the wrong idea," she shouts back at me. "Squally Bay was put together by the Scots! And a few English," she adds grudgingly.

She twists around, glaring into my face. "What about the Indians, you were going to say? Riff-raff! Washed ashore here from all up and down the coast. Father says the real ones were killed off long before we came."

My legs drag through the wet fields. Every few minutes, Agnes swings around with a reproachful look, directed at me or herself, I cannot tell. We reach the orchard, and I can hear a kingfisher screeching over the river, cars humming across the metal bridge. Though I see by her stride that Agnes has already dismissed me, loyalty to Grandma Em boils up within me, and I rush around to block her path.

"Agnes."

She glowers beneath ruffled brows.

I take a deep breath. "This was all Indian land."

The stick lashes out, whacking my shoulder and almost knocking me to the ground. I jibber and dance just out of reach, and then I am running, certain that my legs will fail me and I will not get away. I limp across the bridge, weeping for myself and for the Indians and even for Agnes, for what we don't know and will never learn.

~~~:~~~

Tony loosens the thick, braided rope which attaches the stern of his troller to the tire-buffered dock. With the habit of a lifetime, he lines up the channel markers and guides us across the silted bay. His dark eyes crinkle as he measures the waves cresting beyond the spit, and his ears are cocked to the engine, which he has been repairing, fretting over, for days. This morning a long-awaited part has arrived from Vancouver, and we are giving the *Paquacheenish Point* a test run. A fouled engine could cost Tony his year's income, and as we round the spit he explains the system of openings, when the fishing fleet, limited by licence, is allowed by the government to intercept the salmon migrations along the coast. I marvel at the cycles of nature, bringing back the salmon, but Tony's voice is embittered, a fisherman who with each season feels further distanced from his catch.

The wind lifts my hair through the open wheelhouse window. All week I have been hiding from the rain, but today the westerlies have blown every last cloud away. Behind us, seagulls swoop over the widening froth of our wake. Out on the water I have an entirely new perspective of Squally Bay: a cluster of buildings surrounded by fields, then the hills undulating back to the mountains. Many of the blue-green slopes are crisscrossed by logging roads, their growth crudely and recently shaved.

Tony listens to the thrum of the engine, his hands resting lightly on the varnished wheel spokes. Even when scrubbed his fingernails are rimmed black, and his wool sweater gives off the acrid perfume of diesel and oil. Leaning against him, rising and falling with the swell, I feel as if I have been plucked from my cottage by the hand of a benevolent giant, and placed in a perfect, self-contained world. We have not been able to reach each other lately; he has been preoccupied with his engine, and I have been sleeping too much.

We pass rafts of bobbing ducks, comparing their markings with the illustrations in Tony's bird books. The engine changes tune and I glance up in alarm. Tony has slowed alongside a shoreline broken into channels and islands, some no more than sparsely treed chunks of rock.

"Klinniklinnikaht." He pronounces the word easily. "Goes back a mile or so to a marsh." His hand adjusts the throttle as we churn through kelp and debris stirred up by the tide. "My boat is named after this point here, coming up." He traces a headland on the chart beside the wheel. "Paquacheenish. Most powerful chief ever, on the whole coast."

Shading my eyes, I pick out the white hulls of fishing boats, the mast and stays of a sloop anchored in the lee of the trees.

Tony raises his voice over the accelerating engine. "Once a great village, if you believe Grandma Em. Well, she should know. She married up here. Grandpa Vincent. Just a few shacks left now, and old man Howie's general store. He tows it around the coast on floats. The kids were all shipped out; they had to go to the residential school in Port Albert."

Through the open window I count no less than twelve eagles, catching updrafts, heads and tails flashing in the sunlight.

"Vincent taught me how to use a shotgun, in the marsh." Tony's mouth is skewed by his scar when he grins. "Grandma Em used to say, 'Vincent, you are the last of the Klinniklinnikaht men.' Must've been true. Never saw no one hunting up here but us."

"What happened to all the people?"

Tony shrugs. "Nobody talks much. Earl, he's pretty quiet, you might have noticed."

During my introduction to Tony's family, Earl nodded shyly over his tea. Winnie explained that after years of conversing with the fish, he didn't have any words left.

"Why can't I find either of these names?" I ask, studying the chart.

Tony 's mouth twists sardonically as he puts his finger on the chart. "Estrella Inlet. In honour of the Spaniards, first to set foot."

He takes the binoculars from their hook; trollers are gathering in preparation for the next opening, and he recognizes old friends.

"Where are we going?" I ask.

He moves my hand along the chart. "Quatlukaht. Another hour and we'll be there."

Eventually we round a rugged headland into a bay curved like a crescent moon. I am as excited as a child as the anchor chain clangs over the bow. Tony unties the rubber dinghy and slides it alongside, helping me over the gunwale to a precarious seat below. He pulls the cord on the outboard motor and we plane shoreward, almost airborne on the fat pontoons.

His black hair is streaming and worry flies out of his face. We run parallel with the shore to the sheltered end of the bay then turn sharply, driving onto the beach on the back of a breaking wave. I leap out, staggering with exhilaration and the solidity of the land. With a quick motion Tony is beside me, pulling the boat beyond the surf. Our bare feet test the warm, powdery sand. The beach is a jumble of pearly logs, worn smooth by the sea and rain. "Where does all this wood come from?" I ask.

Tony shows me the sawcuts. "Some break loose from the booms." He caresses a bleached stump. "This one broke off in a storm. Been here a long time."

We climb past the logs to the fringe of shrubbery surrounding the bay. Tony bends over tracks in the sandy ground: river otters, raccoons, and deer. "And cougar," he adds. The museum in Port Albert has a stuffed cougar mounted on a branch, poised so realistically that I could feel the claws in my flesh when I scurried below.

Away from the ocean, the air is fragrant and still. We sit against a grassy bank which has eroded to reveal a midden, layers upon layers of shells and blackened soil. Mounds and hollows are transformed into house sites as Tony describes the layout of yet another village reclaimed by the salal. He shows me the walkways down to the sea, where cedar canoes, not rubber dinghies, once lined the beach.

I shake my head in wonder. "Think of everything that happened here! Think of how ignorant we are!"

Tony's voice is flat. "Not much written down. Grandma Em knows the history through the songs. Maybe you'll hear her tonight," he laughs.

"Tonight?"

"Potlach for Andy's graduation," says Tony. "You are my guest."

Flustered, I turn away. To be exposed to the scrutiny of his family ... and yet, the chance to hear Grandma Em sing ....

Tony unfolds a faded blanket, anchoring the edges with stones. He lies back, sighing, his arm shading his face. Worn down by his problems with the engine, he dozes as I prowl the shoreline, peering into the musty caverns beneath the logs. I am looking for treasure, to mark this day and this place. At the north end of the bay I climb a shallow ridge, and beyond me unravels a ribbon of sand as far as the eye can see. A corner of my soul lifts off, floating over this infinite strip, and as it goes, I feel not diminished but as rooted as the evergreens and the wind-sheared salal.

Tony looks up sheepishly when I return. "Guess I fell asleep."

We unpack the lunch, admiring the profile of his troller as we eat. I lie with my cheek against the blanket, thinking about the people for whom this beach had been home.

All at once Tony jumps up, casting off his sweater and shirt. He pulls off his jeans and swaggers into the ocean, diving beyond the surge.

"I'm purifying myself!" he shouts, laughing at my shock. He disappears beneath the waves, sweeping ashore in a flurry of foam.

He falls onto the blanket, and I wince as his icy thigh brushes mine. "Purifying yourself for what?"

"For the salmon," chuckles Tony. "A hundred years ago I would have been out at dawn, scrubbing myself with handfuls of hemlock. Salmon like their fishermen clean."

I nod, speechless.

"The idea is to get rid of human smells. The touch of my finger on a hook could lose me a big juicy coho." He rubs his legs happily. "I should do it more often."

I follow the curve of his jaw, his shoulder blade, his spine. "And what about a woman's touch?"

"Forbidden for months, until every last bit of meat is smoked and dried and put away."

"Too bad," I whisper against him, tasting the salty ocean and sweat.

It has been weeks since we have been so close. He turns to me, his mouth seeking my breasts beneath my shirt.

Never have I felt so alive as at this moment, within his embrace. I lie back, looking into his eyes, and for a few seconds I glimpse, recklessly, the rest of my life.

~~~:~~~

Squally Bay basks in a twilight glow as we enter the meeting hall on the Reserve. With family, as with everyone, Tony is courtly but guarded; only by a slight stiffening do I guess that his ex-wife is sitting beside their son Andrew, a sprawling teenager. Andrew has the shoulders of an athlete, an asymmetrical haircut, and a silver ring in one ear. I know him already from the weekends he spends with his father, doing odd jobs around the wharves. Intriguingly, Tony chose for a wife a copy of his mother, round and broad-cheeked. She smiles generously at me, undoing my months of dread imaginings, envying the woman with whom Tony shared his early years.

Soon the hall reverberates with people and noise. The lights dim, and metal chairs scrape as the elders take their seats. Children of all ages have gathered around on the polished wood floor which doubles as a basketball court. Rattles and drums come to life in hands which moments before were stirring coffee, or comforting babies. The men start to sing and the women gradually join in, and the crowd quietens as the ancient words and timeless rhythms transcend the utilitarian hall. To my surprise, the leading singer is Earl. The song ends, and he introduces Andrew, whose parents and relatives come forth with good wishes and gifts.

When it is Tony's turn to speak, I watch the scar on his mouth, burning with the recall of his kiss. Not realizing that a potlach meant presents for everyone, I am as bashful as Andrew when Tony hands me a small, square box. Beneath tissue lies an engraved copper bracelet, which he slips over my wrist like a gleaming cuff.

"I can't accept this," I whisper, my eyes brimming.

He slips his arm around me. "Bad manners to refuse a potlach gift."

Earl helps Grandma Em to the front of the room. She kneels on a mat, nodding to her chattering family, to the children racing wildly along the walls. Andrew rises up, managing a speech of thanks which is repeated through the crowd. Tony glances briefly at his ex-wife, sharing the pleasure of their son.

Then, I hear Grandma Em's quavering voice. It is a voice which seems not to originate from Grandma Em but from the essence of the coast itself: the fish and the birds, the trees and the lap-lap of the tides, the rain and the waves, and the people who rode the waves, fierce, resilient, and true.

The bracelet Tony gave me sags on my wrist. I gaze around the crowd, and the faces are hardly recognizable, suffused with Grandma

Em's song. Here in this humble setting, I have found the treasure which eluded me on the Quatlukaht shore.

~~~:~~~

Summer has been good to me, gratifying and routine. The salmon runs are consistent and Tony's engine problems are solved. I meet his boat at the dock, and leave with my cheeks grated and stinging from the stubble he spares no minutes to shave, so urgent are the demands of the silver fish in the hold.

Dr. Conaliki blushes at the rashes on my face. We are getting along well, he and I, consoled by our common status as newcomers to Squally Bay. Agnes has showed up at the clinic only once, making a dramatic entrance with a thorn festering in her foot. Dr. Conaliki removed the thorn and she limped determinedly home; she did not acknowledge me, and there were no more invitations to tea.

Grandma Em is always welcoming. I bring tidbits of gossip, and questions that arise from my wanderings. She has tales from the forgotten villages all over the coast, tales of passion and revenge, secrets buried in the salal. She thrives in the spring, says Tony, and dwindles when the cold weather arrives. She is ninety-one years old, born just after the century's turn. A cousin of hers resides in a Port Albert rest home, still lucid at one hundred and twelve.

Her door is ajar as I come up the path. She is sitting on her mat, facing the September sunshine, and although I sense a resigned weariness she smiles cheerfully as I fill the kettle for tea. I have just been at the Fall Fair, in the Community Hall, a voluminous building erected by pioneers at the junction of the two main roads. I can hardly wait to tell her: finally I have something to add to the button and the letter from Captain Hume.

The Community Hall was filled with tables covered in white paper, laden with squashes, dahlias, needlepoint, and preserves. At the far end was a display loaned by the museum in Port Albert, put together for last year's Bicentennial, commemorating the history of Squally Bay. Artifacts rested on satin in locked cases, and I stood with my nose pressed to the glass: Wolf Head, Bear Mask, Shaman's Rattle. Propped against each other, the chisels and the mauls seemed like sculptures in stone. The central piece of the display was a heavy whalebone club, tapering to a handle carved into the head and wings of a Thunderbird. "War club for a chief," I read aloud. "Found by Donnie and Davie Lavalle while digging for clams, Quatlukaht, 1934." The Lavalle boys lived several miles from Quatlukaht, at what was once the site of a pilchard factory; Tony's chart warns of pilings submerged at high tide.

Photographs from the museum archives were mounted on poster-boards along the back of the hall. Pioneers reclined beside stumps with their crosscut saws and their teams of oxen; the women were on their verandahs, next to flower beds hacked out of the bush. Their hair was neatly parted for the camera, collars straightened, jaws clenched with the seriousness of the occasion. The local schoolchildren had contributed essays, reporting that the Spaniards came but did not stay. Only a hundred and thirty-six years ago, the McPhee family from Scotland settled at Squally Bay.

It was when I came to a photograph of the McPhee mill that I made my discovery. A sturdy black schooner was tied beside a stack of lumber on a wharf in front of the mill. Several men reclined on the lumber, and an elderly man stood on the forward deck. He was thin, almost skeletal, and he gazed over the bay with a proprietal air, one foot resting on a hatch. The name of the schooner, on the bow, was the *Coast Princess*. This was the same name as in my great-great-great-grandfather's letter, and I studied the old man for the longest time, convinced that I had found him at last.

As I talk, Grandma Em mulls over her tea. The light slants beyond the door, another afternoon gone. The air has a nostalgic crispness which only heightens my excitement.

Grandma Em nods towards a box on the dresser, next to a brown enamel radio. It is the kind of box which once contained stationery, and we open it together, our heads bent over the sheafs of photographs inside. Close to me, Grandma Em is a blend of cedar, sweet tobacco, and grass. Her grey hair is loosely braided, tied with a frayed cotton strip.

The photographs tilt across the table and I would greedily grab them, except that they are meaningless without Grandma Em. She shows me a picture of Tony and Elsa on the oyster-shell path; their lunchboxes are shiny and their bangs are trimmed as they wave goodbye on the first day of school.

Then she separates a yellowing, fly-spotted portrait which must have once hung on a wall. An enormous man with a bushy white beard is posed awkwardly in his best clothes, a pipe gripped in his massive hands. He very much resembles one of the men in the photograph of the *Coast Princess.*

"Ah, Jean-Louis." Grandma Em's voice thickens. "He helped build the mill. There weren't any women of their own for these Frenchmen, of course. Jean-Louis courted my grandmother when she was a girl. Pali, she was called." She peers at a date scrawled in the corner. "This was taken in Port Albert just before he died."

Our eyes slide from old Jean-Louis to the two other figures in the portrait. A woman is sitting beside Jean-Louis, holding an infant in her arms.

Grandma Em taps the swaddled child. "This is me. And this," she whispers, "is my mother, Evangeline."

We stare silently, and a draft through the door scuds across the table, scattering photographs, rippling tea.

"What happened to her face?" I cannot stop myself from asking; the words gush out in disbelief.

Grandma Em fumbles for the portrait, pressing it to her breast. She shakes her head, and my question swirls away from us, unanswered, lost to the autumn wind.

~~~:~~~

KAHAMMIS: 1852 - 1863

OVER THE HILLS and down the slope to the bay tore the southeast wind, flattening the grass along the spit, ripping away the last pockets of summer air. Up on the ridge, the giant cedar tree swayed and groaned above the two women squatting in its lee. Kahammis cupped her hands around her bluestone pipe, leaning against Tatatoe, who was visiting from Klinniklinnikaht.

They had spent the morning sorting and splitting sedge grasses, which now swung drying on poles outside the lodge Kahammis shared with the families of her brother and son. She would wake all winter to the golden bundles stored above her sleeping platform, along with the coiled roots and silky bark which formed the warp and weft of her life.

Her pipe had belonged to her father, and she puffed contentedly in the absence of Aneetsick, who was trading at Port Albert. The tobacco was from Jean-Louis, the stranger with the sash who had first come into the bay nine years before, on the day Hiyuyah died. Although Kahammis purchased the tobacco with her baskets, Aneetsick disapproved of her smoking and chafed at her stubborn will. She and Aneetsick were like two trees in the forest, joined at the roots, branches touching, but their crowns reaching for different portions of the sky.

Kalowish and Sa-sat-kis had gone with Aneetsick, their canoes loaded with salmon and roe, and pelts from the fur seals they hunted offshore. Moochinnick also went on every trip to Port Albert; ever since his rescue, he behaved as if Nootseetaht was his rightful home. No one knew how this galled Kahammis, for at night, in the shadows back from the hearth, he became a hulking reincarnation of Tatoosch or Quassoon. Then she would hear his voice, oily and smooth, and she would remind herself that she was safe. Moochinnick wrapped his tongue around the jargon of the fort with ease. Aneetsick let him do more and more of the talking, particularly with the traders; soon, worried Kahammis, Aneetsick might not speak at all.

Pulling her cape more tightly around her shoulders, Kahammis watched Paonea rush out from one of the lodges below. She scooped up a small boy and then joined her mother, ambling through the village. Paonea had turned out to be as plump and matronly as everyone had expected; never, though, had Kahammis dreamed that she would marry Moochinnick. What mattered to Aneetsick was not Moochinnick's personality but his lineage, and all the rights he could claim. He had no interest in his past or his rights, however, and had not once gone north to Quatlukaht, leaving his people at the mercy of the cousins, who were still too busy quarrelling to rule. T'isharth's village was disappearing beneath the salal, and the surviving Mannakaht settlements were barely hanging on to their share of the diminishing trade. Kahammis suspected that Moochinnick stayed south because he was too used to his comforts, and the proximity of Port Albert.

Paonea and Chee-uxqua were supervising the dismantling of the drying racks, shaking sand off the clover roots and putting food away, all the while glancing at the clouds stacked up over the hills. They stopped to help a scrawny woman bent beneath the weight of the boards used to compress the berry cakes. This was Yanis from Klinniklinnikaht, the daughter of one of the women Paquacheenish used to send out to the ships. She had been found by the matchmakers as a wife for Sa-sat-kis.

Kahammis gazed south from her vantage point on the ridge. "Will you go to the fort one day?" she asked Tatatoe.

"Not me," shuddered Tatatoe. "Bad enough Neetsa!"

121

Neetsa was twenty-six years old and strikingly attractive; she had refused every suitor, to her mother's despair. It was Neetsa and Kleeshinnin who worked to maintain the flow of wealth set in motion by Paquacheenish, for Hasallum was too preoccupied with his canoes. Few ships came to anchor now in the lagoon; everyone went instead to Port Albert. Kleeshinnin looked after the cargo and protected Neetsa from the opportunists at the fort, while she did the bartering for the blankets and the tools.

Kahammis recalled her last visit to Klinniklinnikaht, to celebrate the birth of Kleeshinnin's first child. The village had seemed ramshackle and unsettled, and on one of her walks she had encountered a solitary raven, beak pointed skyward, feathers ruffled as if in a shrug.

Her eyes flickered south. Every season brought more stories, more revelations, and more change. Perhaps she might have gone to the fort in the beginning, in her own canoe. It was too late now, the stories had grown too big. Now, even the lands beyond the picket walls were controlled by a chief no one had ever seen. The ships that once sought furs now brought white people and their possessions, and beasts which pulled clanking metal through the soil in the valleys and along the sunny slopes. Except for a few straggling blossoms, the camas fields had been trampled to mud. The village beside the fort had been relocated to the harbour's opposite shore. The old chief had died with his questions unanswered, though his people seemed happy enough with blankets, whisky, and rice.

Kahammis had overheard mutterings about the women who lolled against the fort walls, women contemptuous of men like Kleeshinnin and Kalowish, who hurried past with burning cheeks. Since Hiyuyah's death, Kalowish had carved his emotions into his masks and canoes, and sold them as quickly as they were done. Four hefty logs lay on the delta, awaiting his adze and future buyers from the fort. Amazingly, most of these canoes left Nootseetaht with their bows unadorned, meaning that the new owners were setting out to sea without the security of their crests. From what kind of world, wondered Kahammis, did these strangers come?

Kalowish relied on Jean-Louis to supply him with trees. Jean-Louis and his helpers worked along the coast with huge, ringing axes; Kahammis had heard the axes when she paddled north to the birth feast. She had been flabbergasted at the breaks in the wall of greenery which had stretched from Nootseetaht to Klinniklinnikaht since time began. Suddenly everyone wanted trees, not pelts; Jean-Louis told her that he was cutting the finest spars in the world. Spars, he explained, were the sticks on the ships which held up the sails, the same sticks that were so bewildering to her mother when the first ship had floated into Klinniklinnikaht like something out of a dream.

Lately, not even the treacherous entrance into Nootseetaht stopped the smaller vessels; they arrived and departed on their own random timetables, ignoring the tides. Inevitably they scraped the reefs, or grounded in the shallow bay, and Moochinnick was much in demand guiding them out. Kahammis cared less about the ships than the expression on Aneetsick's face, haughty yet mesmerized as he watched from the shore.

The storm was drawing closer; she could feel it in her bones. The villagers slid the canoes farther along the ramps, covering them with mats. She heard a sob beside her, and turned in surprise to see Tatatoe wiping away a tear. It occurred to her that Tatatoe had been looking at the canoes, many of them made by Hasallum when he lived at Nootseetaht.

She made an effort to keep her voice calm. "He hasn't gone off again, has he?" Tatatoe nodded, and Kahammis sighed. Hasallum had a habit of wandering into the woods, with only his rattles and his prayers. When several weeks went by and he did not return, Kleeshinnin would track him to the rotting log he had tripped over, or the ravine he had tumbled into, seemingly unconcerned. Kleeshinnin would carry him home to Tatatoe, who nursed him at the hearth. Hasallum would resume working, his canoes ever more fantastically embellished, drawing customers from all over the coast. To Neetsa's chagrin, he would not make a single sale. As the mood struck him, he gave his creations away. Then came the call of a certain, perfect moon, a call that Kahammis understood he was powerless to refuse.

Beside her, Tatatoe's miseries were multiplying. "Also," she blurted, "Kleeshinnin would not let me put the cradlepads on his baby's head!"

Neither had Moochinnick permitted the cradlepads for his son, and to the dismay of Kahammis, Aneetsick had approved. Moochinnick had begun referring to himself by the new name of Charlie, and his son was called Henry, on the advice of traders from Port Albert who had sounded out the names of the great chiefs from across the seas.

Kahammis clenched her teeth around her pipestem. Aneetsick had said: our children must not be mocked. The foreheads of the aristocracy, mocked? When she had snapped back at him, across the firepit, he glanced pointedly at her boiling stones. He was reminding her that she was the only cook in the village who did not use iron pots. She had intended to, but when she first returned to Nootseetaht, she had uncovered her mother's boiling stones in the ashes of the family hearth and had used them ever since.

She hurriedly wiped away her own tears as Yanis came running up the ridge.

"Where are the boys?" panted Yanis. "Their canoe is gone!"

When their father was away, the impossible task of minding Callicum and Sea-ossum fell upon Yanis, and she scanned the bay, wringing her hands. She had last seen them splashing on the delta, chasing the spawning salmon into the weirs.

Kahammis chewed her pipe. "Perhaps they have paddled upriver?" Pali, their younger sister, was with a group of girls on the riverbank, picking rosehips to string into necklaces for the winter dances.

"Something is missing from the chief's lodge!" Yanis covered her face. "The chief's harpoon!"

Kahammis coughed. "His whaling harpoon?"

Yanis bobbed her head fearfully.

Kahammis got to her feet. The sea beyond the spit churned between the tide and the wind, and the entrance to the bay was almost obscured by breaking waves. Silver-winged gulls wheeled above the white water, reflecting the late afternoon light.

Hasallum had given the boys their own canoe, telling them it would carry them to the stars and home safely again. Surely they had not set out with Aneetsick's prized harpoon! Then she remembered how they had refused the mussels she had served in the morning; were they purifying themselves, the rascals, for a hunt?

She took off her cape and turned to the cedar tree, thinking of the many years that had passed since she last pulled herself up, queen of her realm. She began to climb, groping for familiar holds, pausing frequently to rest and peer below. Despite the addition of three lodges, Nootseetaht seemed much smaller than when, as a child, she had perched for hours with only the jays and the occasional eagle for company. How old Sa-sat-kis would fret, calling her down.

She picked out Pali amongst the girls on the delta. Pali had been amply mothered by Paonea and Chee-uxqua, and now they prodded Kalowish to begin the marriage arrangements. He took refuge in his carving, not ready for Pali, who so reminded him of Hiyuyah, to grow up and become ensnared by life.

"What do you see?" called Yanis and Tatatoe, as Kahammis rose through the creaking branches.

Though her eyes watered from the wind, she could still follow the tight, circling ascent of the season's last osprey, hovering over the spit on wide, slender wings. Smoke swirled above the village; the women were raking the hearths in preparation for supper. Just as she was beginning to relax, she noticed a speck in the distant waves. It tipped up, then dropped precipitously out of sight. Suddenly another speck appeared, angling across the swell. She rubbed her eyes.

"What is it?" cried the women.

Kahammis stared for a long moment. Yes, there they were, two canoes turning laboriously towards shore.

"It's the boys!" she shouted. "They're coming in!"

~~~:~~~

Jean-Louis heard the wind rushing through the treetops, and he shouldered his axe, heading back to the little cabin he had put up in the bush behind Hoxem. His two Klinniklinnikaht helpers had been hinting that a storm was coming, and though he never doubted their knowledge, they were experts at finding excuses to avoid work. They had already departed for their village, indifferent to his protests. When they ran out of tobacco, they would return.

He quickly launched his canoe, loading his axe, iron spikes, and rope. He had left three prime fir logs on a beach not far from Nootseetaht. The logs awaited towing by steamer to Port Albert, where they would be milled and shipped to the great harbours of the world. He wanted to make sure that the logs were secure, for even after nine years, the tides and the weather caught him by surprise.

His two comrades from Montreal had long since moved on, preferring to be closer to the stores and the saloons. Now, when he went down to Port Albert to replenish his supplies, he found the boardwalks ungiving beneath his feet after the loamy forest paths. He was mortified when the Port Albert ladies ducked behind their parasols, intimidated by his bushy beard, which kept off the mosquitoes, and by his rolling stride. The sash that he saved for special occasions set him apart not as a member of the proud voyageurs but as an oddity, a relic from the past. He was thirty-two years old. Without the company of his helpers, he could lie crushed in the forest and no one would ever know.

He left the shelter of the cove, regretting that he had not paid more heed to the warning about the storm. Scarcely noticeable in the woods, the wind snatched dry tassels of kelp from the shore and tossed them like tumbleweeds into the sea. A wave slapped over his bow, drenching his tools, and he cursed extravagantly. He had learned to curse from his father, sneaking off with his brothers to practise behind the woodpile, giddy with the power of the forbidden words.

How his father would love to be with him now! His father, too, had been a voyageur, wielding his paddle with the finesse that had carried the fur companies beyond the lakes, beyond the plains and the mountains to the glorious coast of dreams. Home to Montreal he brought the stories of bravery and adversity that had shaped Jean-Louis as a boy. Jean-Louis and his brothers stacked their backs with the weight of the portage packs until they toppled over, groaning and amazed. They learned to match their father's forty strokes to the minute, the rhythm which had propelled the birchbark canoes west, loaded with trade goods, then east again with the precious furs. Jean-Louis could have worked on a local farm, or ferried cargo on the river with his ageing father; was it any wonder that he joined the swarm heading off to search for gold, for adventure, for a place in the world?

Was it any wonder that he had stayed here? There were logs to last a thousand lifetimes, and he had made too many friends to leave. He chuckled to think of his deals with Kahammis, when they debated over the number of woven baskets it would take to fill her tobacco pouch. The price seldom varied, and neither did their ritual of sale; Jean-Louis made a show of examining her baskets while she fingered the tiny beads on the moccasins he wore. His mother got the moccasins from the Lake Indians back east, and shipped them to Port Albert. He traded the baskets in turn for dried salmon, and dogfish oil to grease the log skids.

Once, during a visit to Klinniklinnikaht, he noticed that Hasallum was gone. Kleeshinnin admitted, unhappily, that Hasallum had been away for too long, and Jean-Louis had offered to help track him when no one else would volunteer. The old chief had drifted far into the mountains and was light as a leaf when they found him; his leathery face was filled with acceptance, a kind of inner glow. He lay over Jean-

Louis's shoulder, letting himself be carried home. They passed beneath an enormous spruce tree just as the sunlight touched the tree's crown, splintering into a multitude of rays which shot down to the ground. Jean-Louis heard a noise which seemed to emanate from the tree and realized that it was Hasallum, solemnly addressing the spirit of the mighty spruce. Kleeshinnin had translated, a message of such poignance that ever since, Jean-Louis had not been able to pick up his axe without touching the gold crucifix around his neck, remembering Hasallum's gentle voice, commanding man and nature as one.

Paddling hard, he reached his logs just as they began to shift, licked by the incoming tide. He secured them with rope and stood with his arms across his chest, his beard flapping in the wind. Though the weather was worsening, he was confident that he could make it back to Hoxem. Yet he remained on the beach, staring out over the water. Except for his ponderings on the souls of trees, and his annoyance at unscrupulous schooner captains, who fed whisky to his helpers on the sly, rarely did he feel troubled by worries or doubts. Rubbing his beard, shifting from foot to foot, he wondered what nagged him as he stood watching the whipped-up waves.

With a grunt of amazement, he picked out a canoe dipping and lurching like flotsam. Must be strangers, he thought, laughing grimly; only fools such as himself would choose to be out. He recalled his first voyages, swept sideways, backwards, and even upside down by the relentless currents and the swell. He shook his head at the two strug- gling paddlers; they were running from the storm, farther out to sea.

"Jean-Louis!" he exclaimed aloud, leaping to collect his tools. "We are all strangers once! They'll end up in China if you don't help!"

~~~:~~~

"Keep bailing!" shrieked Sea-ossum.

Callicum forced his fingers around the bailer as water gushed back and forth inside the canoe. His eyes were locked on the receding hills. A wave reared up and cascaded over Sea-ossum, wrenching at his paddle. The canoe pitched precariously; Callicum could feel Aneetsick's harpoon sloshing between his knees. Where did whales go in storms? He imagined them far below, in some quiet, safe place. He turned to Sea-ossum and before him floated, as if in slow motion, the worst moments in his life, moments he and his brother had somehow survived. But the look on Sea-ossum's face was more terrifying than the weather, than the coast slipping away. How the two-headed serpent would sing as she sucked them down. Callicum dropped the bailer with a clatter, appalled to hear her already calling, calling, over the waves.

Jean-Louis was speeding towards them, paddling and howling like a madman through the gale. He was in the middle of a rollicking chorus which he remembered, with many embellishments, from the country dances of his youth. He loved to sing like the coast people when he paddled, though he had yet to learn the proper chants.

He drew alongside the floundering boys. "How's fishing?" he yelled.

Sea-ossum moved his lips, but no sound came out. Callicum fumbled for the bailer, open-mouthed, peering through his wet copper hair.

"Well, I'm heading into Nootseetaht," Jean-Louis shouted cheerfully. "You about done for the day?"

Sea-ossum's face was frozen with concentration as they followed Jean-Louis in a wide, careful turn; he was copying every stroke Jean-Louis made. When Callicum looked up, he was stunned to see the spit directly ahead. He grabbed his paddle, shaking with relief.

Jean-Louis slowed as they approached the funnel of water between the spit and the shore. "Rougher than I expected!" he shouted back to the boys.

Callicum and Sea-ossum surged past Jean-Louis. "Follow me!" yelled Sea-ossum, gratefully astonished to have found his voice.

They led Jean-Louis in a wild dash, skimming the whirlpools and hurtling past the gnarled pine tree on the crest of a powerful roller which swept them into the bay. They crossed to the village beach, Jean-Louis yodelling merrily. When Callicum stepped out of the bow, his legs wobbled beneath his weight. He glanced back and saw his brother clinging limply to the stern.

Pali flew down the slope. She hugged Jean-Louis and peeked into the pockets of his worn flannel shirt, hoping to find paper twists of candy. Taking advantage of the distraction, Callicum and Sea-ossum skulked up to the lodge with the harpoon.

Kahammis and Tatatoe came to greet Jean-Louis, their bark skirts billowing in the gusts.

"Tell him he must stay," cried Pali, tugging his hands.

Kahammis teased him about his salt-crusted beard, speaking slowly, so that he could understand. Each village had its own dialect, combinations of consonants and stops, with the slightest inflection altering meaning or tense. Jean-Louis was the only outsider to progress beyond the jargon of the traders, words and phrases thrown together without subtlety or respect. Kahammis wished that the children could be spared this jargon when the men unloaded after a trip to the fort, or when the schooners grounded, the crews shouting rudely for assistance as if the villagers were to blame. For how could such harsh, labelling slang describe this wind, or the hoink-hoink of the geese skidding along the delta, or the soft, bitter murmur of the cormorants at dusk?

No sooner had Pali dragged Jean-Louis up to the lodge than the rain began, skittering against the roofboards and hissing into the hearths. Callicum stood by eagerly with the pole, rearranging smokeholes to suit the cooks. Chee-uxqua dished up the bubbling spawn of the salmon the men had split open at the riverside. Paonea mashed sugar into a vat of salalberries, her toddler Henry peeping from beneath her skirt. The sugar came regularly from the fort, and if the women served the berries unsweetened, the children complained.

Kahammis heaped embers over the potatoes she had been given by Gitti-kang. He always stopped at Nootseetaht on his journeys south, his bow loaded with potatoes covered by mats to protect them from the sun and the spray. He had become even more distinguished looking with age, and more gracious, never failing to comment on the transformation of Sa-sat-kis, from starved waif to accomplished carver and devoted slave. Along with the potatoes he brought canny observations, spinning out the nights of his stopovers with his news.

Most impressive to the villagers, he had once been aboard the Smoking Tree. The Smoking Tree had steamed all the way to Gitti-kang's islands in search of rocks that burned, or glittered, or contained mysteries of no importance to a people whose fortunes were not fixed in stone. Since then, many foreigners had come and gone, and their only useful legacy was the potato, cultivated by Gitti-kang's people with much success. Poking the charred lumps in the hearth, Kahammis anticipated the tender inside flesh, while the children waited, sticky-fingered and with expressions of divine innocence, for Paonea to turn her back on the berry vat.

The harvest of the salmon and the arrival of Jean-Louis gave the evening a festive air, all the more charged with the storm sweeping over the hills, breaking summer's spell. A line of giggling girls fanned out along the central aisle, performing a dance of gladness to the staccato accompaniment of the rain. Jean-Louis applauded especially for Pali, in the lead. He wrestled with the boys, and little Henry beat his fists on Jean-Louis's head. Kahammis noticed that Callicum and Sea-ossum glanced often at the harpoon above Aneetsick's sleeping platform, as if confirming that once again, they had survived.

During the meal, Yanis brought around bowls of rendered seal oil. Kahammis watched her, seeing her own young self bending to please Yatintala and Quassoon. Rarely did she open that desolate place in her mind. She sat chilled with remembering, taken back by the sound of the rain and the smell of the oil and the mask of servitude on Yanis's face.

Yanis had lost three babies in early pregnancy. Three grandchildren for Sheebo, thought Kahammis. She waited until Yanis came around again with the oil. "I will take you into the forest," she whispered to her. "We will pray for your next child." Yanis said nothing, but her back straightened and her face was radiant. Kahammis ate well, her appetite returning with the banishment of the ghosts of Quatlukaht and Yuhktu.

After the meal, Chee-uxqua ladled out the tea that Jean-Louis loved, a fragrant brew in a cedar bowl. The boys had resumed wrestling, and the girls sang lullabies, stringing rosehips in their laps. Paonea, leaning against the wall, nursed young Henry. Kahammis puffed on her pipe while Jean-Louis stretched beside her on a pile of mats, drinking tea.

It was this cosy den of warmth and companionship, reflected Jean-Louis, that drew the greatest contempt of the captains and their crews, trading along the coast. Every now and then, the traders accepted invitations into the villages, and he had heard their descriptions of the filth and the perversions concealed behind the rough cedar walls. How horrified they would be to see him now, to know that he would exchange all the camaraderie of the Port Albert saloons for a night like this, amongst these people who so freely welcomed him into their lives.

Pali approached Jean-Louis, pointing hopefully to a beam where the drying grasses hung. When he smiled, she scampered over and retrieved a small case which he had left behind on his previous visit. A crowd gathered around Jean-Louis as he unbuckled the leather-covered case. The lid fell open to reveal the red silk lining, and the people gasped as they did each time. Jean-Louis got to his feet, and the lodge fell silent except for the rain streaming along the roofboards to the ground. He lifted the violin and placed it beneath his chin with a pang of regret; for him, his music was a reminder of the world he had left behind.

So instead of the folk tunes they had come to expect, he chose a piece his mother had sent him, her smudged inkspots blackening the score. A gifted musician, she taught piano to the children of a prominent Austrian family who lived in one of the manor farms along the river, outside Montreal. From this family she had obtained many musical compositions, satisfying a quest for adventure no less ardent than that which had pulled first her husband, then her sons, out west. Gazing at the earnest faces before him, waiting breathlessly for the draw of his bow, Jean-Louis knew that the piece she had sent him would receive the debut it deserved. He closed his eyes and commenced to play. Pali sucked her fingers with drowsy rapture, and Tatatoe bent her head, weeping soundlessly beside Kahammis. Callicum and Sea-ossum listened gravely, their rescue having elevated Jean-Louis to the rank of hero.

The entrance mat lifted as the occupants of the other lodges crept inside, like moths to a torch. Jean-Louis swayed, and his audience swayed with him, as if it were the essential strings of their being that he so evocatively stroked. He was playing his version of Schubert's "Ave Maria," which he had practised for weeks alone in his cabin, convinced that he had found the most beautiful melody ever composed. When the final note trailed away, he opened his eyes. He saw that a stricken expression had come over Kahammis, and he wondered, aghast, what he had done.

That night the people of Nootseetaht slept deeply, soothed by Schubert's magic, by the food and the rain. Only Kahammis lay awake on her sleeping platform, pinned by the ache that had settled even more fiercely into her bones, and, far worse, by the certainty of change. Ringing axes, trampled fields, scornful traders, and neglected cradlepads seemed insignificant next to this music which had pierced her heart with its brilliance, and its sorrow. Against guns, they had a chance. Against the forces behind this music, they were without defence.

She waited, raw-eyed, for the grey dawn.

~~~:~~~

Two years later, on a drizzling afternoon, Kahammis and Pali worked along the tide-bared bay with their digging sticks, exposing colonies of small, muddy clams. Kahammis paused frequently to lean on her stick, hunched beneath her cape and rain hat. She watched the herons stalk the shallows, stretching their scraggly necks and seizing minnows with victorious gulps.

At the sound of unfamiliar voices, she and Pali dropped their sticks and stood rooted in the mud. The herons stopped in mid-step, erupting into flight as six men emerged from the river path. Aneetsick and Moochinnick came out of the main lodge, alerted by Callicum, who had been sitting by the entrance, whittling a maple whistle.

The six men trudged along carrying rifles and bulging canvas packs. They halted at the sight of Aneetsick and Moochinnick, then one man separated himself and approached. He was stooped with exhaustion, and his thinning brown hair was plastered over his forehead. His men were pale and bedraggled and seemed indistinguishable from one another, as strangers so often do. Kahammis gripped her stick, glancing towards the river as if somehow betrayed.

Aneetsick, a commanding presence looking much younger than his fifty-six years, gestured for Moochinnick to greet the men. Although Aneetsick understood the language of the fort, he relied on Moochinnick as his Speaker, so that he could better listen and observe. Villagers poured out of the lodges, chattering in confusion.

The leader straightened. "We're here on the authority of the government," he announced, unfolding a damp, soiled paper from his pack.

Moochinnick nodded, acknowledging the paper. Aneetsick remained aloof; although he had heard around the fort that there were many meanings to the authority of the government, never before had it justified intrusion from the impenetrable rear. His first assumption was that the men had been shipwrecked, crawling to safety along the coast. Countless boats slammed onto the rocks, discharging passengers and freight into the sea. He studied the rifles and the laced boots, not so sure.

"This is me, Robert Airley." The leader underlined a section of the letter, and Aneetsick's face masked his indignation at being shown a piece of paper which he could not read.

Robert Airley addressed Moochinnick. "What is your name?"

"Charlie," Moochinnick replied affably.

"After the Bonnie Prince, no doubt!" chuckled Airley, and his men barked with laughter, gazing around with increasing confidence.

132

Moochinnick smiled. Although he did not know these men, he knew their type, how they enjoyed a joke.

Airley unfolded more papers, which he sheltered from the drizzle. He explained that he had made maps of the mountains and the coast, tracing his route from the fort. He sketched the bay and the spit, and Moochinnick quickly grasped the concept of the maps; Aneetsick disdained to look. The men lowered their packs and their rifles, staring around the village. Chee-uxqua watched from the entrance to the main lodge, debating the problem of accommodation. The leader could stay with the chief. But the others?

They surprised her by taking their packs up to the ridge, where they laid out a camp. The children crept behind the big cedar tree, and Moochinnick's son Henry went closer, bribed by the older boys. Naked except for his short cape, he held out his hand and asked for sugar, to the amusement of the men.

Kahammis still stood with her digging stick, although Pali had taken away the basket of clams. A raven pecked nearby, amongst the lush carpet of algae and kelp. If only Jean-Louis was with them, thought Kahammis; she placed no trust in Moochinnick, even if he was Speaker for the chief.

The men huddled beneath a tarp, lighting smokes and talking amongst themselves. Aneetsick sent fish, for apparently they were short of food. Robert Airley was busy with his maps in the fading light.

"Look at that savage on the beach," commented one of the men, pointing to Kahammis. "Did you ever see such a sight?"

Pali went down to Kahammis. "Come on, Grandma," she said, taking her by the arm. They came up the slope, into the main lodge.

"We ain't putting foot in there," exclaimed another man, and his companions vehemently agreed.

But Airley did go in, after supper, invited by Aneetsick. He was served tea in a tin cup, and Chee-uxqua offered him bog cranberries, stored in boxes of moss. Courteously he ate and drank and discoursed, through Moochinnick, on his travels.

Kahammis had refused supper and sat with her pipe in the shadows against the wall. Paonea played with her second son, Johnny, close by. Yanis brought tea, and steaming packs of seaweed to place on Kahammis's legs. Though not yet pregnant, Yanis fasted and prayed, with absolute faith in Kahammis, for a perfect child.

Sea-ossum and Callicum slipped out of the bay in the darkness; Kahammis overheard Aneetsick telling them to go to Hoxem, grateful that for once his instincts matched her own.

Airley explained that his expedition had been underway for twenty-one days, chopping through the bush, crossing lakes in borrowed canoes. Using guides from the southern villages, they had mapped the settlements and the topography as they went. No guide had been willing to come out to the coast, leaving them to hack their way across the mountains on ancient hunting trails.

Sitting across from his guest, Aneetsick drank tea out of a bowl carved by Kalowish. He asked himself whether the expedition was merely one more peculiarity of the white men, or was there a hidden purpose? At first the fort had seemed distant enough, but with every year came further, unexpected encroachment. Now, drawings of his people's land!

Morning brought the west wind, hurrying Callicum and Sea-ossum home from Hoxem. Boys no more, they flexed their shoulders with bashful pride as they escorted Jean-Louis to Aneetsick's hearth. Aneetsick had tamed them not through reprimands but through responsibility; they alone collected the precious eagle down from the nests, and they alone dove amongst the breaching whales, filling boxes with ceremonial water.

Grumbling after yet another miserable night, the men on the ridge watched as their leader headed down to meet the new arrival. They commented on Jean-Louis's beard, wilder even than theirs, and on his plodding inspection of the maps.

Though he towered over Robert Airley, Jean-Louis was shrinking from a barrage of questions, searching his mind for the English words he had been taught by his mother.

"You've lived here how many years?" Airley rephrased his inquiry several times, trying to keep the incredulity out of his voice. He consulted his most recent sketch, marking Hoxem. He was particularly interested in visiting a large village which was farther up the coast. Jean-Louis became immediately protective of his friends at Klinniklinnikaht, and he pointed out the wind and the whitecaps, obstacles to travelling north.

The childen cavorted around the ridge as the mildewed tarps came down. Patches of blue sky appeared along the horizon, then vanished behind moving grey walls. Henry piddled unself-consciously into a heap of clamshells, and the men snorted over their tea.

Amusements had been minimal during their weeks of slogging through the bush. Their feet were rotting, provisions had spoiled, and fresh venison had proved as elusive as Airley's hopes that a mysterious inland tribe would show them an easier route. Dried meat from one of the villages had given them violent cramps, and Airley had insisted on scaling every last bluff. With all the land in the world, it was beyond their comprehension why anyone would value this inhospitable coast. Even so, they were tough and stoic men out of the Royal Navy and the Royal Engineers, trained to be loyal despite their doubts.

Moochinnick, bored by the dreariness of winter, brightened at the prospect of accompanying the expedition back to Port Albert. The breeze had freshened and he, as well as Jean-Louis, persuaded Airley not to head north. Aneetsick ordered Kalowish, Sa-sat-kis, and six of Nootseetaht's best paddlers to ready the canoes. Moochinnick was placed in charge of receiving the promised payment at the fort. The passengers took a long time to settle in the canoes, twisting for a last look as they crossed the bay.

"Like a bloody row of crows," remarked one man, indicating the villagers, who watched them leave. "You bloody well can't tell them apart!"

His companions nodded, relieved to be returning to civilization, but as they passed the spit, they gripped the gunwales in alarm at the lift and dip of the swell.

When the canoes were gone from sight, the children inspected the flattened ground of the camp. Henry found a tiny blue bottle containing traces of a white ointment. They all took turns sticking their noses into the bottle, squealing at the smell. Even Callicum and Sea-ossum could not resist a sniff, rolling their eyes in disgust.

Jean-Louis and Aneetsick stood together on the beach. Jean-Louis cleared his throat, feeling that he should say something, though he and Aneetsick seldom conversed.

"What do they want?" growled Aneetsick, before Jean-Louis could speak. "The authority of the government! Who is this famous chief I have never met, who gives away the right to make pictures of our land?" He stalked off towards the river, as if needing proof that all the intruders had left.

Kahammis sat at the hearth, chewing on her pipe. Pali set aside the bark skirt she was mending and came over to nestle with her grandmother.

"Why are you sad?" asked Pali, blinking up at Kahammis.

Kahammis shook her head.

Pali nibbled the tip of her braid. "Jean-Louis promised to buy me a dress, Grandma! Do you know what a dress is?" She smiled and squirmed in her grandmother's lap. "A real dress!"

The expedition reached Port Albert at dusk, driven from behind by an icy wind. At times the canoes surfed with the swell, the faces of the Indians shining with exhilaration and the bear grease they had slathered over themselves to shield them from the cold. Robert Airley was glad that it was only grease, and not the garish red and black paint of which they were so fond.

The hired paddlers scarcely missed a stroke all day, a feat of endurance in utter contrast to the sloth and debauchery Airley had been used to around the fort. When he had questioned why they must swerve extra miles off a rocky point, Charlie insisted that he stand up, so that he could see the vicious rush of tidewater closer to shore. He hastily resumed the security of his seat, aware of Charlie's smirk, and the apprehensive glances of his men. The Indians never took their eyes off the ocean and seemed to communicate with each other through their paddles, from bow to stern.

When they arrived at the harbour, Charlie slyly held out for twice the number of blankets that had been arranged. Sidling closer, he suggested that whisky would settle the price. Airley nearly laughed out loud at Charlie's gall. He had no illusions, however; within hours, the Bonnie Prince and his cohorts would be spewing and squabbling outside the shanties and saloons that had sprung up between the harbour and the fort walls. Inside, of course, would be Airley's own men, celebrating their just rewards.

Later in the evening, after everyone was paid, he spread his maps to dry beneath the oil lamps on his desk. He was chilled to the bone, and still queasy from the motion of the swell. Though the expedition had been gruelling, it was a success, and he looked forward to filling his journal with all that he had observed. He prided himself on his treatment of the Indians, although his men assured him that he was wasting his time. He was too charitable to show his opinion of the native way of life, and indeed, hoped to return to Charlie's village soon.

His stomach would have settled better if he had not missed supper, and he recalled the smoked fish from the village; it had been amazingly flavourful and sweet, devoured by his men. Aneetsick, the hard-eyed chief, had sat like a king beside the huge hearth in his lodge, sipping tea out of a whale-shaped wooden bowl, which he held between his fingers as if it were made of the finest porcelain. Everywhere Airley looked, he had been struck by such scenes. He remembered the old crone on the beach, brooding over her stick; she could have been lifted out of a medieval tale.

And who was that Frenchman, Jean-Louis? Was it true that he had spent eleven years eking out a living in a remote cove? Too remote, for when asked to estimate the worth of the local forests, Jean-Louis had lapsed into unintelligible poetry. Had he rejected society, embracing a primitive state? It was not unheard of, nor was it unheard of to take an Indian wife, although during his travels, Airley had found the native women to be extremely chaste, keeping themselves separate even from their own men. There had been one small incident he could not forget. A young woman had been nursing her baby in the lodge as he drank tea with Aneetsick. Her breasts glistened in the firelight, and his single, shocked glimpse of her swollen brown nipple was burned into his brain. Aware of the stirring in his groin, he bent shakily over his maps.

As he retraced his route, he knew that before him lay a land of unlimited potential, not only for timber and coal but for people, for the beauty and space that people deserved. He had come to believe that mean-spiritedness was as much a consequence of setting as of soul, thinking back to the petty rivalries that had ruled the gloomy English town of his birth. Smiling, he told himself that he was beginning to sound like Jean-Louis! His superiors wanted facts, not philosophy. He assembled his scale and his pencils, filling out the rough sketch he had made of the bay and spit. He visualized the line of cedar houses, the canoes like dories in orderly rows, the comforting layers of woodsmoke. There had even been a bald eagle watching from the top of a fir tree.

During the journey down the coast, he had tried to get information from Charlie, who was remarkably intelligent despite a hulking appearance made worse by a misshapen skull and a foul mane of hair. Several times he had asked Charlie the name of the village, his notebook balanced on his knees as he painstakingly copied the sounds. But what sense now could he make of Charlie's huffs and grunts?

He frowned over his notebook, remembering the gusts that had begun on the beach, chasing them all the way south. "Yes!" he exclaimed aloud. "Yes, of course. Squally Bay!"

He neatly labelled his map and leaned back in his chair, yawning, satisfied.

~~~:~~~

Kahammis shrugged off her basket and settled into the warm grass. She joined a group of women who were resting in the sunshine, their baskets filled with the curly-tipped new shoots of bracken ferns. Across the meadow, a male grouse beckoned its mate, humpha-humpha-humpha, sky and earth vibrating with the passions of spring.

During the night Kahammis had dreamed that she was with Sheebo, in a place of such bliss that upon waking she had pressed her hands to her mouth, bereft. But now, as her glance passed over Yanis, she understood the meaning of the dream.

"Yanis," she called, "no more twisting or turning at the loom for you!"

The women cheered and teased Yanis, who was too stunned with hope to speak.

Pali led the procession back to the village, singing as always, like a little wren. Her puberty had been celebrated over the winter, and although she had received her adult name, Jean-Louis continued to call her Pali and so did everyone else. The naming ceremony had been hosted by Kalowish with his customary thoughtfulness; he gave away exquisitely carved boxes, utensils and tools which he had worked years to accumulate. He had taken on his sons as apprentices, though Callicum and Sea-ossum found many distractions, preferring the axes and the anecdotes of Jean-Louis to their father's quiet craftsmanship.

That night the village feasted on the steamed fiddlehead ferns, and on fresh halibut caught by Jean-Louis. He entertained the crowd with his epic battle to land the enormous fish, all because, the audience howlingly concluded, he had failed to achieve the required state of purity.

Sa-sat-kis and Yanis hid their beaming faces, and not even Aneetsick begrudged the two slaves their moment of happiness, raising his rattle and announcing his gift of emancipation to the forthcoming child. This was a bold move, and Kahammis was deeply touched; she held Aneetsick's gaze for a long moment across the hearth before he returned to the conversations of the men.

The sun lingered over the water, and the children went outside to chase each other around the grassy slope while their parents watched indulgently, wondering how it was possible to run with bellies so full. Loudest and sturdiest of all the children was Moochinnick's six-year-old son Henry, who charged behind his spear, a sharpened stick, bellowing like the young bull sea lions that wintered on the reefs. His hair had been cut to a stubble to discourage lice, and he was endearingly vain, daubing his chest and cheeks every morning with paint. Only Kahammis thought back to his never-mentioned grandfather and great-grandfather, Tatoosch and Quassoon.

Callicum and Sea-ossum were sitting with a group of youths. They jumped up, calling out excitedly as white sails appeared beyond the spit. They were familiar with every vessel that travelled the coast, even to the personalities of the captains and their crews. Every now and then, as a special privilege, Moochinnick would allow them to paddle his canoe to Port Albert. Moochinnick had grown enormous on his favourite meal of rice and sugar; he no longer paddled himself and barely squeezed into the many uniforms he had acquired from the ships. He astutely kept his whisky drinking separate from Nootseetaht; Paonea and Chee-uxqua would have roasted him with their wrath.

"It's the *Coast Princess*!" shouted Callicum. He and Sea-ossum had been aboard once, with Jean-Louis at Hoxem, negotiating over logs. They watched, thrilled, as the schooner tacked slowly and cautiously through the gap, into the land breeze. The sails luffed, and the clank of the anchor chain echoed around the bay. They counted five people on deck: a man, a woman, the captain and two crewmen. Only twice before had vessels anchored overnight, on grounding tides. Moochinnick was ceremoniously paddled out, reporting back to Aneetsick that the *Coast Princess* was delivering passengers to a destination he had never heard of, Squally Bay.

Darkness fell, and the villagers sang and drummed in honour of the fiddleheads and the halibut, and the babe in Yanis's womb. But frequently they came out of the lodges to look at the schooner in the bay, lit by a watery moon.

In the morning, woken by the clattering of oars, the children scampered down the slope as the schooner's tender was rowed ashore. A crewman unloaded a pile of boxes, going back for more. The male passenger supervised, keeping a stern eye on the children and on the rising tide, which constantly threatened the boxes on the beach. The captain came ashore, escorting the female passenger. She carried an infant concealed in her cape, and wore a hat almost as wide as the box on which she sat. She smiled timidly at the children, who pressed closer, clutching each other's hands. Aneetsick leaned against the doorpost of the lodge, keeping track of the comings and goings with hooded eyes.

Kahammis also watched, from her weaving mat around the corner of the lodge. The captain spoke animatedly with the male passenger, and they climbed up to the ridge, gazing around the bay. She lowered her head as they passed by. The captain was very tall and thin, and when he took off his hat to rub his forehead she saw that his hair, as she suspected, was red. Her mouth was dry, and her fingers gripped the bark strands. She could not make herself look away. She thought she had buried the longing to see him, a longing so painfully tangled with her hatred for Quassoon and her love for Kalowish. Now that he was here, she wished desperately that he would leave.

Around noon the anchor chain rattled onto the foredeck of the *Coast Princess* and the villagers, puzzled, set aside their tasks. Kalowish and Sa-sat-kis wiped the sweat off their faces; they were straddling an overturned canoe on the delta, repairing cracks with warmed spruce gum. Silently they watched the schooner, with the captain at the helm, sail out of the bay. The woman drooped beneath her hat while her husband paced the beach. Over the next hour, he transferred the heap of belongings to a new location, on the ridge beside the cedar tree. With elaborate hand signals, he intercepted Callicum and Sea-ossum as they were heading out to check crab traps. Though they had picked up many words from the fort, they good-naturedly joined the pantomime and helped with the move.

Aneetsick's face became more and more drawn. Finally he sent Moochinnick up the ridge. By now the villagers were buzzing with their interpretations of the morning's events.

Moochinnick returned, out of breath. "Welcome to Squally Bay!" he announced, guffawing.

"Squally Bay?" From where she sat around the corner of the lodge, Kahammis heard the sarcasm in Aneetsick's voice. "What nonsense are you talking?"

"Those people up there," Moochinnick waved towards the ridge. "They bought the land here from the government at the fort. They have a map," he added, shrugging blithely, "and on the map, this is Squally Bay."

Kahammis could feel Aneetsick's shock. "Bought land here? Do they not have land of their own?"

"The government told those people, this land is to be used." Moochinnick glanced uphill, where a tent was being unpacked. "His name is Mr. William McPhee." Scowling, Moochinnick thought about the expressions on the faces of William McPhee and his wife as he had gone up to greet them: from her, horrified awe, from him, the same frosty reproach that had been directed at the children. Not even the lowliest chiefs on the coast would reveal such feelings at such a diplomatic moment. Furthermore, William McPhee had held the map just out of reach, as if Moochinnick was not smart enough to recognize his own home.

"What do you mean, used?" hissed Aneetsick.

"The government," Moochinnick replied testily. How could he explain the government? It was a higher spirit which behaved in the most contradictory ways. For example, whisky, which was supposedly forbidden, flowed like a river around the fort, where the people worked harder than slaves, the very same people who had confided to Moochinnick that they had left their own lands to be free.

Moochinnick shifted uncomfortably, recalling an earlier visit to Port Albert, when he had been sought out by a group of government men. They asked many questions about Nootseetaht, comparing his answers with the notes on Robert Airley's maps. The following day, they had wanted to meet with him again, and Moochinnick revelled in his importance. In simple language the terms were explained: all the land now belonged to the white people, but for a compensation of several pounds per family, the village would remain intact and the villagers could still hunt and fish. Moochinnick thought for a while, and could find no fault with this arrangement. The payment was calculated and accepted by Moochinnick on Aneetsick's behalf, for it was well known around the fort that he was married to Aneetsick's daughter, and had the confidence of the chief. Inflamed with good intentions, Moochinnick decided to purchase for the people of Nootseetaht luxuries they seldom saw. The weeks passed until one day the canvas bag of money was empty; the gifts had been gambled away. Disconsolate, he realized that he ought to go home. At home with his wife and family, wonderfully, nothing seemed changed. The money became irrelevant; he was Moochinnick, an already rich man.

"Go back!" ordered Aneetsick, wiping the stupid grin off Moochinnick's face. Since the newcomers had not requested to meet with Aneetsick, he was struck by an awful possibility: had it been assumed that Moochinnick was chief? Even so, Aneetsick refused to leave his post and go up himself. "Find out what this means."

The woman huddled on the box, the baby crying beneath the folds of her cape. William McPhee wrestled with the canvas, nodding irritably at Moochinnick.

Kahammis glanced up from her weaving, watching Moochinnick and listening to the baby's cries. She was struggling to calm herself and concentrate on her work.

She was making a basket for Tatatoe, overlaying, with dyed bear grass, the Mannakaht crest which Tatatoe had explained to her on the day they first met. Forty years later she retrieved the details from her memory: raven, herring, cat with the long, slinky tail. Tatatoe's world was crumbling; Hasallum was no longer fit for his role as chief, and Kleeshinnin was too mild and loyal to usurp his father. Despite Neetsa's efforts to maintain the trade, the legacy of Paquacheenish was slipping away. Many of the best warriors had left for Port Albert, where they gathered by the hundreds from all over the coast, visiting and drinking and gambling, oblivious to the summons of their heritage in their veins.

Moochinnick returned to Aneetsick. "Growing things," he announced grandly. "Just like around the fort. And," he added, puffed up with the significance of his information, "we're going to have a mill for cutting logs, by the river."

Aneetsick looked at Moochinnick as if he were a slug. Though fleeting, it was a look not lost on Moochinnick, tucked into a corner of his brain while he continued to smile affably, pityingly, at his chief. The bays and inlets were beginning to hum with parties of newcomers, building houses and mills. Having missed the chance to dominate in trade, was Nootseetaht going to be left out of this as well? Perhaps, reflected Moochinnick, Aneetsick was getting too old to understand progress. The white men at the fort valued Moochinnick, roaring at his jokes and relying on him to smooth their deals. With his influence, Nootseetaht could become a busy, thriving place.

Kahammis set aside her basket and picked up her pipe. Aneetsick stalked off, most likely heading for the caves upriver, she thought, where he stored his collection of guns. Moochinnick spat scornfully, and Kahammis inhaled as if hoping she could burn out the heaviness in her heart.

Paonea and Chee-uxqua stood beside the main lodge, clasping and unclasping their hands in agitation as they listened to the wailing baby on the ridge. Finally they called Pali, who put on the dress Jean-Louis had given her, a treasured calico gown bundled up at the waist so that she could walk.

Pali went reluctantly up to the ridge. When she approached the baby, the man rushed over, and she drew back, pointing and making rocking motions with her arms. As soon as she lifted the baby from the woman, the squalling ceased. She could not help but giggle, crooning and swaying around the tent and the boxes and the tree. The infant took huge shuddering breaths, gazing over Pali's shoulder with eyes like the tiny blue flowers which popped out of the moss in early spring. The man went over to the woman and helped her to her feet. They walked slowly past the lodges, past Kalowish and Sa-sat-kis on the delta, to the river. Pali followed proudly with the baby, while Paonea and Chee-uxqua peered from behind the doorposts.

In the evening, the villagers assembled in Aneetsick's lodge. They ate the leftover halibut, and the crabs brought up from the traps, and again they celebrated the onset of the harvest season. The voices of the young girls climbed sweetly over the earthy harmonies of their mothers, and the boys and the men stamped their feet, leading with the words of the old, old songs to which, on this night, they instinctively turned.

Sagging against their parents, the children were jolted awake by a commotion at the door. Drums stopped, voices fell away. William McPhee stood at the entrance, his face strangely reddened in the fire-light. For a few seconds, he seemed not to know why he was there.

"Charlie!" he shouted.

Moochinnick heaved himself up off the mats, stepping through the crowd.

"Charlie, this has got to stop!" William McPhee glanced jerkily around the lodge, into the dark, dumbfounded eyes. "This is upsetting my wife! We cannot sleep!"

When he withdrew, everyone turned to Moochinnick, who had begun to perspire.

"This is upsetting his wife," stuttered Moochinnick.

The crowd stared at him blankly.

"The singing! The drums! The noise is upsetting his wife!"

Aneetsick rose, and in a voice ringing with dignity, brought the evening to an end. He thanked his guests, waiting as each one left.

Kahammis woke early the following morning, wondering what had roused her. A breeze lifted the new leaves and a child mumbled, dreaming; the gulls chittered faintly beyond the reefs. A mink slipped stealthily over the grassy spit, whiskers twitching, fur streaked with dew. Closer, closer crept the mink, the oystercatchers trembling on their nest. They waited and they waited, then in dread they abandoned their speckled eggs, fleeing along the shore. Back and forth they ran, peep-peeping their distress.

Kahammis heard them from her sleeping platform, and then she heard boxes banging on the ridge, and she was as bewildered as the oystercatchers at the swift finality of change.

~~~:~~~

Kahammis was given the last canoe made by Hasallum before he died. She had gone up to Klinniklinnikaht in mid-summer for an eelgrass feast, seeking him out in the clearing where he worked over a blackened hull. When he turned at the sound of her footsteps, she saw that his eyes were rambling and opaque under wisps of white hair. He worked his adze to an inner plan, assessing, caressing, amidst a sea of scented chips and curls. When she spoke his name, he laughed delightedly and took her to a small canoe resting on stands in the shade. He had carved the Kalowish crest into the prow, and along each side of the bow flowed a shower of dancing rays. It was as if she stood looking at the canoe which had carried her north to Quassoon and then home again, now rotting on the beach, used as a barricade by the children in their mock wars.

Shortly after the eelgrass feast, the ship they called the Smoking Tree had brought to Klinniklinnikaht a man who requested to meet with the chief. He was not a captain, and he carried himself in an austere manner not seen amongst the trading crews. He wore a long black dress which trailed through the mud of the lagoon, quite unlike any of the uniforms obtained by Moochinnick or Paquacheenish.

Kleeshinnin had acted as interpreter in a meeting filled with pauses, Hasallum musing over each question presented by the visitor. The questions had grown longer and more complex, and the visitor's lips had thinned, his tone sharpening and his grey eyes darting between Kleeshinnin and Hasallum, who, upon sighting a raven over the trees, began to croak and hop on his crooked old legs.

Abruptly, the visitor went back to the ship. Hasallum turned to his son in surprise; he had intended no disrespect and was only illustrating the powerful connection between the coast people and the creatures of their crests. In the days following the ship's departure, however, he became sadder and sadder, as if, in that simple misunderstanding, he had lost the trust which had sustained him for so long. Not even the kisses of his grandson restored his smile. One evening, at supper, Tatatoe realized that he was missing; Kleeshinnin and Jean-Louis searched for weeks without success. In the minds of those who loved him, his disappearance was irrevocably linked to that last, impulsive little jig on the edge of the lagoon.

Again Kahammis went up to Klinniklinnikaht, shearing her hair and rubbing ashes over her face with Hasallum's family. Ravens from afar converged over the inlet, grieving with guttural clucks, and the people consoled themselves thinking that if only the visitor from the ship could have witnessed this black-winged lament, he would have understood Hasallum's point. Kahammis wished that she could bring Tatatoe home with her, but recent events at Nootseetaht would only compound Tatatoe's misery, events from which Kahammis herself sought escape.

Immediately upon his arrival, William McPhee had set to work building a house on a level knoll beside the river path. The house was made from the fir trees surrounding the knoll, felled by Jean-Louis, who came from Hoxem and camped on the ridge while he helped. The McPhees moved in before the roof was completed, fastening canvas temporarily over the beams.

For the villagers, the construction of a lodge was a wondrous, collaborative event. A family would save for years, amassing the cedar boards, the poles, and the feast gifts required. Each aspect of the McPhee house was both novel and controversial; not even Jean-Louis could explain the maze of inner walls and the illogical positioning of the hearths.

William McPhee asked the Nootseetaht men for assistance, and they went willingly, though they soon found the sawing tedious in the heat. After a morning of cutting planks, Callicum and Sea-ossum poked their blisters and meandered away. They grinned sheepishly and retreated to their canoe when William called after them, wagging his finger, "You'll only get half a day's pay!"

No one consumed food the way William did, at exactly the same moment each day, and no one measured work as he did, every hour recorded on paper in a hoarded box. His helpers were incredulous when he read out the day's tallies and tasks; if they worked from one full moon to another, they would receive two blankets, sugar, tobacco, and rice. They believed him, but who could endure?

It was all this and more which Kahammis left behind as she paddled out of the bay one evening at the hot, crackling end of summer. She needed to be alone, to listen to the ocean, and to feel the memory of Hasallum carried within the canoe. Still she searched the kelp beds for the sight of a small, furry head; at Pali's naming feast, Kalowish had given her a dish, an otter with a spiked urchin set into its belly for a lid. Would her grandchildren never know the otters except carved in wood?

She glanced across her shoulder, distracted by the marker on the tip of the spit. Sea-ossum and Callicum had ferried William around the bay while he lowered a weighted rope from the bow, testing the water's depth. He tacked markers to the trees, establishing a channel from the lone pine to one of the last firs beside his house.

The McPhees sat in their new parlour, drinking tea. The windows were draped with muslin, since the glass panes ordered from San Francisco had not yet arrived. Mrs. McPhee, who had asked to be called Julia, was sitting in a wooden structure which all the village children had ridden, on the day that the McPhees had been at Port Albert arranging supplies. Henry had rocked so violently that he had flown over backwards with a terrible crash, and Pali nearly fainted with fright and shame for it was she, guardian of the infant, who had allowed the children inside.

A pile of cedar blocks lay on the delta, cut from a log floated downriver. Earlier in the day, Kalowish and Sa-sat-kis had been splitting shakes for the roof, and the crisp, wet sound of the separating shakes filled William with satisfaction as he supervised from the house, where he was putting up shelves. Long before noon, for no apparent reason, the two men had set down their mauls and vanished. Now William stewed over his teacup, furious at them for quitting work, and furious at himself for relying on Charlie to deliver the glass. He pressed his tired shoulders into a chair he had put together out of plank ends; one of his understandings with Julia was that they would not ever squat on the floor.

His mannerisms, so unlike those of Jean-Louis, intrigued the Nootseetaht people. What appealed to them most was his prominent nose, strangely reminiscent of Paquacheenish, their legendary benefactor. On the rare occasions when they came face to face with him, they were drawn to this nose while quailing before his intense blue gaze. He shaved daily, using a piece of metal sharp enough to slice their skin, when they had secretly tested the blade. His fastidiousness was encouraging after their experiences with the trading crews, for they were a people who knew the benefits of clean living, to the soul.

But his spirit, feared Kahammis, was like the spirit of the osprey which glided over the windless bay at dawn, while William razored soap off his cheeks in slashing lines. He shaved on the porch of his house, just up from the delta, where the osprey hunted with ruthless grace.

Kahammis and the other women had been heading up the river path with their baskets and digging sticks at daybreak, glancing shyly at William on his porch, when the woodland birds had twittered into the undergrowth and an eagle entered the bay, where the osprey was diving for fish.

The great eagle, which had presided over Nootseetaht for many years, took offense at the osprey, and the osprey began to climb, with the eagle in pursuit. The women had turned at the sight of the two birds arcing back and forth across the disintegrating moon. Kahammis had sensed the eagle's outrage as the osprey climbed in ever higher circles, a sculpin still in its talons, a mere speck in the sky, until finally the eagle had plunged downwards and flapped into the trees.

Idling in her canoe amongst the reefs, Kahammis noticed the same eagle beating slowly along the shore. The gulls rose clamorously, and only when the eagle passed by did they return to their rocks.

Jean-Louis was sitting with the McPhees in their parlour, their guest for tea. He watched admiringly as the eagle crossed the bay and landed on a sandy mound at the river mouth, joining a group of yearlings picking over a fish carcass in the dusk. The arrival of the patriarch brought fresh protest from the crows, jeering and feinting from the safety of the conifers along the shore.

"What a racket!" William nodded at the musket propped in the corner. "I'll give them something to complain about!"

"You'll wake the baby." Julia spoke softly, hunched over a dress she was sewing for Pali, out of fabric Jean-Louis had purchased at the fort.

William's attention went back to the cedar blocks. "Why are they so lazy?" he asked Jean-Louis, who sat at the table, cutting leather hinges for doors.

It was Sa-sat-kis who had put a stop to the shake-cutting. William had insisted on shouting at him and Kalowish as if they were equals, although Jean-Louis had explained many times that Kalowish was the master, and Sa-sat-kis was the slave. Sa-sat-kis felt compelled to put aside his maul and go upriver, where he and Kalowish explored the cool, quiet forest for potential canoes.

Jean-Louis stroked his beard. Content for days with only his violin for company, he was slow to reply, a slowness made worse by William's impatience, and by the thick Scots accent that took long moments to decipher. Julia sometimes spoke to Jean-Louis in formal French; she had been to Paris as a girl. Whenever Jean-Louis was near Julia, the blood coursed through his body and he felt tingling and weak.

"I treat them well! I pay them a fair wage!" William glared through the muslin at the lodges.

"Lazy?" Jean-Louis shook his head. "You'll see them out here on the delta when the dog salmon come. Thousands of fish caught and cleaned, enough to feed the village for a year. Enough to give away," he added pointedly. Aneetsick kept the McPhee household supplied with dried salmon and game, freeing William to work.

"Here?" William strode to the window. "Here is where I'm putting the mill."

"Oh no," spluttered Jean-Louis. "Here is where they harvest the dog salmon."

"I own this land! I need to put the mill here, to run the saw."

"There isn't enough water to run the saw," retorted Jean-Louis, his neck prickling against his flannel collar. Julia bent over her stitching, and Jean-Louis refrained from mentioning how the level of the river rose in the spring, with the snow melt and the rains.

"I'll build a flume." William sat down, controlling his irritation.

The work of clearing his land had been overwhelming, and he was clinging to his rituals and his standards with a fervor that was driving him away from Julia, when they should be coming together, united against the wilderness. Daughter of an eccentric Edinburgh scholar,

Julia possessed few pioneering skills. For the entire previous week she had been tracing hearts with a stencil; the native girl, Pali, looked after Maggie, even through the night. It was, he admitted, better to have Julia sleeping at his side than attending to a fretful child. Since the ordered paint had not arrived, Julia had used a concoction from the natives: chewed salmon eggs, ochre, and spit. Now the walls of their first home were decorated with hearts that had dried to the colour of blood.

Certainly he sympathized; it was Julia who dealt with the natives on a daily basis, isolated from her own kind. One night she had woken in a fever, trying to recite all the native words for the wind; he had been shocked at the gibberish coming out of her mouth. The moonlight through the muslin illuminated her skin beneath her nightgown, and he had gently pulled her down, swallowing his distress. In the tent they had slept on makeshift cots, Jean-Louis snoring nearby. Prior to the tent, they had rented a dingy room in Port Albert, and before that had been the months of deprivation on the ship. By the time the house was ready, his desire for her was almost incapacitating; he staggered away from her in the mornings, slapping river water on his face and neck. He wondered at the men toiling alongside him; did they, too, succumb to their women night after night? His only salvation was to exhaust himself on the saw, on his land.

He looked around with a start as Pali appeared at the parlour door, holding his rumpled daughter in her arms. Julia made no move to take the child, waving Pali away. Maggie had been born on the ship, and she and Julia had been sick for most of the journey. By some miracle, Maggie thrived in Pali's care.

Pali carried Maggie down the porch steps and along the beach, skirting the eagles flocked around the fish. Jean-Louis watched Pali through the window; nothing pleased him more than to hear her singing in the kitchen, where she was learning to cook. He finished his tea and bade good evening to the McPhees, stopping at the village on his way back to his tent.

The tide was running against Kahammis as she paddled back through the gap. She swung around behind the spit, looking across at the row of lodges, their roofs bathed in light. The fresh shakes on the McPhee house were also lit up, and what the sun could accept, so must she. Hasallum had told her many times: our wealth is a river, belonging to all living things between the mountains and the sea.

Rumours of land sales did not concern her, for land had always been occupied by heritage. They had enough, she reasoned, to share with the McPhees.

What did concern her was this: why had the McPhees deserted their original home? Who was Julia, with her skin like dentalia shell beneath the hat, wanting to touch the baskets, and to speak the words for the eagle, the wind? To live in a divided box, with only a husband and a baby and no other kin ... this was the fate of a slave, or worse. Yet Julia seemed to suffer more from confusion than disgrace, while her husband greeted each morning like a warrior, not an outcast.

Only Maggie seemed undisturbed; she had woven a spell over the village with her flower-blue eyes. She crawled from one lap to another around the hearth, filching berries and slurping juice from shells, and once she had even grabbed the pendants off Aneetsick's chest, the women tittering behind their hands. Pali, who looked after her, was the envy of every other girl with her new duties, her dresses and hairbows, and her proximity to the treasures in the boxes and chests.

Pacing back and forth in front of the window, William noticed the small canoe by the spit. He stopped beside his wife. "Don't do that!"

Julia blinked over a piece of thread.

"Use your scissors, not your teeth."

Embarrassed at his brusqueness, he squinted through the muslin. He recognized the old crone paddling slowly towards the village; during the construction of his house, he had been forced to pass her several times a day. She was always up on the ridge, surrounded by baskets and children, her black eyes inscrutable behind dirty clouds of pipesmoke. Watching her, he resolved more than ever to maintain his standards and rise to his goals. His vision of Squally Bay would prevail.

It was a vision that drove him constantly to better himself, to challenge the limitations of his birth. He had left the family farm to his five brothers and gone to clerk in an Edinburgh shipping firm, chafing in an office for ten years. Always, over tea in the warehouse, the talk had turned to the possibilities beyond the invoices, beyond the hierarchy of controls in a young man's life. He was twenty-eight when he met Julia, the new organist for the church choir. She wore white, and the sunlight streaming through the stained glass had formed a halo around her golden hair. He could not believe his luck when she accepted his suit.

Julia's father offered them a room until they could afford a place of their own. Julia's parents, he discovered, were freethinkers; he dreaded the day they would meet his father, a rigid and respected Highlander who had served in the military and urged his sons to do the same. His father, however, was too ill to travel to Edinburgh.

After their wedding, escaping the chaos of the household, he and Julia attended talks on the Sandwich Islanders, on the flora and fauna of the Caribbean Sea, on the Maori Revolt. Julia had to leave early from one lecture which included descriptions of scalping and cannibalism in the Americas. They were reassured by an associate of her father, a London scientist, who showed them studies proving the superiority of the British race. Through colonization, the natives would disappear. Why, the scientist asked rhetorically, did the primitive cultures exist at all? William had nodded, but his young wife had fidgeted with the buttons on her skirt. William took her hand, torn between sheltering her and needing her support.

He wrote to the Colonial Office in London, and to his mother's uncle, a prosperous merchant in Montreal. He studied the latest maps of the United States, where land was available for free. When finally the uncle replied, it was with a warning to stay away: his business was almost bankrupt, and the city was ripped apart by riots and rivalries between the British, the French, and those fools who wanted to join the United States.

Then came news of the expansion of the fur companies along the northwest coast. This was the opportunity William had been waiting for: a hospitable climate, and the potential for growth. From across the sea came the cry for settlers to secure the interests of the Crown. He bought passage on a supply barque, selling his share in the barren holdings he had inherited upon his father's death. Two of his brothers promised to follow within the year. He had turned thirty on the day that he and his little family reached Port Albert, too exhausted by the journey to feel more than stupefaction.

At Port Albert he was directed to Robert Airley, chief surveyor for the fledgling government put together to oversee the trading companies, the settlers, and the native people who, despite their declining numbers, occupied the finest harbours and bays. More than a thousand natives had congregated around the fort, transients from all over the coast. He had climbed a corner bastion with the surveyor, from where they could observe the native camp. "Will we be safe?" he had asked, in shocked dismay.

151

Robert Airley assured him that the only real troublemakers were the northerners, for whom the navy stood by. The biggest threat to the expanding colony, explained the surveyor, was the relationship between the Indians and the land. Not even the most insignificant islet or rocky point was without some claim of ownership, based on hereditary connections or, even more obscure, supernatural myths. Battling through the bush had been simpler, he commented wryly, than sorting out the native demands. In William McPhee he felt a kindred spirit, a civility of manner and thought. Few who passed through the fort were educated; for most, what they came to was a paradise compared to what they had left behind.

While the two men consulted, Julia had ventured out of their rented room. Though she remembered the perils so gruesomely savoured by the neighbours in Edinburgh, the long voyage had given her a terror of confinement. The matron of the boarding house loaned her a high-wheeled pram, and she and Maggie jolted along a pot-holed street, veering away from the ox carts and the steaming piles of manure. She had been advised not to go near the harbour, through the shanties and the tents. She had come upon two native women in woven capes and hats like inverted flowerpots, standing with their backs against the fort wall, their expressions implacable, their eyes downcast. She had looked at the charred strips of fish in their baskets, and later asked her husband: is this what we must eat, after gagging over the mouldy bread and cheese on the ship? She had retreated to the overpriced boarding house to nurse Maggie, but when she sank on the bed, puffs of dust rose up from the blankets; William found her later, clinging to Maggie and sneezing, in tears.

Since the best land around the fort had already been taken by the fur companies, to grow food for their employees, the settlers were forced out into the valleys, and up and down the coast. William had scoured the maps with Robert Airley, who, after careful deliberation, recommended a place he had surveyed personally: Squally Bay. Though the entrance was tricky and the anchorage shallow, there was a river and prime stands of trees. The natives, obliging and well-nourished, kept to their village along one shore. Most importantly, the fort was but a day's paddle away.

Native rights to all but the village had been removed by a treaty process begun shortly after the colony was established, based on the survey reports. Robert Airley checked the government records to verify that compensation had been paid. Confident that the McPhees would be satisfied, he witnessed the purchase of two hundred acres along the north bank of the river, an acre a pound. In time-honoured tradition, the McPhees promised to cultivate their land.

So it was not the sunset over Nootseetaht that William saw through his parlour window, as the old crone came ashore. He saw jetties and heard the jangle of ships' rigging; he saw pastures and livestock around the barns. At the periphery of his vision, he sensed the presence of the native people; only recently had he learned that Aneetsick was the chief. Briefly he wondered, what did Aneetsick's hard, black eyes see?

Julia set aside her sewing with a laugh. "Look at this!" she exclaimed, picking up a hinge. "Look what Jean-Louis has done."

Jean-Louis had incised the leather hinges with miniature hearts. William glanced across the table, shaking his head.

Kahammis pulled her canoe along the ramp. Yanis came down to greet her, flushed and depleted in the final days of her pregnancy. They went up to the lodge and Kahammis lay on her sleeping platform, weary from the paddling, and from the worries she had not been able to leave behind. She listened to Pali's description of the new dress, and she watched Maggie sucking hungrily at Paonea's breast. The women had taken pity on Julia, discovering that she could not properly feed her child. Indignant at this latest rival, Johnny helped himself at the sugar bin, pinching Maggie as he slunk by.

Moochinnick was on one of his extended stays in Port Albert. Soon he would return laden with gifts, oblivious to Henry's bullying, Johnny's whining, and Paonea's fixed smiles. The villagers disapproved, yet still Aneetsick depended on Moochinnick's fluency and his connections for trade. Many hoped that Callicum and Sea-ossum would take over from Moochinnick; however, the process of learning was slow, with the risk that they, too, would forget who they were and join the crowds milling around the fort. Better to send Moochinnick, and spare the less experienced men.

As darkness closed in, Aneetsick ordered the fires stoked. Tonight was special: on this night they would summon the dog salmon, provider not only for the people but also for the seals and the birds and the whales, an essential link in the cycle of life and death. Out came the plank drums and the sticks and the rattles, and the voices of the villagers beseeched the Life-Giver. Aneetsick danced beneath an ornate head-dress passed down from his father and grandfather, hooked and fanged and symbolizing the spirit of the fish for which Nootseetaht was famous, the spirit the Wewksah had tried, and failed, to steal. All through the night Aneetsick danced and his people called, and above the drums rose the melancholy sounds of a violin, everyone trusting that far out over the ocean, they would be heard.

Pali had gone back to the McPhee house. She lay on a mat beside the cradle, so that she could comfort Maggie; Paonea had found two more sharp edges of teeth. Lulled by the singing and the tree frogs, Pali slept.

William lurched up from bed, frightening Julia. "What is it?" she cried.

"Drumming again! No wonder they can't put in a day's work." He swung his legs to the floor. "I've had enough."

"Shhh." Julia put her hand on her husband's arm, tilting her head. "Jean-Louis! How superbly he plays!" She sank back. "How I wish I could be there, playing with them." She blushed. "I bought a silver flute, before we left."

William looked at her, aghast.

She turned into the pillow as he pulled away. "I couldn't bear to be without my music," she murmured, barely loud enough for him to hear.

He stared out the window, at the moon rolling like a yolk-yellow ball over the trees. His voice was grating. "How did you pay for it?"

She sighed tremulously. "With the pounds you gave me for dishes and things."

Disappointment dragged down his face.

"But, William," she cried, waving in the direction of the village. "Look how simply they live! What do a few dishes mean?"

"Dishes mean that we are not animals," he replied. "Are you planning that we eat off clamshells? That money was for our company set!"

"I know, I know. But think of the duets," she added, brightening. "Jean-Louis and I can play together in the parlour after dinner." She giggled. "It will be very civilized!"

He looked down at her glowing skin, her hair entwined with the lace on her gown. He could feel her power over him even as he despaired at her thinking; she had been raised with too many ideals, not enough propriety. "We'll buy ten sets," he said gruffly, "with the profits from the mill. We'll have them shipped out from London."

"Are you sure about this mill?" whispered Julia. "Are you sure it must go by the river?"

"Certainly. Where else would it go?"

"Perhaps farther along the bay?" Julia looked up worriedly. "We must not be responsible for depriving them of food."

"What the mill has to offer is a lot more than food!" Through the window, he could hear that the drumming had quickened, accompanied by frantic yells. "When will they stop? How can they do this to me?"

Julia's fingers slid across his bare chest, and he fell onto her with a groan. Maggie stirred, and Pali reached over sleepily to the cradle. All through the night the drummers beat out the rhythms: hunter and hunted, lover and beloved, the fundamental rhythms of life.

~~~:~~~

At precisely the same moment each day, the sawmill shut down.

So sudden and intoxicating was the silence that Kahammis chuckled out loud as she trimmed the basket in her lap. Between her teeth was a fragment of apple skin which she worked with her tongue, chuckling anew.

She was on the ridge beside her tree. The tent that Jean-Louis had camped in all summer was gone. Yanis sat nearby, wiping trickles of milk from her baby's dimpled chin. Sa-sat-kis had thrown himself at the shake blocks, earning wages which he accepted on behalf of Tsuwitty, his new son. The shakes he had split covered the chicken house, the woodsheds, and the boilers that drove the saw, and now Jean-Louis was hinting at building himself a proper house.

Julia came up to the ridge. "Another one?" she asked gaily, offering a wooden bowl.

Kahammis shook her head. Her mouth was still busy with remnants of the first apple, re-experiencing the crispness, the sweetness, the rosy peel. A schooner had arrived from Port Albert laden with everything the McPhees had ordered, and more. Moochinnick was aboard, beaming with munificence, sprawled on the cabin roof, but his two-month absence required a lengthy recuperation sipping Paonea's herbal brews.

The dog salmon run had been the best in years. Aneetsick was able to send to the fort enough dried fish to purchase tea and tobacco, axes and kettles and shovels, metal to make knives and harpoon heads, all the extras which eased his people's labours.

William McPhee witnessed the run: the river was so thick with fish that he could have crossed to the far bank on a bridge of glinting, silver backs. He witnessed the harvesting, the alder fires and the drying racks, and he saw the logic in locating the mill farther along the bay, close to the spit. His brother Donald had arrived from Scotland, bringing the vital components of the saw. Donald was three years younger, loutish-looking but gifted in his comprehension of how bits of clanging metal fit together to do the work of a dozen men. With Donald's help everything became easier, and possible; only a few months after his arrival, the mill was ready to cut wood. When the boilers fired up and the blade began to whine, William realized immediately that Julia had been right, the mill did not belong near their home. He stood on his porch in the evenings, the tension in his shoulders easing slightly at the sight of the distant sheds and stacks of lumber; his vision was filling in.

Julia knelt beside Kahammis, unbuttoning her collar and shaking her hair free of her hat. She reached for the basket Kahammis was holding, and when she twirled it, the vivid colours nearly leapt off the sides. "Beautiful!" she exclaimed, trying out her newly learned words. "Let me buy it from you, please?"

She had given Kahammis a packet of red powder from the fort, and a cube of laundry blueing which they crushed with a stone pestle, dying strands of grass. Now Kahammis was thinking how she could mix in the yellows and the russets and the purples from plants, creating an entirely new dimension to her work. "I'll make you another one," she said firmly. "This one is for my brother."

She presented Aneetsick with the basket that night. His face had become severely lined in recent years, and he moved less swiftly, but with the same aristocratic grace. When he thanked her, she turned away, hiding her pleasure. She had begun to despise Moochinnick, who found hundreds of opportunities to undermine Aneetsick, especially amongst his sons, and the McPhees. His insolence was all the more offensive since it was Aneetsick who had rescued him from the fort and taken him on as a son-in-law. Only Kahammis had known from the beginning: Moochinnick did not belong.

"Hey, what a basket!" Moochinnick lounged on his elbows by the fire. "Make me a big one, decorated with the bear, of course!" His exposed belly shook as he laughed.

No one acknowledged him, gathering instead around Kleeshinnin, who had stopped by to share news on his way home from the fort.

Apparently a trading post had been established at one of the villages in the sound, giving the Mannakaht people access to fort goods in exchange for furs and oil. Quassoon's elderly cousins were still at Quatlukaht, but their best hunters and warriors were long gone. Kleeshinnin noted, with quiet satisfaction, that not a single whale had been taken in the years since Quassoon's death. Moochinnick belched merrily through the conversation, reminding everyone that such troubles were no concern of his. Why should he care about Quatlukaht when his needs were already so well met?

Most interestingly, reported Kleeshinnin, the Sheshalam and the Wasquimaht had turned against each other in a feud too complex and vengeful for outsiders to understand. This news was discussed with relish over pipes and tea, and Aneetsick recalled the carnage in the channel off Klinniklinnikaht, when Ewona and Wikkosum had struck. He thought to himself: how easy it had been to be a hero, then.

As always in the evenings, his thinking came around to William McPhee. A cutter from the fort had blasted its horn and slowed off the spit in the morning, met by the McPhee brothers in their rowboat. The cutter continued north and the McPhees returned to the bay. A short while later, William asked Aneetsick to assemble the villagers on the beach. He belatedly introduced his brother, and then explained the workings of the mill. Just before striding off, he announced, as if it were an afterthought, that the powerful chiefs from Port Albert were on the lookout for the least signs of trouble, with their gunships standing by.

All day Aneetsick had pondered this message, trying to pinpoint the source of the threat in William's voice. His people had gone back to their chores, nervous and subdued; both William and Donald were wearing six-barrelled revolvers in their belts.

The entrance mat lifted as Jean-Louis ducked through. He came from Hoxem where he was passing his hand-logging operation over to Anton Lavalle, a man, like himself, descended from the voyageurs. Anton and his family had given up their farm in Oregon near the site of the first, and largest, fort on the northwest coast. In 1849, when the United States and Britain placed their long-disputed boundary along the forty-ninth parallel, Oregon Territory and the fort fell to the south. But many of the settlers bore no allegiance to the United States, and began looking northward for a new home. The Lavalles remained for six more years, until their farm was washed away in a freak springtime flood. Accompanied by his Indian wife and seven children, Anton was starting over at the age of forty-five. Jean-Louis met the family by chance at Port Albert; to celebrate their safe arrival, Anton had been wearing his voyageur sash. Jean-Louis set aside his plans to sell for a profit and brought the Lavalles to Hoxem, cramming them into his little cabin.

Everyone greeted Jean-Louis, and Chee-uxqua went to find his tin cup. Kahammis studied him through her pipesmoke, thinking that something about him did not seem right; in the morning, she would find out why.

"Terrible business, up in the sound," he commented, settling on a pile of mats.

Heads snapped around. "What business?" demanded Moochinnick.

"Why, the murder of the trader," said Jean-Louis, taken aback. "Well, it isn't certain," he added. "Could've been a drowning. But he's disappeared alright!"

Aneetsick relaxed slightly as William's message immediately became clear. Were the McPhees, he wondered, concerned that they might also disappear? He thought of the gun-filled caves; if only they knew.

During the night, a raccoon snuffled persistently along the boarded edge of the poultry run behind the new house on the knoll. When it finally scrabbled through, the chickens exploded into panic at the yellow-eyed monster in their midst. William rushed out in his night-shirt, cursing and tripping over a tree root. The men in the Nootseetaht lodges half-woke, amused. Never had they imagined such ridiculous birds as the chickens, defenseless but for their cluck. This was the fourth or fifth such disturbance, and the big eagle had snatched a tender meal. If William wanted eggs, they could send some young boys out to the reefs to rob the gull nests in spring. If he wanted fowl, gladly would they snare him a duck, and spare his rest.

William returned to his bed, tossing and fuming until it was time to shave. He decided to hire Henry as a guard. Sa-sat-kis could build a temporary sleeping platform below the roosts.

Nothing fascinated the children more than the chickens. Inquisitive faces ringed the enclosure for hours, marvelling at the sight of the birds ascending and descending the plank bridge into their miniature house. Every once in a while, a flustered hen would deposit an egg on the dirt, and the children would laugh hysterically. Only Pali was allowed to collect the eggs, a duty which she performed with such style and concentration that all the girls in the village imitated her, gliding around with baskets on their arms, noses in the air.

The next morning, Henry claimed his new-found importance with a heavy stick, ripping away at the surrounding underbrush and nearly decapitating Johnny, who tagged behind. Johnny offered his grimy collection of boiled sweets for the privilege of sharing the bed. Henry took the candy, then advised their mother of Johnny's plan. Paonea embraced her young son; she needed him herself, she told Johnny, to keep her warm.

His problem solved, William set off for the mill. Soon the sound of the saw reverberated around the bay, reaching the delta where Kahammis walked. The sandpipers ran confusedly on dainty, almost invisible legs; swooping and swerving, they vacated the bay. Would they return in spring, Kahammis wondered? Would Nootseetaht lose this aerial ballet? She carried the weight of the saw's whine between her eyes, sometimes more, sometimes less, a jangling point of pain.

By noon the sun had warmed the breeze, saturating the air with autumnal glow. Two swans wafted against the far shore, stragglers south. Kalowish worked on the delta over a roughed-out canoe. With him was Jean-Louis, on whom Kahammis was keeping an eye, intrigued. Jean-Louis usually exuded energy like a waterfall; now, his adze stuck in his hands. Kalowish was puzzled, but too polite to refuse an offer of help.

The porch door on the McPhee house banged open, and Jean-Louis jumped as though he had been shot. Pali and Julia burst out in splat-tered aprons, waving long spoons purple with juice. Behind them tottered Maggie, just learning to walk. Pali and Julia were trying to make jelly with the last of the salalberries, but despite their best efforts, no amount of boiling or sugar could produce the taste Julia had hoped for, and they gave up, screaming with laughter and despair.

Kalowish paused over his adze, mystified by the feeble noises coming from Jean-Louis. The day before, at Hoxem, Jean-Louis had experienced a huge, internal shift, as if after experiencing life in shades of grey, he suddenly found himself exposed to a dazzling kaleidoscope of colours. The cause of this was the realization that he loved Pali and wanted her to be his wife. Excusing himself to the Lavalles, he departed at once for Nootseetaht.

But now that he was here, he was overcome with inadequacy and had spent the whole morning bumbling around Kalowish. The sight of Pali, laughing and spinning and covered with jelly, felled him like the final cut to a massive, undercut trunk. He floundered off in the direction of the mill, hoping that William could put him to work.

Kahammis followed him along the beach. So, she deduced, it was their little Pali who had brought him to his knees. She had flitted and danced and was now flown from her nest, for the benefit of the McPhees. Was Jean-Louis such a shocking choice?

She left him at the mill and stayed in the lodge with her pipe all through the afternoon and the evening, oblivious to the bustle and the gossip around the hearths. The women had a bottomless interest in the McPhee household, particularly during the past weeks. Julia had been ill, and Pali, in attendance, relayed her symptoms back to the village. Paonea sent teas, and now Julia was up again, organizing picnics to the meadows, preserving fruit, salting fish. The women feared that she was pregnant again, too soon, in their opinion, after Maggie's birth. With good-humoured ribaldry, they speculated on the love-making in the iron bed almost as big as a ship, in the sleeping room. And they scrutinized William as he marched below the village every day, on his way to work at the mill.

Julia sat by the parlour window, watching the last of the light over the bay. William and Donald conversed, as they did each evening, on the prospects of the mill. Donald had moved into the tiny spare room. The presence of an outsider had a calming effect, providing a fresh ear for the hopes and dreams which Julia had been listening to since Edinburgh, when she and William had strolled the waterfront, waiting for their ship. All going well, another brother, Georgie, would arrive from Scotland within the year.

William looked down at his ledger where he recorded every piece of lumber produced by the mill. Ninety-foot-long spars from Squally Bay were on their way to ports around the world; with the forests of eastern Europe depleted, the northwest coast of the new continent was a valuable source of masts. The demand for pilings, for the wharf expansion at San Francisco, far exceeded what the McPhee brothers could supply. They needed oxen to haul the logs and make pasture of the land. For months they had been awaiting the delivery of their oxen, already paid for, from the fort. William realized that he would have to go to Port Albert himself; it was clear that Charlie had no intention of sharing deck space with a pair of horned beasts.

He closed his ledger, sighing. "We need more workers, that's all there is to it."

When Julia looked up from her rocking chair, he noticed how thin her face was, and pale. At Port Albert he would buy tonic for her, and treats, the tinned biscuits she craved. And a fancy dinner set; his Julia would not go without.

"We need to educate the workers we have," Donald commented drily.

"Educate!" spluttered William. "They're like children! All they think about is eating and sleeping and feasting." He brought his chair down hard on the plank floor. "They're an affront to the human race!"

"Human?" Donald snickered into his fist.

Julia thrust aside her sewing basket, and the two men half-rose in concern as she rushed from the room.

Cracking his knuckles, Donald peered through the darkening window. All day they had been on the lookout for the cutter's return, bringing news of the trader's fate.

"Murdered, I'm certain of it," muttered Donald, voicing the fears that had haunted him since his first glimpse, aboard ship, of the swarming fort camp. "Speared. And gutted. His head chopped off." He drew himself up indignantly. "I heard the talk in the saloons. I'm no fool!"

"Drowned, according to Jean-Louis," William reminded him curtly. "Easy enough to believe, in these waters."

"You believe Jean-Louis?" Donald's mouth fell open. "He sides with the Indians every chance he gets. Why, he's gone Indian himself."

William glanced warningly towards the hall. "Julia needn't know any of this."

"Well, what about ... her?" Donald jerked his elbow in the direction of the kitchen, leaning closer to his brother. "She could be a spy!"

"Pali? Pull yourself together," chided William. "Remember, these are a simple people. They live by the example we set."

Though he abhorred the native way of life, he did trust the villagers at Squally Bay. He trusted them with his daughter, and he even trusted Aneetsick, although the chief still, stubbornly, protested the siting of the mill. By what right, William asked Donald at least once every evening, did anyone protest the legitimate use of Crown land?

From the kitchen he could hear the sounds of the cookstove being opened, wood crackling, the bottom of the kettle snapping as water heated for tea. He noticed the clouds enfolding the hills; by morning the sky would be closed in with rain. He hoped they had not missed the cutter, and, despite his advice to Donald, thought it would not hurt to wear the revolvers for a few more days.

Henry sat staunchly on guard with his stick while the chickens settled and resettled on their roosts. Across the bay, the mink and the river otters and the raccoons lifted their noses to Henry, to the chickens, to the rain. Down the coast flew the sandpipers, fleeing the premonition of winter in their timid, hollow bones.

Kahammis prodded tobacco into the bowl of her pipe, watching her family around the hearth. Long ago, she had been as young as Pali; she had climbed her cedar tree, certain that she could fly. It was a perilous world, even for the bravest little birds.

Tomorrow, out on the delta, she would talk with Kalowish.

~~~:~~~

Two children scrambled over the rocks, their bare toes squishing in the ruffled, emerald seaweed exposed by the falling tide. A raw wind sliced across the bay, through branches laced with morning frost. The mill sat silent on this, for everyone, day of rest.

Maggie leaned over a salty pool, poking her finger into a furling anemone. She had just turned three, and although her companion, Tsuwitty, was only half her age, he had followed her since he could crawl. They roamed back and forth along the shoreline between the McPhee house and the mill; the village, in between, was considered by both children to be their common home. Together they had survived an encounter with a nest of ground wasps, and worse, with a rare jellyfish which had washed up on the beach, a flaccid orange plate that quivered deliciously beneath their feet until they felt its sting. Still Maggie battled with her father over the ladylike boots he brought from Port Albert, which she kicked off every morning as she went down the porch stairs. He would retrieve the boots when he came home for lunch, wondering how it was possible that his daughter ran like a dog with the native pack while he struggled to civilize his land. Julia retreated to bed, with her infant son, from this clash of wills.

From where they worked, around the village or on the delta, Yanis and Sa-sat-kis supervised the children. Aneetsick had kept his promise and proclaimed Tsuwitty free, so that the earnings of Sa-sat-kis went to secure his son's place in the world. William paid the same wage to Sa-sat-kis as he did to Callicum and Sea-ossum, great-nephews of the chief, partly out of fairness but also, he reminded them often, to defy the custom of slavery.

Maggie and Tsuwitty jumped up from the tide pool, alerted by a scolding kingfisher. Jean-Louis was coming along the river path with Pali on his arm. Pali laughed and ran to the children, and Jean-Louis stopped to watch, quietly exultant. Ever after, when separated from Pali, he would see in his mind's eye that tableau on the delta, Pali's braids flying and her slender arms outstretched against the backdrop of the bay.

Kalowish had deliberated for months, unable to relinquish his daughter to a man who, despite his excellent qualities, was still a stranger in their midst. Leaving Hoxem to the Lavalles, Jean-Louis had gone to Port Albert and returned with title to fifty acres upriver from the McPhees. He returned also with Georgie McPhee, William's youngest brother, who had finally arrived after being shipwrecked off Cape Horn. Georgie helped him clear a place to build, although Jean-Louis had been scarcely aware of the passage of one day to the next. His house was ready, and still he lacked his bride.

The village women had ceased their nagging of Kalowish, not wanting to be responsible for the outcome of his decision. Meanwhile, Pali found herself caught between her adoration of Jean-Louis and loyalty to her village, a net of emotions she could barely understand. She sought refuge in the McPhee household, where Julia lay dejectedly amongst the quilts and pillows, her blue-skinned infant by her side.

Life in the village stalled, until at last Kalowish agreed. The marriage of fourteen-year-old Pali to Jean-Louis Mallette was cele-brated during the winter feasts honouring another successful cycle of harvests, at the beginning of the year marked by William McPhee in his ledger as 1858. Jean-Louis wrote his mother, promising at the first opportunity to have his marriage sanctioned by the Roman Catholic Church. He knew she would not sleep easily until this was done. A few intrepid priests had made their way up the coast, heading farther north, leaving a flurry of hope and excitement amongst the believers in their wake. Though Jean-Louis dreamed of a mission chapel gracing the bay, he kept such aspirations from the Presbyterian McPhees.

So, it was not an ordinary morning when Jean-Louis brought his bride down the river path. This frosty Sunday in January marked the beginning of their life together, and as he gazed over the bay, the raucous kingfisher was no less delightful than the ringing of wedding bells to his ears.

Julia saw him from the parlour where, swaddled in shawls, she rocked her son. Neither she nor Pali could appease young William, who howled for hours, his face contorted and his limbs drawn up. Julia was training two village girls to replace Pali, but the task was wearying her almost as much as the misery of her child.

She smiled wanly, indicating to her husband the presence of the newlyweds outside. "Do let's ask them in!"

William rubbed his hand over his eyes. The previous evening, he and his family had attended the final wedding feast hosted by Aneetsick's lodge. So troubling was this occasion that he had hardly slept, his few moments of peace interrupted by his son.

"Fine," he said between clenched teeth, knowing that to refuse Julia would bring on more tears. In his very own parlour, he must now receive his native housekeeper, whom Jean-Louis had married in a pagan ceremony with rattles and masks.

Jean-Louis and Pali came up the steps, their faces sparkling like the ice crystals on the trees. Pali wore a fringed bark cape, woven by Kahammis as a wedding gift. Jean-Louis was resplendent in an over-sized shaggy vest, his bright sash around his waist.

Julia called to her helpers in the kitchen for cups of cider from the pot simmering at the back of the stove. The prospect of serving Pali, playmate since they were babies, sent the two girls into fits of giggles as they wrestled over the privilege of dusting Julia's company tray. Soon there came a prolonged, brittle crash. Julia and Pali dashed in from the parlour to discover that the girls had fallen backwards into a basket of eggs. The mess of shells and yolks set them off again and Julia and Pali joined in, the anxiety of the visit dispelled.

William shook his head as if in pain. He invited Jean-Louis to sit down and braced himself for another outburst from his son, who stared from the wicker cradle with accusing, milk-blue eyes. Seated, his hat on his knee, Jean-Louis could barely restrain himself from reaching over and giving William a manly, affectionate punch. He wanted to express his pride in the status they shared: husband, and provider. It was all that he had ever wished for, now realized by the grinding, glorious process of acquiring a wife.

"Some wedding!" he contented himself with saying, choking on the words. "Some night!" He mopped his forehead with an orange handkerchief which he stuffed into his sash.

William nodded frigidly, gazing out the window, willing Julia to return. Children swarmed over the delta, his daughter amongst them, her golden hair all that distinguished her from the native pack.

He glanced back at Jean-Louis. Though he would never question a person's faith, he wondered how Jean-Louis could possibly describe the events of the previous evening as a marriage, that most sacred of vows.

In his three years at Squally Bay, not once had William stepped past the entrance of a lodge. The villagers always invited him to their festivities; always, he refused. Only because Jean-Louis had helped build his house did he this time agree to attend. He escorted his family to Aneetsick's lodge, stooping below the massive beam supported by doorposts carved into ferocious scowls, leaving behind one world and entering another, the dark and teeming heart of Nootseetaht that only Maggie knew.

He had straightened to find himself in a cavernous, flickering room. Maggie darted off to join her friends, furious at having to wear a pinafore and boots that pinched her toes. When he opened his mouth to order her back, the pungent, smoky air had scorched his throat all the way down to his chest. Every eye in the lodge was upon him, and he felt laid bare, as if the villagers were somehow privy to information about him which even he did not know. The moment passed; he and Julia were led to their seats by two young men who minced through the crowd as importantly as a pair of ushers in a concert hall. Then he discovered that he and Julia were the only ones sitting on chairs, crude but accurate copies of the new furniture in the parlour of the house on the knoll.

Barely had they settled when out of nowhere came a startling boom. A row of half-naked girls pranced down the central aisle, among them his kitchen helpers; crimson with embarrassment, he had hardly been able to look. On the other side of Julia sat the white-haired old crone with the shabby cape; she had a way of appearing in his line of sight around Squally Bay just when he least expected her, like an apparition out of a fairy tale. Julia chatted with her in the garbled talk of the natives, talk which he had forbidden in his home.

"They're dancing our welcome," explained Julia. "How lovely they are!" She waved discreetly to the helpers, who blushed and bumped into each other, losing their step.

Closer and closer swayed the girls, singing and revealing their shapely thighs through the rustling strands of their skirts. William looked for his brothers, Donald and Georgie, squatting on cedar mats across the aisle. To his mortification, they were gawking like school-boys at the girls. Behind them sat the Lavalles, Anton and his flat-faced, native wife whom everyone referred to as Madame Lavalle, their seven scrubbed children filling a row.

The dance ended to a roar of approval from the crowd. Numerous speeches followed, then drumming, rattling, and monstrous beasts lunging from behind a painted screen. Creatures in bizarre masks cavorted so realistically that even William had felt drawn into the meaning of the pantomimes. He had been certain that one of the actors was Aneetsick, the taciturn chief. Protectively, he glanced at Julia. Her face glowed with emotion as she whispered to him that Jean-Louis had first come to the bay on the day that Pali's mother died, after giving birth to his future wife. Not since Scotland had William seen her so animated, her hair twisted up with a jewelled clasp, her perfect profile reminding him with a jolt how isolated they were, how far they had come. Over her chiselled shoulders she had draped a black velvet cloak, open at the front so that he could see the outline of her breasts beneath her ivory silk dress. Young William stared from her lap, for once distracted from his internal distress.

In his role as master of ceremonies, Charlie had grunted to his feet, announcing the food. Huge, steaming vats were brought forth from another lodge, where the women must have been preparing for weeks and weeks. And how the people dug in, as if during all the planning, the preparing, no one had eaten a thing. Entire salmon disappeared in a flash; overflowing tubs of crab legs were snatched up and crunched between strong white teeth. Oil streamed onto heaping platters of roots and rice. In the middle of all this gluttony, Charlie bellowed for more, his greasy belly flopping over his unbuttoned, cut-off sailor pants. William tried to eat, knowing from experience that the salmon was delicious, but with each bite his eyes went to Charlie, the food turning to wood chips on his tongue.

Worst of all, when everyone sat back, groaning and replete, still the vats and trays sailed in. "Leftovers!" Julia whispered. "Kahammis says that for Aneetsick's lodge, this is the greatest moment of the feast. The moment of abundance: look how rich they are! Look how much they can give away!" Gaily she clapped her hands. "It's magnificent, don't you agree?"

At midnight they stumbled outside, and William gazed around the starry bay with the thankfulness of one who wakes intact from a terrible dream. But the contrasts, and the excesses, remained in his mind, and Charlie belched and bellowed through his fitful sleep.

Now he sat with the beaming groom, torn between revulsion and a kind of shocked acceptance of the pitfalls of the frontier. He forced himself to look attentive as Julia came into the parlour with Pali behind her, carrying the tray.

Jean-Louis downed his cider in a single gulp. "That was fine music we made last night," he said to Julia. "Very fine music, Mrs. McPhee!"

Julia smiled, shifting young William in her lap. Part way through the speeches, Jean-Louis had been brought the case which contained his violin. When he stood to play, Julia rose as well. William had watched, dumbfounded, as she withdrew her flute from beneath her velvet cloak. They began to play and the crowd listened, spellbound, until Jean-Louis laid down his bow with a humble sigh. William had mutely acknowledged Julia's return to her chair. At the same time, he acknowledged a lack within himself, a lack which turned an exquisite sonata into the rough scraping of a file against his soul.

Pali finally finished her cider, and as William stood on his porch with her and Jean-Louis, saying goodbye, he noticed a mast beyond the spit. He was expecting Captain Hume on the *Coast Princess,* to deliver a load of pilings to the fort. This was a sloop, much smaller, tacking through the gap towards the most recent addition to the bay, a wharf adjacent to the mill.

Hastily he excused himself, fastening his coat and scarf as he went down the steps. The bright expanse of the bay filled him with energy, restoring his sense of purpose. Already he was making plans for the big house, farther back along the river, a two-storey mansion with a proper kitchen and a balcony off the bedroom, where he and Julia could oversee the comings and goings of the thriving community they had pioneered.

Donald and Georgie had each purchased sections of land between the native village and the mill. Donald rushed to complete his house, hoping that the rumours of a bride ship coming to Port Albert would prove true. Georgie was only nineteen, and William felt that he spent too much time with Callicum and Sea-ossum, capable and strapping youths who had yet to put in a full day's work. Like all Highland laddies, Georgie loved to fish. He and his companions would slip away at dawn, returning when the mill was shut down for the day, loaded with halibut or chinook. Georgie was a favourite with the wagging, old village women; he thought nothing of letting them run their fingers through his shiny chestnut curls.

Only the mess of the village marred the pristine January landscape: lopsided lodges, racks and steam pits, and mounds of debris where the seagulls and crows jabbered from morning to night. William's gaze swung back to the sloop neatly approaching the wharf. From behind the mill came the lowing of the oxen in their stalls; he wondered if Donald had attended to them or was still asleep, Donald's literal and all too frequent interpretation of the day of rest.

To his surprise, Robert Airley was climbing up the ladder from the deck of the sloop. Whenever William was in Port Albert, he stopped by the surveyor's office for long, satisfying hours of talk. This was a first, Airley visiting the McPhees in Squally Bay.

The two men shook hands, wishing each other a prosperous New Year. "I can hardly believe what you've accomplished," exclaimed Airley, laughing ruefully as he gestured along the bay. "My men would have thought me a miracle-worker, had we come out to this on our expedition across the mountains."

"Are you staying?" asked William. "Julia will be thrilled."

"I'm here on behalf of the government, as a matter of fact." Airley lowered his voice as they strolled the gravel beach. "Apparently there has been a misunderstanding. With Chief Aneetsick. He came to my office last month."

"Aneetsick?" William frowned. "Yes, he's probably angry because I won't let him burn the slopes so that more berries will grow. He and his men almost set fire to an entire hillside last fall." William shook his head. "Endangering our lives, for berries, no less!"

"It wasn't about the burning," said the surveyor. "It was about the treaty between the colony and the village, before you came. Chief Aneetsick claims that he has not received compensation for his land."

"I don't know anything about that," exclaimed William. "In my opinion, they have received compensation enough. I offer employment to every able-bodied man, and our schooners supply their every need, at no profit to me."

Robert Airley nodded. "We'll meet with the chief. And with Charlie; if I remember correctly, Charlie knows the workings of the village better than anyone. But first, I'd like to see the site of your new house. And," he added, smiling, "offer my congratulations on the birth of your son."

Aneetsick stood by the entrance mat, watching the two men pass below the lodges. He returned to his place at the hearth, and Kahammis looked up worriedly from her weaving. Tension had been building since early morning, when she woke to the sounds of a confrontation between Aneetsick and Moochinnick in the bushes behind the lodge. The confrontation had ended with the sudden, explosive shattering of glass, then Moochinnick stormed inside, and had been sulking on his sleeping platform ever since.

Paonea and Chee-uxqua slumped at the hearth, worn down by their efforts to placate Moochinnick, who was becoming impossible to please. Paonea tried to quiet the children racing in and out, still high from the excitement of the wedding celebrations. The only person untouched by the tension was Jean-Louis; he was too busy teasing his bride across the hearth.

The Lavalles had departed earlier for Hoxem, in canoes paddled by Callicum, Sea-ossum, and, unbeknownst to William, Georgie. The helpfulness of the young men was fuelled by the three eldest Lavalle girls: fifteen-year-old Lucille, fourteen-year-old Marie, and twelve-year-old Louise, plump and merry companions despite their frugal existence in the remote cove.

Henry and Johnny burst through the entrance, walloping each other with a ferocity that further incited the other children, creating ever-shifting zones of neutrality and war. Such antagonism added to the worries of Kahammis, struggling as she was to keep pace with the changes in recent years. No sooner did her people rally to one change, be it the transfer of trade to Port Albert, or the noise of the saw, than along would come another, requiring entirely new adjustments to the balance of their being. They could not assert themselves; they were too unsettled, too unsure.

Almost overnight, Donald and Georgie McPhee had claimed possession of the land adjoining the village, levelling the forests into slashed, swampy fields. Apart from silently seething, what could

Aneetsick do? His people counted on him for reassurance of their place and their worth, but what noble warrior could fight the stumps, or defend the birds fluttering around their broken nests?

Later in the day, Maggie bolted through the entrance with the news that her father wished to see the chief. Also Charlie, she added, with a skeptical glance at the sleeping platform where he snored.

Kahammis could feel Aneetsick's chagrin at this summoning: three-year-old Maggie with her hands on her hips, urging Aneetsick to hurry because the important Mr. Airley was also outside. Paonea crept over and shook Moochinnick, who swore and swatted her away. She dragged him upright, imploring him to put on his cape. He lumbered bare-chested down the aisle behind Aneetsick.

The two men were waiting on the beach. Aneetsick was greeted by Airley with a handshake; William nodded stiffly. Moochinnick lurched from foot to foot, wheezing in the crisp air.

The surveyor explained that a search of government records had confirmed what he already knew: eight years ago, when the treaty had been made, Charlie had accepted the money on behalf of his chief. Aneetsick listened, stunned with rage and humiliation. He could not bring himself to look at Moochinnick, who shuffled uneasily, one hand holding up his pants below his belly.

With enormous difficulty, Aneetsick managed to speak. "What belongs to us?" he asked, in a harsh, guttural voice.

"The village belongs to you," replied the surveyor, taking a map out of his case. William watched impassively as Aneetsick was shown how the land around the bay had been divided into sections, for purchase by the colonists.

"What if the village gets bigger?" asked Aneetsick. "What if we need more space?"

"The governor has allocated a certain number of acres for each family, all along the coast," explained Airley. "I suppose you could petition the government," he added kindly, glancing up the slope. "Is the village growing, then?"

A grimace of such pain passed over Aneetsick's face that Airley turned away, shaken, rearranging the papers in his case. He straightened, clearing his throat. "Well, if you have any more concerns, you know where I am." Bowing to both men, he set off along the beach with William.

Aneetsick turned to Moochinnick, his black eyes glittering as he looked him up and down.

"What difference does it make?" whined Moochinnick, hugging his bare chest. "You said yourself, white man's money is like dirt."

"Dirt, yes!" snarled Aneetsick. "Our dirt!"

He strode up the slope. Moochinnick stumbled and slid behind him on the frost-slicked grass, and went immediately to his sleeping platform, shouting for tea.

Kahammis worked blindly over a basket frame. The lodge was hushed except for the crackle of the fires, Moochinnick's moans, the tapping of Kalowish's chisel against a wooden bowl. Aneetsick stared into the yellow-blue flames and Chee-uxqua wrung her hands nearby.

The following morning, Robert Airley thanked Julia for the roast chicken dinner and the evening of conversation they had shared. William walked with him to the mill wharf, prolonging every moment of companionship, and together they looked beyond the stump-dotted slopes to the future pastures, the rich earth crumbling beneath the plough. They saw the churches, the stores, children in the schoolyard, playing on swings — the pioneer dream.

William stood wistfully as the sloop slipped past the spit. Julia had been an exemplary hostess, and young William had been dosed with gripewater so that their guest could sleep. Only the meeting on the beach had marred the visit, yet perhaps it had been necessary, to set Aneetsick straight. One could not help but feel compassion for Aneetsick, betrayed by the loathsome Charlie, who would never again be trusted with McPhee business at the fort. Robert Airley had pointed out that for all Aneetsick's stubbornness he was fair and sober, unlike many chiefs along the coast. He also pointed out, ironically, that the native consumption of alcohol supported the colonial government, through yearly licences which the liquor traders were required to buy. Without this revenue, no wages would have been paid at the fort.

"Be fair in return," Airley had advised, "and you cannot go wrong."

"Fair!" retorted William. "Does being fair make me responsible for the native plight?"

He turned his back on the bay, hearing the sound of Donald's axe, like rifleshot in the early morning air. Donald was splitting wood to feed the boiler, an eternal chore. They had received so many orders for lumber and pilings, they could have used another mill just to meet their own needs. But their most pressing goal was to secure timber rights upcoast, the direction of future wealth. If only, he thought irritably, they were not so hampered by a shortage of equipment and good help. Looking around for Georgie, he raised his eyebrows at the empty hook where his youngest brother's coat should have hung. Donald leaned on his axe, shrugging noncommittally.

The *Coast Princess* came in at noon. Prior to the construction of the wharf, rafts of milled wood had to be barged or boomed out into the bay, at the whim of wind and tide. Donald had rigged a system of rails and carts to the end of the wharf, where the crew of the schooner stacked the timbers on board. As William and Donald lowered the last heavy piling, one of the schooner's crew gestured rudely along the wharf. Charlie was waddling towards them, wrapped in a mangy bearskin robe. He squinted hopefully at Captain Hume, who turned his back with an expression of resigned disgust. Charlie was notorious along the coast for his flamboyant promises of presents, rarely delivered, and for his avoidance of small spaces; in sleet or August heat he sat like a giant, furred chiton on deck, while every other passenger took refuge below.

The people of Nootseetaht ignored Moochinnick's shameful exit and continued about their business while the *Coast Princess* set sail. Kahammis made an effort to avoid seeing the captain during his frequent stopovers at Squally Bay, though it did not displease her that he was well-liked and dependable. She saw him instead through Kalowish, sometimes even through Callicum and Sea-ossum: his angular walk, the shape of his forehead, and the colour of his hair. She was confident that to him she was merely part of the landscape, the old weaver on her mat.

The sails billowed and the heavily-loaded schooner crawled through the gap at slack water, Moochinnick clinging to a hatch. Captain Hume tacked slowly south, and William headed back to his house, glancing in annoyance at the clouds over the hills. Changes in the weather constantly preoccupied the McPhees, to the bafflement of the natives, for whom the moods of sky and sea flowed purposefully as part of a greater, assimilated whole. When William or Donald objected to the rain, even the children sniggered at the ludicrousness of their shaking fists.

The afternoon had barely reached its fullness when the first hard splatters hit, and the villagers needed no other encouragement to hurry inside. Moochinnick, the source of the tension, was gone; they were free to enjoy the food and singing and storytelling that turned the winter evenings into their most cherished time of year.

Only the children lingered, awaiting that final, imperative tone in their mothers' voices. Maggie and Tsuwitty scampered off for one last look at the new ducks in the poultry run behind the McPhee house. The enclosure had been enlarged around a muddy pond which drew predators like a magnet and elevated Henry to a fearsome status with his stick. The loss of a chicken or a duckling charged him with revenge, and along one corner of the pen hung a row of bushy tails, severed from dead raccoons.

Maggie and Tsuwitty dangled over the edge of the pen, watching Henry distribute kitchen scraps. Johnny sat on a stump, smouldering with envy as he plotted how he could replace Henry.

"Get offa there," growled Henry, and Maggie and Tsuwitty retreated into the salal, snickering at Henry, who was surrounded by quacking ducks. One disgruntled drake nipped Henry's ample behind, and he hopped into the air with a squawk of outrage. The children smothered their laughter beneath the wet leaves; from the delta they could hear Sa-sat-kis calling for them as he gathered his tools.

"Look!" whispered Maggie, pointing to a slug by her foot. She stabbed the slug onto a twig and crept forward, offering it to the ducks. She turned to Tsuwitty, her conspiratorial grin falling away at a glimpse of tawny fur springing through the underbrush. She threw herself over Tsuwitty, screaming as claws raked across her back and down Tsuwitty's bare legs.

Knocked out of his daydream, Johnny lunged for the stick Henry had left propped by the gate to the pen. The cougar crouched over the children, tail thrashing from side to side. This was the moment Johnny had been waiting for: he brought the stick down in a fury of hope and thwarted desire, and the cougar toppled into the salal. Maggie's screams rose even higher and Tsuwitty gasped at the bloody lines spurting along his thighs. The cougar shook itself upright; again Johnny brought down the stick. Yelping, the cougar bounded away.

Sa-sat-kis reached the pen and fell upon the children with a cry heard by Yanis on the beach, where she was searching for her son. Within minutes the entire population of Squally Bay was at the poultry pen, reeling at Johnny's description of the attack. Between re-enactments, Johnny leaned nonchalantly on the stick, while Henry gaped over the slop bucket.

William carried Maggie to the house. Julia clutched young William, coils of hair spilling over her shawl. They laid Maggie on the kitchen

173

table and pulled away her blood-soaked jersey, exposing her mauled flesh. The native girls sobbed by the stove, where they ladled water into a pot. Maggie was quiet, trembling from head to foot. Her father dressed her wounds with alcohol and wrapped her in linen from one of Julia's trunks.

In the lodge, Chee-uxqua took charge of Tsuwitty, packing his legs with poultices and admonishing him to stay still. Maggie's screams had frightened Tsuwitty far more than his injuries and he pleaded with his parents to let him see her, devastated by the sight of her being carried away.

The villagers slept restlessly, as though somewhere, somehow, important business had been left undone. Kahammis searched back through the years, trying to recall a cougar so close to the village. Why, now? Her thoughts revolved through the night, through Tsuwitty's whimpers, through the preparations of the trackers, who were heading into the forest at William's request. She, too, must go into the forest, seeking not the cougar but the void out of which it had come. She must seek the wounded spirits, and make peace.

~~~¦~~~

Not until the second summer after his wedding did Jean-Louis take Pali to Port Albert, to have the marriage blessed.

Kahammis went down the slope as they prepared to leave. It was early morning, and seven herons waded along the delta, swivelling to the sound of William McPhee's shaving water hitting the ground in a wide, foaming arc. The old eagle, sentinel of the dawn, watched from a tall fir.

Jean-Louis and Pali were travelling south in a canoe which bore the crest of Paquacheenish and belonged to his grandson Kleeshinnin, Klinniklinnikaht's modest and soft-spoken chief. Kleeshinnin sat astern, his paddle across his knees. Neetsa was in the bow, surrounded by boxes of berries and fish, and gaily-coloured baskets made by Kahammis.

Pali threw her arms around Kahammis's neck as she said goodbye. Pinned to the starched collar of her dress was a spray of roses, the intensity of their fragrance overwhelming all other aspects of the embrace. The canoe backed away and sped towards the spit, yet the scent remained with Kahammis where the petals had brushed her cape.

Earlier in the summer, she had walked upriver to see where Pali lived. It had been a walk along a path of bittersweet memories: past the scarred cedars, past the winter camp of her childhood, past the curve in the bank where she had comforted Tatatoe, who still wept; Hasallum's bones had never been recovered.

She came to the small, slab-sided house Jean-Louis had built. There, beneath the muted roar of the falls, Pali spent her time washing her husband's shirts amongst the boulders, or washing butter from the cream Julia gave her, from the new cow, even more marvellous to the children than the chickens or the ducks. During one of his excursions to Port Albert, Jean-Louis had befriended the blacksmith's wife as she cursed and threatened her spade into a plot of clay between the smithy and the street. He came back carrying a burlap sack of tangled roots with a reverence lost on all but Julia, who shared his longing for flowers to surround his home. Henry and Johnny delivered buckets of chicken droppings upriver, in exchange for candy, and into the moist earth on the south side of the cabin went the roots, below the railing where Jean-Louis propped his feet on Sunday afternoons.

The smithy roses bloomed in their first year, and it was these that Pali wore for the trip to Port Albert, blushing at the emotion in her husband's face as he pinned the apricot-tinged buds to the collar of her good dress. With the dress stretched to bursting around her middle, the need for a priest had grown urgent in Jean Louis's mind.

Rumours of the clergy passing through Port Albert had been delivered by Anton Lavalle, who also had news shocking to Jean-Louis and the McPhees, isolated all spring by their push to clear the land. Port Albert had been invaded by thousands of miners buying provisions on their way to the interior, in a frenzied search for gold. The fort was in dire need of spiritual, indeed, any form of guidance as a tent city expanded around the harbour, into the adjoining farms. Land prices had soared, the local merchants could not keep their shelves stocked, and the government clerks were unable to issue licences fast enough to please the adventurers arriving from San Francisco, from all over the world.

So extravagant were the claims of fortunes to be made that Anton Lavalle would not rest overnight at Squally Bay; he had paddled home to Hoxem in the darkness to inform his family that he would be leaving for the interior on the next boat. Jean-Louis felt compelled to travel to Port Albert to hear for himself what he was missing out on, yoked like a dumb ox to his fields. Georgie chafed to join the rush, restrained only by William, who was certain that he would never see his younger brother again if he let him go.

Far more disturbing to the villagers was Kleeshinnin's news, when he and Neetsa stopped on their way south to trade. The week before, two Royal Navy gunships had entered the channel at Klinniklinnikaht, aiming their barrels into the lagoon. Armed men searched the lodges, and Kleeshinnin had been interrogated as to the whereabouts of the supply barque *Ponderosa,* bound for remote settlements in the northern sounds, and long overdue. Finding nothing at Klinniklinnikaht, the gunships continued up the coast to Quatlukaht. A cache of fresh goods had been discovered behind the farthest lodge, including items of marine hardware for which the natives could not account. Two of the elderly cousins had been apprehended and taken aboard. Kleeshinnin learned these details when the gunships anchored at Klinniklinnikaht on their return to the fort. Kleeshinnin was enlisted as an interpreter, so that the navy captain could prepare his report. But the cousins had barely spoken, surly with rage.

Kleeshinnin was renowned along the coast for his uncanny knowledge of fishing, shared freely amongst the visiting crews. This time, however, the officers did not leave their ships even for chinook, convinced that the hapless *Ponderosa* passengers had been massacred, possibly even eaten alive. Such conjecture had dominated their discussions ever since the trader had supposedly drowned in the Mannakaht sound; his body had not yet been found.

Both Aneetsick and Kleeshinnin suspected that the *Ponderosa* had strayed off course in poor visibility, breaking up on the rocky headland off Quatlukaht and grinding to pieces in the swell. But who knew, for sure? Bristling at the thought of armed strangers swarming through his lodge, Aneetsick wondered aloud: could any village be searched, at whim? He advised Kleeshinnin to stay at Port Albert only as long as necessary; more than ever, the coast people needed their chiefs.

The waters of the harbour shimmered at sundown when the travellers arrived, and not only Pali but everyone on board drew back, astounded at the numbers of boats at anchor, and crammed alongshore. No longer did bastions and picket walls define the fort; these landmarks were barely visible amongst the crush of stores and saloons. Kleeshinnin's canoe circled slowly, a shaft of bronze light glinting off the raven's eye embedded in the upswept bow. They found a patch of beach below the native camp and Pali clambered out, clinging to Jean-Louis, her nose pressed into his shirt.

"What is that smell?" she murmured weakly.

The foreshore was littered with foul clumps of sewage and seaweed; as Jean-Louis stared, a small rodent disentangled itself and scurried beneath an overturned hull. Dogs scavenged the tideline, nipping at each other, and a pair of roosters crowed obstinately at the setting sun.

In the morning Kleeshinnin and Neetsa would trade for flour and rice, tobacco and cloth, for bleached bear grass and the rare, sweet camas bulbs that might have reached the fort from some as yet untrampled glade. As they spread out their sleeping mats beside the canoe, a howl erupted in a nearby shack, followed by the staccato summons of the plank drums, picked up and repeated through the camp.

Jean-Louis gave careful directions to Kleeshinnin and Neetsa, arranging to meet them late the following afternoon; he intended to treat them to a meal at the boarding house where he had always stayed. Pali bade Neetsa a reluctant goodbye and stumbled off behind Jean-Louis. At the main wharf, below the fort, Jean-Louis spoke briefly with some men he knew. They continued up the street, and Pali cringed at the boisterous crowds, the nearness of the horses, the dogs that Jean-Louis staved off with a handful of stones. They stopped at a curtained doorway which opened to stairs leading up the outer wall of a saloon.

"Full!" Jean-Louis gawked at the sign pinned to the door. He backed into the street, calling with his hands cupped around his mouth. "Madame Olson! It is me, Jean-Louis!"

A woman appeared on the balcony above the saloon. Tiredly she shouted downwards, "I'm full, can't you see?"

"But Madame," cried Jean-Louis, his voice catching in his throat, "I am here with my wife. Do you not have even one wee bed?"

"Your wife!" Pali peered up nervously as Madame Olson, guffawing, leaned over the balcony rail. She was twice the size of Julia, with stout knots of hair twisted over her ears. "Fine, a bed! That's all anyone can promise, these days."

Whooping with relief, Jean-Louis hustled Pali past the curtain. Madame Olson was waiting when they emerged onto the balcony. She looked at Pali with a squeal of distaste. "It's a squaw! A child, no less." She glared at Jean-Louis. "You know I don't run that kind of place!"

Jean-Louis clutched Pali, who stood meekly at his side. "But Madame, we are married! We have come to Port Albert to find the priest."

Madame Olson snorted. "Jean-Louis, you are a child yourself if you expect me to believe that. Besides," she added, glowering at Pali, "what about the *Ponderosa*? I won't have cannibals in my house!"

Jean-Louis pulled out his leather purse. Coins spilled in his haste, rolling off the balcony and clanging against the boardwalk below. "Please," he begged, "just for tonight?"

Madame Olson sighed and took the money. They followed her along the balcony to a room divided into stale, dark alcoves by blankets draped on ropes. Swatting flies, she pointed to a cot and left them alone.

Jean-Louis sank onto the cot, his face in his hands. Instantly the cot upended, and he crashed onto the floor. He was so astonished, so indignant, that Pali burst into tears, covering him with kisses where he fell.

"My darling," cried Jean-Louis, wiping away his own tears. "Forgive me, please. This has been a terrible mistake. We will leave as soon as the priest blesses us, even if it means travelling home by moonlight."

He righted the cot, shaking out the filthy blanket, and tentatively Pali lay down. Jean-Louis slept beside her on the floor, holding her hand. During the night they woke repeatedly to yells and thumps in the saloon below, to coughing and groaning in the crowded, airless room. Before dawn they were up, Jean-Louis standing guard while Pali used the privy in the rear yard. Pali was pale and shivering; to calm her, they walked the deserted streets, pausing at the shop windows, and Jean-Louis showed her the four corners of the fort. They bought buns and sugar-drenched coffee from a baker and sat looking out over the harbour, their backs warmed by the rising sun.

All morning they searched for a priest, from the waterfront to the farthest farm. A few of the more sympathetic merchants thought they might have caught sight of black robes the day before, or perhaps the week before. The sentry at the fort's main gate scowled derisively when they approached him, aiming a wad of chewing tobacco at their feet. Jean-Louis learned that a passenger boat was due imminently from San Francisco, and as the sun reached its zenith, beginning its downward slide, he convinced himself that surely there would be a priest on board.

Befuddled with exhaustion and the hot, dusty press of bodies, Pali drooped at his side. He knew that for her the priest was no more than a mythical figure out of his past, an inexplicable obstruction to their happiness in their little home. He could not bear to expose her to the mob at the wharf, so he took her back to Madame Olson's, to wait on the balcony for his return. He told her to watch for Neetsa and Kleeshinnin, with whom they had agreed to meet. Rolling her eyes and pocketing a few more coins, Madame Olson let Pali stay.

Pali shifted listlessly along the rail. When she was very still, she could feel the baby fluttering in her womb. Kahammis and Chee-uxqua and the other village women often laid their palms against her dress, and Julia went through her trunks, choosing extraordinary costumes she thought the baby might need. Maggie had volunteered to be an aunt, but only, she announced firmly, if it was a girl. Maggie scorned her younger brother; who would believe, she told Pali, that something so small and hideous could make such a fuss? A nursing mother visited the McPhee house regularly in the mornings and after-noons, while William was at the mill. Young William was finally putting on weight and Julia was regaining her strength, the shadows fading from around her eyes, in a face that for Pali was the most beau-tiful in the world.

Below her, groups of miners swaggered back and forth, bearded and dressed in the bright flannel shirts that Jean-Louis wore. A native couple squatted against an opposite wall, their bent heads touched by the last rays of the sun. Pali had noticed this couple in the same position the evening before. Now and then the woman opened her mouth in a toothless yawn. As the miners approached, she grinned and called in words Pali could not understand. When one of the miners made as if to kick her with his heavy boot, Pali cried out loud. Yet the woman did not flinch, her companion beside her unperturbed, and the dogs slunk nearby, darkness closing in.

From the direction of the harbour came a series of shrill whistles, then cheers and shouts. Pali tilted her head sleepily, her chin in her hands. Cooking smells wafted above the dust, and Madame Olson was slamming pots in the tarp-covered kitchen out back. Searching for Jean-Louis amongst the coloured shirts, Pali was no longer even thinking of the mysterious priest, just wanting her husband and hearing, in the distant cheers, the rush of the river outside their home.

Jean-Louis pushed through the crowds along the walkway as a sternwheeler churned towards the main wharf, trailing brown water in a festive cascade. Passengers from San Francisco crammed the upper and lower levels, calling jubilantly to friends and relatives onshore. A swath of light led past the horde of ships to the sun on the horizon, and the sky all the way to Nootseetaht was aflame with streaks of scarlet, orange, and rose. The gangplank thudded down, and the passengers streamed onto land. Jean-Louis watched the decks emptying, his fists clenched with hope.

Pali peered over the rail as a team of giant oxen came along the street, pulling a wagon loaded with vegetables. When the farmer cracked his whip, the oxen bawled in protest, setting off yells of laughter amongst the men lounging on the boardwalks in front of the saloons. Two familiar figures stepped aside to let the wagon pass, and Pali gave a joyful wave as she recognized Neetsa and Kleeshinnin.

Neetsa strolled along looking neither to the right nor the left, pendants dangling from her earlobes and from the finely shaped nose she had inherited from her grandfather. Her formal bark cape laid claim to a lineage demanding of respect even amongst the mayhem of the native camp. Beside her, his withered arm tucked close, Kleeshinnin walked with the stilted gait of one who is more comfortable on the water, his powerful shoulders almost overbalancing his short, undeveloped legs. Only at the fort did he wear trousers and a shirt, his feet bare.

Pali ran down the stairs, explaining that Jean-Louis was at the wharf meeting the priest; they must await his return. "Come on up," she said, pointing invitingly to the balcony.

Kleeshinnin glanced around, as if seeking the natural tranquillity of dusk in the yellow light and the noise spilling out of the saloons. Miners staggered by, jostling Neetsa, and Kleeshinnin yanked her closer with a reprimand. The trading had gone well but the mood around the fort was too manic for his liking; he was eager to find Jean-Louis and head for home. His mouth felt thick with dust, hunger, and a foreboding that had hounded him since he first set foot ashore. "Not here," he said gruffly. "We will wait at the canoe."

A miner stood watching them from the open door of the saloon. "Hey!" he yelled. "Watcha charge for the ladies?"

Kleeshinnin hurried Neetsa and Pali along the boardwalk. "Keep going," he told them, between his teeth.

"Hey dumb Indian, I'm talking to you." The miner strode out into the street. His high boots gleamed, and his hand nudged the knife sheath on his leather belt. "How much?" he repeated, to jeering approval from his friends.

Kleeshinnin spoke softly. "Let us pass."

"Where's your manners, pointy-head?" The miner nodded aggrievedly. "Just like them savages up north, attacking the *Ponderosa*. No manners at all!"

His words electrified his audience, and the saloon emptied. Neetsa and Pali were knocked against Kleeshinnin in the drunken, hostile crowd.

"How much?" The miner jabbed at Neetsa, who stared back with icy, hate-filled eyes.

Kleeshinnin put his arms around the two women, urging them forward. Suddenly he doubled over, with a whoosh of expelled air. A fist chopped down on his head, and he sank beneath a flurry of boots. Pali could hear bones cracking, agonized groans. Petrified, she reached for Neetsa. Hands clamped over Neetsa's mouth, dragging her backwards as she clawed to free herself. Pali lunged for Neetsa's cape, feeling the bark slip through her fingers. She tried to follow but a man's elbow smashed against her face, then into her breasts, and she let out a desperate shriek.

Jean-Louis turned away from the harbour, trudging up the wooden steps to the street. Another ship was due to arrive in the morning; surely his need would be answered, his faith restored. Disconsolate, he recalled how he had picked his best roses, pinning them to Pali's collar. He tasted the grit in his mouth and thought about the stewpot that was always on the stove when he came in from the fields. Julia had done a wonderful job of teaching Pali to cook; for once, he noted wryly, William's loss was his gain.

A wagon heaped with produce was entering the main gate to the fort. Jean-Louis stepped around the oxen, as handsome a pair as he had ever seen. He reached out to caress a warm, muscled flank, pulling back with a start at the faint but unmistakeable sound of his name ricocheting along the fort wall. He glanced up and down the street and then, in a rush of dread, remembered Pali waiting on the balcony.

Pali felt herself lifted by strong arms and by the force of a stupendous roar, a roar which cut through the frenzied crowd, pawing hands

181

falling away. She scrabbled against Jean-Louis, and the miners muttered and wiped their fists, slouching towards the saloon.

Kleeshinnin lay on his side in the dirt. "Neetsa!" he wheezed, his breath rattling underneath his ribs.

Jean-Louis looked around wildly, as if just realizing that she wasn't there. He ran back and forth, bellowing her name while Pali moaned over Kleeshinnin.

A voice cut sharply above them. Madame Olson gripped the balcony rail. "She's gone," she said flatly. "You won't find her now."

She came down the stairs, holding out a bucket of water and a rag. "You're a fool for bringing them here," she told Jean-Louis. "Port Albert is no place these days for fools." She went back up, shaking her head.

Jean-Louis swabbed at Pali's bleeding face. "Don't leave me," she whimpered, hanging onto his hands.

She limped behind as he carried Kleeshinnin to the canoe. He settled him in the bow, warming him with blankets, lifting a water flask to his lips. Kleeshinnin stared unseeing and unmoving into the dark.

Jean-Louis lay with Pali beside the canoe. Though he had not thought it possible to sleep, he dozed off, waking abruptly at first light. He turned to Pali; her eyes were swollen shut and her braids were matted against her cheeks. He tiptoed away, sick with guilt and grief.

Ships appeared like mirages through the fog over the sleeping harbour, shifting and surreal. Jean-Louis followed the tideline, his eyes downcast, as if searching the rotting debris for answers: what offence had he committed, to bring such tragedy upon those dearest to his heart?

He found Neetsa by the pilings near the main wharf. Mercifully, she had not yet been discovered by the birds or the rats or the mongrel pack. Her neck had been slashed. Blood bubbled and seeped underneath her; she was naked, and even her jewellery had been ripped away. He crossed himself and prayed that his mind would cease to think, that his limbs do the task they must do.

He wrapped her in his shirt and carried her back through the murk. Pali was still asleep, and Kleeshinnin's eyes barely flickered as Neetsa's body was rolled into a mat and lowered into the canoe. During the journey home, Jean-Louis sought relief in driving his paddle through the grey-green water, stroke after stroke. Clouds funnelled over the far mountains, widening south as the day passed. Pali wept piteously, touching her cheeks, staring at the mat, at their zig-zagging wake.

Kahammis was sorting berries on the ridge. Every few minutes she glanced upwards, at the undersides of the clouds tinged navy and rust. She rose to her knees as a canoe entered the gap, and she was waiting on the beach when Jean-Louis came ashore.

Pali stood teetering, rosebuds dangling from her collar. Maggie and Tsuwitty raced down the slope, falling back when they reached the canoe.

And the bay resounded with their thin, horrified wails.

~~~:~~~

Kahammis roamed with her burden basket and her stick, searching for ferns in the forest behind Nootseetaht. Soft, pallid light sifted through the dripping branches as rain showers crossed the southeast straits, restoring the essence of the coast after summer's interlude.

The great forest that had once spanned the bay as far as the eye could see was gone, except for a single tract which belonged to the natives, extending from the village back to the hills. The land that had been lying waste, in the view of the pioneers, now presented an entirely new cycle of growth to the sun and the stars and the moon: mellow browns, vibrant greens, and rich yellows. From the verandah of his two-storey Georgian mansion, William McPhee could gaze over his fields and his expanded mill, inhaling with pride at all that he had achieved.

Increasingly, the natives worked for him for wages, or traded fish; the children had grown accustomed to rice, sugar, and flour, staples from the fort. Kahammis roamed the trails not only to supplement this diet, but for solace, refuge from the ceaseless chock-chock-chock of the mill.

She sank beside a promising clump, jabbing with her stick. She was dismayed to discover that she was breathing heavily, still not reconciled to the discrepancy between her humming, inner self and the years she dragged behind, worse than a burden basket for weighing her down. Her hair was silvery like Aneetsick's, and her skin had taken on the hues of oiled cedarwood. Still she led the bark-gatherers, and still Aneetsick brought in the first whale; the starchy roots she dug would be roasted and eaten with the fat of his harpoon.

She paused at the sound of a commotion from the edge of the forest, where the pasture began. Picking up her basket, she beat through the wet ferns towards a cluster of children: Henry and Johnny, Maggie and Tsuwitty, four-year-old William, and three-year-old Evangeline, daughter of Jean-Louis and Pali, her copper ringlets bouncing as she hopped up and down.

In the centre of the children hissed a baby raccoon. Blotchy-cheeked with excitement, young William pleaded with Henry to lend him his club. Henry was eleven and as husky as a grown man, patronizing with the smaller children but ruthless with Johnny, the usurper and favourite of the McPhees since the cougar incident.

Young William smashed the raccoon to a pulp while Kahammis watched from the trees. A tinny clanging came over the fields, and Maggie and Evangeline dashed off, hand in hand. The boys followed more slowly, young William lingering for a final swipe.

Julia stood on the verandah of the big house, ringing the bell. The children trooped past her to the back parlour, sparsely furnished but cosy and wall-papered, with two windows facing the barn and the poultry pens. Pushing and shoving, they took their places on the fir-plank floor, waiting for the day's lessons.

The raccoon abandoned to the eagles, Kahammis wound her way home. Chee-uxqua received the bracken roots gratefully; the salmon had not spawned in nearly the numbers expected, and the drying racks were bare, the storage boxes unfilled. Warming her hands at the hearth, Kahammis found herself wondering, as she lately often did, at the paltriness of the run.

Was it the curse of Moochinnick, languishing in exile? Rarely did he return, loaded with gifts and charm, the villagers polite but cool and Paonea deeply embarrassed by this husband who chafed at village routine, departing on the next schooner south without so much as a farewell. Nine months after the most recent visit, their daughter Noni had been born.

Or was it the power of the foreign shaman tnat had eluded Jean-Louis? For days Pali had hemorrhaged, and no one had been more surprised than Kahammis when she gave birth, much too early, to the tiny but flawless Evangeline. There was no such consolation up north at Klinniklinnikaht, where Kleeshinnin lived crippled and wordless, and Tatatoe was ghostly with loss.

Or was it the constant comings and goings, the building and clearing, sudden shifts in ancient patterns of light and sound? What did the fish think? Were they disapproving? Were they confused?

184

Meanwhile, the storage boxes sat empty. Aneetsick was away hunting in the marshes behind Klinniklinnikaht, with Callicum, Sea-ossum, and Georgie McPhee. The wintering flocks no longer settled on the Nootseetaht delta, scared off by the shotguns. When the geese passed over, in a honking, swishing cloud, the people tipped their heads and paused in their labours: the men scything, or bundling shingles, the women digging for potatoes under the watchful eye of Annie, Donald's new wife.

Donald had given up waiting for a bride ship and sent for his distant cousin Annie; somehow she had seemed less formidable in recall than in person, flouncing off the gangplank in Port Albert with the scathing pronouncement: "So this is the back of the world!"

Georgie was also married, to Lucille, eldest daughter of the Lavalles. William took scant satisfaction in Georgie's choice of a wife, a choice further diminished by the marriage of Sea-ossum to Marie Lavalle, and Callicum's courtship of Louise.

The marriages of their daughters ensured survival for the Lavalles; Anton had returned from the interior no better off than when he left. The euphoria of the gold rush had fizzled almost as quickly as it began, and Port Albert was once again a placid outpost, except for the native camp. The colonial government had put out the call for settlers, who paid their shillings and pre-empted their chosen acres, and commenced the arduous conversion from forest to farm. And all along the coast, for inspiration, these newcomers looked to the example of the Squally Bay McPhees.

For her school, Julia provided frocks and trousers, and led alphabet drills, and despite Annie's observation that the children attended only for the tea at the lessons' end, the parlour was open to all. William would have preferred some other location; in the evenings, he was certain that he could smell a penetrating combination of smoke, sweat, and manure. Henry and Johnny had progressed from the poultry to the livestock, and although Julia did the milking, she could not have managed without their help.

The children droned along with Julia, sapped by the heat of the woodstove and by their morning of play. Hidden in Henry's shirt was a needle-like thorn which he used to prick Johnny, rousing the room to a brawl. Five-year-old Tsuwitty fingered the ribbons of scar beneath his pants, keeping his distance from the older boys. Beside him, Maggie recited in the sing-song cadence of one whose attention is far away, in the farthest reaches of the forest, where she and Tsuwitty were constructing a guerilla retreat. She was determined to evade young William, who reported her activities every night at the supper table, in a voice sly and prim.

Evangeline yawned dreamily, admiring the wallpaper, cherubs and cottage roses climbing to the ceiling in exotic curls. She laid her head on Maggie's shoulder, listening to Julia's accent. Julia spoke English, Pali spoke the village dialect, and Jean-Louis spoke French; quite naturally, Evangeline replied in a mixture of all three. Jean-Louis brought her down the river path in the mornings, when he worked at the mill, and Pali fetched her in the afternoons, out walking with baby Pauline.

Julia knelt amongst her students, passing out coloured pebbles to help them make sense of their sums. She jumped to her feet at the sound of her husband on the verandah; with an hour till dinner, only an emergency would bring him home.

William was in the kitchen, trying to ignore the two native girls sitting on the rug peeling vegetables, tittering helplessly. After four years they still fell apart at the sight of the man of the house.

"What's wrong?" asked Julia.

"A splinter." Glaring at the girls, he showed Julia the inflamed line beneath his thumbnail. "I tried to pull it out but I just made it worse." He had intended to work until dinner but his thumb, a part of his anatomy previously unnoticed, suddenly got in the way of every task.

Julia clucked sympathetically. "Come along where the light is best."

He went with her along the hall to the front parlour, unheated except for guests, elegantly panelled and filled with furniture shipped out from Scotland. She led him to her writing table, beneath a large, draped window overlooking the bay. She rummaged through her tray of sewing supplies and held his wrist tightly, probing the nail. His jaw clenched, he stared across to the spit, where the clouds met the sea, sodden, leaden, closing off their pocket of civilization.

When the splinter was removed, Julia brushed his thumb with a kiss. He glanced down at her in a rush of appreciation. Her hair was pulled back in a loose knot, exposing her neck. At thirty-one, she was as lovely as the angel in the Edinburgh church, where, deaf to the sermon, he had been swept away by the sunlight crowning her head.

She leaned against his chest, and he realized, with a twinge, that it had been more than a year since she had brought out her silver flute.

He would insist that she play at Christmas, and the New Year. At times she spoke of the simplicity of the early days, in their first house, now used by visitors and christened "the honeymoon cottage" because of the hearts on the hinges and the walls. She had stayed in bed for a week after they moved into the new house, and her helpers had moped in the kitchen, adrift. "It's too grand!" she explained tearfully. Surely she had not expected them to live in the cottage for the rest of their lives?

Now, in this moment of tenderness, he forgave her every inconsistency and held her close. What a distance he had travelled, from the bleak, trodden moors of his youth, where black-faced sheep appeared out of the fog like blots on a conscience, solemn reminders of the stinginess of life. Here he revelled in the lushness of the land, not yet robbed by centuries of travail. He put his lips to her hair, breathing in her lavender warmth.

"What have you been doing?" he asked, picking up her hands.

"Making soap," Julia laughed, trying to hide her reddened skin. The vat of lard and lye had bubbled on the stove all week under Annie's supervision, the native girls holding their noses behind her back. "Clean, clean, clean," sighed Julia, "and it's not even spring."

They left the parlour, Julia stepping into the kitchen to check on the progress of dinner. William continued along the hall, and as he reached for the door handle, a proper knob, not the levers Jean-Louis had carved for the cottage, he heard his son speaking in the schoolroom. He hesitated, listening, not sure what to make of young William; Maggie's forthrightness was a blessing in contrast.

"Wrong again!" young William shrilled.

There was a rattling of pebbles, then a piping voice: Evangeline, elfin daughter of Jean-Louis and Julia's first kitchen maid. Though not old enough for school, Evangeline apparently refused to be left out. Already she possessed the boldness that William had come to see as characteristic of the half-breed, like Lucille Lavalle, seducing Georgie with her indecent bosom and rolling brown eyes.

"Why must I?" demanded Evangeline. "What does it matter anyway?"

"Why?" Young William spoke severely. "Because when you grow up, you are going to be my wife, that's why!"

William fled the house, his moment with Julia forgotten, the heavy hand of destiny squeezing inside his chest. Until now, he had wanted

Squally Bay for himself. He must go to Port Albert; he must encourage Robert Airley to send countrymen out his way. Sharing his dream, he reflected dismally, was his children's only hope for a proper life.

After their lessons, the children played on the beach below the village, unbothered by the rain. They chased the tide with trenches and launched fleets of flotsam, with seaweed sails. Kahammis listened contentedly from where she sat at the hearth, skinning a rod of ironwood which she had brought back from her morning walk. She was making a poker to tend the potatoes in the coals.

First brought to the village by Gitti-kang, potatoes were now multiplying in the McPhee fields. The fields also produced turnips and beans and vistas of grass for the beasts in the barns. The pickers received part of the harvest, counted out by Annie. But the picking came in the same season as the ripening berries, forcing the women to rise even earlier, lifting and stooping all day. How thankful they were when winter came, and they could rest.

Kahammis held the poker to the flames, hardening the wood. She heard an angry yell from the beach, replacing the sounds of the children. She went over to the entrance, where Paonea had lifted the mat, gazing out with baby Noni in her arms.

Annie was stomping along the shoreline, heading for Maggie, whose boots had been tossed aside, her blonde pigtails unravelling.

"Miss Maggie McPhee!" shouted Annie. "Come here at once!"

Young William and the others edged furtively away. Annie's face was white, like the apron covering her from neck to shins. Her hair was fastened with long, sharp pins; she kept spares in her pocket and by the end of the day, she appeared to be wearing a prickly metal cap.

Maggie slopped through the shallows, her skirt tucked between her bare legs.

"What do you think you are doing? Put on your boots! Pull down your skirt! Do you want to end up in the gutter?"

Maggie looked around, perplexed.

Annie made a grab for her, yanking her over her knee, smacking her with grim outrage. When Maggie regained her balance, she stumbled up the slope.

"Where are you going?" gasped Annie.

"To the lodge," muttered Maggie.

"To the lodge?" Annie was incredulous. "Get home and help your mother. And let this be a lesson, do you hear?"

Maggie turned blankly towards the river, young William scurrying behind.

Tsuwitty and Evangeline crept up the slope and went immediately to Kahammis, burying their faces in her cape.

"Does this mean that Maggie has bad spirits in her?" asked Tsuwitty, in a stifled voice. "Was her auntie beating them out?"

Suddenly, from up on the ridge came the crack of splintering wood. Kahammis and the children rushed around to the side of the lodge. Donald McPhee was retrieving his double-bitted axe from the lower branches of the majestic cedar tree Kahammis had always thought of as her own. Annie strode towards him, shouting advice.

Kahammis stared, stupefied. She let go of the children and rushed up to the ridge. Donald was just lifting his axe when she flew past him, into the tree. She faced him, breathing raggedly, her arms outstretched.

Raindrops glinted along the metal blade that he held in mid-air. "Get out of my way!" he roared, Annie scowling over his shoulder.

Kahammis stood unblinking, steadying her breath. As if by a hidden signal the lodges emptied, villagers filing up to the ridge.

Donald lowered his axe. "See this tree?" he said thickly. "See this field over here?"

Kahammis was aware that his property adjoined the natural boundary of the ridge. She did not take her eyes off his face.

"Well," roared Donald, "this tree is blocking my sun!" Annie nodded wrathfully at the villagers.

Evangeline and Tsuwitty knew instinctively to run for their fathers, at the mill. Jean-Louis noticed them coming, and shut down the saw. Sa-sat-kis dropped his bundle of shingles, and William emerged, frowning, from behind the boiler.

Tsuwitty seized his father's hand and ran with him back to the village, William behind them, at a more dignified pace. He climbed up to the ridge, astonished at the crowd.

Donald leaned on his axe with an exaggerated sigh. "Will someone please tell her to get out of my way?" He stepped back, sighting along the huge trunk. "There's enough rails in this tree to fence my entire field! Look how old it is. Why, it'll probably fall down in the next good wind!"

Jean-Louis spoke up. "Where is the edge of your land?" He seldom found time to play his violin now, and his once-twinkling eyes were subdued.

William crossed his arms, studying the ridge and the field. "The tree belongs to the Reserve," he declared, and the villagers exhaled, moving closer, in support.

Out of the corner of her eye, Kahammis saw canoes approaching the spit: Aneetsick and the hunters, home from the marshes. She straightened, smiling to herself.

"I'm afraid this tree is not yours to cut down," William told Donald, barely controlling his impatience. This was the second interruption for the day, when they had a long list of orders to fill. The fence, William knew, was Annie's idea; she was convinced that the natives stole vegetables when her back was turned.

"Wait a minute," protested Donald. "I'm trying to grow food, right?" Annie's head bobbed vehemently. "Food!" repeated Donald, spitting out his words. "Do these people not understand food?"

William looked at the old woman guarding the tree and he shuddered; she would haunt him until the day she died. "Come along," he said to Donald, under his breath. "You'll make a fool of yourself if you don't."

Donald hoisted his axe over his shoulder, and the villagers averted their eyes. He crossed the field with Annie, and the men returned to the mill.

Kahammis stayed on the ridge until they were gone. She had reached back through the decades and found the strength that had defied the Wewksah, and Quassoon, against impossible odds. She held her head high as she went down to the beach, where the canoes crunched ashore.

Georgie disembarked with Lucille, who had been staying with her family at Hoxem. The children danced around the canoes, and the women cheered as the hunters showed their bounty. Georgie slung a pair of mallards over his back and delivered them to the big house. Julia accepted them delightedly, smiling at Lucille, who blushed behind her husband.

The following day was a Sunday, decreed by the McPhees as the day of rest. For the villagers it was a day of celebration; Aneetsick distributed the game amongst the lodges, and the fires were piled high with fresh boughs while the men drank tea and recounted the hunt. The women brought out the best dishes, stirring and mashing and singing: yes, they would eat well tonight!

The oil lamps glowed in the dining room of the McPhee house, where Julia served the roasted ducks. She had invited Donald and

Annie, sparing Georgie the embarrassment of refusal; he and Lucille were upriver, visiting Pali and Jean-Louis. Annie had not acknowledged Lucille, and discouraged any letters to Scotland, with Georgie's news.

The mahogany sideboard was set with Julia's finest china, recently arrived on the London ship. Young William sat watchfully; Maggie shifted in her chair to gain as much distance as possible from her aunt. William waited for his wife at the head of the table, pleased and relaxed. Since January they had cut over thirty thousand board feet of lumber, not to mention pilings, shingles, and spars, their best year yet.

The kitchen girls carried in platters of vegetables, jugs of gravy and cordial, bowls of chutney and pickled eggs. They fluttered at the door until Julia dismissed them with a wave. William said grace, then rose to carve the mallards, which had been stuffed with apples and raisins and rice. Annie took a slice of bread from a woven cedar basket, passing it back with a grimace of distaste.

Maggie glanced meaningfully at her brother. They had made a bet as to whether their uncle would spray food, in one of his fits.

The men discussed the most recent developments, including Robert Airley's promise to send out settlers, and the prospects for expanding the mill. Julia sat quietly, and Annie busied herself with the platters.

"What's this?" Young William stabbed at his plate with his fork.

"Glazed parsnips," murmured Julia. "At least try one little bite." She sighed as he rearranged his food, his mouth compressed.

From beneath her eyebrows, Maggie observed her aunt. She and Tsuwitty were planning to dig a gigantic pit, camouflaged with leaves. Tsuwitty also had plans for a snare, to be tripped by Annie's foot as she chased them into the forest. Maggie chewed thoughtfully, examining every feature of her aunt's face. She had decided that when she grew up, she would look like Lucille.

"Please eat," chided Julia. Young William was as skinny as a cricket in his Sunday suit. "Your friends in the village would love to have such a heaping plate." She bit her tongue as the words came out and Donald groaned, reminded of the altercation on the ridge.

"I can't believe it," he spluttered, his mouth full. "Here they are, complaining about how the fish haven't come, how hungry they're going to be. You'd think they would have some common sense!"

He held out his plate for more meat. Annie, sensing Maggie's stare, glanced sharply at her niece.

191

"Perhaps they are hungry already," murmured Julia, her hands in her lap. The shortage of salmon troubled her; she had missed the spectacle of the delta bustling with cutters, the air smoky and sweet with the drying fires. She had just discovered the shortbread tin inexplicably empty and her helpers had confessed, with many tears. In the village, food was shared according to need. How could she punish the girls when they did not perceive that what they had done was wrong?

William sipped his cordial; he would have a whisky later, when his guests left. "I've been thinking," he said, clearing his throat. "I've been thinking about putting a stop to those ... winter ceremonies."

Julia turned to him, shocked. "You can't do that. It's their religion. It's the same as our Christmas. They look forward to those ceremonies all year!"

Annie choked over her duck. "You call those obscene carvings religion?" She bitterly resented having to walk past the welcome figures along the beach. "You call those bare-naked dances religion?" She glared around the table, knife and fork in her fists.

Maggie and young William were hushed and wide-eyed. Their mother was very still, and their father calmly sipped cordial.

"I'm afraid the ceremonies are merely an excuse to ...," William paused, pursing his lips, "... to overeat, to indulge."

"That's it exactly," snorted Donald. "Indulge!" He shovelled up the last of his potatoes, his face flushing. "Like children! They have no self-control!"

Bits of potato splattered across the table as he spoke. Maggie and young William ducked, exploding into laughter beneath the white linen cloth. Their father rapped the table and they sat up, not daring to look at each other, frozen on the edges of their chairs.

When the meal was over, William ushered Donald and Annie out the front door. They heard drumming from the village, primitive and insistent, and William stood on the verandah long after his guests had disappeared into the gloom. It was not that he disagreed with Julia, but someone had to do the work. Someone had to take responsibility for the future of Squally Bay.

Rain dripped through the smokehole down to where Kahammis squatted on her heels, watching Aneetsick across the hearth. How satisfied Aneetsick looked, to have provided for his people, who surrounded him now with their happiness and song. When she told him about the incident on the ridge, he had nodded, suggesting that it had been necessary for the McPhees to learn that boundaries could work both ways. He had seen enough to know that the McPhees would never understand how the coast people felt about their land. They lacked the generosity of spirit, he told Kahammis gravely, and though it was a regrettable limitation, it need not interfere with village life.

Kahammis scanned the crowded lodge, reassuring herself that all her family were present, and well. When the leftovers were carried out, when the children yawned sleepily, the drummers rolled their sticks to a crescendo of applause, and everyone turned to Kahammis, faces shining with expectation in the firelight.

Her black eyes sparkled and her voice cackled as she told the legends, spinning back through the generations, pulling her people closer, into the heart of the great universe of which they were such a tiny, hopeful part. Onward spun the stories, and her voice grew stronger, not weaker, and the people of Nootseetaht listened, gratified and secure.

~~~:~~~

There were certain winters when the squalls marched in relentless succession down from the hills, across the bay, into the ocean beyond the spit. Just when it seemed that the clouds would last forever, tantalizing breaks would appear, slits which revealed the electric blue sky above, followed by whole hours of sunshine. The people would move about slowly, chins uplifted, palms upturned, as if better to receive this golden elixir they had so missed. It was on such an afternoon that Kahammis walked the spit with the children, the wind whipping back their hair and stinging their cheeks. Lessons completed for the day, the children squabbled over driftwood and climbed the lone pine to the marker, and the raven clicked and complained from across the channel.

Gazing offshore with her hand shading her eyes, Kahammis was puzzled by the continuous flow of canoes, travelling north with the tide but against the fair-weather gale. The raven quietened, as if in confirmation of this unusual sight. Even the children were surprised, although they were used to canoes, reserving their excitement for the supply schooners or the occasional gunboat.

Kahammis turned from the ocean, narrowing her gaze to exclude the cleared land, focusing instead on the activity around the lodges.

193

The fishermen had just brought in spruce branches laden with herring spawn, and Pali and Paonea were setting up the racks. Nearby played their daughters Noni and Pauline, born within weeks of each other and now two and a half years old. Moochinnick had never seen Noni, the village sealing over in his absence.

The herring set off the season of abundance, the dipnets bending from the weight of the wriggling silver fish. It had been several years, however, since the storage boxes had been truly full. Kahammis searched her mind for solutions, and still they celebrated, honouring the first herring, the first coho, the first whale. But they celebrated with a surreptitiousness and a restraint utterly contrary to their purpose, ever since William McPhee's lecture on the harms of the feast. Aneetsick had diplomatically heard him out; inwardly, he had seethed. How could he tell his people, don't sing, don't dance? How could he respect a man who, when discussing the spirit of Nootseetaht, spoke not from his soul but from a mouth twisted up with strange notions of evil?

Now, standing on the windy spit, Kahammis watched Aneetsick step out of his lodge and turn towards the delta, where a canoe had been left on trestles, the carvers otherwise occupied in the fields. She and Aneetsick had shared a lifetime of losses and gains, yet somehow, Aneetsick's pain hurt more than her own. She had her weaving; for the warrior chief, there was no respite. When at times she could not find him, she knew he was upriver with his guns. But the battle for which he had so valiantly prepared had never materialized, and his ammunition had been spoiled by moisture in the caves. Slowly he walked the beach below the village, not looking anywhere but forward, as if the sprawling McPhee homestead did not exist. He stopped beside the canoe, touching the unfinished markings of the Thunderbird and Whale.

Kalowish was building the canoe to commemorate the birth of Seaossum's twin sons. He worked with the toddlers in the shavings between his feet, pestering him with questions, and never had Kahammis seen him more at peace.

Racing to the end of the spit, the children again dislodged the raven from his perch. They pointed to a column of steam coming up behind the canoes, and sure enough, this was one of the vessels that figured so vividly in their imaginations: a gunboat, naval authority of the colonial government, stationed at the fort.

Young William shouted himself hoarse, certain that the appearance of the gunboat signalled the war that his Aunt Annie had been predicting. News of skirmishes with the Indians trickled steadily across the border from the United States, causing the McPhees and all the other settlers to glance uneasily at the dark faces in their midst. Despite the depression that had followed the rush for gold, the native camp at Port Albert had flourished, a black hole of depravity growing wider and deeper around the harbour. Georgie McPhee scoffed at such talk; Julia refused to listen, spending more and more days in bed.

Young William hurled stones across the spit, eager to take up arms. Kahammis moved out of range, tugging at her cape and squinting at a canoe which had separated from the convoy offshore. As the canoe swerved closer, lifting and rolling in the rough sea, she recognized the sweeping northern prow. It was Gitti-kang, his paddlers aiming, drenched and determined, for Nootseetaht.

The children ran to the village in anticipation of visitors. Kahammis stood by the pine tree as the canoe shot past, Gitti-kang raising his hand to her from the stern. She saw with pleasure that he was wearing a hat she had made for him, on the occasion of a blubber feast several years before.

When she reached the village, Gitti-kang was speaking with Aneetsick in a low, urgent voice. Gitti-kang's people remained aboard, staring soberly at the villagers gathering to greet them. Aneetsick called to Chee-uxqua, who immediately mobilized the women and girls. Yanis hurried to the water pool upriver, and the others went into the lodges, coming out with boxes and baskets of food.

Gitti-kang received the food with a formality which further mystified Kahammis, and she moved nearer. As always, she wore her most recent evolution in capes, festooned with past and current treasures familiar to her own people but arousing much curiosity amongst the northerners; the children in the canoe peeked from the sanctuary of their mothers' knees, smiling for the first time. But the smiles of the children seemed to have a reverse effect on Gitti-kang, his old face wrinkling so sorrowfully that Kahammis reeled, looking to Aneetsick for explanation. He stood aside, aloof, his characteristic response to distress.

When all the supplies were stowed, Gitti-kang rose ceremoniously to give his paddlers the order to leave. Then he paused, rummaging beneath the decorated blanket draped around his shoulders. He beckoned to Kahammis, and pushed a small, grimy basket into her hand.

The great canoe reversed, bow swivelling towards the sea. Clouds were smoking along the horizon, and stray gusts frothed up the water inside the bay. Gitti-kang raised his arm in a final salute, and the villagers responded with a song of farewell.

Kahammis remained on the beach as the last chorus faded out over the spit, and then she turned her head, inadvertently meeting Aneetsick's eyes. In all their years together, she had witnessed his victories and his rage; never had she witnessed his fear. Once more she reeled, clutching the basket. She did not want the basket; she wanted Gitti-kang back, feeding them potatoes and stories, making Aneetsick laugh. Her fingers shook as she withdrew the carved loon.

Moochinnick appeared in a borrowed canoe, later in the afternoon. He laboriously crossed the bay, and Paonea watched from the entrance, holding Noni, who squealed to join her companions. Paonea looked as trapped as Noni when Moochinnick lumbered up the slope, trailing his filthy bearskin.

Revived by a meal of fresh spawn, he soon had the young men enthralled with his tales of treachery and triumph over impossible odds, impossible to anyone but Moochinnick. At the climax of his oratory he beat on his chest, slamming Kahammis backwards in time; she crouched over her pipe at the far side of the hearth.

Aneetsick had not spoken since the departure of Gitti-kang. "Why have you come?" he growled finally, interrupting Moochinnick.

"This is my home!" Moochinnick was lathered with sweat in the warm lodge. He winked at Noni, who frowned from behind her grandmother, Chee-uxqua.

Aneetsick spat into the flames. "You came because the governor told you to," he said coldly, and everyone in the lodge stiffened at the mention of the governor, the almighty fort chief. "The governor ordered the natives to leave, is that not true?"

Moochinnick coughed, flustered. He had further expanded during his long absence; unable to fit into pants, he had wrapped a length of soiled cloth around his waist. Mortified, Paonea wondered how she could induce him to wash.

"What about the sickness?" asked Aneetsick.

Moochinnick blinked. "Sickness?"

"The burning-up sickness." Aneetsick's eyes glittered, and the lodge was silent, the little basket hot in Kahammis's hand.

"I don't know any sickness," Moochinnick replied petulantly, slurping tea. He grinned at his young audience and thumped his chest. "Do I look sick?"

Aneetsick got up and went out into the blustery night. Kahammis would also have left, if she had somewhere to go, for it was unbearable to listen to Moochinnick's tales growing ever more grandiose, Henry and Johnny sitting worshipfully at his feet.

The following morning, William McPhee sighted the white plume of the gunship on its way back to the fort. He set out at once with Donald and Georgie, to intercept the ship. The crew of the gunship took no risks with the entrance into the bay, heaving to off the spit while they shouted back and forth with William. This was a scene repeated all along the coast as the colonists struggled to keep abreast of change, secluded in their small inlets and coves.

When the McPhee men returned to the bay, Kahammis was on the delta with the children, watching the carved outlines of the Thunderbird and Whale burst into life beneath the chisels of Kalowish and Sa-sat-kis. Paddling rapidly, the McPhees went straight to the new wharf near the big house. They were using the canoe which had been given to Georgie during his courtship of Lucille. Georgie's possessions were few, and the villagers had been concerned that the Lavalle family would lose status if he could not at least carry his bride in a vessel of his own. They debated the matter of Georgie's crest at length, consulting with Julia and Jean-Louis; along each side of Georgie's bow flared a ripe thistle, flanked with swords.

Etched onto William's face, as he crossed the delta with his brothers, was the expression of stark reproach which Kahammis had not seen since the day he landed at Nootseetaht eight years before. He and Donald strode to the house; Kahammis guessed that Annie was inside, taking over during one of Julia's bad spells. Kahammis watched apprehensively and so did the old eagle, shifting from foot to foot in the tallest fir. Georgie continued paddling upriver, where Lucille was helping Pali ready the garden for spring.

Moments later, the window-doors at the top of the McPhee house flew apart. Julia appeared, her nightgown flapping in the gusts. Frantically she waved and called, but no one on the delta could make sense of what she was trying to say. William enfolded her from behind, pulling her inside. Maggie and Tsuwitty clutched hands, and young William looked up at the empty balcony with a pinched, frightened frown.

A lower door banged open, and the two kitchen girls darted across the verandah, into the yard. Close on their heels ran Annie, swinging her broom. A moment later, William leapt down the steps in pursuit.

He shouted at Annie and herded the two girls back inside, then he stood on the verandah, staring around, distraught. His stare stopped at the children beside the unfinished canoe.

"William! Maggie! Come here at once!"

Maggie and Tsuwitty galloped towards the house, Evangeline and young William behind. William grabbed his son and daughter, gesturing violently for the others to leave. Tsuwitty tried to join Maggie, perplexed by the sound of the bolt sliding in the door. Evangeline hammered on the door until he dragged her away. Maggie and young William shivered in the hall, listening to their mother sobbing in the bedroom above. Annie loomed out of the shadows with the broom.

William confronted her. "Control yourself! The native girls will sleep in the pantry for now. If you chase them off," he added, "who will take care of the children?"

Donald moved beside Annie, smacking his fist into his palm. "Dirty Indians! I knew from the minute I laid eyes on that camp, it would come to this."

Footsteps clomped along the verandah. Annie looked out the window, lifting her broom.

"I'll deal with it." William unbolted the door. Henry and Johnny stood grinning, bringing the milk buckets from the barn.

"Put the buckets down!" commanded William. "Go back to the village."

Henry and Johnny gaped; always before they had been received by the kitchen girls, giggling and teasing with morsels of cake.

"Go! And keep out of the barns, do you hear?"

Henry and Johnny backed away, slack-jawed.

The kettle began to whistle on the stove. Annie pointed to the children. "Bath!" she said piercingly. "Who knows where they've been," she added, glowering at their father.

"I guess I'll finish up at the mill," muttered Donald. "Someone better warn Jean-Louis." He shook his head, as if just realizing more complications. "What a bloody mess."

Alone in the hall, William tried to shut out Julia's sobs. Maggie yelped loudly from the kitchen, and he rushed into the front parlour, closing the door. He crossed the carpet to the window, leaning for support on the back of Julia's writing chair.

The villagers had assembled on the delta and were gazing in wonderment at the big house. The old crone stood off to one side, her head lowered like a turtle into the collar of her motley cape. Henry and Johnny shuffled abjectly, their hands in the pockets of their ill-fitting pants.

William slumped against the chair. He must meet with Aneetsick, he must define the limits of the village, he must keep his family safe. The officers on the gunship had been unconcerned; the natives at Squally Bay were known for their docility, and the McPhees were known for their stern but fair command. Fair! What did fair matter, now? William looked out over the delta with a recoiling horror: who amongst them already harboured the smallpox?

He had seen fat, drunken Charlie coming home to the bay. Earlier in the afternoon, he noticed the villagers giving visitors boxes and baskets of food, when daily they complained of needing more rations for their work. He could feel his frustrations blowing up inside him: Julia's limpness, Maggie's defiance, Annie's nagging, the intransigence of the natives, the never-ending battle with the land. Scarcely could he draw breath, so constricted and constrained did he feel, pinned in his parlour window by the scrutiny of the dark, ragged crowd.

In the evening, when the children were settled, he went up the wide staircase to his wife. Annie had spent the day furiously cleaning, and had been persuaded with difficulty to return to her own house. Jean-Louis was upriver with Pali, and Georgie had gone to Hoxem with Lucille. Watching them leave, William once again despaired at Georgie's poor judgment; with these relationships, what use were boundaries?

Wearily he greeted Julia, grateful to find her awake and composed. For a dreadful moment, when he had first told her the news, he thought that she intended to throw herself over the balcony. He sat on the side of the bed, patting her hands. Now that she was calmer, he could explain what he had learned from the captain of the gunship. The smallpox had been brought up the coast aboard a trading vessel, whose sailors had no doubt availed themselves of the services of the squaws. When the disease broke out in the native camp, the citizens of Port Albert had rallied, wild with fear. Finally the government was forced to do something about the sordid mess on the harbour shore. The governor ordered the natives to disperse; escorted by gunships, they were returning to their distant homes.

Julia covered her face. "What about the people who lived at Port Albert before any of us came?" she whispered.

William sighed. He had no one but himself to blame, for bringing an innocent, unprepared woman into an environment where the Indians would be her only friends. Part of him desperately wanted her to be more like Annie, though he winced to recall the faces of his children when Annie got through with her scrubbing brush.

But Julia's preoccupation with the natives was driving both him and her to exhaustion, and for what good? Everyone knew that the primitive must give way to the superior race. Unfortunate though it was, the smallpox would speed this process, civilizing the world. Furthermore, he reasoned aloud, surely Julia could not condone the drunkenness, the prostitution, and the constant uproar of the native camp?

She regarded him from the pillows, pale and forlorn in the flickering light. "Have you spoken with Aneetsick?"

He nodded, looking pained. He had explained to Aneetsick that every last pile of garbage must be cleaned up; the villagers must bathe and keep to themselves until it was certain that there was no disease in their midst. Aneetsick had inquired about the white man's medicine, taking William by surprise. The protecting medicine was very hard to come by, he told Aneetsick, even for the McPhees. The captain of the gunship had reported that supplies of the vaccine had been used up in the first days of the outbreak. Aneetsick received this news with a haughty grunt, turning away, and William had hurried back to his own house, sympathetic, but relieved. Now more than ever, the natives must know their place.

"What do you mean?" interrupted Julia, with an ironic laugh. "This is their place, right here."

"Of course, darling, but what can we do? We must protect our children."

"Charlie arrived, yesterday." Julia's voice climbed, her cheeks reddening. "I've never liked him, from the beginning! That's what I was trying to tell them, out on the delta, to send Charlie to his home up the coast! But they're very loyal, you know. He's married to Aneetsick's daughter. They would never make him go."

William caressed her slender wrists, taken aback. What else was swarming around in her mind?

"Do you remember when we first came to Port Albert, we saw that canoe full of Indians from across the straits? Do you remember?" cried Julia. "They were ravaged. Ravaged!"

"But they survived," he murmured, holding her tightly. "It will be all right, Julia, I promise."

The days passed, and the mill lay dormant, and a sense of unreality set in amongst the villagers, wounded by a banishment they could not comprehend. Aneetsick gathered his people, repeating what he had been told by William, but he failed to meet their eyes, focusing above their heads as if he was addressing some distant presence, perhaps the Thunderbird of his crest. The snowy-headed eagle spent long hours in the fir tree, calling out in a high pip-pip, and the villagers listened carefully, seeking reassurance for themselves and their chief.

For Kahammis, the passing days brought unanticipated delight, not only because with spring came renewal, but because the stilled machinery returned Nootseetaht to the rhythms of earlier, untroubled times. She would not be drawn into discussions of disease, the roving hand of vengeance which struck here and there along the coast. Disease had decimated the enemy Wewksah; she never doubted that her own people would be spared. The men spoke angrily around the hearths: with no wages, and trading suspended at Port Albert, how would their families eat? But of course the universe provided, as it always had. The canoes went out at dawn and came back loaded with mussels and oysters and clams, and the women went into the forest and returned with their baskets filled.

So when Callicum and Sea-ossum brought in the year's first halibut, Aneetsick quite properly organized a feast. The women hesitated to celebrate amidst such uncertainty, but Kahammis spurred on the drummers and the dancers; the masks and the rattles and the cloaks were concealed in readiness behind the painted stage screens.

Moochinnick, who seldom roused himself from his fetid nest by the hearth, barked orders with mounting irascibility as the hour of the feast drew near. His habitual belching and spitting had driven off even the younger boys, fascinated though they were with bodily functions. His sole authority was now over Paonea, who rushed to stop his bellowing and restore peace. Noni avoided him totally, while Henry and Johnny turned against each other with fresh fury, deprived of their farm jobs and crushed by their father's decline.

On the morning of the feast, Kahammis woke to Moochinnick's snores. Then she heard Paonea's quiet weeping, and she cursed the wicked, far-reaching powers of the fort. But she got up determined to enjoy herself, clapping her hands and summoning Yanis to brush her cape.

At dusk Jean-Louis strolled down the river path with Pauline on his shoulders. Pali was beside him, carrying the violin case. Evangeline ran ahead, and when they reached her, she was looking up despondently at the brightly lit mansion. Jean-Louis ruffled her ringlets with a tender sigh. She had rejected his explanations, broken-hearted at being kept from her playmates and school.

Suddenly she caught sight of Maggie and young William in the parlour window. "Look, papa, look!" She waved, but the two heads vanished as abruptly as they had appeared.

"Papa," wailed Evangeline, "will anything ever be the same?"

"Things are the same already," exclaimed Jean-Louis. "Same heron out there on the delta fishing for his supper. Same raindrops on your nose!" Pauline began to fuss on his shoulders. "Oh-oh," he groaned, "same wee voice crying from the wilderness."

Jean-Louis had been vaccinated against smallpox years before, at his mother's insistence. Thankful now for her advice, he thought back to the letter he had sent her, months after the tragic journey to Port Albert, with news of Evangeline's birth. In painstaking detail, hating himself for his duplicity, he had crafted a meeting with a priest. He would carry forever the burden of that terrible journey, a burden eased only by Pali's love, and his vow to never again impose his world on hers. Even so, she cooked their stews and grew roses with skill that surpassed his own. She was worth a thousand Annies, and he felt sorry for Donald, who looked more beaten every year. Annie had become the watchdog for the sins of Squally Bay, a role she had assumed with relish since the quarantine. She patrolled the McPhee fields, raving if the children stepped across the line separating, in her mind, the savage from the privileged. How she could blame the natives for circumstances beyond their cause or control was a mystery to Jean-Louis, and he roared if she came too close.

Proudly he ushered his family into Aneetsick's lodge. He helped himself from the food trays with both hands, and when the crowd requested his jigs and reels, he was eager to comply. They revelled through the night, and the wind carried the sounds of their merriment far out over the water, away from the McPhees.

The next morning, Moochinnick moaned pitifully; Kahammis assumed he felt slighted, and paid no heed. He shook as if stricken by a chill but when Paonea stoked the embers, he threw a box of water over himself and ordered her away. By evening he was writhing on the bearskin, convinced that an old enemy had stuck a knife in his back.

Aneetsick could take no more. "Roll over," he told Moochinnick through his teeth. "I'll stick that knife in farther if you don't shut up."

Moochinnick howled all night, oblivious to Aneetsick's disgust. The villagers filed past him in the morning and as he dimly recognized their faces, he begged them to strike him dead. They crept away, appalled to hear articulated the wish they had been sheltering for years. Paonea and Chee-uxqua applied poultices to his inflamed throat and recited cathartic chants, and by the third day after the feast, he was cured. Except for a slight hoarseness, and an irregular complexion, he was more obnoxious than ever and the villagers regretted their restraint.

The men departed for the halibut grounds and the women paddled upriver to harvest new shoots from the thimbleberry thickets. Kahammis sat on the grassy slope near the lodge, weaving a cape for Evangeline. Though she did not like to admit it, she was conserving her stamina for the bark-gathering. She was dozing in the sunshine between squalls when the women returned, their bows heaped with greenery. Paonea and Noni came up the slope, and Noni ran to give Kahammis a fresh shoot.

Paonea entered the lodge. Immediately she burst out, quaking and speechless; her mouth opened and closed like a gaffed fish. Noni began to cry, and Chee-uxqua rushed up the slope in alarm. She took one look at Paonea and went inside. Through a wall of disbelief, Kahammis heard her screams.

When the men came home, the village appeared deserted. The women and children were inside, huddled at the hearths.

Moochinnick's face was covered with fiery splotches which seemed to be swelling even as Aneetsick and the other men stared. Moochinnick peered around the lodge, searching for Paonea, who hovered like a ghost nearby. He gestured for water, and the men backed away, fleeing into the sunlight.

The following day, splotches erupted on Moochinnick's shoulders, spreading along his belly to his legs, until he became a continuous rotting, draining wound. He could not speak or sleep or see; he bleated and quivered until finally he died. The men dragged the bearskin down to the beach and lifted Moochinnick into the canoe he had brought from the fort. They towed the canoe beyond the spit and set it ablaze, and they watched until the last smouldering chunks of cedar fell away.

Darkness preceded light, day preceded night: the people of Nootseetaht moved jerkily through their rituals and their needs. Kahammis was awake very early in the mornings, listening, knowing that the owl was out there, close by. Strangely, she had never felt less ready; she could not begin to count up the baskets yet to find their shape, the feasts yet to plan. She listened with detachment, a suspense of the restlessness that had driven her for so long. She found herself riveted by the radiance of the ocean after a storm, and she chortled out loud at the antics of the jays. She studied the fat bottom of the honeybee waggling along the border of Evangeline's cape, as if she had never seen such a remarkable sight. For lost hours she sat clouded in pipesmoke, her fingers clamped around the stone stem, and only later was she aware of the ferocity of her grip.

Yanis scoured the hearth where Moochinnick had lain. Paonea blackened her face and cut off her hair, while Henry and Johnny roamed listlessly, indifferent to the efforts of the younger boys to goad them into a fight. Pali came down from the cabin, singing lullabies to Pauline in a brave, fluting voice.

Aneetsick purified himself, and went out in his whaling canoe to scout for the first migrating greys. Kahammis watched him from the ridge, until he merged with the haze; she was filled with admiration at his refusal to be shamed. Moochinnick's flaming exodus had not gone unnoticed; white cloth strips fluttered from the fences, lest the villagers forget their limits.

The morning came when Paonea failed to get up from her sleeping platform. Noni poked and cajoled, and Paonea turned to the wall-boards, not wanting to frighten her child. Within a few days the enormity of the sickness hit: first Paonea, then Chee-uxqua, Henry, Pauline, Yanis, Johnny, and Kalowish. Callicum and Sea-ossum ferried bodies wrapped in mats to the burial caves. High over the village rose the shrieks of the gulls and the crows and the eagles, a never-ending

204

cacophony of despair. When she did sleep, which was rarely, Kahammis relived the long-ago massacre in her dreams.

Jean-Louis buried Pauline, placing rosebuds like ripening apricots across the small mound of soil. He sat on a river boulder in the starlight, and drew his bow haltingly over the strings of his violin. Reflected in the scabbed, stunned faces of Pali and Evangeline was his gratitude; they would begin again.

One afternoon, filling containers at the flagged river pool, Kahammis realized that it had been too many hours since she had last seen Aneetsick. She launched her canoe and paddled upriver, straining against the green water flooding down from the mountains. As she had expected, Aneetsick's canoe was pulled up on the bank beside the winter camp of their youth.

She went ashore, staggering through the overgrown glade, searching for the trails where she and her brothers had played. She came upon Aneetsick propped on a ledge outside one of the secret caves. His stomach and shoulders were bleeding where he had tried to rub off his sores with evergreens. She sat with him through the evening, through the night. He opened his eyes to the sunrise, and turned to her with such anguish that her breath stopped in her chest.

Her tears spilled onto his blistered skin as she cradled him close. But after a few minutes, he pushed her away. She drifted downriver, her head bowed, her paddle at her knees. The eddies over the delta caught her canoe and twirled her out into the bay.

The McPhees watched her from the upper balcony of their big house, where they stood taking in the morning air. Julia lifted her arm timidly, leaning against her husband; she was almost weightless beneath her shawls. Night after night they had lain awake to the moans and screams of the villagers, the snufflings of the kitchen girls, the whimpers of Maggie and young William. The fields were unseeded and the tools were rusting from disuse. Had it not been for the support of Captain Hume and the *Coast Princess*, they would have lacked provisions as well. Donald and Annie wanted to evacuate to Port Albert; William was convinced that they should stay put, the epidemic would run its course.

As the small, sleek canoe drifted erratically across the sandbars, William was struck by the sight. He stared down at the old woman more closely; unexpectedly she tipped her head, meeting his gaze.

With a jolt he reached inside himself, for a response to the grief in her face. But he felt nothing; he was numb.

A cloud of black wings rose up suddenly from the forest behind the village. William nudged Julia and pointed, and the ravens swirled above the delta in confusion, turning north. When the last raven had passed over, when the old woman had beached her canoe below the lodges, Squally Bay again belonged to the McPhees, sparkling and serene.

On Kahammis's final day, the sky at dawn was that perfect, celestial blue she had once looked to for courage; now, her eyes were veiled like the coast as the day progressed. By evening the rain began, in sheets, then varying mists, mingling with the tide that breathed along the shore, along the spit, where the oystercatchers ran.

The canoes which had set off from Port Albert, on the order of the governor, stopped for food and refuge not only at Nootseetaht but at Klinniklinnikaht, at Quatlukaht, in the Mannakaht sound, all the way to Gitti-kang's islands. Within two years the epidemic did run its course, but a third of the people had succumbed. The royal lineages were shattered, the singers faltered, and the drums were silent. A terrible pall hung over the coast; even the survivors walked as corpses, hollow-eyed with loss.

Yes, the little owl was waiting at twilight when Kahammis died, when her spirit was whisked into the protective canopy of the trees. And thus passed the life of Kahammis: Kahammis, of the spring rain.

~~~:~~~

MARIANNE: April, 1992

"WHO IS IT?" rasps Grandma Em.

Earl is perched on the edge of the visitor's chair, fidgeting with his hands. Though Earl and Winnie had not wanted to admit Grandma Em to the hospital in Port Albert, it seemed only right and responsible; week after week she had lain curled on her mat, and no one knew what else to do. Earl is glad to see me; for all her frailty, I could hear Grandma Em berating him as I came along the hall. She was reminding him that she will not be buried in the mission cemetery, outside the Reserve, where clumps of plastic flowers have been strewn amongst the gravestones, indecently everlasting, like grief. She wants a proper burial, the old way. I have heard rumours of this from Tony, whose aversion to hospitals restricts him to the parking lot, where he contemplates the dusk from the sanctuary of his truck.

Overcome by the sudden intimacy, Earl mumbles goodbye and slips out to join Tony. I sit listening to Grandma Em's wheezing, to the clang of medicine carts, the swish of curtains, the soft tread of the nursing staff on their ceaseless rounds and tasks. But I hear these sounds from an immense distance, momentarily forgetting Grandma Em and marvelling at how far I have come. Grandma Em stirs. Her family is gone and it is only me, an outsider, she has left. She withers into the sheets and is soon asleep.

Her sleeping is nature's gentle revenge on the relentlessness of life. Sleep ought to come easily to the dying, and the sad. But her timing troubles me, for it is spring.

All through winter's long nights and enclosing rains she has been telling me the history of each islet, each clam bed, each point of land belonging to her ancestors. The village at Squally Bay was repeatedly attacked by warriors from across the southeast straits; the last attack would have occurred about the time Captain Hume arrived on the coast, trading for furs. Grandma Em believes that her people have endured because of their crests, their alliances with the natural world. Through her mother's family, Grandma Em received the crest of the Thunderbird and Whale. Earl, through his father Vincent from Klinniklinnikaht, owns the Raven crest. Though I can scarcely keep track of all these inheritances, Tony is clearly, by local standards, a wealthy man.

But as I sit now in this dim hospital setting, I fear that I have asked too much of Grandma Em. I have not forgotten that day in the fall, when she showed me the photograph of her grandfather, Jean-Louis, and her mother, Evangeline. I should never have spoken: before I could stop myself, the words rushed out. We have become so removed from the hideousness of disease. No one mentions smallpox; in the history books, the epidemics are summed up in two or three lines.

A skinny arm pokes through the curtain. Jimmy Joe peeps anxiously, making sure that he has found the right room. He drops something onto the white bedspread and disappears as soundlessly as he arrived.

Grandma Em's hand emerges, grabbing Jimmy Joe's offering, a grubby but still green thimbleberry shoot. Her head pops up, and she chuckles at my amazed stare.

Later in the evening, Tony and I sit together on the porch. I have been breathing differently this past year: deeply, more settled. Dr. Conaliki theorizes about ions; Tony just laughs and asks, how could I live anywhere else? A hummingbird dives for a last sip of nectar, and Agnes calls to her cows through the orchard beside the big house. Agnes occasionally visits the clinic, prim and vacant as she awaits her turn.

208

Agnes knows she belongs here because she is the granddaughter of William McPhee, the first white child born at Squally Bay. I learned this at the museum archives, when I went looking for information on Captain Hume. William married a minister's daughter from Port Albert and raised a family in the house built by his parents, William and Julia, who arrived here from Edinburgh in 1855. Two of his brothers joined the elder William, helping construct the mill: Donald, who left no descendants, and George, who died in 1863. Agnes grew up in the original house, which was also, for many years, the post office. Her father ran the mill and her uncles, Cameron and Maxwell, operated the hotel and the hardware store.

Her grandfather William had a sister, Maggie, and it was through Maggie that I discovered the fate of Captain Hume. In the fall of 1878, Captain Hume and his crew were bringing Maggie home from Port Albert, the final leg of her journey from Scotland, where she had been working as a governess. The *Coast Princess* foundered in a sudden southeast storm: the two crew members survived, but Captain Hume drowned trying to save his only passenger. I read this with a pang though I knew he had been nearing the end of his life; his letter had expressed such pride in his seamanship, and such devotion to the coast people.

There was a small notice of the tragedy in the *Port Colonist* newspaper. A separate obituary, for Maggie, paid tribute to Captain Hume's valour and his many years of service. A memorial ceremony was held at Squally Bay for Maggie, and special mention was made of the native choir, conducted by Maggie's mother, Julia. The ceremony was attended by the former governor, who was in the area on a fishing holiday.

Tony has been readying his boat for the salmon, but without the customary joy of the season; the lovely white hulls of the trolling fleet have been coming into the bay fouled with oil, from a relatively minor spill, a fuel barge far to the south. Conversations at the pub spiral angrily, but it is the anger of impotence.

A warm mist seeps over the delta, and towards morning the rain begins, pattering on the shakes. Tony groans in his sleep, accommodating his body against mine. My fingers slide beneath the pillow, searching for the tiny basket given to me by Grandma Em.

While I am at the clinic, the hospital calls. Apparently Grandma Em has been sitting up in bed, singing through the night. Dr.

Conaliki agrees that her condition has stabilized, and Winnie brings her home. I exhale with relief, watching them rattle through the potholes on the road to the Reserve.

In May we have weeks of fine weather; the early morning chorale of the birds becomes almost frantic with the fullness of spring. On a Friday evening I tidy the clinic, luxuriating in the well-being that comes with the end of work. Tony is having supper in Port Albert with his son. I take my sweater and the walking stick Tony has made me, and follow the rutted path beside the farmhouse, glimpsing Agnes beneath her wide gardening hat. Agnes and Jimmy Joe have been spending long days turning the soil, marking the rows of seedlings with stakes and string.

Despite my mixed feelings for those two, I was touched to read the labels on their prize-winning produce at the Fall Fair: Grown by Miss Agnes McPhee and Mr. Jimmy Joseph. Grandma Em has explained that when the white people arrived, the natives took on or were given simple first names which became the surnames of their children. In her stories Grandma Em adds the old names, the lost names, consonants clicking off her tongue. So to Agnes he is Mr. Jimmy Joseph, but to Grandma Em he will always be Jimmy Joe Sa-sat-kis.

Refreshed by her stay in hospital, Grandma Em is considering a request from the Port Albert Museum for a traditional bark cape. I could see the eagerness in her fingers as she traced birds along a border pattern, confiding that she had not made a cape since she was a girl. No one bothered, when blankets would do; no one had the time.

The fields behind the McPhee homestead are unused except by a farmer who leases the right to run his horses. Finches flit amongst the hawthorn hedges, and two jays perch on cedar rails once stacked high as a man's shoulder, now sliding into the rich earth. The rail fences are a reminder: how many backs were broken, preparing this land? Angling towards the river, I pass the remnants of a barn, rotting timbers and a mossy web of roof. Beyond the barn, a cluster of thorny bushes proffers yellow roses to the dwindling light.

The roses seem somehow unsettling, even more so here than at the abandoned cabin up by the falls. They suggest passion, abundance, and hope. Passion I have trembled close to, in Tony's arms. Abundance was an unknown quantity until I made my way out to the coast, and only recently have I believed in hope. The roses remind me of Grandma Em's stories: despite our short memories and the immediacy of our struggles, we are, all of us, profoundly connected to what has gone before. Once again, a fragment of my soul lifts off, carried away by the scent of the roses, humming and thrumming over the grass.

Tony returns from Port Albert and suggests that we go to the pub, already awash with people and noise when we arrive. As we wade through the crowd, laughter rings hollow like empty glasses, ruddy faces seem grey and cadaverous after the luminous glow of the fields. But tonight the fishermen have put aside their larger worries; good-humouredly they trade accounts of snagged propellers, near-disasters close to the reefs, wasted hours untangling lines. Tony sits next to Dr. Doyle's son, Jock, with whom he has bantered and fished for half a lifetime. Two hundred years ago, whose vision was this?

The pub fills to capacity: the eight ball smacks and the double doors bang, and shouts of thirst ricochet through the smoke and the camaraderie in the vast, low-ceilinged room. The mood is entirely different from previous months; spring provokes the blood. I can see it around me, in the faces of the men as Elsa, Tony's sister, bends over the cue.

Next to the doors, five or six tables are taken up by a group of bikers from Port Albert; we passed their machines outside. Hogs, Tony called them, gritty and menacing in the vaporous lamplight. The bikers claim their section of the action, not saying much, watchful, heavy leather jackets draped over the backs of their chairs. A low rumble turns out to be laughter; Turkey has tripped over the blunt toe of a boot, sprawling with a beer. Turkey gets up grinning, but in his face there is something just as watchful, pulsing, as the moments progress.

Turkey has only recently returned to Squally Bay, hoping to get work as a deckhand on a boat. The cost of the city winter is written all over him, in his pallor and his manic maneuvering from table to table, conniving drinks with cheers and jokes.

I begin to long for bed, and several times we almost leave, then someone remembers another incident, the wry and bonding ribaldry of old friends. The lights flutter at midnight and the noise dips for a second, then surges; reluctantly the crowd trickles outside.

Tony lingers for a last word with Jock Doyle. They are meeting next week in Port Albert, at the government inquiry into the declining salmon stocks. I lean against the wall of the hotel, shutting out their voices and hearing the frogs croaking in the ditches close by.

The cool air seems to have revived the bikers. With a surly ceremoniousness they pull on their gloves, zippering and buckling their jackets, mounting their machines. Elsa clicks across the parking lot towards her sportscar, red and shiny as a child's toy beneath the floodlights. Sometimes she lets Andrew have a turn behind the wheel, on the Reserve. She doesn't even flinch when one of the motorcycles fires up beside her, shattering the quiet night.

Helmet dangling from his handlebar, the biker idles along the pavement at Elsa's heels. By the glare off his balding head I recognize him as Turkey's downfall, a squat and pugnacious man, a mouthbreather, belly pumping in and out as he morosely examined every patron in the pub. Elsa strides to her car as if he did not exist.

The biker suddenly revs his throttle. Jock and Tony are still talking but a few of the others notice, lifting their heads. I see Turkey lighting a cigarette, hugging himself to keep warm.

The wheel bumps Elsa's leg. She stumbles, then spins and lunges at the biker; swiftly and neatly she slaps his face. Tony hears me gasp, turning in surprise. The biker puts a gloved hand to his cheek, and Elsa stalks away. The biker cuts his engine and dismounts. He hits Elsa from behind, knocking her onto the pavement, and the parking lot is silent except for the frogs.

Turkey launches himself out of the darkness with an unearthly cry. He flails at the biker, who holds him off, his boot colliding ferociously with Turkey's ribs. Turkey flips backwards and thuds, head-first, against a curb. Elsa gropes on her knees; Turkey quivers briefly, then lies motionless.

As Tony and Jock and the others advance, the biker defiantly remounts. One by one the motorcycles file out of the parking lot. Through the reverberations, I remember that I am a nurse. I rush to Elsa; her eyes are stony and she fumbles with a bleeding ear. Tony retrieves a silver pendant from the pavement, putting his arms around her, helping her rise.

Kneeling beside Turkey, I am struck by his expression: he seems strangely liberated, at peace. My hand brushes his chest, over the dying echo of his warrior scream. I draw his shirt up to cover his face, and the crowd from the pub gathers around, shocked and solemn, waiting for the ambulance and the police.

The autopsy reveals that Turkey was killed instantly when his head struck the curb; this we all knew. Few of us knew that he was descended from a line of once-powerful whaling chiefs. His family, although living off Reserve for many years, has been traced back through the generations to the heir of Quatlukaht, who married into the ruling family at Squally Bay. Grandma Em is certain of this, from the songs.

Earl reads Turkey's story, prepared by Grandma Em, at the memorial service in the hall on the Reserve. We look at each other and raise our eyebrows: Turkey's flight across the parking lot becomes even more noble, in retrospect. Only Elsa listens impassively, in her jeans and her jewellery. She has gone after the biker with a vengeance, and he is awaiting trial. She does not comment when Tony tells her that the biker's friends have been back, hanging around the hotel.

Tony volunteers to scatter Turkey's ashes. He takes me with him up to Quatlukaht, and we anchor off the crescent beach, beneath a full moon, rocking with the swell. We go out in the dinghy with the canister of ashes, returning Turkey's tormented spirit to the waters of his forefathers. As we drift with the canister, three dark shapes appear through the salal. A mother bear and her cubs step tentatively onto the sand, and later we glimpse the little rumps of the cubs, humping and bumping amongst the logs.

We leave early, coffee simmering on the diesel stove. The eagles and the ravens are soaring off the channel at Klinniklinnikaht, and by the time I have put away the breakfast dishes, we are approaching Squally Bay. Light spills over the hills, pink and gold with the promise of the new day. I find myself recalling certain lines in Captain Hume's letter; this is a moment he would have described. The letter had been his soliloquy: a lonely, old sailor preparing for his final passage along the coast which had claimed his heart. It may have been sent to his grandson Edwin, but it was meant for Edwin's great-granddaughter, for me.

We churn around the beacon, the wheel shuddering in Tony's hands. Two black shapes are racing along the spit. "What are those?" I ask, laughing and pointing at the high-legged birds so earnestly defending their territory where the shadow of the troller skims the shore.

"Oystercatchers." Tony nods absently, lining up the bow with the markers, steadying the worn, varnished spokes.

I twist in wonderment at the flying feet and bright, sturdy beaks; these are the birds on the border of Grandma Em's cape. Every afternoon, for an hour or two, she weaves on her mat. Occasionally she sings, and I listen, amongst the unfinished baskets, the clutter, and the dust. I am waiting for the right time to tell her that I am carrying Tony's child.

Across the smooth water, the street lamps in the village fade like stars into the dawn sky. Tony cuts the engine. Sensing his stillness, I glance up at his face.

He is looking at me so intently that my heart trips in panic. "What is it?" I cry.

"Your eyes," he says gruffly. "Reminded me of something, just then." He seems confused, shaking his head.

The bow nudges the wharf, and he hurries out to fasten the ropes. His lips touch my hand as he helps me down.

"We're home," he smiles.

~~~:~~~

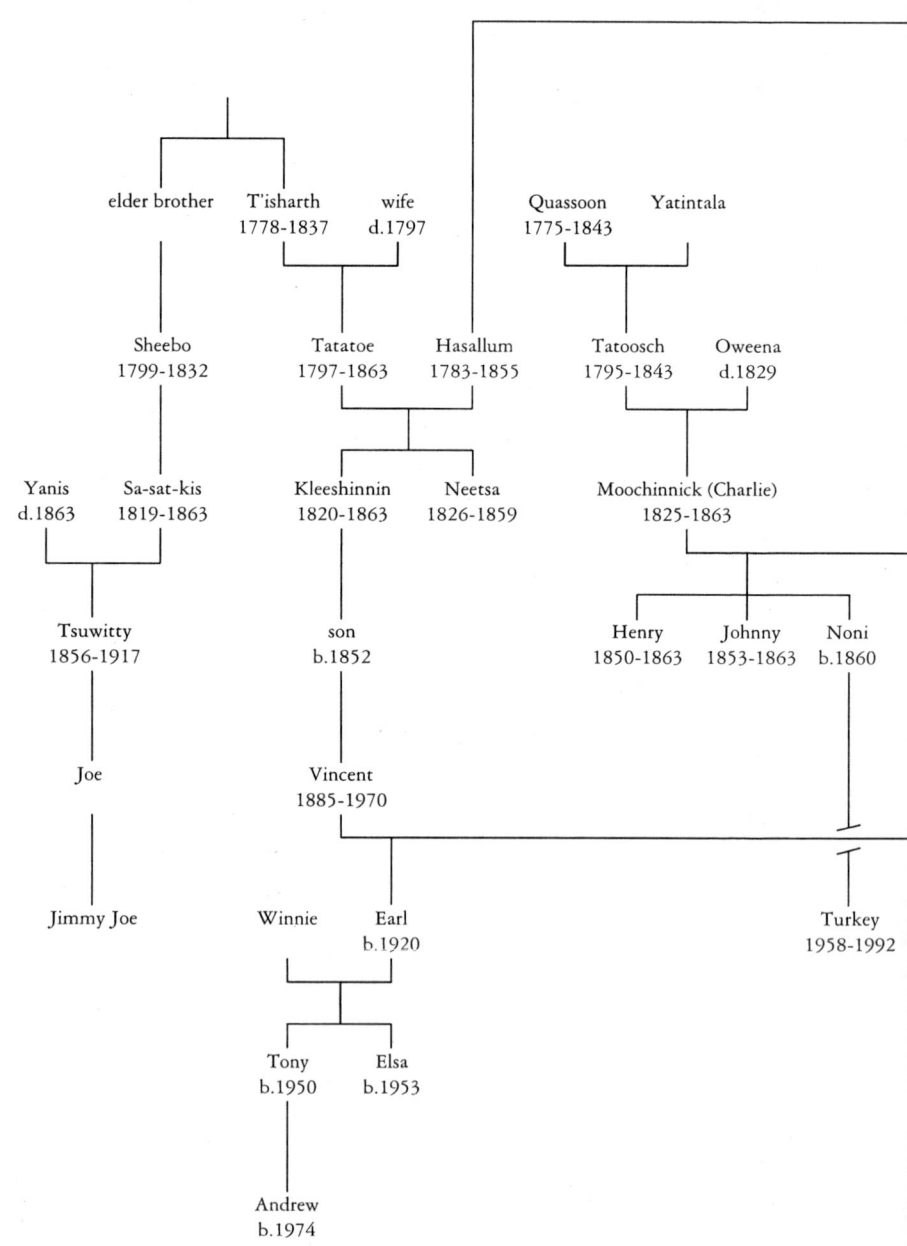

216

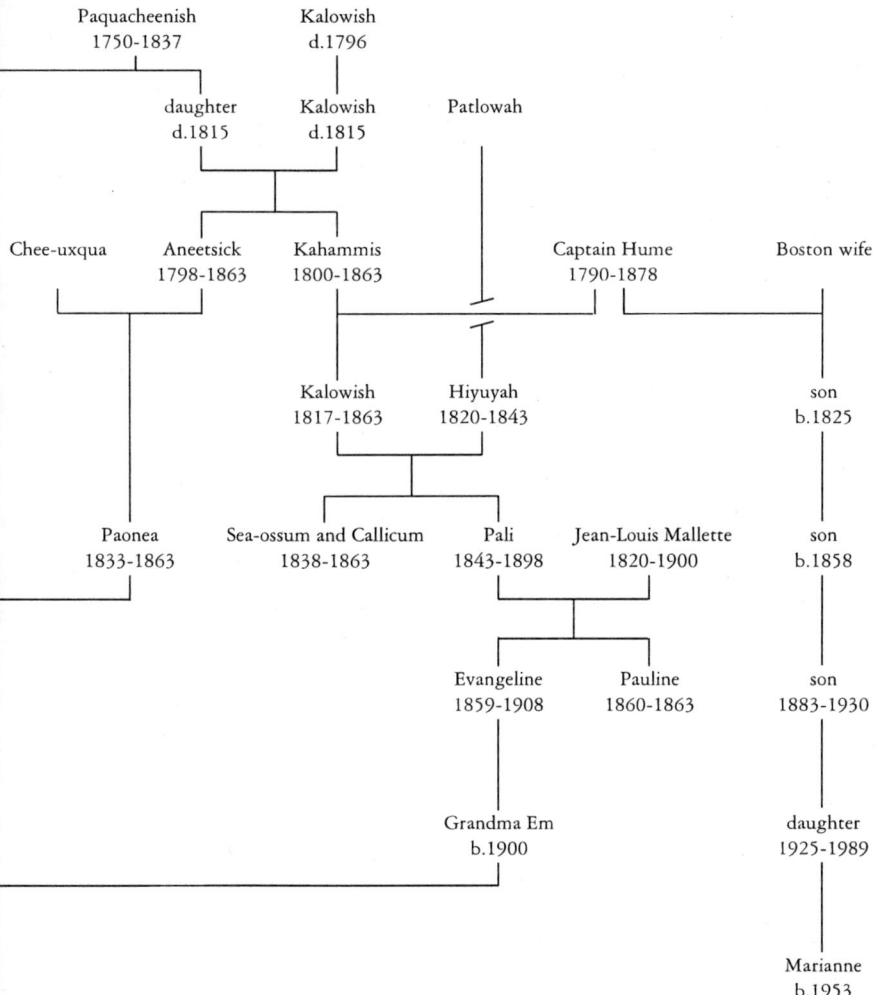